THE ANCESTOR GAME

Alex Miller grew up in London and now lives in Melbourne. He is the author of two previous novels: *Watching the Climbers on the Mountain* and *The Tivington Nott*.

PENGUIN BOOKS

A major new novel of grand design and rich texture.
Helen Daniel, Age

A superb work of fiction. One of the most engrossing books I've read in a long time.
Robert Dessaix, Books & Writing

Alex Miller held me in thrall.
Tom Shapcott, Overland

Richly rewarding.
Jill Kitson, ABC Radio

A mammoth act of the imagination.
Dinny O'Hearn, Melbourne Times

Miller's integrity, his thoughtful and considered treatment of his complex theme, must be honoured.
Andrew Riemer, Sydney Morning Herald

A very fine work . . . garrulous, cerebral, even obsessive, written with great clarity and sense of drama.
Gerard Windsor, Australian

Rich and evocative . . . A profoundly humane and compassionate book.
Sophie Masson, Australian Book Review

A high point in the second wave of Australian fiction that confronts Asia.
Peter Pierce, Bulletin

THE ANCESTOR GAME

ALEX MILLER

PENGUIN BOOKS

Penguin Books Australia Ltd
487 Maroondah Highway, PO Box 257
Ringwood, Victoria 3134, Australia
Penguin Books Ltd
Harmondsworth, Middlesex, England
Viking Penguin, A Division of Penguin Books USA Inc.
375 Hudson Street, New York, New York 10014, USA
Penguin Books Canada Limited
10 Alcorn Avenue, Toronto, Ontario, Canada M4V 3B2
Penguin Books (N.Z.) Ltd
182-190 Wairau Road, Auckland 10, New Zealand

First published by Penguin Books Australia, 1992

8 10 12 14 13 11 9 7

Copyright © Alex Miller, 1992

All rights reserved. Without limiting the rights under copyright
reserved above, no part of this publication may be reproduced,
stored in or introduced into a retrieval system, or transmitted,
in any form or by any means (electronic, mechanical, photocopying,
recording or otherwise), without the prior written permission of
both the copyright owner and the above publisher of this book.

Typeset in 10/12½ Garamond Light by Midland Typesetters,
Maryborough, Victoria
Made and printed in Australia by Australian Print Group

National Library of Australia
Cataloguing-in-Publication data:

Miller, Alex, 1936-.
The ancestor game.

ISBN 0 14 015987 8.

I. Title

A823.3

For Ruth and Max Blatt

ACKNOWLEDGMENTS

I would like to express my thanks to Professor Bao Chien-hsing, of the Shanghai Foreign Languages Institute and to the painter, Yehching, for their generous assistance while I was in Shanghai and Hanghzou. I would also like to express my thanks to Nick Jose, then Australia's Cultural Attaché in Beijing, for introducing me to Ouyang Yu, who was at that time teaching in Australian Studies at the East China Normal University in Shanghai. Ouyang has since become a firm friend. My chief debt, however, is to Barrett Reid, Stephanie Miller and Bryony Cosgrove, from whose concern and candor this book has benefited.

CONTENTS

BOOK ONE

BOOK TWO

BOOK
ONE

DEATH OF THE FATHER

In a wintry field in Dorset less than a year ago, I enquired of my mother, You don't want me to stay in England with you then? She, clipping her words as if she were trying out a new set of shears on the privet, replied, No thank you dear. I waited a minute or two before venturing the merely dutiful alternative, You could come out to Australia and live with me? Thank you dear, but I think not.

We resumed watching a pair of swans. Their pale forms merged with the river and the flat fields and the sky, then emerged again mysteriously, as if propelled by the unseen hands of giant children at play. Nothing else moved. Everything around us was grey, luminously grey, and very cold. We were closed in by fog. There was only the rushing sound from the motorway a mile off. As I stood beside my mother I realised I'd arrived at a moment of decision. Ill-defined anxieties flickered in my mind. I remembered the Chinese refer to these moments as dangerous opportunities.

We watched the swans glissade into and out of our view, on the river that was indistinguishable from the sky, and we waited until the bruised sun had dissolved. Our cold vigil in the field at sunset was our homage to the memory of her husband and my father. There was to be no lasting memorial. There had been no service. There was no patch of ground to remain sacred to his memory. He probably would have liked there to have been: a headstone set among others' headstones and incised with a couplet from Burns: *Nae man can tether time or tide; The hour approaches Tam maun ride*.

But my mother didn't care for headstones, or for her husband's taste in poetry, and so, as she was now in charge, there were neither. There'd been no arguments about these arrangements as my father had had no friends to argue for him, and my mother and I were the only surviving members of the family. She took my arm and walked me back to her home across the frosty fields. To have seen us we must have looked like any English mother and son taking their habitual evening constitutional; persisting, despite the bleak weather, the way the English do persist with such things. In fact neither my mother nor I was really English, and we'd not seen each other more than two or three times in twenty years.

I hadn't returned to England to bury my father, but to be present for the release of my first novel. It had provided me with an excuse for the journey. I'd hoped my book, which was set in England, might prove the basis for a reconciliation with the country of my birth. I'd hoped something might have healed between us by now. And I'd been on the alert for a sign of this healing when I telephoned from the airport to let my parents know of my arrival. My mother sounded put out when she realised it was me phoning. Oh it's you Steven! I thought it must have been the doctor ringing back. Your father has just died.

My gaze roved appreciatively over her lovely English furniture and the porcelain in its cabinets, pieces she'd collected with care over the years, and I saw how deeply she now belonged to this place, how buttressed against dislodgement she had grown in my absence, a successful cultural graft drawing her sustenance with assurance from the rootstock of her adopted country.

Although it was winter she'd managed a dark arrangement of

velvety chrysanthemums. I couldn't resist the impression that these flowers signified a celebration rather than an occasion for mourning. She looked at them when we came into the room in a way that did not ask me to share them. We sat in armchairs on either side of the gas fire, she in her own and I, I supposed, in my father's, and we watched television. It was the London Philharmonic with Solti conducting. My mother moaned and swayed as if she were the cello embraced by the thighs of the cellist. Then, when Britten's symphony ended, she rose from her chair at once, switched off the television and said matter-of-factly, That was lovely. To detain her a while longer I responded to an offer she'd made me earlier, I'll take the book on Nolan then. If you really don't want it?

She paused behind my chair, holding the tray with our cups and the supper things on it, and looked down at the top of my head – I could see her reflected in the screen – and she reminded me, You sent it to him for his sixtieth birthday.

I'd forgotten. In the instant of speaking I'd thought I was selecting the book randomly from my father's things. Something of his to remember him by, not something of my own to recall myself by.

He never looked at it, she said and laughed uncomfortably, impatient. He detested that sort of painting. Anything which reminded him that artists have abandoned the pictorial manners of John Cotman and Francis Danby made him angry. I thought you'd sent it to provoke him. He thought so too, you know.

There was a pause, then she said, I don't pretend to understand you Steven.

She cast off this remark on her way out to the kitchen as if she were casting me off. I heard her clattering the things in the sink. She began singing the cello from Britten's symphony. I realised that she couldn't wait to have done with me so that she might at last get on with living her life quite alone. Her verdict, it seemed, was that if I'd wished to belong in England then I ought to have stayed.

When she came back into the room she did not sit down again

·

but plumped the cushions on her chair and stood and waited for me. She was ready for bed. I wanted to say something to her about how I felt, but I was unable to.

I hope your book does well, she offered at last, as if she were referring to a world composed of a thin unreality that she could not quite bring herself to believe in.

Thanks.

Still she did not move. There was a mute tightening of the congested intensity between us. Then, You never wrote to us Steven! It was years before we heard anything from you. We thought you must have perished in the outback, or whatever it is they have there. Then that book arrived from you, like a taunt. You can't blame us now for this whatever-it-is that's troubling you.

I took the heavy Sidney Nolan monograph to bed with me and sat up with it open across my knees. There was an inscription on the front end paper. I recognised the hand as one I'd tried out for a while, upright and orotund, before lapsing into the backward slant that came more naturally to me – a calligraphy, this, in which my words appear to test the way forward with one tentative, extended toe. *Dearest Dad, With all my love and best wishes for a happy birthday, your son Steven.* It was dated August 1961, the year of the publication of the book. How very up-to-date I must have thought myself then. I remembered writing the inscription. I remembered the fountain pen I'd used. Now, towards the end of my thirty-ninth year, I was the first person to read my birthday message to my father. *Had* it been my intention to taunt him, the antiquary and amateur watercolourist, with this paean to brutal modernism from the far side of the world? How else might he have viewed this unexpected gift from his only son after so many years of silence? It must have seemed to him – this man whose 'eye' had remained adjusted for more than half a century to the nostalgic fragilities of the faded watercolour sketch – to be a coarse rejection of the traditional craft he believed himself heir to and therefore guardian of. He must have shuddered with outrage as he placed the quarto volume on his bookshelf, unopened.

Uneasy with an expectation of what I was to reveal, I turned the page and began to read the essay before the plates by Colin MacInness. *Australia is an Asiatic island that Europeans inhabited by accident*, it began. And a little further down the page, *Everything about Australia is bizarre.* I read until I lost interest in the writer's insistence on a uniquely eccentric nature for Australia and for the 'kingly race' of Europeans who inhabited the continent. Yet I wanted to be reassured. I wanted to believe in the book. I turned to the plates.

There were pictures of Ned Kelly in the bush, and pictures of abandoned ploughs in flat, empty country that couldn't possibly grow anything, and there were carcasses of horses and cows and vast red uninhabited landscapes, and there were ghostly portraits of Light Horsemen with emu feathers in their slouch hats, invoking the Anzacs and Gallipoli. And then, in the midst of these images of soldiery and abandonment and of sterility and failure, there was Leda and the swan, the divine parents of the mythical Clytemnestra and Castor and Pollux, and of Helen of Troy. The landscape was still unmistakably Australian. The swan was white.

What was one of the Queen's swans doing here in this sinisterly brutal world, which appeared to rise less upon a vision of human tragedy than upon a bleakly dispassionate view of a civilisation that had failed: a European civilisation that had failed to take root in an environment hostile to its ageless central icons of the plough and the warrior. I examined the rest of the pictures. The images referred to an Australia of which I had no direct experience. The white swan, I decided, must serve as the cipher by which the other images were to be read. Its persisting whiteness I took to be sufficient evidence that the nature of myth must go much deeper and be less conscious and amenable to manipulation than was implied by the project of the book. It wasn't that the pictures themselves were inauthentic – *they* were undoubtedly the authentic expressions of one man's disappointment. It was the claims being made for the pictures that were inauthentic; the chauvinistic insistence that something unique and non-European had been established in Australia, when what I clearly had before me was an example of a regional vision located deep within the embrasures of a European tradition.

I closed the book and dropped it on the floor beside the bed. A thick pain was pushing up against my diaphragm and there was a whooshing in my ears. I lay on my side with my head over the edge of the bed and breathed shallowly, my arm extended, bracing myself against the book. There had been the failure of my father's heart the previous Saturday. The swift attack that had killed him while I was making my way through the customs at Heathrow. Had I inherited his condition? Was this the revenge his outrage had required? Would my mother be standing in the field watching the swans again in a day or two, on her own?

After a few minutes the pain eased and the rushing in my ears subsided. As my hearing readjusted to the sounds of the world outside my body I realised I could hear music coming from my mother's room. It was the 'Dance a Cachucha' from *The Gondoliers*. I pictured her dancing around her bed in her nightdress, gay and diaphanous, her thin, reddish hair flowing and translucent in the lamplight, celebrating her liberation from the onerous uncertainties of her Scottish husband and her Australian son. I listened gloomily to the catchy foot-tapping tune and to her dum-de-de-da-de-da-da-da and I saw how completely she had always kept her magic to herself. Was I returning to Australia in the morning to continue my exile, or was I going home? The book had been no help to me at all. Nolan and his Leda paintings had found their home in England long ago.

ONLY CHILDREN

At afternoon recess the man and the woman were there again in the staffroom. As before, they were in conversation by the gas heater. The heater wasn't lit as the weather was fiercely hot, but the man held his hand out to it behind him every now and then as if he were in need of its warmth. She was taller than he by several centimetres. She was wearing a grey dustcoat and dark pants and she stood still and kept her hands thrust into her pockets. She didn't look directly at him, even when she spoke to him, but gazed steadily in the direction of an unoccupied table tennis table by the far wall. She moved only when she laughed. She was about thirty. Perhaps younger. He looked to be somewhere between his middle forties and early fifties. But boyish. Small and light-boned like an adolescent. He had a lopsided way of standing, one small, rounded shoulder higher than the other, one hand clutching his elbow when it was not reaching for the heater, while with the other he held a cigarette close to his lips. He repeatedly took long, hungry drags from the cigarette, never removing it more than a millimetre or two from his mouth, so that the exhaled smoke fanned out against the open palm of his hand and enveloped him. He might have wished to conceal himself within it.

Unlike her, he was constantly on the move. They were

indecisive movements, re-balancing himself from one foot to the other and, at certain moments, appearing as if he were about to set off somewhere only to change his mind at the last second and swivel round instead, reaching for the heater again, his point of reference. He was Asian. I preferred at once to refer to him in my mind as oriental. There was a coy and half-concealed refinement about him which insisted on this. He and the woman formed a composition of their own, a mobile triangle with the black heater its fixed vertex, distinct and unrelated to the activities of the other staff.

I was clear about why I was attracted to the man. The woman was more closed and difficult to read. But he looked as though he would know how I felt. Like my father, I had no close friends. I'd always managed well enough without such relationships. Once I'd not noticed the absence of intimacies of this kind in my life. Things had begun to change for me, however. Since my earliest childhood recollections I'd believed that if I could only reach deeply enough inside myself, one day I'd come upon extensive and complex landscapes rich with meaning and mystery, waiting for me to explore them. I'd believed the purpose of my adult life would lie in the exploration of these places. My confidence in the existence of this internal homeland, however, had eroded over the years. It had been my confidence in its existence, my belief in my own uniqueness, which had at one time provided me with an immunity from being infected by the mannerisms and beliefs of my father. Without it there seemed nowhere for me to retreat from him. Without it I saw that it was possible I might eventually grow to be indistinguishable from him.

On Thursday at morning recess the man was alone by the gas heater. He didn't look my way, but as I approached him I was aware of him beginning to wait for me. I indicated the table tennis table, Like a game?

He checked me keenly, as if I'd suggested some extraordinary piece of mischief. Yes! he exclaimed with a throaty rush of breath.

Let's have a game! He continued to smoke while we played and never shifted from the one spot at his end of the table. He flicked the ball back to me with a practised twist of his wrist that was effortless and automatic. I dived and lunged from one side of the table to the other, trying to keep the ball in play, but succeeded in scoring only when he paused during a point to light a fresh cigarette from the stub of his old one.

We should play that point again, I offered. He wouldn't hear of it. That was a good shot, he said. I laid my bat on the table. It's too hot for this. He agreed at once. I gained the unsettling impression that he would have agreed as readily to anything I might have proposed, would have been prepared to fake enthusiasm for it.

There was a disturbing and fixed misalignment to his features. It was as if the right side of his face had been given a permanent upward nudge, resulting in a faintly sardonic expression, an aspect of amused irony stamped on his countenance at the instant of understanding. I was put in mind of my mother's warnings that the wind would change and leave me with an obscene frog mouth and bulging eyes for the rest of my days. The wind must have changed for this man. I thought of him as having been touched, as having been wounded, by the powers of the enchanted world she understood but had been unable to share.

He was of her height and of a similar slight build and he, too, had about him a fey elusiveness. Where's your assistant today? I asked.

He looked uncomprehending for a second. Oh, you mean Gertrude. He chuckled. That's what I'll call her! My assistant. He was shy suddenly, as if he thought he might be in danger of taking the joke too far. Gertrude Spiess. She's a senior lecturer in drawing at the Prahran College of Advanced Education. He delivered this explanation with a formality that was almost ceremonious. She is an artist. A real one. She comes to do some emergency teaching here because she likes to do it.

His upward-tilted right eye observed me coldly all the while he was speaking. I found myself caught between responding to the diffident yet encouraging tone of his voice and the malevol-

11

ence implied by the set of his features. With a seriousness that made the question more than casual, he asked me at one point was it difficult to teach non-English speaking children to read and write English. He awaited my reply as if he expected to hear from me something lucid and definitive.

There was an eagerness, a kind of complete disclosure of his own ignorance, in the manner with which he put his questions to me, that made it appear he must be prepared to accept whatever I might say as God's truth. His manner flattered me with an implied expectation that I would adopt the role of expert in the English language. And I might have adopted it, except for the way he seemed to wait quietly within himself for just such a sign of my acquiescence. He noted my wariness and smoked his cigarette. His name, he told me, was Lang Tzu.

With ten minutes of the morning classes still to run I went in search of his art room. A terrible north wind had descended from the desert. The school grounds were filled with a roaring. A harsh rain of red Mallee dust swept down from the roofs and whirled in drifts about the yard. Through the noise of the storm a child was screaming. A few metres in front of me a boy was thrashing around on the near-molten asphalt. I couldn't decide whether he was at play or had been hurt. I started towards him and he sprang up at once, shouting over and over a word which I didn't understand. Opposite were the Gothic doors Lang had told me to look for.

The air was so hot against my face I felt sure things must begin to ignite at any minute. Plastic bags, milk cartons and other rubbish were being whipped into a vicious tornado by the scorching wind. At the doors I hesitated, fascinated by the fury of the heat storm, my hand on the iron latch, and was immediately engulfed by the fierce updraught of hot plastic and grit. I went in and dragged the door closed against the suction of the wind.

It wasn't a classroom I'd entered, it was a barn. An assembly hall. A great cool echoing place of sanctuary, in which a pale illumination was admitted through several high, pointed windows composed of dozens of diamond-shaped panes of glass. There was an old and somehow familiar smell, composed of mineral turps, oil paint and book dust. Something moving on a cross-member in the open timbers of the ceiling caught my attention. A sedate row of pigeons roosted there shoulder to shoulder, gazing down on to the activity below them. Several children were taking it in turns to run the length of the hall, jumping from one work table to the next, until from the table nearest the front they made a leap of two metres or more, at full stretch, on to the proscenium of the stage, where they landed with a sonorous boom that echoed round the hall as if a drum had been struck. Surprisingly, considering this distraction, most of the students were working, either on their own or conferring with a neighbour. They were painting pictures on large sheets of brown paper.

Lang was standing on his own at a table on the far side of the hall, reading. He had a cigarette notched firmly between his fingers and held close to his face, his eyes tight against the smoke. He was standing side-on to the table, the book pressed down with his free hand, the pages held open with his spread fingers. He looked as though he'd paused to take a quick look at the book on his way to doing something else and become caught up in it. His lips were moving and his body was reacting to the rhythm, or to the sense, of the words.

He didn't look up as I approached him. I saw he was reading Burns' *Tam o'Shanter*. With a mixture of fear and awe and deep fascination, I'd listened as a child to the swaggering tones of this poem more times than I could remember. My father had known by heart every one of its two hundred and twenty-four lines. I'd been exposed to it so often that I'd absorbed entire passages without ever making the effort to do so. At the slightest invocation, it sang in my head with my father's voice. The mention of something Scottish, and in particular Glaswegian, was sufficient to set off in me a string of stanzas from *Tam*.

When I was fifteen I discovered I possessed the ability to reproduce exactly my father's voice, his thick Glasgow accents and the aggressive manner of his delivery. After I discovered this talent I used to pretend to be my father to my mother. I did it despite misgivings of a preternatural kind, despite feelings that I was invoking something sinister and dangerous and greater than myself, something that I might not be able to control. The compulsion to do it, however, was irresistible. At about the time of day when we were expecting him home from work, when the house was quiet, I'd slam the front door and go into the sitting room and call wildly, Are you there for Christ's sake Mary?

My mother would come to the door of the passage and look at me with her clear grey eyes. Though I feared them both in different ways, neither of my parents ever punished me. There was a detached fatalism in their attitude to my behaviour, as if they believed that to seek to direct it lay beyond their charter. As if, indeed, we were not a family but were three unrelated people living in the same house.

When my mother saw it was me who had called and not my father, she would return to whatever she'd been doing. At that moment I would sense my father's presence within me and would fear I had enchanted myself with him. Despite her lack of a reaction, I understood that my mother was quite as disturbed by this trick as I was myself. It drew us into a kind of shared conspiracy against the real man. She never admonished me, even mildly. Her attitude, it seemed to me, implied that if I wished to do such things then I must be prepared to deal with the uncertain consequences myself.

The poetry of Robert Burns was my father's established way within me, it was his right-of-way, a means by which his personality could flourish in me. When I saw that Lang was reading *Tam* I was more dismayed than surprised. I felt offended. It was too personal. Impossible that there could have been any conscious malevolence in Lang's choice of poem, but I couldn't see it as mere innocent coincidence. My gaze was drawn along the lines by his moving finger and I heard my father's voice begin to fill the hall, *The wind blew at 'twad blawn its last; The rattling showers rose on the blast.*

The students stopped jumping on to the stage and watched us. Lang turned to me and urged me to continue, his knowing right eye twisted upon me, his nicotine-stained finger pointing at the poem. He took a deep drag on his cigarette and pushed the book towards me. It was an Everyman edition, its green cloth boards sticky-taped to a broken spine. Go on! He exhaled a dense cloud of tobacco smoke, which engulfed me. The students moved in a little closer. They were Lang's size. He picked up the book and placed it in my hands, then he took a step back and stood among the gathered students.

I looked down at the poem. My father's voice arose at once within me, loud and arrogant, challenging all authority, a voice beneath which aggression strode in time with the rhythm. An aggression that denounced as weaklings and fools any men who did not partake with him of the superior liberties of the Scots – an option he considered unavailable to women. An aggression directed principally at the English, who'd had the unpardonable audacity to abandon the values of the eighteenth century. *The wind blew as 'twad blawn its last; The rattling showers rose on the blast; The speedy gleams the darkness swallow'd; Loud, deep, and lang, the thunder bellow'd* . . .

Fascinated, we listened to the authentic voice of my dead father declaiming the poetry of his imaginary friend and hero, his darkly timbred tone thickening the air of the high cavity of the hall. I could feel his weight above me. A monstrous charge of flesh for the air to carry. Not a tall man but square and solid, heavy and unyielding in thick tweeds and woollens.

After several stanzas the suspended dust caused a stifling tickle in my throat and I gagged on the words, my eyes burning and filling with tears. The students turned away. They'd heard enough. I blew my nose and glanced into the shadows of the ceiling. A figure there foreshortened from beneath, an inverted Dali Christ, my father, dangerous among the old black timbers, the polished studs on the soles of his boots glinting. I wondered how my mother could have remained indifferent, how she'd managed to go on reading her book while he ranted, hobnailed boots and all. I'd made the mistake then of believing it was he who held the key to our share of the magic, not she. For it was he who had freely invoked hobgoblins and apparitions and she who'd eschewed all reference to such things. I'd not recognised his bluster for what it was, nor her unadvertised guardianship of the secret remembrances of childhood.

I sneezed and blew my nose again and wondered if Lang thought I was weeping. He returned from dismissing his class and stood close to me and looked into my face, eager to see what I was feeling. His thick lips were purple and his teeth darkly stained and his short black hair stood straight up from his white scalp as if it were electrified. There was a greedy excitement in his eyes. Come on then, let's go and get a counter lunch!

I'm not crying, I said. It's the dust.

Yes, yes, yes! He was exuberant. He made an expansive gesture in the air with his arm extended, as if he would dismiss the dust back to its concealment for me. I shouldn't let them jump on the stage. This old place ought to be pulled down. He was laughing.

I went with him through rising steam across a concrete yard which had just been hosed and into the pub by the back door. There was a smell of grilling meat and stale beer in the passage. We entered a small back parlour. It was an old-fashioned pub, untouched since the fifties, at which time this room had no doubt been the Ladies Lounge. The tables were topped with thick, scarred brown linoleum. The woman artist, Gertrude Spiess, was sitting at one of the tables on her own. She looked over and waved a magazine at Lang when she saw us come in. There was no one else in the room. Lang introduced us and left us. She offered me her hand. Our fingers touched and we smiled and said hullo and fell silent. Lang had gone to a servery, which framed a portion of the front bar, where there were men gazing upwards to the accelerating voice of a race commentator on the television. Gertrude examined the magazine she'd been reading. I realised she was part Asian.

Lang placed a glass of red wine in front of each of us and sat next to her. Let me see. He took the magazine from her. She watched him closely. He began to read, his lips moving, murmuring the words, at first inaudibly, then more loudly, until we could hear them. 'Born in the colourful Melbourne suburb of St Kilda in 1946, Gertrude Spiess is an Australian Artist with an intuitive grasp of the significant icon.' He made an appreciative noise in his throat and took a gulp of wine. There you are then, he said. An *intuitive* grasp. That means you didn't have to work hard for it. It's amazing what they can tell just from looking at pictures. 'She acknowledges a cultural debt not only to Gabrielle Münter and the German Expressionists but also to China.' He paused to take another gulp of wine and to light a cigarette.

She reached for the magazine. Read it later.

He held on to it. Just a minute! He read on, adopting an overly respectful tone, his voice drifting towards parody.

Lang! She warned him.

His voice dropped obediently to a murmur. His lips still moved, however, and I had the impression that the effect of her warning would soon wear off. His eyes glittered with a mischievous, primate quality of cunning.

Observing them, listening to them arguing about the worth of the article in the smart fine-art journal, feeling my presence with them accepted, and beginning to see something of their friendship, I chose to understand them in a certain way. The way I began to understand them offered me the outlines of a story, something to preserve me from certain disenchantment, to save me from the awfulness of reality. Feeling pleasantly woozy from the effects of the wine, it seemed to me that Lang and Gertrude might occupy the vacated homelands of my interior, which were in danger of being colonised by the chanting spectre of my father. Without considering what I was about, I allowed myself to be charmed by the pretensions of this fiction.

After a while, when they had left the magazine aside and he had drunk several glasses of red wine and had begun to be difficult and argumentative with her, I picked up the magazine and read the article.

It was an extended essay in biography and criticism. There was a photograph on the title page: a black and white portrait of her. She was seated on a lacquered ladder-back chair in a room braced with light. She was leaning a little forward, as if she were about to get up and go towards the object of her attention. One pale hand pressed expressively on her thigh, against the rich woven fabric of the black woollen dress. The dress had a wide V neckline. The photographer had achieved the lustrous sheen of soft pencil-modelling on her bare shoulders and bosom. She was looking through the eye of the camera towards the object of her thought. It was a very clever photograph. A skilled photograph. It made of her an important personage: a woman emerged from a deeply textured life into the view of the camera for us to glimpse for a tiny privileged moment, before she was drawn away once again to where our attention could not follow. I felt sure the photographer must be her close acquaintance. A friend. An admirer no doubt. His name appeared discreetly below the lower right hand corner of the picture: *Ernst Kühn.* I began to elaborate a circle of such people positioned around her.

The article posed as scholarly, but possessed none of the enthusiasm and generosity one hopes to find in a work of scholarship. It was disappointing. It lacked an ardent desire to share understanding, to bring lucidly before the reader certain precious results of a search for knowledge. It was, in fact, little more than a promotion for a one-woman exhibition of Gertrude's drawings, which was to be mounted later in the year at a Richmond gallery. There was, however, another, more concealed, meaning to the text, evident in certain passages: 'The merging of different motif areas in her drawings and the transformation of spatial relationships into flat correspondences gathers towards a distortion of depicted reality and the dissolution of its phenomenal form.' I didn't try to reach the sense of this. I understood the point of it was to transpose the locus of authority from the works to the discussion of the works. The writer had assumed the role of validating authority for the images he discussed. In order to do this he had been required to transform what he saw with his eyes into ideologies that he could 'see' with

·

his intellect. It was not he or his ideas that interested me. It was the biographical information of his subject:

One cannot speak for long with Gertrude Spiess about her work without hearing from her of her father. The facts are themselves unusual. Gertrude was born when her father was sixty-nine. She never knew her mother and cannot recall a time during the first twenty years of her life when she and her father were apart for more than a few hours. She talks of her work, its sources and its challenges, as if she is referring to a parallel life, as if she is referring to a time and a place where she and her father continue their existence together today. Her unusually close relationship with her father, a gentle and highly cultivated man according to her account, obviously remains the principal source of material for this young artist's project.

After a lifetime as a bachelor, she informs us, her father never quite recovered from his delight at becoming a father. 'As a child I always knew myself to be at the centre of his concern. He was very old and I was very young. It was always necessary for us to look after each other.' She will not discuss his death and refers to herself as 'the unpunished child', as if there is a mystery here, the significance of which we ordinary folk will not quite comprehend. One is inclined to believe her.

I became aware that they were waiting for me. Gertrude's leaving now, Lang said. I returned the magazine to her. I'll look forward to seeing your drawings. I found myself being examined by her. The pupils of her eyes were a deeply polished black. They were extraordinarily clear and steady. It was not an unfriendly examination.

When she'd gone, Lang leaned over and took my glass. He was shivering. Let's have one more before we go back, Steven. His smell was of wine and cigarettes and an admixture of the rancid and the perfumed. He rested heavily against me as he got up, and he dragged breath into his lungs as if it cost him a great effort.

The roof iron was roaring and shuddering under the blast of the hot wind and the walls of the building were vibrating. There would be grass fires by now. There were always grass fires on days like this. Crazy people went out and lit them. I could imagine the altered light. The red Mallee dust infused with smoke. And the acrid smell of burning vegetation, which I found delicious. I saw little heaps of leaves smouldering by the side of the road. That is how it had been. The smell of burning leaves on autumn afternoons in Kent, where we had lived then. The black limbs of the chestnut trees embracing overhead as we passed beneath them in my father's family Austin. My mother mounting her dark green bicycle as the impulse took her, and riding away. From me and him, even then. Aching to be alone. Going without a word. He and I at the front door watching her go. Cycling away from us into the slanting sunlight or the slanting rain. And we would not see her again until nightfall, when she returned wind-burned and smelling of fields and hedges and the smoke of burning leaves. My father at the Baring Arms by then. I'm a colonist, she once announced, to me or to the house, inspired by her journey. Standing at the rising stern of the *Arcadia* as the great ship drove into the grey seas of the Bay of Biscay years later, I repeated it to myself. I'm a colonist, I said, in order to reassure myself. To reassure myself that what I was doing was not unprecedented. I'd been unable to explain why I was going. There was something out there in Australia that I needed to reach.

The Chinese understand the Scots, Lang whispered hoarsely as he placed the glass of wine unsteadily beside my hand. He coughed thickly and leaned towards me, We both have clans.

Are you Chinese?

Of course! Yes! I'm Chinese! He was dismayed by my question. You didn't think I was a Filipino Chinese did you? I've been mistaken for a Filipino Chinese before. He gazed gloomily into his wine.

Yes, but I didn't think you were a Filipino Chinese.

I don't look Chinese. Even to people who are clear about the differences.

I didn't say I didn't think you were Chinese. I was just asking *if* you were. I didn't know.

He dragged on his cigarette and took a gulp of wine. There's something else. Something that's the same about being Scottish and Chinese for both of us.

. . . What is it?

He screwed up his murky eyes and pointed his cigarette at me. No matter how hard we try we can never lose it. And no matter what other people do they can't fake it.

I'm not Scottish. My father was. *He* never lost it. He didn't try to lose it. But I'm not Scottish, Lang. Don't think of me as Scottish. I've never been there. I faked the accent.

No you didn't.

What?

Hunched down in his seat he stared at me, alternately inhaling smoke and sipping from his glass. What are you then?

I'm Australian.

He laughed triumphantly. He'd scored. We're all Australian, Steven. What are you really?

It's late, I said. Shouldn't we be getting back?

If you're not Australian what are you?

I'm Australian. My mother's Irish. Or she was. She might be English by now.

He opened his eyes wide, his peculiar right eye opening wider than his left – a pale opening in his face. Your mother's still alive?

She's in England.

He murmured wonderingly, Your mother is still alive in England! And you've just come back from seeing her haven't you?

Last month.

Your mother! He sighed and looked into his empty glass. She must miss you very much. Her only child.

She doesn't miss me at all. And what do you mean, only child?

We're all only children, Steven. He appeared surprised I hadn't known this. You and me and Gertrude. We're all only children. The myths and legends are all about twins. Have you noticed that? You're a writer. You should have noticed. The subject should interest you. All the expert studies are of twin behaviour. Science and mythology aren't interested in us, Steven. They're not interested in one-offs. Uniqueness is a nuisance for them. They want to derive universal principles from their observations, not

.

21

to be entertained by them. Uniqueness tells them nothing they wish to know. They look away in embarrassment whenever they come across it. And they only preserve it in a jar of formaldehyde and store it on a dark shelf somewhere in case another one like it ever turns up. But secretly they think the place for it is in a freakshow. Our parents are just as dismayed as the scientists, but *they* have to pretend to be pleased for the sake of appearances. They have to pretend we're a blessing to them. But the truth is the only child doesn't bring them any closer. One child doesn't make a family. They know it. They know something's amiss so they make a ridiculous fuss of us to try and cover up the truth. It's a triangle. The sole offspring divides and rules, it doesn't draw everyone together into a happy family. You've heard of the eternal triangle haven't you Steven? As if this reminded him of something, he looked at his watch. We're late. He got up. It's not a good idea to keep turning up late for classes.

Come with me after school, he offered, as we hurried from the pub. I'll cook you some pork Shanghai style. There's going to be a cool change later. We'll go to Tom Lindner's gallery and look at a picture for him. He always offers champagne on a Friday evening. You'll be impressed with Tom.

Out in the street it was even hotter than it had been earlier. We were forced to turn our faces aside from flying grit. The sky was thick and dark, as if we were close to an ironworks. And the smell of burning grass was strong in the air.

Lang clutched my sleeve and leaned close to me. He shouted into my ear as we stumbled along together, Why do you think real family people always call the only child a spoilt child? The child's spoilt, they say. And they're right. It's a recent elision of despoiled. Everyone knew what despoiled meant not long ago. They knew what they were saying. Now we repeat it without knowing what we're saying any longer. To despoil is to forcibly seize something that doesn't rightfully belong to you. Spoil is what has been seized from your enemy by force. He stopped walking abruptly, still hanging on to my shirtsleeve, and blinked at me, the sardonic twist of his features momentarily the face of a precocious child; a child prepared to plead and to cajole and to mystify in the pursuit of its secret desire. The only child belongs to the enemy, Steven. He watched me to see what effect he was having. The only child belongs to Shinjé, the Lord of Death. He chuckled and dragged me onward. The only child is a hostile infiltrator Steven.

In the deserted school yard he waved goodbye. I snatched at him, What about Gertrude and her father? She's an only child but they were happy.

They weren't a triangle, he said and left me standing by myself. As I turned to go I saw someone at an upstairs window. The window was protected from stones by a grill of weldmesh. A pale oval face observed me. It was unmoving and squared off by the steel wire. A preparatory study for a portrait. I was unable to resist a suggestion that the face at the window was Lang's. That he'd somehow managed to get up there very quickly. Or that I'd experienced a lapse of attention and more time had passed than I was aware of.

THE LOTUS AND THE PHOENIX

Feng Three tried for eighteen years to have a son. He was twenty-two when he married his first wife. She bore him four healthy daughters and failed to survive the caesarean delivery of the fifth. He did not forget her name: Hsing, which means apricot. She was the only woman he ever truly loved. His second wife, whose name he soon forgot, bore him three daughters before he divorced her. This wife had given Feng Three no legitimate reason to divorce her, so his friend, the sinister Scotsman Alistair McKenzie, Chief of Police, arranged a little something and she was returned in disgrace to her family.

Feng was a Shanghai capitalist, a banker and dealer in international commodities. He married a third wife. On their first night together he told her, Bear me a son within a year or I shall divorce you. He was impatient, and afraid he might be running out of time.

This wife did as she was required and in nine months a baby boy was born to them. The child was dead at birth. Feng Three looked at the little body, which lay swaddled tightly in a white cotton sheet, and after a moment of deep thought he pronounced his conclusion. There was a note of satisfaction in his tone, which surprised the servants who overheard him murmur, So it is possible then. For, after eighteen years of fathering only female children, he had come to doubt his capacity to father a male child. All was not lost. It seemed he was not flawed. Feng was so preoccupied with this new knowledge about himself that he did not notice the detached judgement with which his young wife had been appraising him since he had come into her room. Three months later he got his third wife with child again. In due time Lien, which means lotus, was once more delivered of a stillborn child. This event caused a great deal of consternation in the household, which had been waiting for the birth with much uncertainty and hope. Once again the dead infant was male.

The father of the dead baby, Feng Chien-hsing, the third Phoenix, who had westernised his name and was known as C.H. Feng, came into his wife's room and stood by the bed and gazed at his second dead son. His wife's servant was silent. She did not move. She did not look at him. For three minutes Feng stood there gazing down at the little wrinkly face of his dead son, whose unopened features were the colour of slate. Feng longed to breath life into the motionless body, which seemed to wait at the door of time and reality for a sign from him. Finally, the father's gaze left his child and came to rest upon his wife.

From the moment he had entered her room Lien had been watching Feng. Each with an image of the dead infant in their minds, husband and wife now looked at each other. Feng was forty. He was in the first rank among Chinese businessmen in Shanghai. Physically he was sound. For a price there was little he could not arrange. He was conscious of being at the peak of his powers. Lien was eighteen. She was the only child of Huang Yu-hua, the old literary painter of Hangzhou. She was without power or property of her own. For her position in society and for her personal welfare she was dependent on the goodwill of her husband. As they looked into each other's eyes a heavy rain shower bore down on the house. The sturdy window frames shook and the glass trembled. When the violent squall had passed the silence was broken by the dripping of rainwater.

Feng's longing for a son was great but he did not know what to do now. The rainwater tapped loudly on the iron pipe under the window, the sound pressing in upon his thoughts, pressing in upon his doubts and his anxieties and his suspicions. Pang, pang, pang, sending him a coded message for which he did not yet possess the cipher. With a slight movement of his hand he directed the servant to remove the body of the child. Then, cautiously, he seated himself in the gold brocaded French tub chair which stood beside Lien's bed and he looked at his wife in a way he had never looked at her before. He asked himself, What does this woman want? Not a matter to which he had given any serious thought until now. What does she want? he asked himself, and felt he would be prepared to concede to her almost any reward she might ask of him. He noticed then for the first time the unusual colouring of her eyes for a Chinese of unmixed descent. The dark pupils were incised with tiny flecks of bronze. This discovery came to him with a shock. Could this woman be the girl from the provincial capital whom he'd married? He found the unwavering intensity of her regard distracting and he looked away. Apart from the colour of her eyes, what he had seen in them troubled him. He had seen that she was not ashamed. Even more disturbing, he had detected in her no fear of himself.

He became aware that he was leaning forward anxiously, in a position that might be a little ridiculous, his buttocks painfully tight, poised on the extreme rim of the chair. He coughed and adjusted his position and sought to reassure himself that women can only suffer. But the platitude did not satisfy him. Clearly it was not so for Lien. He was puzzled. He had not been prepared for any of this. He was conscious that she had achieved a certain advantage over him. How great it was he could not yet say. For another minute or two he sat on. Then, without a word, he rose and inclined his head to her in a formal acknowledgement and left her room.

A moment after the door had closed softly behind the departing Feng, the servant re-entered. When she saw who had come in Lien turned her head on the pillow and looked out of the window. From where she lay she could see the blue spring sky framed by the pink cabbage roses of the curtains. You see, I said it would be no more than a shower, she said, as if, before being interrupted by Feng's visit, they had been discussing the unlikely prospects of the weather. The servant sat on the bed and began to brush Lien's hair and to sing to her in a soft voice an old Chinese song from Sikong Tu's *The Twenty-Four Modes of Poetry*. The piece she chose was from 'The Pregnant Mode'. It began, *Not a word said outright, Yet the whole beauty revealed.*

Almost half a year passed and nothing was decided. Divorce was not mentioned. Feng was preoccupied. It was the summer of 1926, and in July Chiang Kai-shek's army began marching north from Canton. It was rumoured the Japanese had given the warlord Chang Tso-lin ten million dollars to fight the southern armies of the Guomindang. The French, the English, the Germans and the Americans, with whom Feng transacted most of his business, were certain to help Chiang against the North, or so many believed. It was a time when old alliances could not be relied upon to hold steady. There were openings for the well-placed and the astute, and, therefore, also hazards. It was a time of crisis, a time of dangerous opportunities.

When Lien informed Feng in August that she was pregnant for the third time and wished to discuss certain matters with him, he cancelled immediately an important meeting with certain foreign bankers and accepted at very short notice her request for an appointment with him.

She wore a dark green tailored suit, which had been made for her by her English dressmaker. She stood at one of the tall windows in the first floor drawing room and waited for him. While she waited she watched the nannies in the English park across the road. Along the shining paths they confidently stepped in their blue dresses and their grey stockings. Nannies pushing babies in big-wheeled perambulators and nannies with toddlers clasped by the hand and nannies with small children who ran ahead of them bowling hoops. At two o'clock on a Wednesday afternoon, the world outside Feng's white villa was filled with the cries of children.

In profile against the light it was observable that Lien possessed the long features characteristic of the northern Chinese. When the clock struck the hour she turned from the window and walked across the room. She was tall and moved with the tutored, slightly self-conscious manner of someone who might once have been a dancer. She sat in a straight-backed Carolean chair. She felt more comfortable, more alert and more able, on the hard oak and black hide than she did on down-filled cushions. And while she waited she smoked a cigarette, tapping the soft American packet repeatedly against the intarsia surface of the small circular table before her. The ivory scenes on the table were Italian, men with javelins hunting deer and bear on horseback. Her repeated tapping at last dislodged a tiny piece of hoof from one of the leaping deer. She attempted to press the piece back into its place, and when it wouldn't go, but stuck to her finger, she impatiently flicked it to the carpet. A moment later she consulted her watch. The time was approaching three minutes past two.

The resemblance this fine large room bore to a European drawing room was just that, a resemblance. Though there were a number of English pieces the room was not English. And despite a richly decorated French vitrine with marquetry panels and ormolu mountings, which stood between two of the windows, its shelves filled with lustrous pieces of a Sèvres coffee service, the room was not French either. The room was 'European' in the sense that a room in Sydney or London might be said to be 'Chinese'. That is it reflected the desire of its owner for a certain effect. To a genuine European there might have seemed to be something incongruous about the furnishings, something possibly to cause amusement, especially among the English who often found themselves amused by the Chinese. *They* might have detected an element of burlesque, of unintentional parody, in the resolute elaboration of the 'European' theme which was set forth in the furnishing of the room. For there was no object in this room, nor indeed in the entire house, that was Chinese. Not even one or two of the chinoiseries one might confidently expect to find in a real European room. And although this omission might have been considered by an observant English visitor to the house to exemplify the unintentional parody, it was not an oversight, but was by design.

C.H. Feng, to whose design the furnishings of this room and of all the other rooms in the house conformed, was accustomed to express his commitment to internationalism with a degree of purity that was considered, by those who knew him, to be eccentric. The English looked for no explanation of his behaviour beyond their own assumed superiority. That a native of a country they had exploited successfully for more than a century, a country which had never offered them any serious opposition, should mimic them seemed only natural.

Feng had long meditated upon an aversion to the traditional cultures of China and was contemptuous of those who wished to preserve them and the memory of them. Though many thought this no more than the affectation of a powerful man seeking to impress upon his peers the uniqueness of his own character, Feng was in fact not without good reasons for his attitude. He had not furnished his home in order to please anyone but himself, however, so despite the unkind comments of certain members of the International community, no grey-glazed stoneware bowls from the Northern Song, or pear-shaped porcelain vases from the kilns of the Ming, and no exquisite turquoise bronzes from the tombs of the Western Chou stood about in these elegant rooms to impress visitors with his fastidious connoisseurship of the ancient arts. Feng was not a connoisseur. He was a disappointment to those of his Western guests who anticipated viewing something more exotic in this Chinese banker's home than Bow shepherds and shepherdesses. And in their disappointment they often found it diverting, when among their own countrymen, to ridicule what they took to be Feng's imitation Europeanness. It never occurred to them that it was they and not he who had misread the situation, and Feng himself was too certain of a natural endowment of equality to ever attempt to enlighten them by explaining his view of history in justification of his behaviour.

Feng's aversion to Chinese traditions did have its limits, however. With his blessing, two of his daughters had married German army officers and one an Iowan missionary, and as a consequence of this he enjoyed the reputation of being liberal in practice as well as in theory. For the English there could scarcely have been a more revealing test of the authenticity of Feng's liberalism than this. None of their daughters married anyone but Englishmen; or, if they did, they were not blessed by their parents for doing so. The limit of Feng's European sympathies, however, was reached when he thought about the son who was to follow him. He could not think of the boy as being other than Chinese, as other than of direct Chinese descent. His three wives had all been from old Chinese families. They had all been Han. This had surprised no one. No one had ever thought of taking C.H. Feng to task for being inconsistent when it came to choosing a mother for his heir. Everyone had understood perfectly.

As he came through the door she resisted an impulse to put out her cigarette. Instead of putting it out she drew on the smouldering tobacco and held the smoke deep in her lungs, half closing her eyes and counting to three before releasing it. He was standing by the table in front of her. She crushed the butt in the ashtray and only then looked up at him. It was exactly five minutes past the hour. He apologised for his lateness and she responded by apologising in turn for the interruption to his arrangements.

May I sit down?

She inclined her head, indicating the chair opposite her. Feng did not hurry but moved cautiously, deliberately, approaching the unknown. He lifted the chair and examined its seat before placing it back some distance from the table. Then he sat down. Neither spoke. Beyond the silence was the distant screaming of the children in the park. When it seemed at last that she would not speak before he did, he asked, When is it to be? He was a short, heavy man, shorter than she. His black, oiled hair was close shorn above his ears. The white collar of his shirt pressed into the thick muscles of his neck and his brown silk tie was knotted tightly – a polished almond at his throat. Lien began to speak of her childhood. He blinked and listened,

·

but did not react to this development, though he had not expected it.

Despite being scrupulously clothed in the attire of a modern Western businessman it would have been easy to think of Feng as a pirate, ashore from roving the South China Sea. There was a wildness and a disorder about his features. His upper jaw bulged, revealing a set of yellow misshapen teeth. His thick purplish lips remained parted all the time, making him look startled. Even composed, his features gave the impression that he was aroused. Every few moments he forced his mouth closed against the pressure of his teeth and swallowed with a gulping sound, his lumpy adam's apple plunging up and down beneath its sheath of skin, as if it were a live thing he had swallowed. His eyes bulged and from their outer corners loose folds of skin flowed down his cheeks and under his jaw, following the line of a soldier's hat strap, indicating the erosion of tears. His nose was wide and flat and African. In the centre of his forehead was a deep cleft, like an old battle scar, which added an impression of permanent puzzlement to his animated expression. Feng's feelings seemed to sit openly upon his features for everyone to see. He looked like an honest, violent, vulnerable pirate, bemused by life's complexities. One might know where one stood with such a man. It might be some comfort to be certain that as he cut one's throat he did so because it was the sort of thing pirates do, and not from personal malice. Strong though it was, this impression of openness was false. Feng was, in truth, complex. His motives were hidden. He shared his thoughts with no one.

She did not look at him while she talked. She looked past him, sometimes through him, and often out the window to where the nannies were striding about under the plane trees and making circuits of the rose beds. She did not look directly at him until she came to make of him her particular demand, the immediate cause of this meeting. She ceased speaking and turned her attention from the window and looked confidently into his astonished bulging eyes. You must permit me to visit my father, she said uncompromisingly. Then added more persuasively, My health will suffer if I cannot hope to see him again.

Feng blinked, and finally it was he who disengaged his gaze once again from hers. Her boldness astounded him. He had forbidden her to contact her father. The prohibition, imposed before their marriage in the Gothic Holy Trinity Cathedral in Jinjiang Road in front of nearly a thousand guests, had passed as no more than the ordinary exercise of the arbitrary and tyrannical power invested in a husband by a tradition that seemed to Feng to be as much honoured by the members of the international community as it was by the Chinese. Lien had seemed to agree to the condition in return for his assurance of a substantial subsidy to her father so that he might continue to live in comfort in his own vast house in Hangzhou. Feng had imagined till this very minute that Lien had accepted the arrangement as part of their uneven bargain; even as she had wordlessly received on their wedding night his demand that she bear him a son within twelve months or face the disgrace of a divorce. Feng did not know what to think. So he smiled broadly and nodded and made a few sympathetic sounds.

Lien's attention remained fixed steadily upon him all the while.

His hand went to his face. He was seeing his dead sons. The stone faces of his boys. Both of them at once. Side by side on a flat white sheet. Identical. The same death repeated. The same death twice. Failing to be born at the last minute. He groaned and brushed his palms together. If you see your father will it bring me a living son? He asked. He did not say *us*.

It seemed to Feng that people cannot be read by their actions. That people do not make conveniently revealing gestures expressive of their hidden intentions, showing to an attentive world their private motives, as characters are made to do for literary purposes in the *Chin P'ing Mei* or in *A Dream of Red Mansions*. People, real people and not their fictional ghosts, he had observed, pass along in life without showing their innermost selves at all. They share nothing by signs and gestures, but remain concealed. So he was not trying to read Lien. He would have seen no point in that. To attempt to see into the thoughts of another

.

person must be to risk confusion in one's own. Feng was trying to read himself. What if a few visits to the old wen-jen artist in his rotting house in the provincial capital were not enough for her? If he conceded this much, he enquired of himself, could he afford to concede more without compromising his position? This was what he looked inside himself to find the answer to. He breathed heavily and struggled with the hard knot of this question. And all the time he was conscious of Lien sitting composedly before him, the vessel within which his precious seed must be ignited, harbouring her priceless capacity to bear him male offspring. He struggled with himself and pushed hard with his foot against the rug until the front legs of his chair lifted and the seventeenth century English oak joints began to give out sharp snapping sounds. He dug deep into the quick of a nail with his teeth and bit.

Lien waited. She had decided she could gain nothing by answering his question and had decided therefore not to answer it. She was watching a British warship nosing its way up the river against the current, its grey guns thin and dangerous, pointing towards the Settlement, pointing, indeed, directly at her, black smoke churning from the forward funnel and adding its darkness to the heavy overcast that lay upon the city. The nannies had begun to leave the park. It was time for the children to have warm milk and biscuits and an afternoon sleep. Shanghai was not the place she had imagined it to be. She had inherited her father's scepticism concerning the motives of all foreigners.

Feng winced with the sharp pain and examined his finger. A pearl of dark blood swelled against the oily sheen of his nail. He sucked it. Have you had a letter from him recently? He let the chair down with a thump and swayed towards her.

She turned from the window and picked up the packet of cigarettes. She tapped one from the packet and considered it, rolling it back and forth between her fingers and thumb, before lighting it.

Is he in good health? Feng persisted, probing anxiously for some encouragement to his line of enquiry. How he loathed admitting that such relics as her father still survived in China.

Literary painters plotting to reincarnate the bedraggled corpse of Empire. The absurdity was humiliating. It disgusted him to think of them. He bore towards them violent impulses. To be the nemesis of the old families was a dream Feng frequently entertained. It soothed him to think of a China disinfected of five thousand years of their superstitions.

I believe he is not in good health, Lien replied at length, revealing nothing, except perhaps her satisfaction at his anxiety. She would not admit to a forbidden exchange of letters with her father. But one might always hear certain things concerning a loved one's state of health.

With a studied deliberateness that was not to be overlooked by her, Feng said, When you see your father, please tell him of my concern.

She smiled and thanked him.

His child in her womb floated before him in his mind; a fragile bubble tossed back and forth upon dangerous airs.

THE WINTER VISITOR

Beside me Lang was silent, making himself small, the demon in him stilled. The cool change he'd predicted had arrived two hours ago, a chill blast from the Southern Ocean. If you'd gone to sleep after lunch, when you woke you wouldn't have known you were in the same country. We'd been transported to a temperate hemisphere and might have been driving now along a crowded boulevard on a showery spring evening in Paris. The existence a little to our north of Nolan's fiery desert had been forgotten by us once again, and we'd returned to pretending we lived in a Europe of the South Pacific. The hot wind and the burning grass had alarmed us, forcing the truth on us, but only for a moment.

In High Street, Persian carpets hung out on the footpath, and displayed in the lighted shop windows were Italian shoes and French perfumes and German motor cars. In every other shop there were antiques from a Europe whose style we wished to emulate, a Europe that had ceased to exist long ago. Antiques and paintings. And numerous chinoiseries. An abundance of them. It was all there, glowing; everything we could possibly need and much we might never need. Lang pushed the door and I followed him inside. It was a glass door swung upon substantial bronze hinges with, just below eye level, the single word, cursive

·

and gilded, LINDNER. From outside it was not possible to see inside, as there were heavy curtains across the door and the window. You either knew what LINDNER implied or you didn't know.

A buzzer sounded once for each of us and at the far end of a long gallery three people looked our way. Two men were standing together, and a woman was seated behind a desk. The walls and ceiling were white and the floor was of lacquered Baltic pine. The impression was of an intense illumination. Lang set out across the glassy boards and I followed. My mother had frequently set off with adventure in her heart and precious objects on her mind, whistling down the hill above Hastings as if she were an avenging Celt, her feet off the whirling pedals and her hands nowhere near the brakes, concentrating upon the wind in her face and the smell of the salt sea. Other women who were also alone made her welcome, inviting her in to their houses for tea. Their precious things not wasted on her. And after an appreciation of their Coalport or, if they were rich, their Nantgarw, she was away again. Tucking her coat beneath her bum upon the leather saddle and waving with her gloved hand as she leaned forward, pressing on the pedal with the sole of her sensible court shoe, some little piece, a souvenir, about her person.

Lang was a couple of paces ahead of me when the younger of the men started up the gallery towards us. I had a moment to observe him. He appeared to be no older than thirty and was of average height. He moved, however, with a slight stoop, as if he wished to affect the appearance of being older than his years or to appear distinguished by a visible peculiarity. He was wearing a slate grey blouson shirt with the cuffs turned back and a loose green and gold bowtie. Heavy spectacles swung around his neck from a chain. His most arresting feature was a lush and droopy moustache. It was hennaed. When he'd approached to within a few metres of Lang he held out his arms and smiled, Lang, my dear fellow! There was a weariness in this salutation, apology and self-deprecation, a wish to indicate a particular gratitude, a debt even. He might have called his doctor out on

·

a dirty night to attend more to hypochondria and uncertainty than to a genuine illness. As they met he slid one arm around Lang's shoulders and turned and proceeded away from me. It was with a little shock of mortification that I realised Lang was not going to include me. He was going to behave as though I were not with him. I felt it was just possible he'd forgotten I was with him.

Abandoned by my guide at the edge of the Desert Pierreux, I directed my attention to one of the ink drawings that lined the walls on either side of the gallery. As I approached I wondered what I was looking at. Initially I took it to be a calligraphic representation of the sacred rock Uluru, but as I drew nearer I realised it was a female nude and that what I'd imagined from a distance to be the weatherings of aeons were the dark canyons between the hilly buttocks and breasts of the anonymous model, who was without head or hands or feet. The artist was Horace Brodzky. I'd been studying the drawing for a minute when I realised I could see Lang among the group around the desk reflected in the picture glass. He was in close consultation with the man who had led him away – Lindner, I assumed. The other man, the taller and older one, who was dressed in a dark business suit, stood apart as I did and observed them. He was attentive, a person striving to follow a conversation being conducted in a language of which he possessed only a slight knowledge. I observed them, mirrored in a deeper place than Brodzky's black line, until they moved out of the frame and I was forced to turn round and watch them openly if I were to follow what they were doing.

The older man had gone to a bookcase which stood against the back wall and taken the paper wrapping from an unframed canvas. He placed the canvas picture-side out on the floor leaning against the books and stepped away from it. Neither he nor Lindner nor the woman looked at the painting. All three watched Lang, who went over to the picture and stood in front of it. His pale blue slacks were purplish in the bright gallery lighting. They were shiny and thin, the material on the point of disintegrating. They did nothing to hide the shape of his narrow buttocks and skinny legs. There was a configuration of smudgy chalk lines on his left leg, as though a student had been doing graffiti on him.

After looking at the picture for a minute or so he went up close to where it stood on the floor, to within a few centimetres of it, and squatted in front of it. It was a real squat. His feet flat and the seat of his pants brushing the floorboards, his knees jacked up under his armpits and his arms looped over them. Smoke from his cigarette drifted slowly upwards through his spiky hair. He looked as though he were tending a small cooking fire. I thought of the Koories out there as they had once been, in the now sadly depleted interior. But that wasn't quite right. A Chinese peasant perhaps, squatting on the bank of a flooded river, waiting patiently for the water to recede so that he might go home. The scene before me was familiar. It was like a memory. Looking at Lang, I could have been looking at myself. As I had once been. Ages ago. On the bank of a river somewhere, waiting to attempt a crossing.

Lang snatched the canvas from the floor and stood up. Holding it at arm's length he jabbed his stained forefinger at it. Cigarette ash cascaded over its inclined face, catching in the impasto surface and spilling in divided streams like larva. He handed the picture so carelessly to Lindner's companion that it nearly slipped to the floor between them. It's him. That's Dobell. Who else do you think could have done it? He made no effort to disguise his contempt. And when the man looked doubtful he snatched it back and jabbed it repeatedly, Here! There! Look! I expected flakes of pigment to fly off. You don't need a signature, you've got the picture. He walked away from the tall man, dismissing the issue. His gaze roved around the empty spaces of the gallery, settling on me momentarily – a figure occupying his middle distance – then moved on without registering recognition.

Before we left Lindner's that night he bought a painting. It was a full-length portrait of a naked girl of twelve or thirteen years of age. She was of part-Asian descent. It was a cold, humorless picture in the tonalist manner. He was drunk by the time Tom Lindner fetched the picture out from storage and showed it to him. We were all a little drunk by then, but Lang I judged to be seriously drunk. He didn't pay for the painting but took it on approval at Tom Lindner's insistence. From the street I retained a last impression of the three of them standing in the brightly lighted window of the gallery with the curtains drawn aside, the woman in the middle, each of them holding a glass of champagne, watching us struggle to get the portrait of the girl into the back seat of my car. As we drove off they waved. They looked like the cast of a play taking a curtain call. Incredibly pleased with themselves.

His home was on a hill overlooking the city, just over the river from Richmond. It was a polychrome brick mansion and was in a state of serious dilapidation. He claimed his great-grandfather had built it in 1876. I stayed till dawn, till he passed out on the rug in front of the gas fire in the front room, which was cluttered with antique furniture and paintings and empty wine casks and old newspapers and which stank like the back parlour of the pub where we'd had lunch with Gertrude Spiess. I turned off the fire and put a coat over him and tiptoed out into the grey morning. Even though he was safe sleeping on his own hearth, I felt ungenerous for leaving him. I felt I was abandoning him and ought to have stayed till he woke.

At the end of his entrance hall, facing the front door, there was positioned a very large movable mirror in an ornate mahogany frame. As I turned to pull the front door to I saw my reflection in this mirror, apparently entering a garden hidden within his house. Resolutely departing from it, I witnessed myself penetrating more deeply into Lang's domain. Leaving him, I could not resist the impression that I was becoming the person inhabiting the landscape within his mirror. I closed the door and stepped back into the porch. Above the lintel was a sandstone plaque. It was set within a framework of terracotta and ochre bricks. I paused to examine it. It was circular and depicted a pair of dancing phoenixes. Beneath the mythical birds was the word RESURGAM, as if this were the family motto. Eight bouquets of vine leaves adorned the outer circle of the plaque.

I made my way across the dewy grass to the street and drove

•

home through the empty streets. In sleep he had looked even more like a child – small and vulnerable and abandoned, his cheek resting on his two hands, palms together, and his knees drawn up towards his narrow chest; as if someone once in authority over him had instructed him always to sleep in the orthodox manner expected of a child, and he had not been able to disobey them.

The next evening I took a book he'd lent me to bed. I was very tired and intended to read a few pages of it so that I could say something to him about it when I next saw him. It was an old hardcover, and must have once been a smart edition, though now it was broken-backed and stained. Its cloth covers were a rich golden yellow. On the upper cover there was a blind-stamped design. I'd been holding it closed in front of me, resting it on my raised thighs and wondering if I weren't too tired to read any of it, when I realised the design on the cover was similar to the one in stone above the lintel of Lang's front door. I sat up and held it obliquely to the light. A pair of phoenixes confronted each other symmetrically. The birds appeared to be engaged in a ritual dance preceding either mating or combat. I counted eight bouquets of vine leaves clustered round the outer circle. There was no legend, no proclamation of faith, beneath this one. I opened the book. A not unpleasant mustiness was released; a complex odour in which I detected tobacco and wine and the dampness peculiar to Lang's house. The title page bore the following: THE WINTER VISITOR. And beneath this a sub-title, *A Life in the Northern Hemisphere*, followed by the author's name, Victoria Feng. There was an epigraph from the Threnos, or lamentation verses, of Shakespeare's poem 'The Phoenix and the Turtle':

> Beauty, truth, and rarity
> Grace in all simplicity,
> Here enclos'd in cinders lie.
> Death is now the phoenix' nest;

Here, then, was the explanation for the missing legend, RESURGAM.

Unlike the builder of Lang's house, his great-grandfather, it seemed Victoria had not hoped for a resurrection from the cinders to which she had presumably consigned her own particular phoenix. I was tempted to look at the last page, and was on the point of doing so when my eye was held by one final piece of information at the bottom of the title page: the name of the publisher of the book. It was the name of my own publisher. Only the address differed, given here as The Strand. The date of publication of this book was 1912, so presumably The Strand had then been the location of my publisher's premises. The coincidence pleased me. I turned to the first page of the text:

After absences lasting more than half a year he came to me each time as if from a strange apartment which communicated with the part of the house in which I lived by a hidden staircase or passage. When he was absent from us I spent many hours searching for the entrance to this secret way and often imagined I had found it. For a time after his departure I learnt to dull the sharpness of my grief with a resort to the fantastic, and in my daydreams I joined him in a land of pure imaginings which, for me, must lie beyond the hidden doorway. Together he and I, like the mythical *feng* and *huang* of the Chinese other-world, the heavenly emissary which appears when the land enjoys the gods' favour, journeyed side by side and danced our benevolent dance in perfect harmony upon the land which blessed our presence. Daily reality in Coppin Grove by comparison to this fanciful world seemed to me for some years during my childhood to be a meaningless folly pursued by persons of an unmitigated and grim practicality. A world of persons who did not deserve my compassion. No word from my mother or sisters, no matter how kind or well-intentioned, drew from me for years anything but disdain. Until, at the last, one by one, they had all reluctantly abandoned me to my folly, seeing in my presence among them not a daughter or a sister but a stranger in their midst.

On each subsequent visit he was always changed from the way he had been when I had seen him last. And so, I am certain, was I. We met on each occasion as new people, freshly burnished from our travels. The father with whom I dwelt for months at a time in my imaginary landscape was forced to retreat into the shadows of fiction whenever my real father arrived. He always came unexpectedly and unannounced.

On a bitterly cold day when I was eleven – it must have been the winter of 1889 – I was practising Franz Schubert's Fantasia in C – how could I forget, for it is based on his beautiful song '*Der Wanderer*'. I was lost to my surroundings, struggling to master the unfamiliar fingering, when I became aware that someone was near me. I ceased playing and swung around upon the stool. He stood in the doorway. We gazed at each other. In that moment I felt for him the purest, the most distilled, love. We did not embrace. We never embraced. But gazed upon each other's beloved countenance in wonderment. We dwelt in splendour. Schubert's chord loitered in the room as if it were the ghost of that great sadness which all humanity must bear.

'Please don't stop,' my father implored me gently.

'I have just finished, father,' I replied and I slipped quickly from the stool and hurried from the room by the door furthest from him.

He called to me, 'Stay a moment Victoria. I have a present for you.'

But I could not stay. I ran to my room and locked the door and stood dry-eyed before my mirror and solemnly announced to my faithful sister from the other-world, 'The Phoenix has returned to us.' I did not see him again until dinner. The formality of this occasion rendered our meeting easier for me. The ceremony, that is, which was required from each of us shielded me from emotions which I might otherwise have found it difficult to deal with. I believed he too, and that he alone of all those present, understood this exactly as I understood it. His gift to me was waiting in my place. They watched me while I opened it. For my eight sisters there were fine silks from Hangchou and for my mother a carpet from Tibet.

From its bed of silvery wild grass, a grass so soft it was like the fur of a young rabbit against my fingers – a grass so unlike

·

the coarse grasses that grew beside the Yarra and in the paddocks around Hawthorn that it could only have come from the other-world – from this nest I drew forth an earthenware horse glazed with subtle green and orange glazes. It was a horse of fine proportions, realistically formed. It stood with its head slightly turned and its mouth open, alert to the will of its rider. It was caparisoned with a Persian saddle and rosettes of green frogs on the harness. This tall, noble steed I recognised as none other than the legendary *Tianma*, the heavenly horse of the West. I looked at my horse with pride. This supernatural beast would carry me safely and swiftly to the furthest lands which my father might ever visit. It was a horse perfectly fashioned to inhabit the unearthly shadows of my fiction. Carefully I replaced it in its nest of wild grass and put it to one side. I did not need to look at my father to share with him the meaning of this gift. I understood that henceforth I was to travel with him.

My mother did not resist suggesting, 'I am sure Victoria wishes to thank you.' It was her way of letting me know that she acknowledged on my behalf no special preferment with my father. I raised my eyes and looked at her with a contempt that the dead might well bear towards the living. How little you can know or understand of this, my look was intended to convey. I remember she blushed. She was a loving and sensitive wife and the kindest mother ever blessed with eight dutiful daughters, an abundance of worldly goods and a robust constitution. But she was also Irish and her anger could be sudden, implacable and violent in its expression. But I was not afraid of her. How should I be? For I had my secret. So I smiled and waited for her to tell me to leave the room and to go to bed without my dinner. I knew my father would not intervene. My mother was the empress of this world, the mistress of the house at Coppin Grove, her domain bounded by the road and the river and by the summer-house, and by the edge of the native trees yonder. But not extending beyond these boundaries. Beyond her domain lay my freedom. And his. I did not care for this world at all, nor for its rewards. I laughed at them. When Katherine married the mayor and they moved to their great house in Brighton I felt sorry for her. I saw that she had been taken to a prison from which there could be no escape.

How many years was it from the gift of the horse to the terrible day I learned that not only the existence of my mother and sisters but my own existence as well had never been made known to my father's Chinese wife and son in Shanghai? That day I learned I had not existed for him in the Northern Hemisphere, with his number one family, as it became clear. Though I am not certain that in his youth he meant this to be so. I believe it was something deeper than himself which eroded our validity for him over the years. There are certain actions for which people should not be held personally accountable. There are ancient forces which make their way through us as rivers make their way through landscapes, reshaping features we had thought permanent, moving what we had thought to be stilled for ever, and wearing away resolves in us that are not touched even by our strangest imaginings. We are not only that person we think we are, but more. As my father I knew he loved me. But he was also a man from China.

This bright autumn day with the sun warm against my shoulders, the twenty-seventh of May 1908, he is dying. My half-brother from Shanghai, who is wholly Chinese, is with him. I can see my brother's shadow at the window. He stands behind my father's chair and waits to become the second Feng. He is a practical man. I believe Australia means nothing to him ... I would like to cease writing and walk among the trees, among that remnant of bushland which lies yonder, between the riverbank and the road ... The shadow of my brother has gone from the window. My father, the first Feng, is dead. I am alone, now, with my horse and my fiction. I am in my thirtieth year. I have been many years in preparation. Now even Shinjé, the Lord of Death herself, could not be better mounted for such a journey as I intend to make.

The light beside my bed was still on. The book lay on the covers near my hand. I picked it up and remembered I'd finished reading it before going to sleep. There were three hundred and two pages. I closed my eyes again and it was all still there. I watched her cantering away into her fiction on her orange and green horse through the patch of sunlit bush. I watched her setting out on her journey, riding bravely into the unknown landscape of her fiction, aware of her inevitable solitude. Her black hair streamed out behind her and the hooves of her supernatural horse threw a fine golden dust into the bright summer air, a dust which rose into the branches of the slim gumtrees and lingered there long after she had gone. Watching her I *was* her, the way one is the character within whose persona one transcends oneself; and strives with that person, as vulnerable as they to the dangers and difficulties which are encountered; hope and anxiety and fear dancing together in one's brain. Opposed to us on the journey was the dark sign with which she had announced her work: Beauty, truth and rarity, grace in all simplicity, here enclosed in cinders lie.

NO ORDINARY CHILD

Huang Yu-hua, the old literary painter, was sitting at his writing
desk in his study in the provincial capital of Hangzhou. He was
re-reading a letter from his only child, Lien. Huang was wearing
a black fur coat, which fastened high and close about his skinny
neck. The coat was more than fifty years old. It was bald on the
shoulders but was still proof against draughts and damps and
sudden chills, providing they were of the summer kind and not
too severe. A Kazak trader from the Kirgiz had sold his father the
twelve Syrian bear-cub pelts which had been required to make
this precious garment. On his shaved head Huang wore a black
silk skull cap with a gold emblem at the front, like a watchful
eye. Between the skull cap and the black fur his face shone in
the lamplight. His skin was the texture of waxed blondwood and
was stretched tight over the framework of his bones. From either
side of his upper lip silvery grey whiskers languished against the
sable fur, as two branches of a mountain stream might pass on
each side of a rocky prominence.

Huang's lips moved as he read and he nodded all the while,
measuring the rhythm of Lien's thoughts. Since she had gone
from his house two years ago he had become more sensitive to
cold and damp. There was no need for the fur coat this evening,
for the air was pleasantly mild, but should anything happen,

should an unexpected chill arise, for example, with his fur coat on he felt sure he would be ready for it. And he would rather have suffered the discomfort of too much warmth than the wretched anxiety which must arise from being unprepared. He had been nineteen, Lien's age now, when his father had presented him with the coat. He read her letter once again, this time with even more care than before:

My Dearest Father,

Feng sends you his greetings and trusts that you will soon have recovered your former state of good health. Can you believe this? Is it possible that you are reading these words from your daughter, or are you dreaming them? Or, is it that our dream is to come true? I shall keep you in suspense on this matter no longer. Here is what I have to say. I shall be arriving in Hangzhou next Friday. Everything must be just as it was! Nothing is to be out of its customary place! Yes, we are to be together again! But first we must wait almost a whole week. How shall we bear it? By the time you receive this it will be one day less. How lucky you are to be one day closer to me than I am to you, revered parent! Concern yourself about nothing. Do not disturb your routine. Experience no anxiety on my behalf. Everything will be arranged. I shall be travelling by train and his Russian will go ahead by road and meet me at the station with a car. I am hurrying to write this. Be assured my dear Father that I shall not be coming as an important guest to your house. So make no arrangements for the reception of the wife of C.H. Feng. *He* will not wish to know anything of how it is done. He would rather it were not done. Do not greet me at the principal gate with the assembled household. Keep my visit a secret from them. Tell only Yu. Consider that I am returning from an excursion to the temple at Lin Yin. I shall re-enter by my customary way.

Behind Huang hundreds of dusty books were piled untidily one on top of another on pearwood shelves. Apart from his writing table and the books there was little furniture in the room. The floor was composed of large irregular-shaped flagstones the colour of lead. They were worn into smooth undulations from the passage of many generations of slippered feet. The faded carmine and green casements were open and through them could be seen the red-lacquered posts of the verandah, lustrous in the evening light as if they had been made of polished metal. Beyond the verandah lay Huang's formal garden, now in a state of neglect. Huang ceased reading. He folded the letter carefully and placed it in a pocket inside his coat. The sun was setting. Through the casements a bank of cloud could be seen lying across Langdang Ridge, a forested hill which rose from the western shore of the lake, and which was visible to him above the roof of the furthest section of his house – that section of his house, beyond the courtyard of the little red doorway, through which she was to return to him. The temple of Lin Yin was situated on an outcrop of rock within the ridge among the hills, concealed by the forest. He watched until the gilding had faded from the edges of the cinnamon clouds, then he withdrew her letter and once again began to study it. His attention lingered on the ideograph *father*. A tear slid down the side of his straight nose until it encountered the cup formed by the rise of his nostril and the curve of his cheek. When the unbidden servant, Yu Hung-meng, came in and placed the lamp on the writing table, it appeared Huang wore a diamond in his nose. He dwelt lingeringly upon each of her brushstrokes, seeking remembered aspects of a terrain with which he had once been familiar, muttering to himself of rocks and withered vines and dewdrops about to fall, seeking his daughter through her expressive script. A script he had taught her himself. Though she had done him the honour of using the brush, her letter had been written in a hurry and he found only fragments of the old ground they had shared.

He murmured her name and was startled by the unexpected voice. He had not intended to speak her name aloud. It whispered around the walls. He fancied he heard the silk of her gown brush against the doorpost as she entered. He stared about him, distracted. The lamplight illuminated only the flagstones. He was afraid.

Behind a blue-painted screen near the door Yu Hung-meng eased his joints. The scholar's pain was his pain. The scholar's anxieties his. He had served no other master. Since Lien's letter arrived he had been waiting for the signal to rejoice. He bore the old man's misery impatiently. The painter's tears made him groan aloud. How often had they wept together? Were they always to be the ones who must weep? From the folds of his gown he drew out a little box, carved in one piece from the root of a wild thorn tree. She had given him the box to keep his tobacco moist. He tugged off the lid and held it close to his nostrils, breathing the aroma of the dark leaf. The voice of his master called to him then and he rose, slipping his treasured gift back into its place of concealment. As he crossed the study the joints of his knees creaked and snapped, giving out the sounds of someone walking over bamboo trestles. He had tried often to imagine what it must be like for her in Shanghai. The city of the Lord of Death. He knew that much. The infernal regions raised above the earth, where the tower of the Phoenix looked down indifferently upon the misery of a people. A city ruled by foreign devils who knew nothing of Kung or Mung, or of any morality.

While he fetched hot water for the scholar's tea Yu Hung-meng asked himself the question once again: could Lien, their Child of Light, whose birth had elevated himself and his master to a place in heaven – from which they had since fallen back to earth – could their child return from Shanghai untainted by the powers of evil? And if she returned would they not all be worse off than they were now, enduring her absence? At least in her absence they possessed their memories and their dreams. With considerable realism and courage he asked himself, could she humiliate Feng in this way and yet elude his vengeance? He groaned and spat and distracted himself from these forebodings by considering in detail the cigarette he was planning to smoke.

Though forbidden by Huang, he had capitulated to Lien's persistence and given her her first suck on the charmed weed ten years ago, when she was nine. The recollection of the event cheered him. With the action of a dancer blowing a lingering kiss to her departing lover, she had stood in the prow of the boat touching the cigarette to her pink lips, drawing the smoke into her lungs and holding it there. She had closed her eyes and swayed and smiled. A smoker and dancer both, of great natural ability. The recollection of the spectacle still possessed the power to entrance him. Oh my dear friend Yu, she had exclaimed, her strangely speckled eyes alight with the excitement of projected conspiracy, promise me you will persist in this deception of my beloved Father! What a way to put it! He recalled his panic. But she had won him round with flattery. And from that day until her departure for Shanghai with the banker C.H. Feng, he had shared with her his precious supply of tobacco. She was addicted to the pleasure of the weed from her first taste, and he to the enticements of her youthful rapture. This secret pledge with her renewed his confidence in life at a time when he had ceased to derive pleasure from recollecting the exploits of his youth. Perhaps she would bring him a present of a carton of American Camels. The city of the Lord of Death might yet possess virtue. And surely the girl who had done what other girls had only dreamed of doing, the girl who had laughed at dangers which had caused men of nerve to pause and become cautious, surely she would have proved herself a match for the devils of Shanghai, the equal, even, of the Third Feng himself? For was there not within her, Yu Hung-meng reflected, a demon which was the peer of any man's? Who would not sleep lightly if Lien were numbered among his enemies? He approached Huang's table and kow-towed. He was feeling much better.

Huang looked out upon his garden, the failing light concealing the signs of his neglect. The scene before him was leached of colour now, the burnished timber pillars were grey, the column of porphyry was grey. Only the branches of the winter-flowering plum were black against the metallic sky. The shriek of a night heron calling to her mate from an island on the lake startled him. The bird's cry seemed to him an omen, a voice calling a warning to him from the darkness of the other-world. And was a shadow not moving stealthily through his garden? He strove to see more clearly what lay before him. The answering cry of the male heron came from far above him, high in the moonless sky. With what ornate subterfuge had Lien beguiled Feng, he asked himself wonderingly, that the banker had given his permission for her to return home? Huang had great difficulty these days recalling the manner of his existence before Lien's birth. She had entered his life like a comet entering the known firmament, a heavenly body of unknown origin and mysterious purpose portending great events and casting her unearthly light upon the familiar objects around him and making them new and unfamiliar. A disorienting force. She had woken him from a deep slumber into which he had been unaware that he had fallen. Nothing had ever been more unexpected nor more illuminating to him. She had rendered him vulnerable to time. An ancient resistance within him had given way before her presence, and she had led him forward into a garden of infinite delight.

He stared into the night. Now she was to return to him from the cursed city of Feng, the solitary phoenix. Huang had never been there. He could only imagine the horrors of a place such as he believed Shanghai to be. On the other side of Hangzhou, steaming across the iron spans of the Quiantangjiang Bridge, an evening freight train sounded two long blasts on its whistle. He turned away and told Yu to close the shutters. He busied himself searching in the cupboard below the bookshelves. There were boxes here of many shapes and of different materials, some of bamboo and others of lacquer or fashioned from rare and unusual species of tree. Yet others were intricately carved or painted. There was one cast in iron. Into the black face of this box there had been set the likeness of a landscape, a tracery of gold thread, wherein minute travellers made their precarious way through a deep gorge among wild mountains. Such a fragment as the painter Sung Hui-tsung himself might have reflected upon in his old age. The boxes contained Huang's collection of teas. He opened first one then another, sampling a pinch of leaf and rubbing it between his fingers before holding it to his nostrils. It was a particular memory he searched for among the fragrances, but he did not find it. Before Lien's departure, each of the boxes had carried its silk tie, on which there had been inscribed a description of its contents; the variety of bush, its location, the temperature of the day and the time of year at which the leaf had been picked. After she had left, one by one the ties had fallen off and he had eventually stopped bothering to replace them. They now lay about untidily among the spilt tea leaves on the shelf. It had not taken long for his own slackness to affect the rest of the household. He pretended not to notice the servants standing around smoking, or sitting together in one of the courtyards playing cards, or gossiping with servants from a neighbour's house in the sun by the second gateway. Of late they no longer even got up and shammed industriousness whenever he passed by. He had overheard Yu reprimanding them, and had seen that this had little effect. He poured hot water into the pot and watched the steam rise before dropping in a few leaves. He sat in his chair and sucked the brew through his whiskers. It was subtly aromatic, a highlight of citron enduring on his palate. He considered it pleasurably, his eyes very nearly closed, and decided it was almost certainly a local bush. From a random choice, surely this was to be taken as a good omen.

He had married but once and knew what it was, therefore, to be judged an eccentric by his peers. He had first taken a wife when he was fifty years old. He scarcely remembered her. He had married her to satisfy his relatives in the south, who had insisted he repay his debt to the family for his education by bringing a son into the world. His wife had not survived the birth. He had taken no other wife. The debt had remained unpaid. Only since Lien's absence, and in the face of his own advancing demoralisation, had this matter begun to make him uneasy. For by what means might such an outstanding debt be accounted for in the final balance of his life?

Until Lien's birth he had thought of the coming child as no concern of his own. When he heard her, alone and crying pitifully through the nights after the funeral of her mother, however, he had found he could not ignore her. He believed he detected an appeal in her cry which, he was certain, was directed to no one but himself. He responded, and soon she began to distract him from his work; from his pursuit of a kind of static perfection, a mirror of the work of Hsia Kuei, a Sung master of the late twelfth and early thirteenth centuries. He made no resistance to a desire to give advice to the nurse on how to care for the baby. The woman resented this unheard-of interference, so he sent her away, recruited a new wet nurse and took over the rest of the duties of caring for the baby himself. It wasn't long before he couldn't bear to have her out of his sight for more than an hour or so at a time. And even then he thought about her, wondering how she was getting on without him and resenting helplessly the possibility that she might be finding the wet nurse's company more congenial than his. Once she was weaned he kept her by him all the time, day and night, for he feared that a terrible accident waited to befall her if he should allow her out of his reach. Although he did not speak of this even to Yu Hung-meng, to whom he spoke of nearly everything else, Huang was convinced the little girl did not rightfully belong to him, and had been placed in his care through a mistake in the working out of destinies. He lived daily with the fear that the mistake would be discovered by the powers who order these things and that the child would be taken from him. And, of course, all this time, locked away in a dark place at the very back of his mind where even he did not care to venture very often, was the knowledge that he had failed to pay his debt to his family, the knowledge that he had failed in his obligation to the ancestors. His life with Lien became more and more secretive as time went on.

For a week she screamed and there was nothing he could do to comfort her. It was a warm spring night and he was carrying her against his body under his gown, walking in his garden, when she at last stopped screaming. He stood still, exhausted and relieved, and he looked down at her upturned face. When she saw him she smiled. Gleaming in the moonlight, like two little polished grains of rice which had been set into her glistening gums by a craftsman of great skill, were her first teeth. Deeply moved, he gazed at her in wonder. As if she understood everything that was in his heart, her serious eyes returned his gaze. It was with a feeling that now he must break the most powerful taboo by which his life had been ruled, that he placed his mouth close to her ear and whispered, My search is over. I shall look no further. He kissed her hair. His whiskers tickled her face and made her sneeze. He groaned with happiness.

As the years went by Huang became confirmed in his belief that Lien was no ordinary child. He devoted all his time to her education, eventually losing touch completely with his former students and seeing his friends and fellow scholars so seldom that they ceased to refer to him in the present tense. Indeed, unless they were reminiscing about the old days, when he had been one of their number, the eminent Hangzhou scholars never mentioned the name of Huang Yu-hua at all any longer. He knew this and there were times when it made him sad to think of it. But he could not change the way things had been determined. He had abandoned their way and the purpose of his life had become a secret project, the nature of which was known only to himself and to Yu Hung-meng. Whenever he felt uneasy, Huang sniffed the scalp of his child. And quite often he sniffed it when he was not uneasy. The fragrance was of another world and kindled in his imagination images of sunlit gardens and bright musical harmonies that sang to him of an infinite, untroubled wellbeing. This became the subject of the poems he now regularly wrote and illustrated, and which he showed only to her and to Yu.

Together he and Yu Hung-meng were gazing at the sleeping child one night, as they often did, when Yu observed in a whisper, We are two old roosters who have found a golden chick. The next day Huang painted a picture of two huge dark roosters and a tiny golden chick. He wrote beside the image, *The sight of you brings spring sunshine*.

Impatient to see what she would do, he introduced her to his art before she could walk. Soon he was watching her use the four treasures of the scholar – the paper, the ink, the ink-stone and the brush – and marvelling at the speed of her progress. It was not many years before the power of her brushstrokes seemed to arise from within her without conscious effort, as they had only ever done for him on one or two blissful occasions during a disciplined lifetime of striving to master the ancient forms. By the time Lien was twelve he might have passed her work off as the very strongest of his own. It was a kind of heavenly anguish for him to watch her. Amused by life now, he often asked himself, Why did I strive and suffer so foolishly for all those years, when it is really so easy for those who possess the gift? Working with her every day as her teacher, those early years seemed as though they were going to last for ever. But this was an illusion. When she was thirteen something happened which changed their lives. The crisis was undoubtedly preceded by small signs, but it was only in retrospect that he identified these.

He had begun to relax. He no longer worried every day about the powers who order destinies. Her work had begun to rival the best he had ever seen, past or present. It possessed power and grace and spirit and such a paradoxical union of wildness and control that it seemed Nature herself must be working directly through the girl's hands and eyes. It was a winter day and the dark red plum blossom was visible through the open casements when the demon emerged at last. Lien was working at the table in his study as usual. The sun was shining through the open shutters and the air was frosty. The atmosphere in the study reeked with the wholesome smell of freshly ground ink, which she had rendered to the consistency of horse blood. She had finished numerous paintings, and these lay scattered about the floor where she had carelessly thrown them. Huang was watching her.

All at once she stopped painting and held the loaded brush poised above the painting. Huang rose to his feet slowly. Why was she hesitating? He strained forward, trying to fathom her intention. He saw Yu watching them. What was it? What struggle was going on within her? The work which lay before her was bold and large and was possessed of a confident ugliness, its gestures deep and struck from side to side by energies of contradiction. How can she add more, Huang asked himself, to such muscular perfection as this? Without uttering a sound, Lien scored the loaded brush through the length of the painting. Huang snatched the ruined work from the table and looked at her with horror . . .

The cup had grown cold in his hands. Slowly he placed it on

·

the table. His throat was parched. He refilled the cup with the luke-warm remains of the brew in which the lingering note of citron had so pleased him, and he drank. The painting had been a masterpiece. Of this he had no doubt. With the tears running freely down his cheeks he asked her, Why my daughter? Why have you destroyed your finest work?

She laughed at his question and the bronze flecks within her eyes flickered. She ran to the open casement and jumped through onto the verandah and turned and confronted him. Because the donkey needs a tail! she screamed, and again and again she screamed it at him, dodging from one window to the next along the length of the verandah, screaming her nonsensical message at him.

In his sorrow and bewilderment he ordered Yu to burn all her paintings. When she heard this she stood still and ceased screaming, but looked on. While Yu collected her work from the floor and from the earthenware pots in which the scrolls were stored, she stood by looking into the room, her oval features grave and sad, framed by the green and red casements as if she were a formal portrait of herself. Behind her in the garden the deep red of the plum blossom stood out on the black tracery of leafless branches.

The demon's laughter remained in Huang's head for days, for weeks. It remained there until he could no longer distinguish it from the mocking voice of his own self doubt. As if they had been a father and son, he and Lien had always taken their meals together. Now they ate in separate apartments. Huang was alone once again. Each day he enquired of Yu how she was. But Yu had little to report, except that she did not wish to see her father. Huang did not know what to do. There was no one to whom he might appeal for an opinion, for theirs had been an eccentric relationship and had been disapproved of by everyone who had come to hear of it. During this time, with nothing else to occupy his mind, for he was unable to find solace in the poets, Huang began to see that he had committed a great folly in raising his daughter as if she had been a boy, not even requiring her feet to be bound and directing her in every way as if she were destined to bring honour to his own family, instead of to the family of the man whom she would eventually marry.

He needed so badly to talk to someone that he at last began to think of going to see his friend Fan Ping-chen, a great scholar and the leader of their old group. When the spring came and the estrangement from Lien had still shown no signs of healing, Huang got up his courage and ordered a huakan and he went to see the old scholar. Fan Ping-chen lived in a fine house on Geling Hill. The sun was shining as Huang rode along and he opened the curtains and looked about him at the people hurrying along the busy streets. He was reassured to see that nothing had changed and he quickly forgot his fear of seeing his old friend again after so many years, and even began to look forward to the meeting. Why should he not be readmitted to the enjoyable intimacies of old associations? When he arrived, however, Fan Ping-chen greeted him with such an excessive degree of formality and lavished upon him so much honour that Huang was deeply humiliated and was forced to realise his mistake at once. They parted without saying anything of interest to each other.

After this terrible rejection, which he knew must be the cause of endless gossip among the people of Hangzhou, Huang became so despondent that all he could think of was his own death. He visited the local temples, which he had not done since before her birth, and observing the great serenity of the monks he imagined, for a week or two, that he might find peace of mind among the devout Buddhists. But this also proved to be a false hope, for he soon discovered that, for those who dwelt there, beneath the appearance of tranquility within the temple there existed a double of the discordant world that had already brought him so much suffering. After the temple life failed him, Huang stayed home and lay on his bed all day without moving. He refused to eat the food brought to him by Yu.

When Yu informed Lien gravely, The literary painter Huang Yu-hua is waiting for the Lord of Death. You will soon be surrounded by your father's weeping relatives, who will surely wish to claim their property, Lien realised she could depend on no one but herself to redeem the situation. She had already understood that no question can have only one side, and that no person can be only one and solitary. So she went to her father's study and she ground ink and painted a small handscroll depicting a fragment of mountainous scenery in the pure manner of the Sung scholar Sung Hui-tsung, permitting herself no gesture which might identify her own style. Alongside the image, with a small and unpretentious brush, she wrote, *How foolish it is to rejoice in our own draughtsmanship when the masters teach us all we know.* And, as a coda above her seal, she added – henceforth an ironic maxim for her in which the unhappy outcome of her project was to be endlessly recapitulated – *Any girl can learn to draw.* Then she dressed in her finest green silk gown and decorated her hair with her most precious ornament, and she went into her father's bedroom and kowtowed to him before presenting him with the handscroll.

After this she set about establishing her authority with the servants, and soon became the undisputed mistress of Huang's household. No one, not even Yu, ever referred again to her great gift, and it must have seemed to everyone that she had capitulated. Privately Yu was not convinced of this. It seemed to him that the demon of such a gift as hers must be of the spirit and therefore immortal, and if one entrance to expression is stopped up against it, then such a demon will busy itself burrowing to make another.

Lien proved to be a harsh mistress, exercising the prerogatives of a woman without the tempering quality of compassion. There was even cruelty in the manner of her rule, as if she wished to see everyone suffer a little for the sacrifice she was herself forced to endure. And so things continued uneasily for a number of years. Until the Shanghai banker, C.H. Feng, came to the provincial capital one day on business, and encountered the daughter of the literary painter, Huang Yu-hua, under Locking Waves Bridge.

PORTRAITS

Except for a headscarf or bandeau, like the one my mother sometimes wore about the house, she was naked. This 'scarf' presented the only point of cheerful colour in the painting, the remainder being cold flesh against the brown drapery of a curtain. She was pale and sharp featured and her head was much too large and too old for her child's body. Her left hand held a towel pressed to her side, and her right hand, and indeed the whole of her right arm, was held back out of sight behind her, so that she appeared to be thrusting forward with her bony chest and belly. She was looking directly into the eyes of the artist, and her examination was derisory. Her expression reminded me of newspaper photographs I'd seen of wartime women in London's streets. She had decided there was no more to be expected from men.

I realised it was a bath towel, not a scarf or a bandeau, round Victoria's head. It was a towel wrapping her wet hair. As soon as I'd decided this, the situation of the painting's composition suggested itself to me. She had, of course, been returning to her room from taking a bath. She had been wearing the larger towel, which she was now pressing to her side, as a covering. She had met the artist on the landing of the stair. The meeting had been foreseen by her, for she had known he would be

·

there, drafting the dimensions of the upper hall for her mother.

She had begun her secret project with him a year earlier, just after he had arrived. Initially she had stood before him in the open air while he had sketched, positioning herself so that her presence had inhabited a corner of his composition, and persisting until his repeated measuring glances had included her. With the passage of time, and with the increments of further adjustments, she had here at last come to occupy his entire canvas, had come to comprise his only subject, and no doubt to take possession of his entire life. In the portrait her project was complete. No more was to be expected of him. Their relationship had been intricate and strained beyond belief, for him an exquisite and cloaked desire, a mortification to her eight sisters and a torture to her mother. He had rendered her skin grey and cold. He had not signed the painting. Her derision had been reserved for his despair.

In 1908, as a woman of thirty, Victoria might have written of herself then, as a child of eleven:

The girl who stands at the edge of the thin, dry forest observing the artist at work on the green sweep of lawn before her, keeps a private journal of her own. Into its pages at night, when she is alone in her room at the top of the house, her thoughts of herself and her findings concerning the northern hemisphere are written. She writes of the English painter carefully, deliberatively, with the kind of loving and solitary joy of a writer. She is accurate with her observations and careful to resist the proffered image. She is aware of the temptation to become fanciful and knows the dangers are real. Fiction, she has discovered, though it is conducted in the isolation of the mind, cannot be permitted to become madness. She does not know what her researches will reveal. She does not know the end of her story. She writes not with an end in mind but with a desire to make the material of her scrutiny her own, to possess it by means of the location of herself at its centre. She enters it by degrees. She insinuates herself. She is in fear of and is fascinated by her power to entice and to mock the artist. She composes fragments: *From the verandah outside my room I watched my mother walking in the garden with him after dinner when he was newly arrived and talked of nothing but Monsieur Legros and the Slade, as if these had been his own inventions and he not simply one of their less gifted students. That night a yellow moon was reflected in the slow brown waters of the Yarra River. My mother and he did not enter the summerhouse, but hesitated when they drew near to it, unsteady with the closeness of its concealing darkness. My mother's voice was clear and round and sad in the night as she enumerated the features of her domain to him, her left arm extended, pointing, sweeping in a half-circle from the bank of the river to the remnant of native bush. I would like you to paint all this, she told him. A nocturne would be most acceptable. But first I must have the interior views we have spoken of. And then they walked once around the summerhouse, sailors circumnavigating a mysterious island. They did not venture as far as the boatshed – as real sailors might have done – but behaved as if it was not there. Yet, as they left, I saw him turn and look towards it, to where the willows made Vs in the current and the vacant shell of the boat invited thoughts of taking passage with a woman.*

The girl, who is myself, remained upon the high verandah and observed the smoke and the white columns of steam rising from the chimneys in Richmond on the other side of the river, where the poor of the city live and work. On the lawn below her the darker trace of her mother's gown and the painter's footprints mapped their journey upon the dewy grass. She thought of him, and by the light of the moon began to enter her material.

His pose was of a decided superiority as he painted his sombre, uninhabited interiors. But she persisted and in the open air, removed from the house, he admitted her at last to a large oil which was to hang on the east wall of the dining room. The composition was horizontal and extensive, broken in the middle distance by the summerhouse with its oriental eaves and its elaborate finial pointing towards the sky. Beyond this feature of the middle distance were the slim native trees. The attentive eye, led away by these toward a suggestion of less civilised regions, might pursue the meanderings of the river. And here, where the river slid away into the distance, he inserted a dab of alizarin crimson. A solitary figure, it must appear, stood at the edge of the trees.

He permitted her to understand that he had included her merely to gratify her desire to be noticed by him, that he had humored the daughter of his employer. The truth was more sad and more romantic. The truth was that her image within his picture mitigated for him, in a most secret and precious way, the pain of his larger failure, the cause of his unhappy exile. For at the Slade School he had been misplaced. His fellow students had not struggled as he had been required to do in order to comprehend the mysteries of drawing and painting, but had shone effortlessly, a society of gifted luminaries for whom art and literature and Society were but Nature's way, an accessible and effortless path to be illuminated by works of extraordinary generosity. He had not been vouchsafed their largesse of spirit. The best he had been able to manage had been a letter of introduction from Eugène von Guérard, an artist of some past standing who had once held the position of curator of the National Gallery of Victoria, and had been the Principal of its art school until his retirement and return to England in 1881.

He knew he was not, as his mentor had been, an adventurer, but was an exile. He knew he would never see his beloved England again. In this Hawthorn house he found a certain kinship, he was invited to court a friendship with the solitary girl who gazed at him with her mysterious oriental eyes, as if she alone of all the world understood most sensitively the difficulties and disappointments of his life. As if, indeed, she shared his exile from the Northern Hemisphere.

When the painting of the lawn and the summerhouse was finished, when, that is, the dab of alizarin crimson had been inserted, she made him wait upon her and chose with care and numerous hesitations and revisions her own disposition in certain of his canvases. She grew and matured as his most favoured subject. Until the picture of a girl playing a piano, which her mother's friends commended so enthusiastically. With this picture, which required many sittings, she came to her ambition

·

of a full-length portrait, to the ambition of being herself his entire subject matter. To sustain herself upon him, just as the dark mistletoe sustains itself upon the weak branches of the gumtrees along the river, and as he drew her to draw from him her fiction of the Northern Hemisphere. And what then? What when she had done with him? A child is immortal. She was not concerned with the end of her story but with its process. She would travel yet to China on her orange and green horse.

It was two o'clock in the morning but still she wrote and did not notice the chill of the night air until the first cloud from the south-west passed across the descending moon and darkened her page.

Victoria's portrait had been resting against a china cabinet in the front room of Lang's house since the night we'd brought it from Lindner's. He interrupted my reflections on it with a petulant request that I come and examine one of his own paintings, the *only* painting of his hung in the house so far as I knew. That's not a good painting, he said, gesturing with his wineglass at the naked Victoria. You shouldn't be wasting your time with it. Jokingly, I accused him of being jealous.

I had begun, in fact, to think of the house as being as much Victoria's as his. I'd begun to experience it through a combination of my readings of her *Winter Visitor* and my own new preoccupation with the attempt to recast his parents for him from the accounts of them he'd given me. An uncertain project, which was not entirely his nor quite my own. What in February I'd regarded as a state of genteel neglect, a result of Lang's lack of sufficient funds for repairs – a condition which endowed with a certain elderly charm a number of the other large houses in Coppin Grove – by the autumn I'd seen to be the result of several decades of Victoria's studied disregard for the upkeep of the place, her conscious neglect of her mother's old domain, and her single-minded allegiance throughout her long life to the concerns of the other-world of fiction. Lang had increasingly begun to seem to me to be a late and somewhat incidental occupier of what was essentially Victoria's house.

The view of the house that was presented as one drew up to it along Coppin Grove was of a once stately residence of the early boom period which had been severely tampered with. The taste for renovation was evident not only inside, in the choice of the second-rate works of the English artist, but outside even more strikingly in the vaulted Gothic portico which had been built on to the fine Victorian facade. Over time a wilderness of shrubs and trees and climbing vines, which festooned the verandahs and leaned against the walls, had rendered the clash of styles less violent. Under the inspiration of Victoria's neglect a purple bougainvillea luxuriantly dominated such less aggressive species as *Clematis clycinoides*, the traveller's joy of Eastern Australia, and a fragrant jasmine, which had managed to retain a corner of the ground-floor verandah. A temporary equilibrium, as of exhausted wrestlers, had been established between the garden and the house; between the contending influences of mother and daughter. In this mise en scène Lang's was not a determinative presence.

When I accused him of being jealous of the close attention I'd been giving to the work of the English painter he made an irritated noise and turned his back on me, standing as near to the gas heater as he could without catching alight and looking pointedly at the painting which hung above the fireplace, too vexed to offer a response.

Among the dozen or so paintings and drawings in the room, besides Victoria's, there were three other portraits of young women. One was of a girl viewed from behind, seated at a piano. The interpretation was colourful and decorative, but it was unmistakably the work of the English painter. Then, between the windows, there was a head and shoulders of a young woman in a flowered hat, the subject contre-jour in the manner of Sickert. Lang claimed it was the work of Nan Hudson, Sickert's friend. He considered Sickert himself to have been, along with Whistler and Degas, one of the greatest painters of his time. He argued that the relative neglect of Sickert's work marked exactly the degree to which the world of Western art had gone off in the wrong direction, a development he placed at the beginning of the First World War. He defended this view at great length, and in doing so revealed a detailed knowledge of the period. Despite his persuasive scholarship, after I'd heard the argument a few times I got the feeling that in defending Sickert he was, in some sort of disguised and elliptical way, really offering a defence of himself as a neglected artist. The undisclosed argument invited a parallel between himself and Sickert, in which the undisclosed purpose in recasting his parents became a rehabilitative biography of himself, the Australian/Chinese painter Lang Tzu, who was absent from the record.

In a way, of course, it was his own fault if I was spending more of my time attending to Victoria and her painter than I was to him. It was he who'd first drawn my attention to her by convincing me I ought to read *The Winter Visitor*. Now he refused to discuss the book, or evaded by every possible means discussing either it or the English painter. It was as if he were afraid that by attending to Victoria's affairs I might be led to fashion a parallel not between himself and his hero, Walter Sickert, but between himself and the sad English exile for whose despair Victoria had reserved only her derision at the completion of her own project. Ironically, it was Lang's very fear of this that drew my attention to its possibilities.

Above the gas fire, a position which, in the circumstances, bestowed an unlikely authority on the picture owing to its prominence overlooking the other pictures in the room, hung the third portrait of a young woman. Lang had painted it when he was twenty-five and in love with the subject; or, perhaps, in love with the idea of being the companion of such an ideal creature of the Western world as she appeared to have been. It was a picture of a beautiful Englishwoman in the luscious early manner of George Lambert. If it had been painted in 1910 instead of in the fifties it would no doubt have aroused some interest in the young Australian/Chinese artist who'd painted it. I could see nothing of Lang in it, however, and when he'd told me it was his I'd had to disguise my disappointment.

He blew a cloud of smoke at the picture. Do you know why I keep her there? She was my wife. He laughed and coughed thickly, doubling forward and spilling wine on the hearth. For a year, he added gaily, parodying the way some people might boast of having had in their possession for a time an expensive car or a racehorse they couldn't afford. When he'd recovered, he came over and took me by the arm, gripping me just above the elbow and urging me along, the way one might encourage a blind person to enter an unknown place. The strength in his fingers was surprising. I'll show you something that *will* interest you, Steven. He propelled me towards the dining room.

Occupying the centre of this room was a mahogany table of magisterial proportions, around which was arranged a matched setting of eighteen balloon-backed dining chairs with their original buttoned leather seats. Where had Victoria been seated the evening she'd opened her father's gift? The family gathered here in this room and seated at dinner, the mother's Tibetan carpet draped across a chair and the colourful Hangzhou silks for the other daughters. Their attention on Victoria, waiting for her. The last to open her present. Had the painter been seated here too? Near her? Next to her? But an image of them that evening resisted me. To visualise them I had to refer to my recollection of her account in the book.

The curtains were drawn across the windows and the air was stale. Completely covering the ample surface of the table, to a depth of half a metre or more, was a disordered heap of unstretched oils and watercolours and sketches and books and catalogues and other marginalia relating to Australian art; a collection, a hoard really, which Lang has been amassing indiscriminately since his student days in art school at Ballarat thirty years ago.

Look at it, he said. I'm ashamed of it. He was boasting, he was proud of it, it represented plunder, the life's gatherings of a bandit. A pirate's treasure trove harvested from auction rooms and junk shops and private houses and from expensive galleries like Lindner's: whatever had turned up; the individual items in it connected only by their Australianness.

Lang poked at it, securing bits of paper that were threatening to fall out, lifting the corner of a painting and releasing a breathy exclamation of recollection. Still holding my arm, he turned to

.

66

me and looked into my face, examining my features as if he were searching for attributable painterly characteristics, his warm breath touching my cheek, his cold right eye observing me, unmoved and disinterested. *Her* stuff's under this. He waited for me to absorb the information, then released my arm and laid the flat of his hand emphatically on the pile before us. Under here, Steven, that's where she is. Under *my* stuff.

We stood silently staring at it – we might have been waiting for a sign, a movement transmitted to the surface from what lay beneath. See! he exclaimed, delighted with my silence. I put mine on top of hers. Just for a day or two, when I moved in. Till I could find the time to sort it all out. You should see the mess she left. He pushed at a protruding Joel's catalogue, a relic of the days when these had been stapled lists. And look! It's all still here! I haven't touched it. He moved away from me, along the table, examining this and that at random, taking care not to shift anything from its place – an archaeologist respectful of each item's position within the matrix of the strata: we shall only know the meaning of a thing if we know the place we encounter it.

I keep putting more on top, he said. I've thought of pretending to have a nervous breakdown so I'd have the time to deal with it. Archly he looked across at me. What do you think of that idea? He continued his inspection. Compo, he murmured, wonderingly.

He stopped on the far side of the table, his hoard a rampart between us. We could sort it all out, Steven. Together we'd have the time. We could work our way through it. Starting from the top and working our way down. He waited, watching me. She was half Chinese, he said. You won't understand her. There are things you can't guess. You'll have to go through my stuff or hers won't make sense to you.

His telephone was ringing in the hall. He let it ring, watching me, enjoying the moment, before going to answer it.

She was absent from the official record. I hadn't expected to find an entry under FENG, *Victoria* (1878–1968), in *The Oxford*

Companion to English Literature. I'd never imagined it was going to be so easy. But I had felt a little hopeful when I'd consulted the index of authors at the end of Nettie Palmer's prize-winning essay *Modern Australian Literature,* the purpose of which, in 1924, in the publisher's words, had been 'to stimulate an interest in our own literature'. Published in 1912, *The Winter Visitor* fell exactly in the middle of the period covered by this essay: 1900 to 1923. But there was no reference in it, or in any of the other histories of Australian literature, to Victoria or to her books. I'd tried the antiquarian dealers. They'd never heard of her but expressed an interest in seeing *The Winter Visitor.* There was nothing in Ferguson's seven-volume *Bibliography of Australia,* and the vast index of the State Library contained no clue.

I placed my hands on the unsteady pile in front of me. A good shove would topple it. I could feel her there, under my hands in her documentary form, waiting to be recovered. I rocked the pile back and forth experimentally. The table creaked and something beneath it shifted. I bent down and looked to see what had fallen. The space under the table was crammed with stuff. I made out a paint-spattered easel among boxes and cartons and bundles of magazines and newspapers. Beside it there was a large ceramic pot filled with artist's brushes. I knelt down to see better. From the doorway Lang called, That's it Steven. You're getting warmer.

He came over and put a glass of wine on the carpet and sat beside me. There's some of my mother's gold in there. We gazed in through the chair legs at this secondary hoard. He reached through and dipped into a carton. Here, he said, handing me a thick bundle of what looked like new banknotes. Shanghai bonds. I've got thousands of them. They were worth a fortune one day and nothing the next.

He worked to free the chair from an obstructing leg of the easel. That was Gertrude on the phone. She's got hold of something at an auction. It belonged to my grandfather. You should have come earlier if you'd wanted to know about Victoria.

I watched him struggling with the chair. 1878–1968; she'd survived almost right through the sixties. I found it impossible, however, to imagine her watching the news of President Kennedy's assassination. For me she was a woman of thirty at the end of the first decade of this century writing about herself being a child at the close of the nineteenth century. And the woman and the child persisted; they possessed an ahistorical existence parallel to my own. It was only a matter of bridging the gap, somehow.

He freed the chair and pushed it to one side. I'll show you something Steven. I'll show you something that will interest you. He lit a cigarette and released a thick yellow cloud of smoke, as if he were a Chinese conjurer and this were his preliminary theatrical effect. His crafty gaze flickered at me. With care he pulled out a cube-shaped Liptons tea box from under the table. It was a very old box. The cinnamon wood was stained a few centimetres from the base by a dark line, like the wavering shoreline delicately inscribed on an explorer's chart. Victoria wasn't interested in me. You should have come earlier and you could have talked to Gertrude's father. He placed the box between us. Look at this Steven. He opened the lid.

I was more than half-prepared to see Victoria's Tang horse, Tianma, her heavenly horse of the West. There was a skull in the box. It was very clean and white and it was lying face up. A heavy-browed individual with a perfect set of beautifully even teeth. Dorset, he said, with a kind of awe. Let's have a drink.

THE MOTHER

HOMECOMING

Lien got out of the car and stood in the middle of the road. It was three in the afternoon and very hot. There was no one about. She breathed in the familiar Hangzhou dust, the essential smell of summer. She told the chauffeur, who was standing uncertainly beside her, to go away. She knew he was thinking of Feng and was unwilling to leave her alone with only her maid. In English this time, she said, Did you hear me? Leave us. He got back into the car and drove a little way then stopped. She wanted to be alone. She waved at him to go and the black Pontiac rolled forward a few more metres, unable to resist her, before coming to a stop again. She could see the Russian twisted round in the driver's seat watching her. She made an obscene gesture at him. There were dark sweat stains in the armpits of her linen suit, which was crushed and soiled from the train journey. She bent down and picked up a stone the size of a walnut from the roadway and turned and threw it hard. It struck the rear window of the car with a loud crack. The Pontiac jumped forward and stalled. Her maid giggled nervously. Lien picked up another stone. The Russian re-started the car and accelerated away, the rear wheels throwing up a scatter of gravel. Lien dropped the stone and lit a cigarette. She instructed her maid to stack the luggage in the shade against the wall and continued to stand in the sun herself, the wide brim of her pale straw hat casting her features in shadow.

She was facing the long, rear wall of Huang's house. The doorway before her was the second entrance. It was the doorway through which she had told her father she would return, as if she were returning from an excursion to the temple at Lin Yin. The door was scarcely more than two metres high and a little over a metre wide. She wondered now at her insistence on re-entering her home, indeed her father's home, by this means. It was a servant's entrance, or a child's entrance. Only now did she observe the method of its construction, though she had known it all her life. It was made of adzed planks set within a heavy rectangular frame, and towards the top in the centre there was a little trap through which the gatekeeper might safely observe visitors. Why the construction of the door should be significant she could not imagine. It was the peculiar, detailed way she was seeing things. She thought of it as a Shanghai way of seeing things, and she resented discovering it in herself. A stranger's way of seeing. The door had once been a bright vermilion, but had faded to an autumnal sepia. Above it, providing an area of shade around its base, there was a tiled roof with upturned eaves. When it rained, street vendors sometimes took shelter here and smoked a pipe while they waited for the weather to clear, and beggars were permitted to sleep here undisturbed at night. When she had been planning her strategy in Shanghai, when she had been dreaming of returning home, when it had seemed to her that she might never realise the dream, during that time she had thought of this doorway and of the courtyard to which it gave access as her principal goal. Now, standing here in the hot sun on the roadway, she thought, I am no longer the child; today I am the woman carrying the child. And she began to fear that she had miscalculated.

When she was very young, between lessons with her father, she had often come to sit on the bales of rice straw at the window of the storehouse that overlooked the courtyard of the little red doorway. From under the dark, sheltering eaves she had watched the rain falling onto the grey stones of the yard and had pursued

71

her solitary enchantments. And through the rain, always the little doorway in the wall, the doorway to the other world, to the lake and to the mountains and to the temples hidden in the forest. Shanghai had not existed for her then. On hot summer days, such as this, Yu had opened the door and they had cut up watermelons and given the refreshing slices of fruit to thirsty passers by. It had been through this doorway, too, that she and Yu had secretly gone at night on their smoking excursions to West Lake. On those strange and wonderful occasions she had disguised herself in the clothes of a boy.

It was too late to recall the Russian and his car. And anyway, she had been too imperious with him to bear his scorn. She dropped the butt of her cigarette on the road and ground it under the heel of her shoe, and she went up to the door and thumped on it with the flat of her hand. The sound echoed within emptily, seeming to touch some sensitive vital muscle deep inside her own chest. Several seconds passed. Then the trap was opened and the gatekeeper's daughter-in-law looked out, her eyes narrowed against the sunlight.

Lien was aware suddenly that her western clothes made an intruder of her. The woman's eyes were unhealthy, fatigued with laziness and habitual inaction. Why hasn't the dust been laid today? Lien asked her softly.

The woman blinked.

See that the roadway is watered at once, or I shall have you flogged. Are you going to make your mistress stand in the sun all day? Fear came with recognition into the woman's eyes and she quickly unbolted the door and stood to one side, kowtowing repeatedly and begging Lien to forgive her. Lien ignored her and stepped through the door. How could she have imagined it would remain the doorway to her childhood?

Before her was a squalid and narrow space closely surrounded by darkly stained brick walls. The courtyard resembled a portion of an alley behind a cheap Chinese eating house in Shanghai. A mixture of rotting cabbage stalks and straw and duck droppings littered the paving. A broken water pot lay where it had fallen, a desiccated weed rising through the shards. She lit another cigarette. At the touch of the smoke her stomach contracted uneasily. She sensed her maid and the gatekeeper's daughter-in-law waiting behind her with the luggage. How amused Feng would have been to have witnessed this abbreviation of her domain. How he would have smiled to see the poverty of her resources; he whose spaces were vast and whose resources were princely. She visualised him in the citadel of his white villa within the unbreachable lines of the International Settlement, and she felt herself to be provincial and vulnerable. She imagined his voice, low and ironic and dry: So this is your enchanted courtyard that I must fear?

Her project seemed hopeless. The vision of a madwoman.

In four hurried strides she crossed the courtyard and reached the entrance to the storehouse. The air within was heady with the acid fumes from a layer of fermenting poultry droppings. Her heartbeat thickened and slowed as she stumbled forward, her shoes slipping on the mess, and a moment later emerged into the sunlit rectangle of the chrysanthemum courtyard. Here she must be safe, for here she had cultivated her flower garden, staking the slender stems of the dark velvety blooms with golden slivers of bamboo. The raised garden bed was dry, the earth cracked and uncultivated. Then she saw the sunburned beggar squatting against the wall. He was picking over a heap of rubbish, which he had gathered together between his raised knees. His shorn scalp was bare to the blazing sun and he was naked except for a wisp of rag about his hollow loins.

He was watching her, his frightened gaze clinging to her, as if he would immobilise her with the force of his fear. There was a terrible, disfiguring scar across his neck, which terminated in a deep cavity where his collarbone should have been. It appeared as though someone had once attempted to behead him. He was keeping very still, except for his long fingers, which, like crabs, scrabbled together the rubbish and folded it into a filthy piece of cloth. When it was tied he took up this bundle and eased himself half-way to his feet. He did not rise to his full height, but remained crouched, and in this attitude moved with surprising agility to the open archway at the far end of the storehouse.

A hot gust of wind drove down into the yard from the surrounding roofs, sucking the dust and particles of straw and a stray duck feather or two into a whirling spiral: she perceived a demon rejoicing and mocking her, for he had just that moment transformed the chrysanthemums of her youth into the sinister dark-skinned beggar.

Never again, she resolved, would she deny herself the full dignity of her position. Instead of arriving unannounced and a day early through the second entrance, as if she had been divorced by her husband and were ashamed to show herself, she should have arrived at the principal entrance, chauffeured by the Russian in his uniform, with the entire household assembled to meet her. She should have kept them waiting in the hot sun for an hour, at least. There should have been banners and fireworks and feasting in her honour. No matter what her secret aspirations, she knew – and she knew all this in a flash of comprehension while the dust and feathers whirled around her – that she should have returned to Hangzhou as the honoured wife of the Shanghai banker C.H. Feng, a man whose name was feared and respected throughout the province. It terrified her to think how poorly she had exercised her judgement in this matter. Another such grave tactical error, and surely her project must be defeated.

Even now that possibility remained. For the air of abandonment about the courtyards and buildings made her wonder if her letter had actually been received. Or had her father and Yu gone to the lodge at Huang Shan to escape the heat? Perhaps the apartments were empty and she would find her unopened letter waiting for them. For a wild instant she imagined herself retrieving the letter and returning to Shanghai, her father and Yu none the wiser, then going through the entire exercise again properly. She turned to the gatekeeper's daughter-in-law, who stood behind her, a large suitcase in each hand, waiting sullenly. Is your master at home?

The woman did not reply, but looked past her towards a point over Lien's shoulder on the far side of the courtyard. She turned round. Yu was standing in the doorway opposite, his hand raised, shading his eyes from the glare. Relief swept through her and she took off her hat and opened her arms. It's me! she cried. It's me, Yu!

The old man hesitated, then shuffled towards her.

She ran to him and embraced him, hugging him tightly to her. Oh my dearest Yu! I'm so glad to see you!

He cackled with delight and struggled to draw breath. I thought you were a foreign devil, he wheezed.

She released him and looked at him. They held hands. How is he?

Your father will be very glad to see you, Yu said breathlessly.

Did he get my letter?

Yu smiled broadly and pointed a long sallow finger towards her flower garden. That is why nothing has been planted, he said, in the manner of one who has that moment encountered enlightenment, certain the neglect of two years would be accepted by her for the oversight of a single day. We weren't expecting you till tomorrow. He told her maid and the daughter-in-law to take the luggage to their mistress's apartments, then he took her arm and drew her into the shade of the doorway. He placed his hands one each side of her face, cradling her cheeks, and examined her with a kind of mischievous reverence, as if he were searching for secret signs. He made an approving noise through his nose, a little moan, which he repeated a number of times.

She took his hands in hers and held them before her. I've brought you a thousand cigarettes.

You will shame me, he said happily.

She closed her eyes and put his hands to her face again. You smell just the same. Now I know I am really home!

He is not ill, Yu said cheerfully.

She frowned. What is the matter then?

Yu shook his head, awed. A thousand is many more than I had hoped for. I dreamed of a hundred.

Five cartons of Camels. Will you take me boating on the lake at midnight tonight?

He hesitated.

You think I can no longer pass for a boy. Well, you shall see.

.

Then I shall take you.

He sounded serious and perhaps a little sad, she thought. She remembered that the last time they had gone boating on the lake together had been the occasion of her meeting with Feng. She decided to disclose her important news to him at once. Yu! she said.

He looked startled.

I'm going to have a baby. Unless through rumor or gossip, they knew nothing in Hangzhou of the stillborn sons.

He did not react. It was a very complicated matter. Incredibly complicated. What could he be certain of? How long will you stay with us?

Just tell me you're pleased. She gave his shoulder a reproving shake. Tell me you're still with me, Yu.

He groaned and clasped her hand tightly and looked down unhappily at the paving. Feng, the foreigner who was not a foreigner, who had come here only once and to whom she had gone, surprising everyone, her demon burrowing out. To the infernal regions. To the city of the Lord of Death. Was Feng Chinese or not? It was very difficult.

Do not disappoint me. It has not been easy to make my way home.

He looked into her eyes. I have never possessed courage such as yours.

I shall feel myself to be utterly alone if you persist in saying such things.

How was he to bring himself to consider the fact that she was carrying Feng's child? People said Feng had no ancestors. What sort of a person could such a child become? He looked at her belly. There was no sign. Does it make you happy?

Yes! But she sounded as though she were saying something else.

Then I am happy.

Tell no one, yet.

You are like a general, Miss Lien. You fight a campaign that the rest of us do not wish to understand, because we are afraid to understand it. He saw how tired she was and he was ashamed.

·

They had spoken enough. He took her arm and tucked it against his side and led her towards her apartments. He knew how to look after her and to make her strong. It thrilled him to think of having a hungry person to cook for once again. Given an occasion, Yu Hung-meng was the finest cook in Hangzhou.

MEN

The heat of the day had passed. It was evening and Huang was alone in his study. He was seated facing his garden. He had slipped behind the polished surface of the present and was in that pleasurable and dangerous state of consciousness which lies half-way between considered reflection and the free association of images from the memory when, in a drift of cool air from the open casements, he detected the familiar perfume of crushed amaryllis bulb. He became alert. Then he heard the rustle of silk against the door. He turned. She stood at the entrance to his study. She was dressed in her green lily-flower gown and wore her hair in a chignon clasped by a red-flowered headdress. With small steps she came towards him. He struggled to rise from his chair.

Ten minutes later, Yu brought a variety of sweet dishes, a little wine and hot water for tea.

A tremor passed through her womb. She was waiting to see if it would come again. It had not been a movement but a thrilling of the nerves, a message of *being* from the child. She placed her hands on her stomach and pressed. Tomorrow she would tell Yu to call the wind-and-water expert. Then she would have one of the old women determine if this child was to be a boy or a girl.

She had woken from a confusion of unfinished, anxious dreams, believing herself still in Shanghai, and had looked in wonder at the white moonlight where it cast on her wall the sharp black shadow of a branch of the winter-flowering plum tree. Had the silence woken her? Or the calls of the night herons? Or the child? The fretted canopy of her bed aroused memories she could not reach. What was she being reminded of? What lay below the surface of her mind like silver coins at the bottom of a well? The mosquito net was stirred by an uncertain breeze which blew in through the open casements. The air had crossed the lake and had picked up along its margins the perfume of the camphor laurel trees. Her bed seemed narrow and hard and her mind to be on guard against something which she could not specify: the secret dispositions of the enemy, perhaps. A general, Yu had said. She considered the old man's comment. She got up then and went out on to the verandah, intending to smoke a cigarette. But the first puff made her feel uneasy again in the stomach, and there was an emptiness about the night, a close concealing silence, which she didn't like. So she went back to bed and pulled the mosquito net down. The breeze had dropped and the air was thick and humid once more. First she lay on her back and then she lay on her left side and then her right. But it was no use. However she arranged her limbs her hips ached dreadfully within a few minutes. It was as if she had forgotten how to lie comfortably. Briefly she drifted into a light sleep, only to wake again. In the stillness she could smell the lake water and realised it must be nearly dawn. That is how they had met . . .

The boats had collided, head-on: the violent encounter of two travellers going in opposite directions. An omen they had chosen to regard with contempt. The prows bumped and the gunwales slid along each other with a rumbling like a roll of war drums in the cavern beneath the stone arch of the bridge. He was returning from the Back Lake to the Outer Lake and she was going to the Back Lake with the intention of visiting the peony gardens. Their lanterns swung about wildly as the boats struck, casting a red and dancing light on to the seeping stones of the bridge.

He was a giant, an ogre, a monstrous spirit who must lie in wait under the bridge to waylay innocent travellers and devour or enslave them to his will. In the stern of his boat was an even more alarming creature. White as death and hairy, clasping the boat pole in both his hands, the Russian chauffeur stared with infatuated wonder at his ugly master. Feng leaned from his boat, which swayed and jumped about dangerously in the confined space, driving waves against the stones of the bridge with the sound of glass bells, and he grasped the gunwale of her boat with both his hands and thrust his face close to hers. She did not flinch.

He searched her features. His eyes were yellow and clouded and down the centre of his forehead was a cleft, as if his head had been split in two many centuries ago by a blow from a battle-axe in a desperate fight with the other ogres. She had noted that the halves of his head were poorly joined, and had concluded that this unreconciled condition no doubt rendered his wrath a certainty. He had determined, she supposed, that if he could not defeat his fellow ogres, then he would torment human beings; whom he no doubt fancied must be easier prey than his peers. She was surprised and deeply excited to find that she was not afraid of him.

The red lanterns swung back and forth and his face appeared to be splashed with the blood of freshly devoured victims. She imagined a scene of carnage in the Back Lake, the scattered debris of many lives floating among the peonies. But it was his teeth that had most amused her. And she'd had a good look at them. They were huge and misshapen and seemed to have been thrust hurriedly and without regard for order into his mouth in a great double handful by the tooth-giver. They glinted with many stars of gold. His hands gripped the gunwales, locking their craft together. The stern of her own knocked against the stones of the bridge, knocking for admittance, as if this were to be her last contact with the world of the living. His dark smudgy eyes gazed deeply into hers, and he seemed to see through her disguise and to search for a glimpse of her soul.

She returned his gaze without recoiling. If she was about to die, she was pleased to discover that she would die defending herself. For she felt an energy and coldness that delighted her and made her ready. It was the same feeling she had experienced while she was painting her masterpiece. An exultation, a fierceness, elevated her above the impermeability of present reality, or drove her beneath it. There was no difference. With this feeling she knew she could fight the giant and would not run away from him. There was even a desire to die fighting him. Or was it a desire to live fighting him? Surprisingly it amounted to the same thing. It was something she'd known all her life but hadn't actually come face to face with till this moment.

It was as if she were both the fierce person in the boat who saw life and death as one and the same thing, and at the same time was an onlooker, a disinterested observer gazing down from a great height on the two craft and their occupants. There they were, two aroused beings, so unlike each other or anyone else that they must share a peculiar kind of kinship, locked in conflict under the bridge between the two lakes, neither in one place nor in another, but uncertainly placed where one thing did not necessarily lead to another.

Then he spoke and the splendid illusion of gods and demons was broken by the tuneless hissing of his Shanghai accents. What kind of girl goes out on the lake at night with only an old man to defend her virtue?

Release my boat or I shall instruct my boatman to thrash you.

He did not let go of her boat but addressed his companion. How has this girl, who wishes us to think she is a boy, gained the permission of her father and mother to go on such an outing? What kind of strange Chinese family can she come from? Am I supposed to believe there are such oddities living among the grave and haughty gentlefolk of Hangzhou?

I shall not warn you again, she said.

He let go the gunwale. He laughed. I meant no offence. I'm sorry if I startled you.

You didn't startle me.

He held his boat steady by raising his hands and pushing against the low bridge, as if he were indeed a god and were required to support the heavens. I've been here nearly a week. You can't imagine how boring it is for me. You people do nothing but drink tea and creep about your houses plotting all kinds of idiocies. He smiled, his thick purplish lips drawing back from his massive jaw with relief.

She said nothing.

I've been visiting your governor, he said, with mocking

·

condescension towards the official referred to. I suppose you know him? I suppose your father drinks tea with him? He hopes to borrow a large fortune from me, and I shall probably lend it to him. Do you think I should? He laughed. You're not going to pretend to be old-fashioned, are you, after dressing up like that? I'm from Shanghai. There's no need to be old-fashioned with me. It's a much more interesting place than this, I can tell you. Hangzhou's a dump. It's stuck in the past. You ought to know. There are plenty of people in Shanghai who'd appreciate that a girl needs to dress as a boy here if she wants to do anything. Plenty of them. One or two of them might even surprise you.

Another boat was attempting to pass under the bridge. She told Yu to go on.

Feng called after them, You can't escape from me that easily. She heard him laugh and say something in English to his companion. The following day he called at the house. He was even uglier in daylight, without the theatrical effect of the red lanterns. He arrived wearing a richly embroidered gown, which made him look ridiculous and dangerous. Like a wild animal that's been decked out for a ritual. His boatman of the night before had turned into his uniformed chauffeur of the daylight, a man with unreadable features, as impassive and empty as a loaf of white European bread.

She remained hidden throughout the visit, spying on them. Feng was rude. He was openly contemptuous of her father's delicate formalities and evasions. She watched them through the half-closed casements of her bedroom, which was situated on the opposite side of the formal garden from her father's apartments. Feng was large and real, an intruder in her father's study. But it wasn't Feng she was afraid of. Her fear was that this event would slip away in a day or two and become the past. Her fear was that she would fail to snatch from it a kind of splendour, a kind of perilous splendour that she knew she must have from life by some means. His voice carried across the garden. I intend to marry your daughter. But I'm not going to hang around forever waiting for your answer. I'm due back in Shanghai tomorrow. I've talked to people. I know how you stand, Huang. Who's going to make you a better offer? Someone in this city? You know you're never likely to get a better offer than mine. You won't have to worry about money ever again. She heard her father say Feng paid him too much honour, and saw him withdraw to consult with her.

He is insane, Huang said, stricken. What are we going to do? She saw how truly terrified her father was. Huang asked miserably, Shall I send him away? She observed Feng through the casement. He stood very still, unnaturally still, staring into the garden. He didn't pace up and down or look about him with curiosity, as an impatient man or a stranger to the house might have been expected to do, but stood perfectly still. She observed how entirely suitable the word *man* was to describe him. The way the word *horse* describes a horse. He was as wealthy as a warlord and undoubtedly as accustomed to power. Where another man might have gained a certain courtliness of bearing, a distinction and increase of dignity, by wearing such a gown, Feng made it the costume of parody. She giggled. She saw that the gown infuriated him. And that he was impotent. She could imagine him revenging himself on everyone who saw him wearing it – the demigod who must destroy every mortal who sees his face, for those who see his face see the limit of his power and cease to live in awe of him. She said, Tell him he must return here in exactly one month from today to receive his answer.

Huang groaned.

Tell him, she said, still looking through the casement, that you will give him his answer then. She stood up and turned to her father. Go, honoured parent, and give the Shanghai banker our message. But Huang did not move. You see, she began to explain, taking his arm and walking him gently towards the door, if we turn him away without any hope at all, such a man will be certain to destroy us.

Huang was aghast. Then we are in his trap!

But on the other hand, she continued, if we permit him to gain his end too easily he will not respect us and may decide to destroy us anyway. We must hold him with something. At liberty he is too dangerous.

But what shall we do in a month when he comes for his answer?

She took his arm again. If you do as I advise today, we shall have gained a month to consider that.

Huang resisted and drew his arm from hers. And what if he doesn't accept our condition? he asked with anguish. What if he says a month is too long for him to wait?

She considered this. Then tell him, she said, that there is a reason for the month, but that you cannot disclose it to him.

What reason is that?

She smiled. There is no reason father. But how shall he insist on knowing what it might be?

Dazed, and unable to think of any further objections to her plan, Huang permitted himself to be ushered towards the door.

Through the casement she watched him speaking with Feng. The two men kept a wide distance between them. She saw Feng cast an angry look towards her casement and she drew back a little, Su Shi's line coming into her mind: *Seen from our boat the mountains race like horses.*

THE CAMPAIGN

Under her command, Yu and Huang and the company of the household restored the rooms and the courtyards and the gardens of the old house to their former well-cared-for state. On the last evening of her visit before returning to Shanghai, Lien asked her father to pronounce upon the varieties of tea which had been collected for him on her orders. She had painted new silk labels for the collection. The smell of freshly ground ink lent to the study an air of well ordered industriousness. She had found, when she came to paint the ties, that she had ground the ink and applied the loaded brush to the silk in a manner that was determined and energetic and practical, a manner she despised. She'd had to make an effort to resist offering a sardonic commentary as she proceeded with the task, which she had found particularly irritating and tedious.

There you are, honoured parent! She placed the last of the tea boxes in the cupboard and stood back to admire her handiwork.

Now you are a connoisseur again. She heard the note of irony in her tone and hoped her father had not detected it.

She did not enjoy behaving in this way. But she was unable to correct it. The child troubled her at night and she was unable to sleep. She felt tired all the time, and besieged by a kind of violent intolerance. The smallest ineptitude among the servants made her lose her temper and see in their action an attempt to thwart her. To be sure, there had been some real initial resentment to her new regime among the members of the household, and she had found during the first week or two that her orders had sometimes not been carried out. But she knew, considering the difficulties, considering the irregularities in the situation, things had not gone too badly. She did not regret an early action during the campaign. A particular man and his wife had talked of *the daughter who ought to have remained in her husband's family.* It was the gatekeeper's daughter-in-law who brought her news of this sedition. She did not pause to consider the woman's motives, but went immediately to the couple and had them beaten and turned out into the street. The other servants were very subdued and obedient after this. The two who had been turned out hung around the little red doorway for a few days, being fed secretly and encouraged to hope for mercy by their colleagues within. She will soon relent! After a week, however, Huang was forced to receive a deputation and he agreed to reinstate the man and the woman and to intercede on their behalf with his daughter.

That was not wise of you, father, she said to him, as soon as the gatekeeper's daughter-in-law informed her of what he'd done. And she went at once herself to where the terrified couple were washing bedding and told them that if she ever saw them near her father's house again she would have them arrested and sent to the mines. Huang was shocked by her severity. But they have been in my house all their lives, he pleaded. They have no money and no hope of finding positions elsewhere. They will be forced to live among the scavengers. I am certain they will not offend you again. They have learnt their lesson.

It is not to them that I am teaching a lesson, honoured parent, she explained patiently, hearing, however, that she sounded as though she were addressing a senile aunt and not the renowned scholar Huang Yu-hua. It is the servants who remain with us to whom I am teaching the lesson.

She refused to discuss the matter any further. She was suffering. Her body was no longer her own. Enjoyment had been denied to her. She was governed by a compulsion to put everything in order around her, a compulsion to establish for herself a kind of orthodoxy of her own. A rampart against irregularities. To give herself a place. This had nothing to do with a motherly instinct for nest building. *She* was not a part of the child's strategy, the child was a part of hers. She bitterly resented not being able to enjoy a cigarette and the other western habit she'd acquired in Shanghai, a cup of coffee. They both made her feel sick. And she couldn't sleep. Her bed was hard. It didn't welcome her body. The child was like a huge round ball of clay inside her the instant she lay down. It seemed to roll around freely. But worst of all, her mind seemed not to belong to her any more. It surprised her with the hysteria of its responses. The harder she tried to be pleasant and tolerant the more provoked she felt.

She tried to talk to Yu about it. He sat and listened and smoked a Camel and gazed at the foot of her bed, and every now and then he nodded. There are two of me, she said. As if I am myself and my sister. She laughed. I've never had a sister. *She* is sophisticated and westernised. All the things I loathe. *I* am loyal and determined to defend the verities of my childhood. There is no question of not loving my father and you and this house and our way of life. It isn't that. It isn't that simple. It is just that it all irritates me beyond belief. I don't feel as though I'm in control. She saw the look of bewilderment in his eyes and she gave up. Leave me. I'm exhausted. He crept out.

She felt so stifled she could hardly breathe. No matter how great the affection between a man and a woman, she realised there would always be some things that the nature of men would prevent them from understanding. For the first time in her life she wondered what she might have remained ignorant of for not having known her mother. In Shanghai she had observed, and she had seen it here too, that women, even women who were not friends but were rivals, were capable of exchanging a special understanding with each other when there were no men present. An understanding which transcended their rivalries and their social roles and their individual accountability to certain men whom they honoured. An understanding in which something deeper than all that, something universal and unavoidable, was acknowledged. She had never seen this exchanged between women in the presence of men. There was a secret in it, it seemed, the efficacy of which would be jeopardised if men should ever come to hear of it. Was there, she wondered, something in her own nature which disqualified her from receiving this charmed perception from another woman? Had her upbringing as a boy subtly damaged her womanhood?

These thoughts depressed her and made her hungrier than ever for the consolation of a cigarette and a cup of coffee.

It was her last night. She had asked the gatekeeper's daughter-in-law earlier, Is it true you are all waiting for me to return to Shanghai so that you can laugh again? The woman had been too confused by this directness to reply. Lien looked across at her father, who was sampling one of the fine teas. They were seated side by side with a table between them, facing the newly reconstructed formal garden and watching the fading light of evening play upon its surfaces. She hadn't told him yet. The reason she hadn't told him was she lacked an overall plan. And without the foresight such a plan would have provided her with, she feared to be questioned by him. Her plan, her strategy, was evolving. It was unfolding as she entered it. She was required to proceed cautiously.

Does not Fan Ping-chen also have a very fine garden? She was dismayed, and at the same time fiercely gratified, by the mischievousness of this question. She had been looking for the right moment to tell him about the child since the day of her return. Now she had run out of time and was to be forced to disclose her news to him whether the moment was propitious or not. The old women had not been able to agree. One had said it would be a boy and the other that it was certain to be

·

a girl. They had blamed her for their lack of agreement. She knew this. It was the irregularity of her position which had confused the interpretation of the signs for them.

At the sound of Fan Ping-chen's name Huang drew himself up and smoothed his whiskers and sighed and reached for his cup, remembering his humiliation.

She leaned across the table and before he could pick up the cup she placed her hand over his. He looked at her. Dusk was gathering fast now and it was difficult for her to read the expression in his eyes. I am with child, she said. His hand went very still beneath hers. She heard Yu's knees creak behind the blue screen. It will be in the winter, she said.

Huang whispered, It is what Feng desires.

He called to Yu to fetch the lamp and he removed his hand from underneath hers and got to his feet and poured hot water into the teapot. He grunted and sighed and shook his head. Yu placed the lamp on the table. He looked quickly at Lien and she saw he was pleased she had told her father. Huang busied himself adjusting the wick. Feng is different from other men, he said, so quietly she almost missed hearing it. Such men as he are like floods and storms. It is no use people such as we are resisting them. He replaced the globe and looked at her, his features lit by the yellow flame, a mask set against the darkness of the garden behind him. His whiskers were trembling. They possess a mandate from the Lord of Death to accomplish their will without hindrance from mortals. They are admired and feared and befriended by governors and generals and by the viceroys of foreign powers for this reason. Men such as Feng cannot be defeated, daughter. Once we have come to their notice we are theirs and must serve their will until they no longer need us. He leaned his weight against the heavy table. He looked as though he might weep. Fate is with them, Lien, and only when fate abandons them is it safe for us to abandon them also.

Although he had used her name, she realised he had been talking for his own sake. And she saw that the famous wisdom of old men is nothing but fear, a loss of nerve in the face of enfeeblement. She thanked him gravely for his words and rose and embraced him lightly. She apologised for being tired and excused herself on the grounds that she must prepare for her journey tomorrow. His skin was chill and moist. As she left the study Yu rose from behind the blue screen and grinned at her. He held up a packet of Camels and whispered fiercely, Shanghai! as if this were to be their battle cry henceforth, the dusty plains upon which together they would meet their enemies and destroy them. Shanghai! he repeated. She had gained the gallery when she heard her father call after her, Your courage means nothing to him! Only a son will appease him.

SIGNS

It was an overcast autumn day in Shanghai on 11 October, 1927, nine weeks to the day from the expected birth of Lien's child. She remained in bed past her accustomed hour and kept her eyes closed, making no attempt to eat the light breakfast of cereals, buttered toast (with the crusts removed) and fruit juice, which her maid placed on the table beside her. And when the maid returned, Lien told her to call Doctor Spiess.

Doctor August Irenicus Wilhelm Spiess was the leading, indeed the only, specialist obstetrician among the considerable German population of the International Settlement. In an extended Chinese way he had become related to Feng some time ago through the marriage of Feng's eldest daughter from his first wife, Hsing, to a German army officer who was Spiess's second cousin and who was also from Hamburg. Medicine, and indeed his particular specialisation, had been Spiess's father's choice of a profession for him. August himself would have preferred to have been a playwright. He was fifty. He had offered a variety of reasons to the same people over a period of time as to why he had chosen to come to Shanghai and as to why, having chosen to come, he chose to stay. Because of this increase of reasons over time, reasons which came to sound more and more like excuses, Spiess's acquaintances assumed the true reason for his prolonged residence in Shanghai must have been too disagreeable to be openly acknowledged by him; an unfortunate youthful excess involving boys or girls or gambling debts or some such thing, for which he had been banished by his father for ever. He was a very good doctor, however, and so they were glad he chose to stay among them and they did everything they could to make him content and not to embarrass him with awkward questions about his past.

He was not attached to one of the great merchant houses, and August Spiess himself did not know why he had originally come to Shanghai, nor why he chose to stay, and on each subsequent occasion that he was asked to account for his exile he made up a new lie, having usually forgotten by then the lie he'd previously given as a reason. From the distance of Shanghai and with the passage of time it was not difficult to imagine that all sorts of things might have taken place in Hamburg. He often spoke of his old home without inhibition and even talked of returning there from time to time. The city of my fathers, he called it. His friends noticed, however, that whenever a boat prepared to steam down the Whangpu for that distant German port straddling the Elbe – a frequent occurrence – Doctor Spiess made no effort to reserve a berth for himself on it. There are always plenty of boats going to Hamburg, he would reply cheerfully, if a newcomer to the European enclave pressed him on this point. Indeed Hamburg and Shanghai have in common a regular exchange of goods and merchant tonnage. I can go whenever the fancy takes me. He left an impression that he might go at any time and at barely a moment's notice. This impression persisted for more than twenty years, until it could be said that August Spiess succeeded in acquiring an air of permanent impermanence. One or two intellectuals of his acquaintance accounted it very Germanic and philosophical of him to have achieved this ontological instability. He did not care for philosophy himself.

With a delicate flourish he clasped Lien's wrist lightly between the ball of his thumb and his index finger and consulted the dial of his watch. And he stood thus beside her bed, watch in hand, counting the pulses of her heartbeat for approximately fifteen seconds. He was a small man. His blond moustaches drooped expressively and their ends curled upward. His features had about them something that seemed to ask for approval, approval for his cerise silk cravat, possibly, and for the splendid gold pin with a pair of African diamonds that held it neatly in place as if it had been a hunting stock. One golden eyebrow was cocked permanently a fraction higher than the other. Behind his careful, professional manner, sitting ready in the corners of his clear amber eyes, there was a suggestion of a smile. The smile promised to be an open and generous one. It appeared eager to be invited out to share its perception with his patient. The perception the smile seemed to promise was, *What a grand amusement it is to have lived!* Just that. In the past perfect. To celebrate the opposite, it might be said, of the *Grand Guignol.* It was this that he had not yet given up hope of one day writing plays about. The impediment was his father, whom he respected and did not wish to disappoint. His father, Herr Doktor August Ulrich Carossa Spiess, who at eighty-three still resided in Hamburg and continued to practise obstetrics there and who was very much opposed to any member of his family having anything to do with something as suggestive as the theatre. And August himself saw no point in going to the considerable labour of actually writing his plays unless they could be produced in Hamburg. For he knew that only audiences who understand Hamburg society would understand his plays. Despite this it would have been wrong to conclude that August was either unhappy living in Shanghai or was waiting for his father to die so that he could go home and write plays. He was perfectly happy where he was. News of the death of his father would have upset him greatly. August's plays – the Platonic ideas of his plays his intellectual acquaintances might have said – existed quite comfortably for him for the time being in an imaginary life which ran along on the other side of the world parallel to his real life of Far Eastern doctoring. He did not make notes about them on bits of paper. They were not his hobby – geraniums were his hobby. But his plays were a great comfort to him whenever the genuine *Grand Guignol* of greater Shanghai made him feel dispirited about the nature and purpose of humankind.

As if it had been a fine white dish of fragile *Ch'ing Pai* porcelain from the Sung Dynasty, of which the doctor was a respected collector, he replaced Lien's wrist on the blue coverlet and replaced his watch in the pocket of his waistcoat. Then he stood, not saying anything, gazing out of her bedroom window towards the ochreous tides of the mighty Whangpu River.

Lien observed him. After a considerable time she said, Well, Doctor Spiess, I see that my pulse presents you with a great mystery.

His attention did not leave the river, but at the sound of her voice his hand absently patted his waistcoat pocket, checking from long habit that it had actually deposited the watch there. August was thinking. He was thinking, with a feeling of awe that mere human ingenuity could be responsible for it, of the vast tonnage and diversity of cargo that was disposed of through the port of Shanghai each day. He shook his head in a gesture of bewildered admiration for the mysterious energy of his own species. Then he looked down at Lien. At once the enthusiastic smile which had been waiting to be called forth transformed his features. Why Madame Feng, he exclaimed, you are the healthiest young woman in the whole of Shanghai. There can be no doubt of it. To himself he added, and the most beautiful. He would gladly have taken a glass of champagne with her to celebrate both her abundant good health and her refined beauty, if there had been one handy.

Lien waited until she had his attention, then she said levelly, I am unwell, Doctor Spiess. And you had better decide quickly what is the matter with me.

His smile faltered only slightly. He was accustomed to her acerbity. He did not take it personally. When, at Feng's insistence, he had attended her after the still birth of her second child, she had told him that she detested Germans. She might as easily have said Europeans, or foreign devils. He accepted her contempt and even secretly delighted in it, seeing it as a special way she had of dealing with him and with no one else. A challenge. Indeed a compliment. He felt himself to have been singled out from among the other Europeans with whom she came in contact as being particularly worthy. Clearly she trusted him not to make a fuss about her lack of respect, as others might have done. She trusted that he would not consider himself insulted or the dignity of his race impugned; that he would not seek to elevate such incidents to the familiar test of wills between the Chinese and the European styles of honour.

As the daughter of a renowned scholar, and as a practitioner of accomplishment herself of the ancient arts – so he understood – Lien exemplified for August certain particularly alluring intensities of his lifelong fascination with China and its past. He harboured a fervent ambition to visit her father's home in Hangzhou. He understood from his enquiries among the Chinese and from talk that went about at the clubs, that no Westerner had ever been admitted to the house of her father, Huang Yu-hua. As a collector and scholar he dreamed of the rare treasures such a sanctuary must contain. But even more than treasures, with the antiquarian's longing for a reanimation of a romantic past, he desired to himself inhabit, if even for a brief moment, the grave atmosphere of untouched originality which he imagined must imbue the house of the literary painter with a profound and poignant intensity; an atmosphere which he thought of as being a distillation of all that was classical and Chinese. Thinking of it, August was reminded of the mustiness of a monastic library he had visited with his father while they were on a tour of Italy when he was a boy – a kind of dim stone cavern, he remembered, reeking with the visions of entombed scholars. It was delicious to consider. Thoughts of Huang's house aroused spiritual longings in him and he sighed for the opportunity to undertake a pilgrimage to its doors. And was there not something divine, some ineffable mythical reasonance to be found in Lien's shiningly youthful embodiment of those antiquities?

She was aware of her uncertainty of him as a tingling on the surface of her skin. If he should attempt some further physical examination she was determined not to submit to it. She watched him delving in his bag. She knew him to be the friend of her husband's only friend, the Chief of Police, Alistair McKenzie. On coming to Shanghai a little over two years ago she had been told, to her bemusement, that Spiess and McKenzie, and the rest of their western confréres of various nationalities, existed in a state known as extraterritoriality. They might thus have been classified for her as beings not from present reality but from another, less certain, location along the perceptual continuum. She had not imagined before leaving Hangzhou that such a condition as extraterritoriality was possible, at least not for human beings. It had been patiently explained to her by one of her husband's American visitors that technically the term merely denoted the continued jurisdiction of their country of origin over foreign nationals resident in the International Settlement. She had found the tone in which the explanation had been delivered insulting. Did this mean, then, she had wished to know, that these people had travelled to the far side of the world from their ancestral homelands and yet had managed to remain at home? Her difficulty with the concept of extraterritoriality irritated Feng. But the difficulty persisted for her nevertheless. And she persisted in voicing it. It was the metaphysical aspects of the notion rather than its legal definition, however, which most attracted her speculations and which eluded the comprehension of her husband's visitors.

Watching August Spiess searching in his bag she perceived him as not quite real. As if he could not be understood by her as an ordinary human being might be understood by her. As if, to understand him adequately, she would need to apply to him a standard that was not entirely human. For it was apparent to her that he and his fellow foreigners had not emerged intact from their acquisition of the condition of extraterritorialness, but had forfeited a precious aspect of their humanity in the process. She saw theirs had been a less than complete transition from the land of the living to the land of the dead. She saw they had become inhabitants of a No-land, where gods, ghosts and ancestors, as well as numerous other unregistered categories of demons and demi-humans, roamed about in a hazy state of speculative indeterminacy, neither entirely alive nor entirely dead. Partly dead, indeed, was how she had come to think of the foreigners;

their pallor making this categorisation seem even more appropriate. They had suffered a *kind* of decease, a departure from life and its supporting structures sufficient to prevent them from returning home to their loved ones, but not sufficient to have delivered them into the tomb. Her own inclusion by them, therefore, as an honorary European, did not impress her. She viewed theirs as a state no Chinese could possibly rejoice in. And it amused her to hear them speculate at dinner parties as to why Spiess did not take the boat home; for it was as if they performed a charade, in which they had agreed among themselves that this option was still a viable possibility. She knew, of course, that it was not. At home in Hamburg or London or some other place, these extraterritorials would have had to behave once again as human beings, which manifestly they could no longer do, since they had forfeited their precious link with the moral imperatives of their ancestral homelands during the transition to extraterritorialness. In Shanghai they might not actually *be* gods but they could behave *as though* they were gods, immune from the laws and the responsibilities and the constraints of civilised custom; privileged colonists of a terra nullius in which they might deem the natural inhabitants and *their* customs to be not fitting for themselves, irrelevancies which imposed no duties upon them. She was fascinated. She saw extraterritoriality as signifying both an enviable liberation and as a fate more terrifying than any she had imagined. It was clear to her their race could not long endure its habitation of such an imaginary place as the International Settlement. She saw that their race was doomed to extinction and she was repelled and intrigued. Superior to their destiny, with a mixture of pity and scorn she came to think of them as the forgotten children of the Lord of Death. A shimmering, half-real existence on the imaginary edge of China.

Among them only Spiess had been forced into a form of intimacy with her through her husband's insistence that she submit to his western doctoring. The situation had afforded her with an opportunity to experiment. One result of this experimentation was that she had concluded it was not possible to offer this man an insult. She had found him to be without a care for his own dignity. This she understood to be undoubtedly a consequence of his having been removed from the oversight of his family and the bearers of his ancestral worth. For she was entirely convinced that Spiess would not have endured her insults and her mockery without complaint if his father had been a witness to them.

Open please! He slid the chill thermometer between her lips. There is nothing the matter with you, Madame Feng, believe me. I am familiar with the signs of ill health. You exhibit none of them. On the contrary, may I observe that you possess the extraordinary appeal of all young people who are in the very best of health. The signs, Madame, are important. They are the hieroglyphs that men of my profession must decipher if we are to succeed.

She removed the thermometer. If I should lose this child, Feng will hold you responsible.

Gently he took the thermometer from her and replaced it between her lips. I doubt that very much. Your husband, I have observed, is a sane man.

She took the thermometer out again and saw Spiess smile indulgently. My husband is Chinese, Doctor Spiess, she said evenly. No matter what other impression he desires to give. He has placed me in your care in order to ensure the delivery to him of a healthy son. It would be unwise of you to insist on my good health when I tell you I am not well and that there is cause for concern. She quickly replaced the thermometer herself before he could reach it and observed his smile withdraw to its place of semi-concealment. She was pleased to see that he had begun to ponder deeply. He was once again looking out of the window.

She had heard he took his doctoring to the destitute Chinese refugees who were daily crowding into the International Settlement, seeking a refuge from the conflict in the Chinese city, and that he administered to these people without charge. She could not fathom such a persistent trade in charity. What might be his recompense? She watched him reach for the thermometer and read it. He was thoughtful as he replaced the instrument in his bag. Do the hieroglyphs reveal the nature of my complaint yet, doctor?

He was uncertain, his eyes questioning her. Perhaps I should make arrangements to have you admitted to the Catholic hospital for observation and some tests. His hand went to his moustaches and he smoothed the blond hair. It would be for no more than a day or two at the most.

She laughed. Make your diagnosis here, doctor. In the presence of my servant. I'm not asking for your opinion. Do you understand me? She gazed steadily into his flickering eyes.

He smoothed his moustaches once more. Ah, he murmured, his fingers twisting the extremities of the hair. Ahhh, he breathed again, as if the elongation of the sound might bring him closer to his goal.

She wanted to giggle. He seemed to levitate, an inch or two, waiting for confirmation to return him to the equilibrium of the level ground, light streaming through his pale hair. I see that you enjoy the view from my window, doctor. She spoke without mocking him. Inviting from him, even, an observation upon life if he should wish to venture one, an indulgence, something of an old man's wisdom if he cared to part with it. At the sound of her voice he came to earth with a slight bump.

The world passes your window, Madame, he said with enthusiasm.

You may sit down, she invited him, as if he had passed her test. She indicated the rotund French chair which stood beside her bed. Do you know Hangzhou? she asked, when he was seated. It is my birthplace. The air there, doctor, is particularly healthy. She smiled and saw that he was listening to her with great attention. There is the gentle recreation of boating upon the calm waters of our famous lakes in the evenings, at which times one can quote poetry with one's friends and watch the moon rise. Such pastimes in those surroundings restore well-being more efficaciously than do medicines. Are such signs as these read by men of your profession?

Oh indeed they are, Madame Feng. Most assuredly.

I am glad to hear it. The air in Shanghai oppresses me.

I believe I understand you.

I hope you do. She looked beyond him to the sky. She felt him waiting. The clouds bubbled darkly like the surface of an evil soup. And how are your famous geraniums? *They* do not seem to wilt in Shanghai's air.

They laughed softly together.

Perhaps if you were to prescribe a tonic, she suggested. It may take you a little time to convince my husband of my needs. He is very preoccupied with the situation at the moment. Arrangements will need to be made.

He drew out a notepad and flourished his fountain pen above it. Do you prefer a powder or an elixir Madame Feng?

They looked into each other's eyes. The sound of gunfire which had been audible from the outlying suburbs for some days, had drawn closer during the morning. Neither remarked on it. She had had no friends. She had not joined with parties on the lake and quoted poetry, but had talked with Yu and smoked forbidden cigarettes, concealing her sex beneath the clothes of the gatekeeper's son. What could this man know of China? An elixir, she said, I believe would suit me. Thank you.

AN INTERLUDE IN THE GARDEN

Towards the end of the autumn we made an advance into Lang's back garden. It was I who insisted on the move, believing it to be a necessary extension of my territory. The garden had been where Victoria had written *The Winter Visitor*. She had worked at a table in the summerhouse. I knew little more than this. I mowed a path through the long grass from outside the kitchen door to the centre of the lawn, where the ground cover was thin and dry and had scarcely grown at all during the autumn. There was a mound here, a convenient vantage from which to view our surroundings. The rest of the garden fell away from this eminence, at first gently and then more steeply as it approached the bank of the Yarra. I scavenged two battered cane chairs and a table from a lean-to attached to the back verandah and set them up in the middle of the mound. Reluctantly he came out to see. Standing in the sun hunched up in his lopsided manner, his head shrouded in smoke, he blinked uncomprehendingly. It's our base camp, I said. He grunted unhappily, but he stayed.

The landscape we'd entered was open to the sky, except in the direction of the house, which loomed heavily behind us, and in the direction of the summerhouse; the direction we were facing. It was not the structure of the summerhouse itself which occupied space in that direction, however, but a great pale

·

twinkling tree of a species my mother had always referred to with fondness as the aspen; in fact *Populus tremulosa.* A dense thicket of suckers from this parent tree enclosed the remains of the summerhouse and rendered it completely inaccessible and, except for the wrought-iron finial adorning its roof, almost invisible.

It was the end of the first week of the May school holidays and our third occasion at the base camp. We were sitting in our cane chairs reading. The day was windless and the sun warm. It had begun with a fog, which had cleared by lunchtime. Gertrude had given me her father's journals to read and I'd brought one of the volumes with me, but I was finding it impossible to concentrate. Lang seemed to be unaffected by the drowsy stillness of the weather and was sitting upright at the table. I observed him through half-closed lids. The Fourth Phoenix. He was reading my draft of *The Lotus and the Phoenix, No Ordinary Child* and *The Mother.* I hadn't wanted him to see it yet, but he had insisted. We'd had several arguments about its progress. It was still too uncertain to bear a reading. I was sure he would not be pleased with what he read and would misunderstand my intention. I was not clear about my intention myself. All I was clear about was that the manuscript was a further consequence of me being a writer and of having understood, with a kind of passionate intuition that first day, that I needed his friendship.

The sun was warm and golden through my lids . . .

Parasites customarily recognise their hosts by means such as passionate intuition. The recognition is instinctive. In burrowing into the substance of their hosts, from which they are to draw their sustenance and proceed to the fulfilment of their life's purpose, they are setting out on a predestined journey, a project about which they are unable to exercise choice. To proceed with it is their only allowable activity. They have no other purpose in existing. If they do not respond to the signal to advance then they and their species perish. One would not speak of motives and aims in such a matter, or of conceptual certainty. The sustaining substance reacts to one's entry into it. It is not what it would have been if one had not entered it. The result, therefore, cannot become a biography of one's subject. Nor a history, either, of one's own progress. The result must be something one has not foreseen.

One goes ahead blindly, not accountable to verifiable facts but to feelings and intuitions; accountable not to an objective reality at all, but to a subjective one, to the mysterious truth one feels, not to the truth one is able to adduce.

And through all the lies and the distortions and the false images which mark one's way, the endeavour must be to sustain a subjective life for oneself and one's species, and to do this despite the impermeable face of present reality. This is the only purpose one can have. It is why one continues to burrow deeper day after day.

In these thoughts I wasn't exactly quoting Victoria, or even rephrasing her words, but was gathering into a single place remarks of hers which I'd found scattered throughout her work. She and I had been campaigning together for months on *The Chronicle of the Fengs*, the working title I'd given the project. A chronicle of recovery and exploration. Her *Winter Visitor* was its inspiration. Her book was the model by means of which I'd received my authorisation to deal with Lang's material. I'd followed her among the slim gumtrees that strained towards the white sky of summer, hungry for light, the remnant of native bush lying between the river and the road above. Her place of refuge and concealment. I'd walked there often and looked back towards the house from the point at which the dab of alizarin crimson appeared in the painting on the dining room wall. Placing myself at the place where she had first insinuated her own presence into the landscape, insisting on my own existence in the place from where she had observed the artist at work on the lawn of her mother's house. Observed him at work on this very mound where Lang and I reposed in the reflective sunlight of autumn, *our* base camp now. An ideal site for the young painter from England, a painter employed in the topographical and picturesque tradition, whose entirely approachable landscapes my father's 'eye' would have approved without reserve. But too exposed to be the ideal site for the painter of rapturous attachments she had made of him, displacing in the end his approved material and replacing it with herself.

Victoria had become the landscape. She had determined the way I was seeing it, directing my attention towards the significance of certain features and away from others. *He* trailed off in her account, a loose end, leaving behind him, besides her portrait, only a ghostly impression of his sojourn. She'd used him up and moved on to a greater campaign, mounted this time not on a man but on her supernatural horse, *Tianma*, the magic horse of the West. Despite his paintings it was her landscape we inhabited, not his.

The screen door at the back of the house banged and I turned to see Gertrude coming along my mowed path. She waved something at me, a bottle, and called, I could have been a robber. Her hair was tucked under a pale bandanna, tied tightly against the roundness of her skull like a cloche, and she was wearing an old, loose tee shirt and jeans. I realised she must have come straight from working. The place is wide open, she said. She came up and looked at us. I've been watching you from the kitchen window. She had an uncorked bottle of wine and three glasses. Stay there, she said as I went to get up. I'll sit on the grass. I'd rather. She put the glasses on the table in front of Lang and poured the wine. She indicated her father's journal, which lay open on my lap. What do you think then?

I've just started it. I saw that she was in that glittery disembodied mood that is induced by a long session of intense work.

You both looked so old-fashioned from indoors in your white shirts. I wished I'd had my camera. She handed me a glass of wine. It was a pale amber – the colour of her father's eyes. I caught a whiff of fruitiness, as if a perfumed shrub were blossoming nearby, hidden in the wilds of the garden. The aroma was European and autumnal, and suddenly I was reminded of an orchard in Kent when the fallen fruit is rotting sweetly in the long grass and wasps are busy.

·

Lang murmured a greeting and went on reading without looking up. With deliberation he turned a page and groped in the air with his other hand. She fitted the glass to his fingers and he drew it towards his mouth and drank thirstily. Then she stood behind him and looked over his shoulder.

I watched them uneasily, afraid of their reactions, their criticism, afraid of hers more than his, of my unfinished work. We hadn't seen her for a while. She'd been working hard preparing for her show. I'd never seen her in her working clothes before. The left thigh of her jeans was smudged darkly where she must repeatedly clean the charcoal from her fingers. I imagined her standing back from her work, unconsciously kneading the material of her jeans with her fingers while she worked at the drawing with her mind. She read for a minute or two. Then she turned to me and raised her eyebrows. Interesting, she said. And I saw how careful she was being to say nothing, to touch nothing, how careful she was being to leave it alone. She moved away from Lang and sat on the grass, choosing the highest point of the mound. What a fantastic day, she said, as if she really were grateful and surprised that she had been allowed to come out and enjoy it. She turned her face to the sun and closed her eyes.

I watched her. I knew she knew I was watching. I thought how important she had become for me, she and her work, which I had never seen but which I imagined. I'd often wanted to say something to her about the likeness I saw between her and Victoria. Lang said I was imagining it and that they were not a bit alike. I'd had the feeling she might be offended by the comparison, the emotions in the portrait of Victoria being so subjugated and drained of warmth. The likeness between them had seemed too complicated a thing to just remark on, to state simply without being drawn out of a particular context. And then there was the matter of Victoria's posed and aggressive nakedness.

Seated on the dry mound in front of me now, her hair bound up in the bandanna, as if in intentional parody of the towel around Victoria's hair, the likeness was distracting. I wanted to get Lang's attention so I could convince him. For the sake of something to say, I asked, How's the series of China drawings going? Have you finished them? As soon as I'd said it I regretted asking the question.

She didn't move but made a little grunt of annoyance. I don't want to talk about work, Steven. Do you mind? She turned to me and gave me a lop-sided smile, forgiving me. You know what it's like. She held her glass of wine up to the sun. Isn't it lovely! It's a German romantic, or a romantic German. Whichever you like. She squinted at the sparkling burst of light that trembled in the glass, the reflections shimmering on her face. The resemblance to Victoria had vanished. She was Gertrude again.

She took a sip and quoted softly, *Das küsste mich auf deutsch und sprach auf deutsch (Man glaubt es kaum, Wie gut es klang) das Wort: 'Ich liebe dich!' Es war ein Traum.* Not everyone likes it. Some people think it's too sweet. She was looking into her wineglass once more.

I saw an image in my mind of our mound overgrown again and deserted. I drank from my glass. The wine wasn't sweet. It was deliciously fruity. Voluptuous. It's perfect, I said. What was the poem?

She hesitated and gave a small laugh. 'It kissed me in German and said in German (it's hard to believe how good it sounded) the words "I love you". It was only a dream.'

Lang lifted another page of the manuscript and turned it. I felt the afternoon close around us. The silence was punctuated by the calls of the whipbirds among the willows down by the river and the muffled thump of traffic racing across the bridge a kilometre away.

Heine, she said at last. It was one of my father's favourite poems. He often recited it. It begins, 'Once upon a time I had a fine country of my own where I was at home. The oaks grew tall there, the violets beckoned gently. It was a dream.' It's his fatherland that kisses him. It's called '*In der Fremde*'. In exile. It didn't make my father unhappy to think of it. He was only ever at home in exile. Now it's one of my family heirlooms, the poem is, from the old world. Something from a German culture neither of us really had very much direct experience of. Me none at all. I haven't been. I don't intend to go. But all the same I love it! she said with passion. I love everything about it. I can't be critical about Germany. I'm sure it's not a bit like I imagine. She laughed and changed the subject. I was watching you both from the kitchen window just now. Neither of you moved for ages. You wouldn't believe how long. I nearly didn't come out. I almost decided to go away again without letting you know I'd come over. You both looked . . . it looked idyllic out here. A bit unreal. Like a still from a movie. That sort of timeless impression you get when you're looking on. When you're not part of something. You know what I mean? When you're looking on at other people, before you go into the scene yourself, it's not complicated. Is it? Their situation isn't. You just get the fact of them being there. It was odd. It started the minute I arrived. I didn't expect to find the front door open. It never is, is it? And I was expecting to have to rouse you both from the darkness of the house. I had a picture in my mind of you working in the gloom of the dining room among all the junk and stuff and of having to drag you out into the sunlight. I called and no one answered. The place *felt* deserted. As if you'd both been warned to leave. My reflection in the hall mirror as I came through the front door gave me a start. I thought for a split second it was someone coming to challenge me and ask me what I was doing. The front room, when I looked into it, was so still it seemed as if no one had been there for ages. I mean for years and years. That awful portrait sitting up against a cabinet. I went through the house to the kitchen feeling like an intruder. Like people opening the tombs in Egypt must have felt. Then, when I got to the kitchen, I saw you both out here. I mean, I'd actually been wondering if I'd be able to *entice* you out of doors, and there you were! Sitting out here on this little hill in the sun. I'd never noticed there *was* a hill here before. Something had been altered. As if I was in another place. It was so unexpected. It was disorienting. The cane furniture. Where did that come from? And you both in your old-fashioned white shirts with the sleeves turned back. You looked as if you could have taken off blazers and ties and straw boaters

..

a hundred years ago, and somehow you were still here, reading and drowsing in the sun, while everyone else in the world moved on. You could have been anyone. I didn't know you. Two friends in an old garden. Like a Rupert Bunny.

She drank the rest of her wine. I stood at the kitchen window and watched you. And you know what I thought? I thought, if I don't go out to them now, this is how I'll remember them. If I never see them again, if they really have heeded a warning to leave, this is how they'll be for me forever. For the rest of my life. Steven and Lang. The world and I really will go on without them. Two friends in an old garden. That's all I'll have. And eventually, one day, I might begin to draw things about them. Eventually. Not for ages though. Years. And, well, perhaps never.

She was silent for some time. Then she pulled off the bandanna and shook out her hair. O, that's better, she said and lay back on the dry grass and sighed with contentment. She held the stem of the empty wineglass loosely betwen her relaxed fingers and she stared straight up at the sky. The glass toppled slowly, flashing the sun into my eyes. She looked like someone who'd been drugged. Or bewitched. Her work glowing in her. One of Lang's collection of drypoints. A sensuous Félicien Rops' woman, half-satyr half-woman, in the flawed pastoral idyll she'd predicted. Dreaming lustful thoughts behind half-closed eyes. Waiting for a lover. She'd come out. She'd completed the composition. There was the triangle now. She'd joined the men. She said, matter-of-factly, as my mother might have said it, effacing the image I'd been developing of her, I know what it is. I've just realised the Australian sky is innocent. She rolled onto her elbow and looked at me intently. I had to get out. I couldn't stand it a minute longer. I was working, I was in the middle of work and suddenly I thought, suppose I had no one to go and talk to.

I remembered them both as I'd first seen them standing by the unlit gas heater in the staffroom. Yes, I said. She rolled on to her back again. Anyway. I love this weather. I love dry autumn days, don't you? She held her empty glass out to me. I stood up and my shadow lay across her. I refilled her glass from the bottle at the table.

·

My mother, I said, told me about something which changed her life. I knelt beside Gertrude and handed her the glass of wine. She half sat up. What is it, she said, that changes people's lives? What can that mean? People say it don't they? *It changed my life.* I don't think anything will change my life. You'd have to change inside. You'd have to become a different person, wouldn't you? Perhaps I'm conservative. Do *you* think I am? Sit here, she invited me, touching the grass beside her. Tell me about your mother's experience.

I sat beside her on the mound. I was in bed. With a real illness or pretending to be ill. I can't remember. They never made me confess my lies so I don't know whether the things I remember are memories of real events or of events I made up. The effect on my parents was the same in either case. I don't think they noticed. She came and sat on my bed, but instead of asking me how I was feeling she looked off into the distance through my window, and told me she was a colonist. It was the first time I'd heard the word. She and people of her caste, she said, had colonised England. I ought to be proud. As if I was ill, or pretending to be ill, which was the same thing, because of a lack of ancestral pride. At first they'd been refugees. I'd been spared that. The turning point, she said, was something Lord Acton would never have guessed. After she left Ireland and was looking for work she got a position – a 'place', she called it – as a chambermaid in one of London's West End hotels. It was at The Grosvenor. Not one of the really posh ones, but all right. It was during the First World War. She was a girl. There was a fuss in the street outside the hotel one day. When they looked out the window they saw a crowd. People were pointing at the sky. There was a German Zeppelin several hundred feet above London's great buildings. It was stationary. It was the first one and no one knew what it was. It was black. It looked, she said, like a big black grub. A huge maggot that something horrible was going to hatch out of. It hung there above them, its shadow lying on the ground, like a terrible message from a giant they'd thought had died long ago. (I realised I'd begun making it up.) A modernist's version of the Trojan Horse. The beginning of the death of beauty. As if everything familiar was to be returned to the larval stage and reconstructed along unfamiliar lines.

Gertrude laughed softly. Now you're making it up.

No, I'm not. Honestly. It's the way my mother used to put things. It's just the sort of thing she said. She always talked to me as if she was a guest speaker. There was never anything I could say in reply.

Go on! Gertrude urged me.

Some people laughed at the Zeppelin and went back inside their clubs and had another brandy. Others wept and caught the bus home to their children. And some went on as they had been and pretended it wasn't there. When brave people looked for it again in the morning and saw it had gone, they realised at once that its absence was somehow even more sinister and portentous than its presence had been. Some of those who hadn't seen it, and even quite a few of those who had seen it, started saying it hadn't really been there at all but was a rumour being spread by the enemies of England to undermine the morale of the populace. People stopped talking about it in case they were thought to be somehow siding with it. But it stayed in everybody's mind. For the English, my mother said, the sky was never the same again. The English had never before in their history cast furtive glances towards the sky. Their sky lost its innocence to the Zeppelin, she said. But it was from that day that she dated her own self-assurance. In an intuitive and visionary kind of way, which is possible at seventeen, she'd seen in the unsteady reaction of the English to the Zeppelin that they were not indestructible but were a fragile race nearing the end of their term. In this vision she saw that the disenfranchised polyglot from the far-flung corners of Empire, and from the nearby provinces as well, were one day going to achieve the ascendancy. Perhaps not in her own lifetime. But she'd seen it coming and she was happy. She knew now she was the equal of the English. Historically. Individually she'd always known she was their equal but that hadn't given her a sense of destiny as this did. The irony is that once she'd seen that the English were a doomed race she of course fell in love with them. She's never attempted to be *like* them. As a colonist occupying their homeland she observes them sympathetically and collects their artefacts – porcelain shepherds and shepherdesses and that sort of thing – but she doesn't ape their manners. She has never 'gone native'. She has retained her youthful vision and it is this which enables her to mourn their passing while assisting in it.

Lang leaned over me, blocking out the sunlight. He placed the manuscript on my lap. His cold right eye gleamed at me malevolently. You could have been there, Steven, he said.

It should have been a compliment. There was something so begrudging in the way he said it, however, that it came out as an accusation. Gertrude sat up. But you don't seem very pleased about it Lang?

He laughed, knowing and bitter and uneasy. He lifted up the wine bottle from the table and squinted through it. Then he came over to us and very deliberately poured the last of the wine into our glasses, leaving the merest dribble for himself. His hands trembled. The demon in him was abashed. Unable to rise up and mock. Reeling about in there biting its own tail.

Lang stood with his back to us on the outer edge of the mound looking towards the tremulous poplar. What did he mean, *You could have been there*? Been where? Not Shanghai or Hangzhou in 1926, for he hadn't been there himself then. I supposed he'd meant, whether he quite realised it or not, that I could have been in his mind. Wasn't I to understand from his begrudging affirmation that I'd written an acceptable reconstruction of what he'd always *imagined* things to have been then? Before he was born; an understanding put together from evidence left behind by other's memories of those events. Not China but an Australian fiction of China, like Gertrude's Australian fiction of Germany. I watched him standing there prodding the empty wine bottle with the toe of his shoe. But I knew it wasn't the wine he was regretting sharing so generously. How was he going to recover his own version of those past events now? How was he going to rid himself of my images, so very nearly coincident with his own that he'd been forced to acknowledge them. But not his own. A distortion of his own. How was he going to expel the intruder?

Or was it already too late to think of that? Was he going to have to accept my version of his past? My mother identified our caste as both refugees and colonists. But isn't that, sooner or later, what everyone must become? Victoria would have agreed with that. Did I need to defend and justify what I was doing?

As if he found himself to be suddenly exceedingly weary, Lang bent down and picked up the bottle from the grass and said, I'm going in.

Gertrude came and stood beside me and took my arm in hers, and we watched him walk back along my mowed path towards the house, carrying the empty wine bottle. He's my whole family, she said.

I was moved by the realisation that she saw in me an entirely reliable ally. On that fiercely hot day back in February, just after we'd met, he'd said to me, We are all only children. I remembered it now. I pressed her arm against my side and she returned the pressure. After a minute she said, What are we going to do? I didn't know what she was asking me to decide. Arm in arm we stood there on the mound, like a couple. The sun had dipped behind the tree and already there was a chill in the air. A soft mist was drifting across the face of the river below us.

A MEMOIR OF DISPLACEMENT

PAGES FROM THE JOURNALS OF DOCTOR AUGUST SPIESS,
TRANSLATED FROM THE GERMAN BY HIS DAUGHTER, GERTRUDE SPIESS:
MELBOURNE 1966

9 am, 18 December 1927 Hangzhou, at the house of Huang
Yu-hua the literary painter! I am elated and exhausted. That I
am here at all seems still to be a dream. I have just this minute
returned to my room from speaking with Feng on the
telephone to Shanghai. He was reserved. Perhaps even
unmoved. His reaction not as I had expected. I told him she
must rest for at least a week. She is deeply exhausted and there
is a risk of puerperal fever. Was he subdued by a surfeit of
emotion? Or unfeeling? I am not sure. The line, as usual, was
poor, but he seemed merely to grunt. He agreed with my
advice, I suppose. I take it he intends to await our return and
not come down. He has waited twenty years for this.

My emotions compel me to record the event. Two hours
ago, at seven o'clock this morning, Madame Feng was
delivered of a son after an heroic labor of more than twenty-
seven hours duration. When I left them a moment ago they
were both sleeping. A little after one this morning, at that hour
when the human will sinks to its lowest point and the aged
and sick give up the ghost, I believed she was entirely spent. I

.

110

decided there could no longer be any hope of saving them both. Despite the certainty that I would thereby earn Feng's undying enmity, I decided without hesitation to sacrifice the life of his son in order to save the life of his wife. I saw how Madame Feng was slipping deeper every minute into a state of great depletion. Without either assistance or the proper facilities, and in her weakened condition, a caesarean delivery of the infant was not possible. I did not consider it, but readied myself for the gruesome task of butchery that lay before me. As I prepared my instruments by the uncertain lamplight in her cold room, observed all the while from the shadows by the two old women who had been attending her before my arrival, I reflected with a strange detachment upon the fact that I felt no fear of Feng. As the moment approached for me to use the knife it was not of myself that I thought but of the child, whose torso and limbs hung helplessly from her body, its head locked firmly behind the android formation of its mother's ungenerous pelvic bone. When I moved to the side of the bed to do my work Madame Feng must have sensed my purpose, for she opened her eyes and spoke to me. I do not know by what means she roused herself from the deep exhaustion into which her labors had driven her; there is no sufficient medical explanation to account for such a re-awakening. It was as if she had visited a secret shrine hidden within the far recesses of her soul and there been granted a renewal of her will. Her splendid eyes keenly searched my features, seeking for a resolve in me to match her own. Do not kill my child, she said. We must not give up, Doctor Spiess. I was abashed and moved by the calm assurance of her words.

·

Midnight, 19 December 1927 There is a sharp frost, but I have left the casement open, for outside my window, illuminated by a full moon riding in the clearest sky, there lies the original of this world's formal landscaped gardens. I am indeed in the city of heaven! It has ever been my view of a normal birth, in which the infant presents head first, that it puts on life like a new set of garments, that such a happy child mounts upward and is

·

received into a welcoming world. The infant born in the breech position, on the other hand, struggles blindly against its birth, is thrust downwards unwillingly through the dilating cervix by the crushing pressures of the muscles of the pelvic floor into a cavity which has opened mysteriously beneath its feet. The infant so born enters at once upon a blind and threatening passage in which its life is placed in danger at every turn. Surely in the primal memory of the child who survives this awesome journey there lodges the perception that at the very beginning of its life it set out in the wrong direction? Must not every such child carry with it throughout life an unshakeable conviction that it has never arrived at the place where it was destined to go? That another destination, a truer world than the one it inhabits, awaits it if only it can locate the singular doorway through which it must pass in order to reach this homeland?

I was so delivered into the world myself and do believe this fact accounts for my own sense of displacement – the unease with which I daily confront reality. How often have I sought to reason with myself on this matter. Be content August, I say. You are a grown man and a respected physician and ought not to be any longer bedevilled by such doubts. Uncertainties such as these are for the young. How you arrived in the world does not matter. Whether coming up or going down makes not the slightest difference. The point is, you are here. The world is the world. There is only one of it and you are firmly in it. Accept that as a fact which you cannot choose to alter and you will enjoy contentment for the rest of your days.

And yet, within my mind this other voice persists. It is a voice that quietly reflects upon experience and which knows better than to be so beguiled by mere reason as to accept the overwhelming evidence of appearances as a barrier at which our deepest longings must be turned aside. It is the voice of an intuition and will not be silenced. You are lost, August, this voice murmurs to me sadly. Go at once in search of the entrance to the true world or your existence will have been in vain. Looking back upon my life I see it has been the discontented murmurings of this voice that I have obeyed. Even when I have thought I was being directed by practicalities alone, it has been the irrational urge to respond to this intuition that has driven me from one end of the world to the other in search of something I have been unable to describe even to myself. Though I was born in Hamburg and loved by the dearest of parents, as a small child I knew I did not belong there. This knowledge cast a sadness over everything I did. If I rode beside my beloved father upon a sleigh through the forest, my mood would be affected by the wistfulness of nostalgia; as if the scene before me was never to be of my own experience, but must remain elusive and lost to me. As if, indeed, it belonged to the experience of another child in another time.

When I was urgently called to attend Madame Feng in her apartments, my brief sojourn in this exotic and beautiful Chinese house of the scholar Huang Yu-hua had induced in me a peculiar state of receptivity. I was prepared, as it were, to encounter the magical in this place. My life seemed to have been leading me towards this meeting. When I entered her room I saw that labor was well advanced. It was immediately clear to me that the women had hoped to deliver the child without my assistance and that they had only called upon me now because a disaster appeared to be unavoidable. Understandably, they preferred that I rather than they themselves should be held responsible for this state of affairs.

The room was poorly lit and I indicated my need for another lamp. The instant the light fell upon her and I saw that the infant was presenting in the breech, I felt a certainty grip me as strongly as if it had been a powerful blow upon my shoulder – such as I used to receive from my old professor of anatomy whenever he caught me day dreaming at a particularly tricky moment during a dissection. Now look here Spiess! he would admonish me. Be alert! Make no mistake! You have arrived at the place through which you must pass successfully if your life is ever to amount to anything. Go to it!

One of the baby's legs had emerged, the other being twisted

back up against the torso inside the distended birth opening, which had suffered a deep and jagged tear. The situation had apparently been in stasis for some time. At this point I was not aware of the android formation of Madame Feng's pelvis and decided to assist the birth to resume and proceed by the natural means. Was I not, in reaching this decision, however, influenced by another, a greater and more powerful consideration than medical science could have provided me with? From the account of it which I had heard from my father I saw that confronting me here in Marco Polo's 'City of Heaven' at this very moment was a duplication of my own troubled descent into Hamburg fifty years earlier. It was as if an eternal clock had struck the hour for me. As if at the passage of half a century, at the opposing point on the globe from Hamburg, I had at last arrived at the true time and place of my entry into life. All at once the puzzling tenderness which I have felt towards the Chinese since the first day of my residence in this country was made explicable to me. It was as if an angel had descended into the room and swept her molten wings across my eyes and dazzled me with a vision of my own birth. As I stood there I was engulfed by a great compassion for Madame Feng and her unborn infant, a warmth of feeling the like of which I had never before experienced, a sense of my own deep vulnerability to the dangers faced by these two people at this hour. I understood that I had at last come face to face with myself.

But I am a doctor and, dazzled by visions or not, I couldn't stand about doing nothing. There followed many hours of struggle, during which I applied the accumulated skills of my lifetime of experience to seeking the release of the child from the deathly grip of the pelvic bone. But to no avail. The head remained obstinately fast within her body. It was then I was brought to the terrible decision that I must sacrifice the precious life of this child if I were to save the life of its mother. And it was then, as I approached her with this purpose in mind, that Madame Feng raised herself from her exhaustion and in an unearthly voice commanded me not to kill her child.

By the uncertain lamplight we confronted each other. I saw she would not tolerate the half-measure I proposed. That she would countenance, indeed, no retreat to a position of compromise from which a future campaign might be mounted. The expression in her eyes told me that if she did not succeed this night then there would be no future for her. I did not doubt that she had resolved to wager everything on this struggle and to die rather than give it up. Humbled by her resolve, I silently laid aside my instruments.

As if I were some horrible ogre seeking to disembowel her, knowing I inflicted an unendurable measure of pain, I knelt before her and with great difficulty inserted my hands into the deeply lacerated birth opening and placed them around the head of the child. With all my strength I gripped the cranial bones and began to force them into a misalignment, shaping and moulding as if I wrestled with a stubborn ball of clay, until it seemed I dealt not with a single head but with two detached sections. By this primitive and brutal means, uncertain whether the infant lived or expired, but kept to the task by the fierce and unnatural exhortations of Madame Feng herself, who rose upon the passion of her suffering like a martyr upon the flames, I succeeded eventually in passing the infant's unjointed cranium through the acute angle of the android pubis. When the head emerged I saw my manipulations had resulted in a lateral sugar-loaf distortion more grossly pronounced than anything I had ever witnessed in an infant that survived. The crushed features appeared to have been composed from the poorly joined halves of two separate faces, as if the maker of this creature had lacked the refinement of skill necessary to the fashioning of human symmetry, the basis upon which our notions of form and beauty are founded. I was amazed to see that the child breathed. There was evidence of permanent damage to the area of the right eye.

At the sound of its cry she roused herself and asked to see her baby. When she saw it was a boy she murmured thanks to the fates who decide these matters. She seemed indifferent to its appearance but laid the unresisting newborn to her breast with a contentment that I marvelled at. It seemed child and mother had reached each other by so arduous a journey they asked for no more now than the singular comfort of each other's embrace. I stayed and watched while they slept a deep sleep of exhaustion. I have never felt more vividly the nature of birth and motherhood, wherein the new being is grown from the old flesh. Two beings where there was one. Two creatures separate but united. The same flesh parted and become two. As I stood there, tired, relieved, elated, ascended as it were upon the uplift of my emotions the way a bird ascends without apparent effort upon a thermal updraft and scans the desert and the mountain below, the mystery of the origin and destiny of the human race seemed to lie before me in all its infinite extent and uncertainty. What other certain knowledge, I asked myself, could there be than if these two who slept before me were one that I was one with them? Surely there could be no family but one family, and no homeland but one homeland. I was moved then to perform in silence what seemed to me to be a secret ceremony, the significance of which shall remain known only to myself. I acted in this as the priest of our fellowship. The midwife and mediator at the nativity of this child and the rebirth of myself. In this little ritual of my own devising I bestowed upon the infant the name Lang Tzu; two characters which in Mandarin signify the son who goes away. I wished him well on the journey I knew he must one day embark upon in his restless search for a homeland. The journey, if he were to be as fortunate as I, which would reunite him with his beginning.

There, I have written my account of it. The moon has long set and the garden is in deep shadow. The frosty sky is filled with stars. The painter's lines come into my mind: *Midway through life I set my heart on Truth And have come to end my days by the Southern Hills.* I should like to walk in Huang's garden, but dare not in case such an action offer him offence. How little I know the customs of these people.

·

3 pm, 21 December 1927 She maintains a low fever, but the

·

signs of a strong recovery are already present. Lang Tzu feeds well. The realignment of his features will never be complete, but she gazes upon him with a mother's love and sees before her the most beautiful child that ever lived. She is loath to relinquish him even for a moment to the nurse, and will not permit him to be carried out of her sight. I heard her call him Ho this morning, which means harmony. I have not told her of my intuitions concerning his future. Neither of us has said anything about the peculiar likeness he bears to Feng.

I returned to my quarters here half an hour since, groaning from another feast. I cannot refer to it merely as a sumptuous meal, for this daily gastronomic event is observed with such strict and orderly ritual it seems more the fulfilment of a religious office than the performance of a domestic duty. As with all priestly services, this one also partakes deeply of the theatre. I succumb willingly to Yu Hung-meng's culinary arts! Am I not for him the King of the Sacred Rites, to be sacrificed at the appointed hour (whenever that may be) for the common good, as was done in antique times in the priest-ridden cities of Zela and Pessinus? Or might I not be the nurse-frog in disguise, *Alytes obstetricans*, the obstetrical toad herself, whose displeasure they dread to arouse lest I turn my arcane powers against them and betwitch their women into having ugly babies. Whatever marvel I might be for them, for myself dinner has become the highlight of the day! Here is the role I have dreamed of creating since I was twelve years old, at which time, to my astonishment, I attended a performance of Schiller's *Die Rauber*; the moment, that is, when I saw that theatre must be greater than life, for in theatre and not in life did I for the first time witness the free expression of that idealism which is natural to the souls of all humankind.

Awaited sombrely by my attentive audience I make my entrance and sit in solitary dignity at a bare teakwood table which stands at the centre of Huang's vast, unheated reception hall. This table and the carved chair I sit in are the room's only furnishings. My costume is the magnificent fur coat which Yu presented to me with much kowtowing and nervous mumbling on my first day. This coat, so I understand from Madame Feng, was fashioned from the pelts of eighteen grey foxes. It is a princely garment, fastening closely about my throat and enfolding me in draughtproof snugness to the very tips of my boots. In it I appear to be more than twice my actual size. An impression I greatly enjoy presenting to the world. In this coat I am a giant. A figure of fantastic proportions. I am no longer myself.

Cocooned in the silvery grey fur, on the first day I sat in the chair and waited for my dinner; curious as to my new surroundings but a little impatient, for the meal was a long time arriving and I had scarcely eaten for two days. Facing me was the open doorway to the principal courtyard, a wide and vacant space of parade-ground proportions, across which Madame Feng and I had driven in Feng's Pontiac, with all the pomp of visiting royalty, on our arrival. It presented a view with little in it to distract me from my hunger. The only thing that moved in the barren courtyard was the yellow dust, which was plentiful and which was blown about in fierce eddies by a cold wind. I had begun to think I had been forgotten, when a peasant came and stood in the open doorway and stared at me. She remained perfectly still, gazing at me on my throne as if I were incapable of a response and were not another human being such as herself but an exhibit in a museum, a reconstruction of the stoic mastodon from the Pliocene. In a few moments this first peasant was joined by another, who stood beside her and looked at me with a like measure of curious detachment.

Within the half hour a small crowd had gathered before me silently, entirely filling the wide doorway and obscuring my view of the empty courtyard. Some squatted on their haunches, while other stood with a kind of vacant nonchalance upon one leg, and yet others – as if these determined souls were intent upon remaining for the entire five acts – fashioned little cushions from rags and bundles and sought to make themselves comfortable upon the flagstones. They did not converse with one another but observed me all the while with a fixed and serious attention, as if they were confident their patience would soon be rewarded by a spectacle worth having waited for; as if, indeed, they possessed a more certain knowledge than I of what was to take place. I nestled deeply into my mighty fur and gazed at the great beam above the doorway, as if I were loftily indifferent both to their stares and my own fate. I had plenty of time to muse upon my condition and the appearance I must present to these people. I likened my appearance in my present disguise to that of a fat and shapeless grub; a larva of one of their famous silkworms – which they have reared in countless thousands here in Hangzhou since long before the Venetian visited them in the thirteenth century – waiting to be fed my due apportionment of mulberry leaves.

Etymology, so I have found, frequently sustains the casual images we think we take at random from the teeming possibilities within our minds, and reveals our seemingly haphazard choices to have been guided by forces – should I say cultural and historical forces? – far deeper than the blithe gesturings of consciousness. Something of this consideration urged me to pursue further the image of myself as a larva, which it seemed to me I had based upon nothing more subtle than my gross physical resemblance in the heavy fur coat to such an amorphous creature. It was not many moments, however, delving this way and that and proceeding by association of one thing with another, musing and speculating as one does at such times without an exact discipline but with the freedom to consult whatever rises to the surface of one's memory, before I recalled Montaigne's observation that fear *sometimes representeth strange apparitions, as their fathers' and grandfathers' ghosts, risen out of their graves, and in their windingsheets: and to others it sometimes sheweth Larves, Hobgoblins, Robbin-good-fellowes, and such other Bug-beares and Chimeraes.* Here, then, was the word *larva* in its original usage! For in Latin it signifies a mask or spectre whose true form is hidden, a form yet to be revealed. I realised at once that our adoption of the Latin word into our own language and

·

application of it to the metamorphic insect in the primal stage after its emergence from the egg must itself have been an act of imaginative association, a metaphor rather than a literal or scientific description. The discovery excited me. It was but a short step from this ancient Roman notion of the larva as a mask, to the full-blown idea of the fantastic and motley character of the masque itself – a masquerade of my own devising in which I was to be the only player. With this discovery the magical possibilities of my childhood seemed to be restored to me. I had only to desire something to be so for it to *be* so.

I come in daily instalments. For my audience – who are not at all like our cinema audiences in Shanghai and never hiss or boo if the action is a little slow – I am Hamlet today, conversing with the ghost of his father, and Schiller's robber, Karl Moor, in the Bohemian forest tomorrow. A steaming savoury dumpling may be for my attentive audience the equivalent of an entire principality sequestered to prop the fortunes of a tottering empire. For the silent gathering of ragged peasants in the doorway before me, I am convinced the fates of dynasties are decided upon the rising and falling of my eating bowl. Seated in solitary state in Huang Yu-hua's great hall, attired in my phantasmal vestments, and waited upon by Yu Hung-meng and his assistant, I am liberated from the burdensome responsibilities and banal ambitions of Doctor August Spiess, late of the International Settlement, and am exalted to the status of a king or god of the theatre, a mysterious and powerful being who conjures with the secret desires of his devotees at the appointed hour each day. Here in the City of Heaven there is no inner voice insisting that I am lost and must go in search of the real world. Here, for an hour or two each day, I inhabit the real world! And should I doubt it even for a moment I need only raise an eyebrow or crook my little finger in order to receive the instant reassurance from my audience that everything I do is meaningful. Here not a single gesture of mine is wasted! My actions are not whirled away and lost for ever in the blizzard of time the very second they occur!

August, seek no more! my reflective voice urges me. Here you are at home!

If only I could confront my schoolmasters once more and tell them of my discovery! How I detested the study of philosophy which they forced me to undertake! How even the names Kant, Hegel and Schopenhauer, and even more the terrible titles of their books, made my stomach turn and twist with disgust! What a torture for me their exacting formulations were! How I wish I could take those old masters aside for a moment here in Hangzhou and reveal to them that a theatre, a storyteller and an audience are all that are required for the fulfilment of every human desire.

.

I am not alone. Beside me on the teakwood table while I wait for Yu to bring the dishes of steaming food there rests the black handset of a new telephone – an incongruous article of the modern world in this old hall of the classical scholar. We are Feng's conditions; an obstetrician and a telephone. But although we dine alone we have little to say to each other. This telephone, which I would rather were not there, is nothing less than the sign of my legitimacy. For is not Feng himself concealed within it? It is his will that has endowed me with the power to be here; the only Westerner ever to be admitted to this house. The telephone and I are Feng's forces of occupation; our presence here insists upon his primacy in the face of his wife's determination to establish the ascendancy of her own house. And am I not also an agent of her conspiracy to this end? These are the complicated mechanics by which the universe I inhabit here is driven. Fortunately the telephone does not ring, and for the most part I am able to ignore it. I cannot ignore it, however, when I see the gaze of one of my audience stray to it and linger upon it. This I take to be a sign that my performance lacks authority to distract from mundane fears. At such times it is me against the telephone, and even though it does not ring, it interrupts.

Among the duck, pork, veal, the three varieties of fish, the fungi and the fluffy dumplings, the fruits and vegetables of

.

many kinds and scalding mountain of steamed rice – smoking like Vesuvius and ostentatiously and repeatedly renewed by Yu's determined assistant despite my indifference to it; is it the same mound of rice brought again and again to my table or a different mound each time? – among all this I say, there was today a garnishing that troubled me. One particular dish was adorned with freshly plucked petals from the blossoms of the winter-flowering plum tree which blooms at this time in Huang's garden, and which I have admired from my casement. In the middle of winter this tree fills the air with the perfume of spring! The petals, which looked at first like bright drops of blood, I took to be a sign from the scholar; an indication that he also watches my performances. From a place of concealment, his box at the opera, as it were. Are these plum blossoms, however, from which the petals detach themselves as readily as do the wings of swarming termites, a sign of his approval or of his disapproval? If I should ask for her opinion on this matter when I go to visit her and the child this evening, after we have exchanged courtesies and are sipping our scented tea, I am certain she will not enlighten me but will, as always, offer some gentle evasion. There is no direct way here; everything is within a maze and must be sniffed out with great finesse if it is to be uncovered and not startled into some deeper hiding place.

I have always found great solace in flowers – my geraniums in terracotta pots outside my blue door are famous throughout the International Settlement – and am reluctant to see in these floral garnishes tokens of ill-will or emblems of decay; *Fleurs du Mal*, as it were, of Monsieur Gautier's haunted friend! But they were there and stood out so dramatically against the grey glaze of my bowl I could not ignore them. They seemed to insist upon being the bearers of a message. I stared at them floating in the soup and was put in mind of the coagulation test we applied as students to droplets of fresh blood, tilting the paraffin-filled test tube every few moments to observe the exact instant at which the blood would begin to clot. The petals of the winter-flowering plum turned black as I observed

them and stuck with a tenacious adhesiveness to the sides of
the bowl. They clung, indeed, to every surface they came into
contact with and were soon everywhere.

·

Evening, 2 January 1928 Christmas Day and New Year passed
here without anyone remarking upon them. I am glad. They
belong to the world I have left behind. Her fever has quite
gone. She is returned to health. Not, to be sure, to her full
strength, but one senses the restlessness of her youthful
ambition. She requested that I walk with her today. The air was
cold, but the sun shone brightly. Together we paraded Lang
before the servants in a little courtyard on the far side of the
principal storehouse. People came in from the street through a
small gateway, which had been freshly painted in bright
vermilion, and they admired the child and cast curious glances
my way. I felt that Madame Feng intended to parade me, also,
as an exotic acquisition from the strange land of Shanghai,
which I am certain they think of here as the centre of Western
Christendom, that is to say the place where all the devils live.
Walking at her side I felt rather as the Africans in the
seventeenth century must have felt who were taken as
amusements to the royal courts of Europe. I was wearing my
silvery fur and maintained an inscrutable and dignified manner,
while observing everything that went on about me with the
keenest interest. Among the people who crowded round us I
recognised no one from my audience. These folk of the
storehouse courtyard were an altogether better dressed and
more prosperous caste than the hungry crowd that gathers each
day to watch me dine.

Yu accompanied us, fussing around her and Lang all the
while and pretending to keep the curious at a respectful
distance with threatening motions of a bamboo stave. A ritual
gesture it seemed, for there was no real need for him to do
this as their manner could scarcely have been outwardly
more respectful than it was. I noticed, however, how they
signalled to each other secretly with movements of their hands
and eyes, either to warn of something or to comment in some

·

forbidden way upon the proceedings. It went on the whole time and was an undercurrent which I can only liken to the nervous twitterings and flittings of ground birds at the appearance in the sky of a regal hawk. They smiled broadly all the time and giggled and kowtowed to her repeatedly, some offering presents, which were taken up by Yu's assistant, the same short dark and determined man who serves me unwanted rice. I believe Madame Feng possesses the power of life and death over these people and would not hesitate to exercise it. Huang, as ever, remained hidden. Though I felt he watched our progress from concealment. I have not met him yet. His is a secret life. He is another of their silkworms, shielded from contact with ordinary folk and mundane cares by the cocoon of his exquisite refinement no doubt. Yu is his emissary to the world, his forward scout and quartermaster.

The City of Heaven, 24 January 1928 When I visited them this evening Lang was lying upon the skin of a snow leopard. He cried when I went to move him from it in order to examine him. Madame Feng saw in his attachment to the fur a good omen, as she does in everything that touches upon his life. But how can there be ill omens when she herself presents him with only those things she desires him to come in contact with? As I bent over him his protuberant right eye gazed up at me coldly, seeming to remind me of our secret relations and at the same time to indict with a degree of bitterness the limitations of my craft of midwifery. It was an emotional moment. I felt myself to be accountable to him for something larger than his immediate welfare. She would insist he already shows extraordinary gifts. I know nothing of this, but certainly he is not like other babies of a few weeks of age to look at. His features appear to be those of a grown person. There is something old and sad about him. His are the features of experience. And his likeness to his father is startling, even to the dense mat of spiky black hair that shoots straight up like grass from his scalp. She forced into his tiny grip one of her brushes, and when he waved it about – as he could not help but do for it is beyond an infant of that age to relinquish anything – she cried out with delight, as if he had crawled over to the corner and snatched up the brush himself. Were I to force him to cling to my moustaches he would undoubtedly do that as well. But would she see it as an augury? I say nothing, knowing it is not possible to discuss with her what she does not wish to discuss. I am her African.

·

The City of Heaven, 29 January 1928 Observed closely by my faithful following, I was sucking the last delicious vestiges of juice from the crevices of a steamed pork chop this afternoon, a pork chop which had been steeped in a rich dark sauce the consistency of molasses, when the telephone rang. As the sudden shrilling of the bell sounded the crowd at the door scrambled back a good pace. I myself jumped and almost dropped the bone. Hurriedly wiping my fingers I picked up the telephone and placed it against my ear. At first all I could hear was a crackling and buzzing. Then I began to make out the sound of many voices, remote and indistinct voices, whose disembodied tones seemed to send forth messages into a kind of eerie infinity, as airy whisperings which were not meeting up but were passing through each other's tracks like the traces of stars left upon an exposed photographic plate. Messages bound for no destinations! I listened in wonder to mysterious beings conversing in the uncanny deep, then cautiously I repeated my greeting: Hullo! I called, This is August Spiess at the house of Huang Yu-hua! Thin and far away, subsumed one moment beneath the celestial choir and the next rising faintly above it, I heard Feng's answering voice calling my name: August! Is it you? The sound of the telephone had brought Yu and the rice carrier to the door of their kitchen. Like a nervous stage manager and director of the play, they stood in the doorway and watched. Pressing the telephone firmly against my ear and mouth I shouted into it that it was indeed I, August Spiess. I heard nothing but hissing and sharp electrical discharges shot through with those inhuman cries, then Feng's

·

voice struggled to the surface once again, like the voice of a drowning father, August!

He spoke at some length, I was sure of it. But his voice might have been one starling among a mighty flock of thousands wheeling against an evening sky for all my ability to follow it. The boy, August? These were the only words I could distinguish at last. And again, fading, The boy?

He is well! I bellowed, and once more with even greater force. He is well! He thrives! I listened for a long while but could not again locate Feng's voice among the whispering multitudes. Slowly I replaced the handset in its cradle. They were watching me. Yu and his assistant also, from the wings. The hall echoed with my bellowing. Had I overdone it? There was no applause, and without that convention it is difficult to tell how one has done. Yu and his assistant glanced at each other and returned to their kitchen. The others watched me; as before, waiting with apparent assurance of witnessing sooner or later a satisfying denouement to this affair.

•

Hangzhou, 10 March 1928 I can no longer bring myself to call this place the City of Heaven. My audience has been gratified. It came about in this manner. It is spring and I knew my departure for Shanghai could not be delayed much longer. Knowing also that a return visit here could not be counted upon, I resolved a few days ago to undertake an excursion which had long been a fond wish of mine. Fearing she might not approve and would find the means to prevent me from proceeding with it if she were to hear of my plan – for since our arrival we have not ventured beyond the gates – I said nothing to Madame Feng. Normally I sit for two and sometimes even three hours over the midday feast. I determined on this day to take no more than a light snack and then to set out at once on my journey.

So, apparelled in my ghostly fur, with the addition of my straw hat with its gay cerise band, after eating only two small dumplings, I got up from my throne. At this unexpected sign from me, those who were seated at the front of the doorway

•

also stood up. Instead of making my exit as I usually do via the rear of the visitor's hall and returning to my quarters, I strode boldly towards my audience with the intention of passing beyond them to the principal courtyard from where I could gain access to the road.

I smiled broadly and made a hesitant kowtow when they did not fall back at my approcah but stood their ground solemnly. Before stepping down from the table, in my imagination I had visualised something like a performance of, say, *Ariadne* by the Vienna Staatsoper and myself as Lotte Lehmann going among her adoring audience during the interval. In this fable my own little audience had parted respectfully before my approach like the Red Sea parting before the rod of Moses. As they did not move, however, I was unable to proceed and was forced to stand my ground before them. We gazed at each other nervously. The powerful smell of their bodies enveloped me and I recalled my weary nights administering to the poor and the sick in Shanghai's forsaken hovels south of Siccawei Creek in the Chinese city. Only now I was not accompanied by an interpreter. There was no mediator with me who might reveal to these people the benign nature of my intentions. I encouraged myself with the thought that they were so awed by my nearness they had become frozen to the spot. Smiling broadly, I forced my way among them, murmuring reassuring platitudes and placing my hands upon the shoulders of an old woman here and upon the head of a cringing child there, gently encouraging them as if I were the Pope himself among his congregation at Easter time. They did not move aside but resisted me more strenuously, nudging me and shouldering me, indeed bouncing me back and forth between them as bullying boys do in a schoolyard when they have entrapped a victim in their midst. By this ungracious means I was at last delivered from one to another into their very centre, whence all movement among them ceased. I was out of breath and my hat was over one ear. I was surrounded by their staring faces, on which I read a sullen disagreeableness. Now that they had me, however, it seemed they were at a loss to know what to do with me. I saw at once I must take the initiative while they wavered in their purpose and so, with a shout of alarm, I barged my way suddenly through them to the open courtyard. I half expected they would follow me, but my aggressive action seemed to have cowed them, for they did not. When I reached the gates I turned and looked back. They still stood tightly together, like a flock of sheep frightened into the corner of a field, watching the wolf depart hungry. I laughed aloud with relief and with a flourish of my arm bade the gatekeeper open his gates. I decided my unexpected behaviour in leaping from the table and confronting them had so bemused them they had not known how to respond graciously but had taken my action as some kind of challenge which they had felt called upon to meet with a show of physical resistance. Thankfully a poor show as it had turned out.

Once in the public road I put the incident quickly from my mind and strode forward cheerfully, the drumlike knocking of the black-lacquered gates closing behind me sounding in my ears. I had no thoughts of omens, auguries or signs, being confident in my mind that it was I who was the principal dispenser of such things among these people. It was a fine day with a cold breeze blowing freshly from the mountains. A perfect day for walking. I rejoiced in my freedom and looked forward to adventures ahead. It was the first day of Spring in the City of Heaven and it belonged entirely to me! I might have asked myself, implying a degree of self-congratulation, if there could possibly exist anywhere in China a more fortunate being than myself this day.

As I strode along the wide thoroughfares beneath the budding plane trees and the early blossoms I was cheerfully untroubled by the many curious glances cast my way. My thoughts were filled with expectations of treasure. In my thoughts I was already fossicking among the ruins of the ancient kilns and turning up a fine harvest of shards of the famous *Nei-yao*, the original palace ware celadon of the early Southern Sung court, the most prized of all glazes to western scholars and collectors. These would be specimens from the source, taken with my own hands from the venerable ruins in which they had lain for centuries, specimens of such undoubted authenticity I would be able to employ them as touchstones to assess the quality of certain pieces in my own collection and any I might consider acquiring in the future. But it was much more than the possession of a few pieces of broken pottery that excited me. I was making a religious pilgrimage. That is why I made a mistake which might otherwise be inexplicable to me.

If I had paused to reflect for a moment as I went along, I might readily have recalled, for I knew it well enough, that the kilns of Fenghuang Hill, towards which I had set my steps, had been buried long ago under repeated rebuilding and had never been found, and that it was towards the later kilns of Chiao-t'an, a mile or so to the south-west, that I should have been directing my steps if I merely wished to collect shards. But I did not pause to reflect. My head was full of visions. A blind enthusiasm gripped me. I had leaped from my stage in the middle of the banquet and made for the buried kilns of Phoenix Hill as if the voice of Kuanyin herself had commanded me to go there at once.

As I walked along the dusty roads, which became narrower and more crowded with peasants as I ascended the hill, I was thinking of a happy occasion during my childhood. Feeling myself to be nearing the end of a search, I suppose my thoughts turned naturally to its beginning. At the age of eight or nine I travelled with my parents and my sister to Rome. I have always had a memory from this holiday of my father and myself on our hands and knees beside each other in a wide open space. It is like an image from a dream, but I know it to be in reality a memory of an actual event. Though I did not of course realise it then, at the age of eight or nine, on my hands and knees beside my father that day was the moment I became a collector and began my search. I don't know where my mother and sister were on this occasion. They may have been watching us or absent on an adventure of their own. I don't know. They may even conceivably have been on their hands and knees beside us. They are not, however, included in the memory. There has never been a place for them in it. In the remembered image, though undoubtedly not in the true history, my father and I are alone. We are searching for pottery shards, or for coins or fragments of broken statuary, among some ancient Roman ruins. We are devout, awed and deeply conscious of our own unworthiness. We are at the source of our civilisation. We are worshippers at the source. We are true believers. Today, in these modern times, as we all gaze confidently towards the future, it has become a heresy to suggest we might also look to the past. It seems, indeed, absurd to us that generations looked for their inspiration towards the past. But they did. My father's generation, those of them who survive, still tirelessly expound to us the values and virtues of classical antiquity and still see in those remote times the source of everything that is good and right. Although I no longer possess the certainty of childhood, I think I shall never be entirely free from a conviction that my father was right to think as he did. What my mother thought of it all I don't believe she was ever permitted to say. I remember only how sad she was when I left Germany. She seemed to know she was never to see me again.

Above the crouching figures of my father and I, the Italian sky is a splendid azure with little white fluffy clouds floating gently. All around us are the dazzling pavements, the marble steps and broken columns and the shattered pediments of the ancient settlement. Sprouting from fissures and crevices among the stones are thousands of yellow dandelions. Here and there are the downy heads of those which have gone to seed. I pick one of these trembling spheres and blow upon it, and as I blow I make a wish. The wish was of the greatest importance to me at the time of making it. But what it was I can no longer recall. Of that particular action the only recollection which has persisted undimmed to this day is that of the feathery ball of seeds quivering as I held it before my mouth.

Walking along towards Phoenix Hill, I was feeling a sense of wonderment at what a mysterious fiction our memory is, when suddenly my hat was knocked from my head. As I bent to retrieve it I received a push in the back and was sent sprawling on to my hands and knees. As I fell forward I felt no alarm, for it seemed to me I must have become involved in an unfortunate accident and that in a moment all would be explained and restored to normal. Indeed I did not even feel sufficiently put out to interrupt my thoughts. I sensed, or believed I sensed, a kindliness all around me which I did not think to question. On my hands and knees in the roadway I had plenty of time to study the texture of the dust. I was struck by the contrast of this yellow earthy Chinese dust with the dazzling marble pavements of ancient Rome. In the brief moment that passed while I was still expecting to feel helping hands assisting me to my feet and to hear the voices of apology close to my ears, I considered what a wealth of proverbs and wise sayings had been composed upon the subject of dust.

When no one came to my assistance, however, and I began to get to my feet, turning my head as I did so to see what or who had knocked me to the ground, a stone struck me a glancing blow above my right eye. Close around me the excited voices of my assailants encouraging each other suddenly broke into a wild chorus. It is the coat, I thought. They have mistaken me for one of their unscrupulous landlords. They will realise their mistake in a moment. But sticks and stones continued to beat upon me and I was forced to raise my arms to shield my head. About a dozen or more young men and women were gathered around me. I tried once again to rise in order to reveal their error to them. As I did so, however, in their eyes I saw a terror of what they were doing and at once I, too, began to feel afraid. They shrieked and darted at me in ones and twos, hurling their stones and swinging their sticks so wildly and with such an excess of fear and excitement that they as often hit each other as me. Fortunately, the thick fur deadened their blows, which I felt as dull proddings.

A small crowd quickly gathered. My plight was observed by these passers by in that emotionless way the Chinese peasant has acquired through the centuries, which seems to suggest that the misfortunes of others are witnessed through a sort of hole in time. It is all the same, this expression implies, a woman giving birth to a dead child in a doorway in Shanghai or a foreign devil being beaten in a back street in Hangzhou. There is nothing to be done. One pauses to observe and passes on. One cannot intervene, for these are not human beings upon whose misfortunes one gazes but imaginary beings. I recognised one of my audience among the onlookers. It was the woman who had been the first to arrive in the doorway to the courtyard and who had looked at me seated at the teakwood table in Huang's hall as if I were an exhibit in a museum. She was looking at me now with exactly the same expression in her eyes. This then, it appeared, was the final scene, in which the young people kill the hairy old mastodon.

The continuous blaring of an automobile horn cut through the air and my attackers dropped their sticks and stones and thrust themselves through the encircling cordon of onlookers, who let them pass with looks of mild surprise, as if the actors had unexpectedly invaded the stalls. The Pontiac glided slowly towards me and came to a stop. The Russian chauffeur got out of the car and helped me to my feet. I thanked him. The expressionless audience continued to gaze at us. An unforseen turn in the plot. The Russian removed his leather gauntlets and offered me his white linen handkerchief. When I looked puzzled he indicated a point above his own right eye. He watched me while I wiped the blood from my face. There was very little of it. Just a smear. In his gaze I read a sardonic amusement. I had heard Feng say this man claimed to be a prince, but I think it was a claim many of the Russians made. I wondered if he, too, were living for the duration of our stay in Huang's house. I had not seen him since our arrival. He ignored my protests, took my arm firmly and led me to the rear door of the car.

Madame Feng gazed at me from the blue interior. I climbed in and sat next to her. She asked me if I were badly hurt. I reassured her that I was not and told her the coat had saved me

from serious injury. And anyway, I said, surprising myself with
this for I did not believe it, I really don't think they meant to
do me any great harm. I was feeling strangely elated, as if I'd
just had a strong drink. I wanted to smile broadly. I restrained
myself with an effort and tried to look suitably serious.
Madame Feng was looking particularly grim. The car rose and
fell slowly, the body twisting on its chassis as it rode over the
uneven surface of the crowded roadway. I leaned forward like
a drunken man, my face for an instant close to hers. The
Russian sounded his horn continuously. She sat in the corner
of the seat, turned towards me and inspected me coldly. It is
difficult to believe, she said eventually, in quite the degree of
credulity that remark implies, Doctor Spiess.

I held myself against the backrest of the seat and blinked at
her, trying my hardest not to smile or to lurch towards her.

They would have killed you within a few more minutes, I
assure you, if I had not arrived.

Oh no, surely not, I protested. If you had seen them you
would have seen they were far more terrified than I was.

They were bent upon murder. And murder, even for
assassins, is a terrifying business, she said, as if she were
explaining something to a person from another time who
could not benefit from the information.

I couldn't bring myself to believe in the seriousness of this
affair. Despite everything, I still felt myself to be under the
benign influence of the memory of Rome, the blue sky and the
golden dandelions sprouting from the shattered marble. The
onlookers, I felt, had been right. The figure on the ground in
the fur coat a moment ago had been an imaginary being. I
turned to Madame Feng. How did you know where to find me?

The whole of Hangzhou knew where to find you, Doctor,
she said, with undisguised contempt. But not where you were
going. I felt she was running out of patience with my attitude,
but I was not able to make an appropriate adjustment to my
mood.

I told her I had been bound for the kilns.

Then you were lost, she informed me.

It was now I realised my error in going to Fenghuang Hill instead of to the kilns of Chiao-t'an to the south-west. I was shocked by my failure to have seen this obvious mistake sooner. My silly need to smile vanished. I had been behaving, it seems, in a way which had been slightly out of control. It began to seem quite possible I might even have experienced something like small blackouts, selective little patches of memory loss, as if something in me had been carefully concealing my true purpose from me. On considering it I found I had no recollection of the route I had taken after leaving the main road outside Huang's gates. The fine, earthy yellow dust inches from my face as I knelt upon the roadway was the most real thing about the morning.

Why didn't you *ask* me before you went? She was very angry. Yu might have accompanied you. Then you would not have got lost. She looked away. I might have come with you myself.

You shame me Madame, I said miserably. I felt I had failed a standard which she and I had tacitly contracted to maintain between us; an unspecified but an absolute standard all the same, of making the right choices about matters affecting our unusual existence in Hangzhou. I had been a disappointment. I was not the person she had thought me to be. Would I ever regain the ground with her which I had lost this morning? I knew even before I spoke that my apology was going to sound pompous. It was my father who composed it for me. I heard it in German in his voice before I spoke it aloud in English. I see I have made a grave error of judgement and put you to a deal of unnecessary trouble on my behalf, Madame. She made a snorting noise. I cleared my throat and continued, I am heartily sorry and do most sincerely apologise for it. She said nothing, but looked out of the window on her side of the car as if I'd not said anything. The silence was very unpleasant for me. I wanted to be forgiven. After a while I could stand it no longer and said, It is as well that no real harm has come of it.

She laughed bitterly, It is certain your attackers do not share that view, she said, watching the peasants trudging along under their immense loads, loads so large it seemed they must be carrying them for a bet, or that they were living in a land ruled by an ogre. The most obscene perversity can seem normal if one is exposed to it for long enough. It takes a shock of some kind to make us see the absurd and the unjust in human affairs for what they are.

No real harm! she said and turned to me, her eyes alight with fury, with dislike, with contempt. I involuntarily drew back into my corner. You have been in China twenty years and you have understood nothing yet, Doctor Spiess! It is impossible to insult you! Only Feng's power protects you here. If your absence had not been reported to me the moment you left the house you would be dead. The consequences of your death would have been incalculable. As it is, your stupidity has already made inevitable the deaths of those who took advantage today of the opportunity you gave them to attack you. They will die, not you. This time. For there is nowhere here that such people as they can hide for very long. Feng and your friend the Chief of Police will put up a reward. It will not be a very large reward by your standards. But it will be large enough. *No real harm has been done!* Infinite harm has been done! she shouted, unable to contain her fury. There is no end to the harm you have done! It will go on and on, Doctor Spiess, and no one will ever be able to stop it! Even when you have all left China it will go on! You understand nothing! She leaned close to me and asked softly, Will you attend the executions of these wretched people? Will you? Answer me that! When they are lined up in the little yard behind the police barracks with their arms pinioned, humiliated by their captors, tired, hungry, frightened and dirty and without any hope, will you walk up to them arrogantly and spit in their faces to let them know how pleased you are to watch them die? Will you let them know you hate them as implacably as they hate you? Will you grant them this assurance, that they are dying for a reason and have been defeated by a real enemy? Will their deaths dignify you, Doctor Spiess? In some way? In a European way I have not understood? If that is the case, explain it to me and I shall be satisfied. Extraterritoriality? What does it mean to you? Why invent such an idea for the occupation of a country? What is the point? I think I understand. She sat back against the soft blue leather and drew deeply on her cigarette. You won't spit in their faces will you? You will withhold your hatred from them, the only thing that might give some meaning to their deaths, and you will meekly forgive them. And they will die all the same. She laughed with genuine mirth. You see Doctor Spiess, although you have not understood us I have understood you. It is human life you value isn't it? Not its worth. Just human life. As if it were gold and could be neither good nor bad nor worth more nor worth less but must always be worth the same no matter what. One human life is one human life to you. You are absurd! Like your democracy, which you imagine you got from the Greeks, who had slaves. One vote for each person. What a stupid idea! The worst in your eyes possess the same value as the best. You have no way of differentiating between them. The cigarette smoke curled from her lips. I suppose you'll try to have them reprieved so they can have another go at killing you in the future. She turned away.

The car lurched over a deep pothole in the road and we lurched with it, over to the right then back to the left, our shoulders pressing together briefly, flung about like marionettes in a booth, some kind of travelling East-meets-West Punch and Judy show, even to the little blue curtains over the windows. She was right. The likely fate of my youthful attackers appalled me. We drove on in silence, gazing resolutely out of our respective windows at the dismal scene of desperate poverty and filth and unspeakable human degradation and suffering through which we were passing. I had noticed none of it this morning. Just the sunshine and the blossoms. The Russian blasted away continuously on the horn, having scarcely any effect, nudging the buttocks of people with the bumper of the car before they showed any awareness of our presence or attempted to move from our path. The Russian was forced repeatedly to bring the car to a halt and to wait while a top-heavy load was got to one side. And while he waited he pressed on the horn. No one objected. How much more quickly I had covered the distance on foot. I had been in a dream. The dandelions of Rome indeed!

As if she wished to make certain I was left with no possibility of any comforting illusions about what had happened, when we were approaching the gates of the house, which stood open ready to receive us, Madame Feng said, I did not drive out here to save your life Doctor Spiess. She made the words *out here* sound as though we had ventured beyond the frontiers of civilisation. She turned from the window and looked at me. I came out here to save my own life and to secure the future of my son. The violence of her anger had left her. She observed me without interest. You are a child who has been left alone in the kitchen and has burnt himself and very nearly set the house on fire. It is not you, however, who will be punished for this. It is the person who left you alone in the kitchen who will be punished for it. I hope you understand that. I want you to understand that.

∙

These events took place a little over a week ago. Everything has changed. During all my years in China I have never felt myself to be closer to these people nor such a blind stranger in their midst. I have been sitting here at this table in my room by the open casement writing this account for the past four hours. It is two o'clock in the morning. It was raining earlier, now snow has begun falling in the garden. My fingers are so cold I cannot feel the pen. The snow is settling on the edge of the verandah, a greenish phosphorescence out in the darkness. Since that day I have been unable to sleep. I wake in the middle of the night and try to remember what terrible event lies just outside my mind. Then I recall the terror in the eyes of my assailants. I have seen how it is done. The prisoner has a rope around the neck and another above the elbows binding the arms behind the back. The prisoner's hands and ankles are also bound. These children have become my victims. I am to be their murderer. Are there no innocent bystanders to the horror? Are we all murderers, and if murderers then torturers and rapists and thieves also? Villains of the lowest order? What good is our

∙

morality if there is no escape from culpability? Every hour of the day and night I expect the telephone to ring and to hear from Feng that they have been arrested.

The only thing that has not moved but is now more sure than ever, is my love for the boy, my fateful offspring, my namesake, the other Lang Tzu, delivered by my own hands downwards into the disintegrating place of his departure.

·

Hangzhou, 15 March 1928 My portmanteaux are packed and stand ready here beside me. The Russian is to arrive with the car at five thirty and I shall leave for Shanghai by the evening train.

She has not relented. I am not to be given an opportunity to take my leave of Lang. When I entered the guest hall the day following her rescue of me on Fenghuang Hill, the doorway to the courtyard was deserted. It has remained so ever since. Wearing the fur I sat at the table and waited. No one appeared. The courtyard itself remained deserted also. An hour passed and Yu did not bring my dinner but still I continued to sit and wait. Did Huang himself observe my humiliation from his hidden place? I almost expected the woman to come and look at me again and make an object of me. What am I now? What would she see now? The woman who was the first and whom I had seen among the onlookers when I was crouched in the dust and being beaten. Was it she who went ahead of me to prepare the attack.? Eventually Yu brought me a bowl of soup. He was alone. The soup was a poor affair and I was given no spoon. I lifted the bowl to my lips and drank. The rice carrier did not appear. I looked out upon the empty courtyard. Once I was a great actor. Now I am an unworthy beggar. This land is filled with unworthy beggars. We each carry a giant's load.

Yesterday I at last met her father, the literary painter Huang Yu-hua. How different was our meeting from the experience I once imagined it might be. Despite Madame Feng's determination to make them work unceasingly to repair its fabric, this house is decaying. It is falling apart. It is collapsing upon itself. The strange thing is, I have only noticed this during

·

the past week. The place is sliding into ruin and her efforts to restore it will fail.

Wrapped in my fur, which seems now to accuse me, I was returning from the hall. I was stiff from waiting, my hunger unsatisfied, yet I was suffering from indigestion. Giving in to an ungenerous impulse – a state of mind which I believe to be foreign to my nature – I was relishing my discovery of the evidence of decay all around me. As I passed along the gallery beside the faded carmine columns which dignify the inner entryway, I observed how the foundations had begun to subside unevenly beneath them. Then, looking up into the ceiling, I saw that the pediments had cracked and shifted. Here and there I was able to see the sky. So, I thought with a bitter satisfaction, this house will not last much longer. Lang himself will scarcely remember it. Suddenly I realised a figure stood before me in the dark passage. I stopped. Was I to be waylaid in the house itself? It took no more than a moment, however to see that the figure before me offered no threat.

He stood a few paces outside the entrance to his study and his private rooms, at a point along the gallery where a visitor to the house catches a first glimpse of the formal garden lying beyond a small secondary hallway, in which there are usually some chairs with furs on them, as if at a particular hour someone is accustomed to sit there. Huang was waiting for me. He is of much the same build as I, a little shorter even, with a small frame. Despite his slightness of figure, his presence was imposing. He wore a long dark gown or coat, and his hands were clasped in front of him. His head was inclined a little forwards. When I saw him a small hope began to grow in me. I thought to myself, the posture of this man, this head of the household, signifies contrition, humility before his much-abused guest. He wishes to dissociate himself from the punishment inflicted upon me by his daughter. Remembering the last time I had kowtowed, I approached him and bowed in the European manner – a style of obeisance which preserves the dignity of the person who makes the gesture. At this he thrust his clasped hands towards me. I wondered what he intended until I saw he held a small cylindrical object. This he was clearly offering to me. Aha! I thought, a little gleam of hope leaping warmly within me, here is the gift of atonement! I took the box from him and thanked him. Before I could attempt any further speech, and without saying a word, he turned upon his heel and retreated into his study, closing the door firmly behind him. I stood there looking at his door, my thoughts busy with things to say. I had half a mind to knock on the door and insist that we pass at least a few moments together, that we share with each other something of the common courtesies. What had he given me?

I made my way here to my room and opened his gift. Within the cylindrical box there was a small object nestling in a bed of very fine wild grass, which filled the room with the smell of autumn haymaking and made me think of picnics in the country. It was not until I cleared away the grass that I saw it was a piece of celadon. With care I took it from its nest. The gift was a teacup fashioned in the shape of a lotus flower.

It is the finest piece of palace ware celadon I have ever seen. It lies before me now upon this table, its chameleon glaze a bluish-green, like ice reflected in the warm flame of my lamp against the cold light of the day. There can be no doubt this piece was made on Phoenix Hill by the artisans employed by Shao Ch'eng-chang for an emperor of the Southern Sung. If collecting can be dignified with the notion of a quest for the object which embodies the aesthetic ideal of the collector, then this teacup must mark the end of my search. Or, let me say with great sadness, that it *would* have so marked the end of my search, begun that sunny day among the ruins of ancient Rome on my hands and knees beside my father, if I had still been searching. If, that is, I had acquired such an object before my attempt to visit the kilns of Phoenix Hill. While I was still sufficiently blind or innocent or stupid to search for such things, as if I were a blameless child in a world of ceramic visions, and not a murderer.

Huang has given me his finest lotus, his Lien! But it is not something I can possess. As I put my hand out and take it up

·

this moment and hold it before me, its colour becomes a dove grey and the fine crackling of its clear lustrous glaze is made apparent in the altered light. How emotional I feel. This beautiful and precious thing is not mine. I can never own it. But I shall not return it to Huang or it will surely perish with him when this house falls into ruin. I shall receive it into my care. That is what I shall do. Then one day I shall return it to Lang. Here! I shall say, handing it to him in this box of wild grass, here is the finest piece of palace ware celadon to survive the centuries. It belongs to you. Once upon a time it belonged to your grandfather, the great literary painter, Huang Yu-hua, in whose gracious house I spent a few precious months of my life. I shall keep it and its memories safe until then. For me it can never be anything but a chance survival, a souvenir which ought to call to mind the quiet elegance, the restraint and the introspection of a civilisation long dead, but which calls to mind for me instead something else. A sad memorial of such things. Yet I do not feel bitterness now. I feel surprise. What is it I want? Perhaps I have never really been an antiquarian. Can I have done with antiquity? Scholars may look to the past but murderers must look to the future if they are to redeem themselves.

·

Shanghai, 17 March 1928 I went to bed very late after returning from Feng's villa, where we dined together. My report to him was a peculiar fiction. How could I tell him the truth? I applied a selective artistry to my account and spared everyone, including myself. I suppose he believed none of it. He didn't seem to listen to me.

I cannot believe I have a son, he said to me. For almost all my adult life I have had an idea of my son in my mind. That is the only son who will satisfy me. Not this one. What do you suggest? What should I do, he asked me, to rid myself of this ghost and replace it in my affections with the real child?

But he scarcely listened to my suggestion that he exercise patience and spend some time with his real son. That he get to know him. You will grow together with time, C. H., I said. With

·

a certain wistfulness he talked then of his regret at never having visited Australia and his relatives there. There has never been a time during my entire adult life when I could safely have left my affairs here and returned to find myself still master of them. He looked at me and asked, Are you happy August? Is there something you have not done that you dream of doing?

I replied that it took little to make me happy. I was not *un*happy, I said. But he was not listening to me. He played with his glass of Médoc, pushing it back and forth upon the table. He does not like claret, but drinks it in order to prove he is truly Western. He said to me then, I have no desire to see him. He watched for my reaction. Is desire to see one's son anything like the desire to see one's mistress or a friend? Is desire desire or isn't it? He surprised me then by lifting the glass to his lips and draining it. He poured another. Hunger, he said impatiently, is no different if it is hunger for pork or hunger for rice. Is it? If one has a choice one chooses between them but if one has no choice either will do. I hunger for the son in my mind. How am I to satisfy *that* hunger?

He was in a difficult mood. A mood which became more difficult by the glass. I could not talk to him. He wished only to tell me the riddles that obsessed him, not to hear my suggestions for their resolution. He was like an angry dog. He only wanted to argue. He wanted someone to disagree with. When I was leaving he came with me to the door and apologised for having been such poor company. Then he placed his arm around my shoulders and said, We know two of them and we are watching these. They will soon lead us to their friends. Have no fear August, we shall have them all for you.

But I know it is not for my sake they hunt those poor doomed children of Phoenix Hill. There is not room enough in this little journal of mine for one so large as Feng. He is a duke in the affairs of State here and needs a Machiavelli to write him into history. What do I know of his world?

•

Shanghai, 20 April 1928 This is the dream. I had it again last night. I have now had it several times. I forget how many. It

•

differs only a little each time. It is not 1928 but 1926, and the three of us are together attending the funeral of Rilke. The country where the funeral is taking place is not Germany or China. We are in the midst of a large crowd and at first everything is all right. Then I look round and see that Madame Feng, with Lang in her arms, has become separated from me and is being carried away from me by the press of people. We smile and wave and try to reassure each other and we struggle to get close to each other again. But the distance between us grows greater all the time. It is now that I am beset by a feeling of hopelessness and despair. Around me the multitude is indifferent to my plight. The throng of silent mourners moves forward, carrying me with them, and I fear I shall never see Madame Feng or Lang again.

All at once I am brought by the crowd to a wide thoroughfare. It does not surprise me to see Feng riding in his Pontiac at the head of the dead poet's cortege, the Russian chauffeur blasting away on the car horn, which produces the sound of a cello. Feng is serene, princely, and he is smiling just enough for me to guess that he possesses the secret of human happiness. With a small effort I am able to see into his thoughts. I discern his secret. It is this. At the interment of Rilke's remains in a few moments, petals from the eighteenth-century poet Novalis's blue flower of romantic longing for death will be scattered on the coffin by the priest. Feng himself will, at the same time, scatter petals on the coffin from the winter-flowering plum tree in Huang's garden, the same petals which were put into my soup. The red and the blue petals will react with each other to prevent the coagulation of Rilke's blood.

This absurdity possesses for me in the dream the force of a mystical revelation unbinding the secrets of the inner life. I know that if I can reach Madame Feng in time and tell her of my new understanding before the petals are mixed then all will be well between us and my past errors will have been atoned for. Suddenly, I am beside the grave. Madame Feng is standing on the far side. Lang, who is now eight or nine, stands beside her. As with his mother, his head is bowed and he appears to be listening to the service. His disfigured right eye, however, which he is unable to close, stares unblinkingly into the grave, and I know he sees his own future. Neither he nor Madame Feng are aware of my presence on the other side of the grave, and when I try to call out to them I find I cannot. The priest is already scattering the blue petals and Feng is scattering the red petals. As they flutter down into the grave I feel the reaction beginning to take place inside me and I know that nothing can stop me now from reaching my interior homeland. I see Feng smiling at me with understanding, for the country where the funeral is taking place is Australia, his own ancestral homeland. I no longer struggle against the reaction. It takes me away from them. I know that because I have failed to warn Madame Feng, Lang is destined to become an estranged and paralysed man in the crowd of mourners, forever gazing into his own tomb. I feel a great sadness and guilt at this knowledge and I wake with this sadness and guilt heavy upon me. As I lie on my bed for the first few minutes after waking, the dream seems more real and more important to me than the reality that surrounds me, and I long to return to the dream and warn Madame Feng of her husband's secret knowledge, which is the power to destroy her son, a warning I cannot impart to her in the waking life.

Since the morning on Fenghuang Hill, the International Settlement here in Shanghai can never again seem to be my home, as it has for so many years. I feel it is appropriate for me to end this entry in my journal with a poem of Heine's, which has long been a favourite of mine and which has now acquired a new meaning for me: 'Once upon a time I had a fine country of my own where I was at home. The oaks grew tall there, the violets beckoned gently. It was a dream. It kissed me in German and said in German (it's hard to believe how good it sounded) the words "I love you". It was only a dream.'

BOOK
TWO

THE ENTRANCE TO THE OTHER-WORLD

The last of the yellow leaves had turned brown and fallen from the poplar by June. It was now too cold, most days, to sit out on the mound. Lang had retreated to the gas fire in his front room. Nothing I suggested would shift him. He agreed readily, and even with apparent enthusiasm, to all my proposals, but he *did* nothing. It became obvious he was determined to proceed no further with me. I persisted, however, looking for ways to cajole him. None of it worked. We both just ended up drinking more and staying up even later than usual. It began to get a bit exhausting after a while.

Then I arrived at Coppin Grove one Saturday at my usual time, shortly after two o'clock, and found he wasn't at home. This had never happened before and I realised that it might be all over. I might not be able to retrieve the situation. These thoughts scrambled through my mind as I stood at the front door waiting longer than I knew was sensible. I felt a bit shocked, afraid for the first time of how it was really going to turn out for me. I was trying not to remember that my old illusion that I could go back to England if Australia failed me, the myth I'd dragged out and given a shake every time there had been a crisis in my life, was no longer available to comfort myself with. Trying *not* to remember it induced a pang of homesickness, a moment of vivid nostalgia for England and safety.

Certain he wasn't going to be there, but unable to face turning round and just going away again, I went to the back of the house and knocked on the kitchen window and called. I didn't want to be forced to acknowledge just how much Lang and *The Chronicle of the Fengs* meant to me. I wanted to be getting on with it, to keep going at it. I didn't want to glimpse, however obliquely, my extraordinary vulnerability to him. He *wasn't* there of course. Through the brownish film of grease on the window, I could see the mess on the kitchen table. Empty winecasks and junk mail mostly, with bills from the SEC and the Board of Works scattered through it, and fine-art auction catalogues, dozens of them. And a piece of mummified roast pork-on-the-bone, which had been lying there since the night of my first visit to the house in February, when he'd insisted we dine on pork Shanghai style at three o'clock in the morning.

I stood on the verandah for a long time wondering what to do, for at least a half hour, staring out at the garden. A drizzling rain had begun to fall. Which made some sort of sense of standing under the shelter of the verandah. If I didn't do something at once, if I didn't make something happen which was so major and so decisive that he could neither ignore it nor fail to be drawn into it (if I wasn't able, by some means, to worm my way into a vital region of my host) then the project was over. I would have been defeated by his fear and by his alcoholism, one the symptom of the other, and by the impossible inertia of the house and its contents, those mountains of unexamined memorabilia belonging to his past and to Victoria's, which lay there on the English mahogany dining table gathering dust like furnishings for the after-life in the tomb of an extinguished dynasty.

I stood outside the back door looking towards our old base camp, thinking these thoughts and feeling let down and bitter towards him. He might at least have telephoned me to say he would be going out today. No doubt he would claim he *had* and that I'd failed to answer my phone. But he wouldn't have.

For to have done so would have meant risking a confrontation. To have phoned me would have meant bringing his reluctance to continue with our project into the open and talking about it. A reluctance he denied feeling. So how could he talk about it? It was all in my imagination, he would claim. He would challenge me to show some evidence of it and would insist I was being paranoid and unfair to him. Hadn't he always been enthusiastic about my ideas, about the work? I was stuck, that was my trouble, he'd suggest, I had writer's cramp or block or whatever it was called and was looking for a scapegoat. He'd take the blame for that too if it would make me feel better.

I would emerge from any such discussion scarified and exhausted. His logic would be irrefutable. He would gently imply that while an apology from me would be nice he wasn't going to insist on one. He'd let it pass. It didn't matter to him. Things like that, dignity and saving face and such like, were of no consequence to him. There were bigger things for some people to worry about in this life than who was in the right and who was in the wrong. And while I was rendered mute and angry *he* would seize the initiative and urge that we begin work at once on the next section. Come on Steven, cheer up. Let's get on with it. Look at all this stuff. We haven't *touched* it, yet. You can't see where we've been. Let's get my mother's gold out and have a look at it. It's in here somewhere.

But if I were to take him up on the offer, by some means the work would get frustrated and only the drinking would get done. We'd be unable to find his mother's gold, or anything else of interest. The truth was, and I knew it, I was supposed to read his indirect messages only and to behave accordingly. I was supposed to capitulate without a fuss. And if I wanted something to do, I could always recite Burns to him when he was feeling low and have a drink to keep him company. Possibly I might even consider going away altogether for a while and waiting soundlessly until I was summoned, one evening when he was feeling lonely again.

Gertrude's question made complete sense to me at last. What was I going to do? I knew exactly what she'd been asking. I had

.

no idea what the answer might be. The rain was sheeting across the garden now, a heavy mist driven by a cold southerly. One of the cane chairs had been blown onto its side weeks ago in a storm. I decided this was the moment to right it. I went out along my disappearing path to the mound, which looked less of an eminence in this heavy light than it had in the clear dry weightlessness of autumn, when it had seemed to float a little above the rest of the garden, drawn up as much then by optimism and by Gertrude's amber wine as by the refractive qualities of the light, no doubt. I set the chair on its legs and tried to brush the leaves from its seat, but they clung flatly to the wet surface of the cane. I gave it a firm shove, so that its legs were forced a little into the earth, which was spongy from more than a week of heavy rain. Then I stood behind the chair with my hands on its back, as if there were someone seated in it. Someone content to sit and gaze towards the summerhouse through the leafless coppice. As if I were their companion, an attendant to their needs, occupying a place with them somewhere between that of a friend and an employee. An amanuensis, possibly. A servant really, but enjoying the peculiar dignities bestowed by an intimacy with the employer's person and most private thoughts. If it was to be Victoria in the chair then I didn't mind, I had no objection to my questionable status. She could depend on my loyalty.

I was getting wet but I didn't want to leave. The garden was a miserable sight, bare and cold and dripping and black. Still I didn't leave. He'd been right. There were things I had to know. Things I couldn't hope to guess. If he denied me access to the material, then I would be unable to go any further. My fiction, just as Victoria's had been, was dependent on a supply of reliable information. It couldn't subsist on invention. At best the task was always going to be an impossible one and its successful completion therefore an unlikely paradox. The task, the *only* task I could see as being worth attempting, was to penetrate the impermeable face of present reality. I must do it despite the impermeability of the barrier, and I must do it rather than go around the barrier or ignore it. I must get beneath the hard surface by one means or another, because that is where the fictional strata lay, under the polished face of the great enigma of reality, that huge sculpted monolith, a massive object of worship constructed by our ancestors so long ago that no clue as to the means of its construction survives. The puzzle we find our attention bound to despite our efforts to look elsewhere, despite our efforts to find a place in our consciousness which is not within its shadow.

To get beneath the impermeable barrier of present reality, I believed my writing would have to acknowledge the existence of the barrier. My writing would have to contain the barrier. It would have to *be* the barrier itself. Verisimilitude, on at least one of its operational levels, I considered vital to the enterprise. I knew I needed the facts as reference points if I were to have any chance at all of encountering the feelings and the intuitions which I sought. She had thrown off Coppin Grove and her mother and her sisters in order to locate her fiction of the northern hemisphere within herself. I was required to do something similar.

Without their leaves, the straight grey poles of the poplar suckers looked like a monstrous cereal crop of some kind. A whimsical mockery of old agricultural practices and far-eastern influences. I could see the entire assemblage laid out in one of the courtyards of the National Gallery. Sculpture for the people. I began to feel an intense resentment towards the suckers. I *did* need a scapegoat. But doesn't everyone? Did this make him right about everything else as well?

I can't be sure, but I rather think I may have said this aloud; to Victoria, whom I knew would appreciate its silliness. She might have leaned back in the chair, making the cane creak, and have reached up with her hand for mine and have given a soft laugh. I realised it is possible to love the dead whom one has never met.

The rain had set in more heavily. I felt helpless standing there with my hands on the empty chair. Had he gone to see Tom Lindner? Should I abandon this nonsense and go to the gallery and drink champagne with them and discuss the price of art?

What is the price of art? Should I join them? I am ready, I would say. Let us drink to something. And then let us go on drinking. I ordered myself to count to three and on three to release the chair and leave the garden. But I couldn't go through with it.

When my mother had reminded me that the Sidney Nolan monograph related to my own past and not to my father's, I'd felt so defeated for a minute or two that I couldn't think. She might as well have revealed to me that something as implacable and incontrovertible as Providence or Fate was against the realisation of my conscious intentions. The kind of thing Huang warned Lien about Feng having on his side. He is in league with Fate. He might as well have said the Devil. Don't waste your energies trying to get the better of that. You'll fail.

The wind had dropped and the rain had begun to fall heavily almost straight down, as it does in Hokusai's woodcuts. The summerhouse was fortified by the suckers. As if the ground around it had been staked, the way the defenders of the village in Kurosawa's *Seven Samurai* staked the ramparts with sharpened bamboos to keep the bandits out. Taking the chair with me I left the mound and forced my way through the suckers to the summerhouse.

There was a strong smell of cat spray. The boards sagged a bit but did not give way, and the wide upturned eaves provided shelter for more than three-quarters of the interior. I put the chair down. There were three empty teachests lined with silver paper and there was a small table and a chair. The table and chair were broken. Not smashed, but fallen apart, the joints weathered out. It wouldn't take much to repair them. And there was some other junk in a pile in one corner. As if someone had come along and had a go at cleaning up but had abandoned the task. I pulled out the silver lining from one of the teachests and spread it on the wet seat of the cane chair I'd dragged in, and I sat down and looked out at the rain. As the heat of my thighs began to warm them through, my trousers gave off a vapour and a pleasant self-smell. My silver-lined chair was windproof and cosy. I was comfortable. I felt relieved that I'd avoided being entirely frustrated by his absence from the house. The rain continued heavily. I was glad of its grey, intimidating screen. I was glad to be made invisible by it. I stared out at it, feeling that I'd reached a sanctuary, pleased now that Lang was not at home and grateful to have achieved a respite from him and from the exhausting manoeuvrings of the game.

From where I was seated the mound appeared insignificant. It was not a prominent feature of the landscape from the perspective of the summerhouse. The dominant elements of the view – and these opposed each other in an interesting way – were, to the north, the opaque mass of the house, blocking off the light from that source as if it signified an end, as if there could be no going any further in that direction; and, to the east, the tall, open stand of eucalypts, the remnant of native forest, which glowed in the rain with a cold interior phosphorescence, promising diffuse and interesting spaces to the curious traveller.

These two vertical features, the house and the forest, confronted each other across the open area of lawn. The mound from here was a no-man's-land. It was an abandoned base camp. Abandoned by everyone, by the mother and by the daughter and now by us. I began to see that the summerhouse was positioned at the trig-point of this triangular arrangement. The summer-house, neither itself quite house nor clearing nor alluring space, but possessing elements of the features of all three, was in fact the interstitial place from which, with the cunning trigonometry of her fiction, she had surveyed her landscape. The summer-house was the indeterminate feature by means of which she had located herself and engineered her escape from Coppin Grove.

I knew I'd realised something that ought to have been obvious to me for a long time. Something that had been obscured, however, until this last week or two, by the tremulous mask of aspen leaves, the dense thicket of suckers that was at last leafless and no longer able to conceal the secret hidden at its heart. It was a shock to find myself seated there. It seemed I had found my way there, not by any conscious deductive process, not as the result of careful observation, but by the instinctive homing intuitions of a true parasite. It seemed that I'd been making my way towards her workplace all the time. Going out to the mound had not just *seemed* like the establishment of a base camp, it really had been one, a preparatory stage towards the eventual occupation of the summerhouse. I was delighted by this extension of my metaphor, of myself as a parasite, as 'one who eats at the table of another'.

The rain was slackening. When it stopped altogether, I resolved that I would go to the lean-to where I'd found the cane furniture and I'd get the axe I'd seen there and hack a pathway through the suckers to the steps of the summerhouse. The path would signify my occupation. It would be undeniable. I would knock her table and chair together and he would find me already hard at work, as if I were Victoria returned from the northern hemisphere – as Gertrude had it in her image – one hundred years on. The summerhouse would be my winter quarters. He would be required to approach me along *my* path. *I* would abandon *him*.

When he returned from drinking with Lindner, he would find that I had not retreated in confusion from his door, defeated, but had inserted myself into the interstice created by his momentary absence, and that I had thereby seized the indirect initiative myself. He would see, to his dismay, that the situation had changed during his absence, but not as he had foreseen, nor as he had planned. He would see that if he wished to reinstate himself, then he would have to read *my* signs. I'd been too clever for him. He'd underestimated me. He would not be able to ignore the challenge to the interpretation of his material implied by my occupation of her worksite. It was a masterful stroke of indirectness.

She had written, 'This bright autumn day with the sun warm against my shoulders, the twenty-seventh of May 1908, he is dying. My half-brother from Shanghai, who is wholly Chinese, is with him. I can see my brother's shadow at the window. He stands behind my father's chair and waits to become the second Feng. He is a practical man. I believe Australia means nothing to him . . . I would like to cease writing and walk among the trees, among that remnant of bushland which lies yonder, between the riverbank and the road . . . The shadow of my brother has gone from the window. My father, the first Feng, is dead. I am alone, now, with my horse and my fiction. I am in my thirtieth year. I have been many years in preparation. Now even Shinjé, the Lord of Death herself, could not be better mounted for such a journey as I intend to make.'

From where I was seated it was not possible to see the upper storey windows of the house. I got up and moved my chair closer to the edge and sat down again. I looked up towards the large bay window at the back of the house, which I took to be the one Victoria had referred to. Lang was up there, standing at the window, watching me . . .

In the house he handed me a glass of wine and remained close beside me, his shoulder just touching my upper arm, sheltering beside me. He seemed extraordinarily fragile. I recalled an impression I'd formed of him even before we'd met, that he might not be going to have a middle-age but might carry his arrested youthfulness all the way to old age and even to the moment of his death – a solitary figure far out from shore on the dangerously thin sea ice, moving away slowly. Then when I looked again he was gone. The landscape was empty. It was a northern winter landscape I saw him in, almost the icy fogbound river where my mother and I had held our brief vigil in memory of my dead father. I knew I would wake one day to find that Lang no longer existed. A line from *Tam* came to me and I spoke it aloud: *Like the snow falls in the river, a moment white then melts for ever.*

He moved away and leaned on the window sill, his face half-turned towards me, the sardonic tilt of his features caught by the watery sunlight, that aspect of irony which the trauma of his birth had stamped permanently on his countenance and which subsequent experience had done nothing to erode. His right eye examined me distantly – from the other-world – and he chuckled hoarsely and dragged on his cigarette. Burns, he said, appreciatively.

You'd get on my with my mother, I said, seeing this for the first time. Despite Burns. She hated him.

He looked pleased. I remember your mother. I have an image of her racing down a dangerous hill on her bicycle with her eyes closed and her feet off the pedals and her red hair streaming out behind her like the flames of a rocket.

It was a child's drawing of my mother.

In my picture there are thatched cottages and a castle rushing by. He laughed. I've never been to England. She has forgotten that you and your father ever existed.

I knew my mother would understand Lang completely and intuitively. They would understand each other. They would not be surprised or puzzled but would begin conversing at once in a language unknown to anyone else. A secret language for which they would not need the portable icons of white swans and Ned Kelly masks. Their communication would not be on that level, but would be on a level older than that. Objects would glow for them with an interior light, an illumination which had its source in geological, not in historical, time. My mother's advice to me would have been to avoid him. She would not have believed me capable of benefiting from a meeting with Lang. I felt something between us that was almost a family tie, something I'd never felt before for anyone in Australia.

Lin Yin, he said, the temple of hidden spirits. He was looking out the window again. Did you know the gazebo is a Chinese invention? I left the table – where Gertrude's drawing lay; the reason for his earlier absence from the house – and I went over and stood beside him and looked down into the garden. The pale yellow sunlight of the winter afternoon was shafting through the naked branches of the poplar and sliding between the pillars of the summerhouse below us.

You're right to work there Steven, he said, in the solemn, regretful voice he often used when he spoke of Gertrude's work. A gazebo was originally a lookout for the enemy and was built into the roof of the house. Thousands of years ago. Before civilisation. He was telling me something I could never have guessed, reminding me – even though he knew I did not need reminding – that Spiess's journal and Victoria's *Winter Visitor* were not, on their own, enough for me to go on. The father of the village went up into the gazebo as dawn was breaking over the fields each day and he watched for the approach of the enemy. And after many generations, when it was no longer necessary to watch for the approach of the enemy in this way, when the kingdom had been pacified by the benevolent rule of the Yellow Emperor, those who'd sat for hours and watched began to miss the solitary time they'd spent in the gazebo, gazing down on to the countryside and the busy comings and goings of humankind. The long hours alone had revealed to them something which they could otherwise never have discovered for themselves in the world at ground level. Alone in the gazebo they had learned how to reflect on their experience. They had discovered the hidden beauties of solitary contemplation. To gaze inward had become an established custom with them, and they found when they came down that they could no longer live happily without it. For what they had seen in the interior world had amused and entertained and gratified them far more than anything they'd ever seen in the world at ground level. In the busy world of the daily routine of the village, where no one ever had a moment to stop and think but where everyone had to either get on or risk falling behind, those who had come down from their gazebos now found themselves to be strangers, even though they were surrounded by the dear members of their own families. Sadly, they realised that they could never again be content without the interior life of their reflections. So, without attempting to explain themselves – for they knew no one would understand their rejection of reality – but satisfied to let everyone think they were mad, one by one they abandoned their families and their responsibilities and they returned to their gazebos to think. Eventually they removed, or were perhaps asked to remove, their gazebos a little distance from the house. This retreat from worldly responsibilities and from the family was the beginning of the literary arts. It was the beginning of civilisation. It was the beginning of history. And it all started with the need to keep a sharp lookout for the enemy.

·

He turned to me, restless, unsatisfied, the demon awakened in him now. The gazebo isn't an English summerhouse, Steven, for people to take afternoon tea in. It's the entrance to the other-world. You didn't know that did you? He drained his wine and looked around, as if he feared that while he'd been talking the enemy had cut him off from further supplies. Westerners, he said, searching for the cask and struggling not to sound too contemptuous, think the distinction between fact and fiction is self-evident.

He pointed his wineglass at me, like a shaman pointing a bone. She was Chinese; remember that. Chinese, Steven! he repeated, as if he were reiterating a law of the occult that I, his lazy, dull-witted apprentice, was stubbornly unable to acknowledge; a law which placed Victoria and her imaginative life beyond the reach of Western understanding. He snatched Gertrude's drawing from the table and headed for the door.

The erotic was there, but it was concealed. The erotic was in fact the *most* important element in the picture; the thing that made you want to keep coming back. You couldn't sate yourself with it. It didn't lose its effect with repeated looking, but grew quietly more evident, more disquietingly evident, with one's increased familiarity. It wasn't in the girl's nakedness. Her flesh had been made inert. It was grey, with cold, purplish shadows, as if she were suffering from an abnormally high concentration of reduced haemoglobin. The child's bones, her ribs and her pelvis and her knees, poked out, like the bones of other creatures bundled up inside the envelope of her skin. Pictorially the portrait was sinister. The flesh had been rendered unapproachable. One's attention was directed away from the flesh to the eyes. It was in Victoria's eyes that the erotic was implied. She was looking levelly into the eyes of the painter. In her gaze was an acknowledgment of his fear and his guilt and, if one looked long enough and keenly enough, his desire, his lust. And in his attempt to legitimise, to normalise, his lust he had made her features appear much older than her body. Lang claimed

·

to have detected all this at once, the moment Tom Lindner brought the picture out and showed it to him. It took me much longer. But eventually I pieced together the erotic as she saw it, in the mind of the painter, not in his picture. The erotic was withdrawn from the pictorial. It had its existence elsewhere. In dealing with it one's imagination was drawn away from the painting, not into it.

She stared at us in the light of the gas fire: 'The girl who stands at the edge of the thin, dry forest observing the artist at work on the green sweep of lawn before her keeps a private journal of her own. Into its pages at night, when she is alone in her room at the top of the house, her thoughts of herself and her findings concerning the northern hemisphere are written. She writes of the English painter carefully, deliberatively, with the kind of loving and solitary joy of a writer. She is accurate with her observations and careful to resist the proffered image. She is aware of the temptation to become fanciful and knows the dangers are real. Fiction, she has discovered, though it is conducted in the isolation of the mind, cannot be permitted to become madness. She does not know what her researches will reveal. She does not know the end of her story. She writes not with an end in mind but with a desire to make the material of her scrutiny her own, to possess it by means of the location of herself at its centre. She enters it by degrees. She insinuates herself. She is in fear of and is fascinated by her power to entice and to mock the artist.'

Lang coughed, doubling over against his hand. He stayed doubled over for a couple of seconds, then he breathed deeply and drew himself up with difficulty and lit another cigarette. He stabbed his stained forefinger at the portrait. They hate this sort of picture, he said hoarsely, struggling to breathe, in pain, presumably meaning all art-loving Australians. He'd been telling me the story of the painter, the true story, the one occurring briefly in the record. The painter had met with misfortune after he left Coppin Grove and the service of Victoria's mother and, despite his letter of introduction from the magisterial Mr von Guérard, had not managed to make a decent career for himself in Australia. He had, it seemed, painted other naked children. There had eventually been a scandal, a trial, and when he emerged from this he had walked into the breakers off Point Lonsdale and ended his life, facing back towards England.

You're Australian, Lang said, as if he were reminding me that I'd had myself tattooed while I was drunk. He blew out a cloud of smoke. He was gleeful. You told me you were an Australian. Remember? Remember that, Steven? He laughed and waved his cigarette at me. He didn't require an answer. His spiky hair shivered and sent out gleams in the firelight. His ankles were bone-white above his socks, brittle plaster-of-Paris casts. He sat cross-legged on the rug and rocked himself backwards and forwards, the wine slopping about in his glass and spilling on his old blue trousers, his left eye watering and blinking with the optimistic, greedy innocence of a child, his right eye swivelling about independently, the elder, the remote sensing organ of the lookout in the gazebo, on the alert for the approaching enemy. It steadied on me fleetingly, Would you like to see the lotus cup my grandfather gave Spiess.

It really exists then?

Of course it exists! Of course it exists! The eagerness of my interest gratified him. The lotus cup, he said. There's plenty of time. Let's have a drink first. You do want to see it?

I'd love to see it.

Good. Good. I remember everything. He drank deeply, abandoning caution, becoming master of his past again, empowered to reclaim it breath for breath and to deliver it to me, intact, its smells, its texts and textures, the precise weights and measures of things and of circumstances, the gravity and the levity of events. And to prove it, he would produce for me the celadon teacup from the Sung kilns of Fenghuang Hill, the fragile antique heirloom saved miraculously from the ruins, which Gertrude's father had held honourably in trust for him. To prove his capacity, his friendship and his largesse, to prove that it all still belonged to him, he would disclose Huang's lotus, his lien. He would produce for me not merely his mother's gold this time, but his mother herself. He would produce whatever I might

.

desire for my concoction. Nothing was too sacred. Nothing was too precious. He was protected from his fear of saying too much, of revealing too many of his secrets, by the confessional veil of alcohol. He aspired to demonstrate abundance. Completeness. An unflawed trust that would never have permitted him to react suspiciously, as I had done earlier, to his absence from the house. He intended to prove himself to me and to rebuke me in the process for my lack of generosity of spirit. His estate was invulnerable to my incursions. It was too large and too grand to be noticeably depleted by my appetite. He would account to me for his past in its entirety. He would present me with the problem, not of what to put in but of what to leave out. He would dazzle and disorient me. He would leave me confused and uncertain.

He refilled our glasses with the heavy red cask-wine and we clinked them together. I remember everything about my childhood, he boasted. You only need the first ten years. That's all you need. The Nanking decade: 1927 to 1937. The entire period of my life in China. The worst years, the hardest years, for my father and for all the Shanghai capitalists. After ten years it's too late. After a child reaches the age of ten nothing can be changed. His bleary gaze struggled to locate me in the fug of smoke and radiant heat from the fire. He reached out and clutched my sleeve. He swayed. Did he see *me*? You're my only friend, Steven, he said hopelessly and let go my sleeve, half-regretting the excess immediately.

I saw that his bravado would be easily disabled; I saw in him a kind of sorrow and a kind of love and a deep inconsolable regret, a kind of horror of what lay before him, each emotion discrete, like colours in an oily puddle, circling slowly, trapped within his eyes.

I said, And you are my only friend.

He grinned sheepishly, breaking the surface, for a split second the boy experimenting with being grown up. What do you *really* think of me? He laughed, abashed, unsteady, unable to hold to one direction. We're a partnership aren't we. That's what we are. D'you know who said that? Tom Lindner. Yes. He said to me, how's your partner? I just laughed at him. He thinks we're secretly dealing in paintings. He thinks we're up to something. He's clever. No, I mean it. You might think he's silly because he dyes his moustache, but he's not. He's successful. He doesn't know much about art, he doesn't know *anything* about art, but he knows a lot about dealing. And what do we know about art anyway? He knows a thing or two. He knows his own business. That's more than you can say for us. He's rich. We shouldn't forget that. We'd go broke in a minute if we tried doing what he does. He gestured at the pictures on the walls. They'd all be gone in a week. Where d'you think we'd find someone to give us two thousand for Victoria. Take it away, they'd say. It's horrible. And they'd be right. It *is* horrible. I like horrible things. We wouldn't be able to *give* it away. We'd wonder what had happened. The dealers would clean us out. We'd just have the walls to look at. We'd discuss the unfaded patches of wallpaper. Other people would come in and find us talking about Victoria's portrait and all they'd see would be a dark oblong of wallpaper. They'd think we were mad. They'd think we were off in our gazebo. But we'd have money for renovations. That's something. Sometimes I feel like inviting them in. I think of ringing Tom and telling him to come and get them. The lot. Everything. Just give me what you think's right and take them all away. We could take a cask out to the garden, out to the gazebo, and watch them cart it off. They'd think they'd won Tatts. He paused and looked at me quickly. Are you planning on renovating the gazebo? That's what they do to these houses. They renovate them. They like everything to be normal. That's when they're happiest. An Australian gets excited at the prospect of everything being normal. He fell silent and gazed wearily into the gas fire, leaning so close to the flames I smelt him beginning to scorch. Gertrude's an Australian, he said, swaying towards me. She'd be happy if I renovated this place. She's renovated *her* place. Have you seen the way she keeps her house? He watched me closely, mistrustful, calculating again, Have you been there? Have you been over to her place? You could have come this morning. I think she expected you. I rang you, you know. You must have already left. You could have come with me and had a look at her drawings. But she probably had you over when she gave you her father's journal. Did *she* invite you to her place or did you invite her to your place? Did you have dinner together by candlelight? He cackled, You might become a couple. When I'm out of the way. She could renovate this house while you renovate the gazebo. He suddenly reached out and clutched my shoulder and dragged himself to his feet and hurried out of the room. I heard him laughing thickly and coughing in the bathroom. He shouted, I'll get the lotus cup in a minute.

He was gone for some time. When he returned he dropped something into my lap. I was startled and jumped. I'd been expecting the fragile teacup. I should have known better. It was a copy of the poems of Robert Burns.

Read *Tam* first. He arranged himself again cross-legged within scorching distance of the gas fire. He waved at the book, Read it Steven! Read it for me. He searched around for his wine, made a grab for it and knocked it over. The claret made a red pool on the rug. He watched it. The wine didn't sink in to the rug but lay like a ruby lens. You've got the voice for it, he said, staring at the spilt wine, and perhaps wondering if it might somehow be got back into the glass. I had a friend at St Patricks who had the voice for it. He won the Crouch Prize later, when we were at art school together. He looked at me belligerently, as if he thought I wouldn't believe any of this. He lives in Tuscany half the year and in Mosman the other half. They all thought I should have won it. Everyone did. Even *he* said I should have got it. He rubbed his finger over the wine, spreading it. I got a Highly Commended. I can show it to you. Do you want to see it? Nineteen forty-seven. Read *Tam o'Shanter*! Read it! *Tam skelpit on thro' dub and mire, Despising wind and rain, and fire.* How does it go? *Nae man can tether time or tide; The hour approaches Tam maun ride.* You might have heard of him. He's famous. He said nothing for a little while, then he looked up and stared steadily into my eyes for several seconds. He seemed to be utterly sober. Do you think, Steven, that I could ever have represented Australia? Lang Zoo, he said, mockingly, attempting an exaggerated Australian accent. Mr Zoo. That's what the students call me. He reached for the cask and dragged it towards him. Please read Burns for me Steven. I know you hate doing it but just read it anyway. The Chinese are right. You only need the first ten years. My father left it too late. Nineteen forty-seven, Steven. The Crouch Prize. I could have won it. I could have gone to the Slade on a scholarship. Everyone said I should have got it. *Ye banks and braes o' bonie Doon, how can ye bloom sae fresh and fair; how can ye*... He broke off. I will show it to you. Don't worry. Just read a few verses of *Tam*. We've got all night.

REFLECTIONS FROM THE GAZEBO

THIRTY-FOUR DAYS

Just after nine o'clock on the morning of 28 January 1932, at the moment when the first groups of soldiers of the Chinese Nineteenth Route Army were engaging invading Japanese soldiers on the flat northeastern outskirts of Shanghai, Lang Tzu and his grandfather were standing together holding hands beneath the upturned eaves of the garden pavilion at Hangzhou. The old man of seventy-three and the boy of less than six years were admiring the blossoms of the winter-flowering plum tree, situated against the far wall of the garden about thirty metres distant from them across a freshly raked bed of sand. The garden wall's rendered surface was grey and smudgy with stains. From the distance of the pavilion it resembled a bank of fog, such as often lolled over the lake and hung in the valley late into the morning in winter. Against this background the branches of the plum tree stood out as if they had been black lines in a woodcut on old paper. Lang Tzu and the scholar had been standing in the pavilion looking at the tree for more than half an hour. The morning was very cold, and they both wore fur coats that reached to their ankles.

Neither the scholar nor the child was aware that China subsisted in a helpless state of civil war. Scarcely a rumour had troubled them concerning the floods and the famines and the bandits who were every day killing thousands of Chinese in the countryside around them. And even if they had given the larger situation some thought, they could not possibly have guessed that less than a day's journey to the northeast the Japanese were at this very moment attacking Shanghai, which was not only the commercial and industrial heart of China but was also Lang's other place of residence in his dimorphic existence. For it was true, like a specially grafted fruit tree which produces both pears and apples from the same rootstock, Lang existed in two distinct forms. In Hangzhou he was a student of the classical arts of China and in Shanghai he was no less than the child of honorary European expatriates in the International Settlement, where he studied European history and mathematics and French and German like all the other children who were not yet old enough to have been sent to boarding schools in the home countries of their parents. In Hangzhou he wore Chinese clothes and spoke Mandarin and was forbidden by his mother to do otherwise; and in Shanghai he wore European clothes and spoke English and was forbidden by his father to do otherwise.

The contradictions of this double existence had intimidated Lang until Doctor August Spiess, his friend and his German tutor, and the only person who seemed able to see both sides of his situation, confided to him one day that dimorphism was more a divine gift than an impediment to life. They were working together in the schoolroom upstairs in his father's villa in Shanghai on the congenial task of translating certain of Goethe's *Romische Elegien*, number V of which began with a line that August always found heartening for some reason: *Here on classic ground I feel joyously inspired.* Two-headed Janus, the doctor remarked, was the Roman god of the doorway and embodied the interior view and the exterior view with equal felicity. So why should you not do likewise? Have no fear, there are many happy dimorphic phenomena in art and in nature. The doctor said this confidently, delivering it as information well known to all worldly men of letters, such as he undoubtedly was himself.

·

Thinking of his own imminent return to his mother's home, Lang asked the doctor what there might be in Hangzhou of this double kind? For a moment the doctor was nonplussed. His gaze went glassy as he thought back to the time he had spent with Madame Feng in the scholar's house. He remembered many things, but he could think of nothing that would illustrate his confident assertion. Then he recalled the petals which had floated portentously, like so many drops of blood, in his soup one day. Why, he exclaimed, relieved that he would not be forced to disappoint Lang, there is the winter-flowering plum tree, which sends forth its perfumed blossoms in the midst of winter and so embodies a double image of life and death. Which is no doubt what has made its beauty so poignant to your poets for centuries. It is truly the janus tree.

Standing in the pavilion now, in Hangzhou, beside his grandfather, watching the first rays of the newly risen sun strike the red flowers of the plum tree in the wintry garden, Lang felt an assurance within himself the like of which he had never felt before. He felt as if he had learnt something real about himself and his condition at last. Something permanent. Something which would not be swept away by his father's contempt for Chinese values when he returned once again with his mother to Shanghai. The freshly opened blossoms on the black branches reminded him of the yearning beaks of fledglings in the nest, striving confidently towards the worms and insects which the parent birds would soon bring to them. Looking at the flowers he felt a warm happiness in his belly, just as he did whenever he drank a steaming bowl of sweetened lotus root tea. I am kin to the plum tree. She is my sister. I, too, shall bring forth my splendour in the midst of winter's grey. He composed this poem silently and with a kind of passionate secrecy. Aloud, because he knew it would please his grandfather, who claimed the author as an illustrious ancestor, he quoted from a poem by the eleventh-century statesman Wang An-shi: *Sprigs of plum by the corner of the wall Are blooming alone in the cold.* Huang murmured appreciatively and squeezed his hand. Six was not too old for such a gesture of affection.

Since the intrusion into his house, almost six years ago, of the German doctor, behind the high rendered stone walls with their coping of glazed tiles, nothing distressing or contradictory had ever been spoken of again in Huang's presence. Yu and Lien had kept their worries from him, and he had lent himself without complaint to this pretence that all was in order with his world. Nothing he had not wished to discuss had been discussed. Ever since Lang's birth, indeed, for the two occasions had coincided, Yu and Lien and the entire household at Hangzhou had behaved as if the scholar was too fragile to bear the truth any longer.

Huang spent most of his time sitting in his study, completely still, gazing vacantly into his garden. For the past six years he had maintained a suspenseful equipoise, during which no aspect of his condition had altered, except the duration of his silences, and these, like his beard and his fingernails, had grown a little longer. Every now and then a noise or a smell or some little incident caused him to become aware of the tragedy of his circumstances, and he was opened momentarily to the reality of the present, and once again he felt the pain and the futility of inconsolable regret. On these occasions he wept, silently, his tears sliding down his aristocratic nose to tremble like jewels in the fine hairs of his beard. At such moments he longed for nothing more than to hear a last, kind forgiving word from his old colleague and friend, the literary painter Fan Ping-chen, who had lived on Geling Hill and who had possessed the finest garden in Hangzhou. Had Huang but known it, Fan Ping-chen was dead and his house and garden were no more.

Since the visit of the German doctor, since that intrusion, that trespass upon his orderly life, except for the smell of French and American cigarettes, which was often stronger than the smell of incense, and the occasional ringing of the telephone whenever Lien was present, daily life was carried on by Huang without any impressions from the outside world. Since the doctor's fateful visit, life among the crumbling courtyards and galleries and the numerous rooms of the old house had been performed as if it were a play of epic length, slowly unfolding its sombre theme in a theatre long closed to the public's gaze. As if, after all, the

.

doctor *had* written one of his projected plays without quite meaning to. As if the doctor had become a playwright despite himself. As if, indeed, his presence alone on that occasion had been enough to cast each of these people into a role from which only the death of the protagonist would eventually liberate them.

Lien, of course, did not sit for long periods in silence gazing vacantly into the past but got on with the running of the household. She experienced no difficulty grasping a full understanding of the realities of their precarious situation in Hangzhou. She freely acknowledged to herself that there was to be no possibility of a continuation of the old ways in the house once her father was dead. Yet, despite this clarity of mind, she performed her role in the fiction as willingly as everyone else; with, indeed, an even more passionate commitment to its unfolding than the others. While she knew it to be an impossibility, she nevertheless behaved as if her son were one day to assume the scholarly mantle of her father, as if Lang really could become a literary painter and carry on the traditions of her family – a family to which, of course, *traditionally* he could never belong. She lived for the present. She offered her willing collusion in perpetuating a situation she knew to be entirely fanciful.

For Lang the events of that day, 28 January 1932, constituted a decisive turning point, ushering in a new phase of the drama in which he bore the responsibility for one of the principal roles. Once again the influence of Doctor Spiess, if not his direct authorship of the events themselves, was crucial.

Inspired by the conjunction of the blossoming tree and his newly acquired confidence in the prophetic nature of his own dimorphism, all that day, without pausing to take any nourishment, Lang painted pictures of the flowering plum tree. And all day, seated no more than three metres from where he worked on the table, his grandfather gazed through the open casements into the formal garden, unaware of his grandson's activities.

One after another Lang painted pictures of the plum blossom

without once looking up and referring to the tree itself. He was not thinking of the real tree. He painted with his metaphor of the beaks of the fledglings in mind. On the right-hand side of those paintings which he judged to be the most expressive, he wrote in black ink the four-line poem he had composed that morning in the garden:

> I am kin to the plum tree,
> She is my sister;
> I, too, shall bring forth my splendour
> In the midst of winter's grey.

He wrote the poem in the expressive *Li-shu* script, which his mother had made him practise for two hours each day since he had first been able to hold a writing brush. Late in the afternoon he chose the very best of his plum blossom paintings and, first having Yu formally announce him, he took it to his mother and presented it to her. The other paintings he later gave to Yu and told the old man to burn them. Standing before his mother in her apartment, Lang had felt dazed and happy. He knew what it was at last to have done something good that would not fade with time.

When Lien showed the painting to her father later that evening the old scholar's eyes brightened. It is very good, he said. They stood shoulder to shoulder at the writing table in his study and by the light of the extra lamp which Yu had brought they admired Lang's poem and his image of the plum blossom. It was many years since Lien and her father had shared such a moment as this over a painting. You have made a scholar of Feng's son, Huang said at last, his voice shaky, awed and sad.

The following day he could not resist watching Lang at his studies. He had been standing behind the boy for some time, when he reached over his shoulder and took the brush from Lang's hand and with two deft strokes painted a shrike on the pine branch next to the shrike Lang had just painted. Huang's shrike had a ragged patch of white in the middle of its back, a feature which was poorly represented in Lang's shrike. The old man and boy watched the ink drying. Then Lang grasped the brush and loaded it from the shallow depression in the ink stone and repeated Huang's two strokes, executing them confidently, as if he had been practising them for days. Huang breathed with delight and he reached for the brush again and demonstrated another combination of strokes. Again Lang duplicated his action fluently.

Lien was writing letters when Yu came to her apartments and called to her. She left her work and followed him. Together they stood near the entrance to her father's study and, concealed by Yu's blue screen, they observed the old literary painter and the boy working side by side. Huang and Lang worked with one mind, intent and absorbed, as if they had long been master and pupil.

After a time Yu leaned close to her and whispered, The master has come back to us. Lien touched his hand in acknowledgment. She said nothing. In Lang she was seeing herself again as she had been when she was a child and she and her father had thought of nothing but painting and writing. With her trusted friend Yu, who knew everything, she watched the play, and while she watched it she was happy.

It seemed for a time that Yu had been right, and the master had really returned. For, two weeks after the day of the shrike, Huang ordered him to have a boat and refreshments prepared. We are going out on West Lake this evening to look at the moon, Huang announced to everyone's astonishment and disbelief. And as their boat was gliding past the southern end of the island of the Three Pools Mirroring the Moon that evening, Huang rose from his cushions and took the oar from the boatman and with a seemingly effortless movement drove the heavy craft across the shining water. Is the master a young man determined to impress us with his strength and skill? Yu asked. Lien laughed with happiness and she and Lang composed several poems. To conceal his excessive joy Yu averted his face and spat into the water, where he saw the eyes of the carp gleaming in the moonlight.

Despite having achieved total military control of the situation and finding himself and his army in no danger from the defeated and demoralised Chinese troops, on 2 March the Japanese general commanding the occupying forces in the Chinese city of Shanghai – he had not occupied the International Settlements – unaccountably ordered a withdrawal. For this inexplicable stupidity he was to be assassinated on his return to Japan. The day the Japanese departed, the road and rail links between Shanghai and the provincial capital of Hangzhou were reopened, And Feng at once sent his chauffeur to fetch his wife and son home.

In later life Lang was to look back on that brief period of thirty-four days, between 28 January and 2 March 1932, and to think of it as having been a period of years. That was the way life was for us, he would say, speaking of himself and his grandfather, as if everything had always been harmonious between them from the day of his birth until the age of six, when the ancestors had appeared without warning, like bandits through a breach in the wall, and destroyed his peace of mind.

Lang was to remember difficulties as having arisen *after* the thirty-four days in Hangzhou and not as having existed in some other form before that time. He was to look back upon his early years as an untroubled golden age. Also, in reconstructing that time, in going over it in his mind and recounting it to himself, he was gradually to substitute his grandfather for his mother as his teacher of his early years. The betrayal, when it overtook him, seemed to him to come from every quarter – except from his German friend, August Spiess; who remained, so it seemed to Lang, both detached and constant in friendship throughout the period of his war with the ancestors.

WAR

Once Lien and Lang had departed for Shanghai, Huang's courage left him. He stayed in his bedroom all day, lying on his bed. For if he ventured out the terrible sound of the telephone seemed still to be ringing among the empty rooms and galleries like the mocking laughter of Feng. During the day he dozed and at night he lay wide awake. In the darkness he was visited by fearful presences. Feng sent his son to mock him. A spectre. The boy a hideous replica of his demonic father, his white eye floating in the blackness. Huang moaned and cried out and Yu hurried to his side and lit a lamp and made potions and massaged the old scholar's bones. I am rebuked by my troubled ancestors, Huang cried, weeping bitterly. Was I thinking of *her* welfare when I brought her up as a boy? Yu did not answer, but kneaded the old man's wasted thighs with his bony fingers. It was my own selfish love of painting! Had I brought her up as an orthodox young woman she would never have married the demon Feng. She would have brought honour to the family of a gentleman and peace of mind to my final years. Huang wept and wondered if he was about to die and he trembled and couldn't get warm. And when Yu would have left him to return to his own bed, Huang clung to him. I made a terrible mistake, he confessed, clinging to Yu's gown. Bring me my book of the ancestors.

From a secret compartment behind the cupboards beneath the bookshelves in the scholar's study, Yu carefully removed Huang's book of the ancestors and took it to his master. All that night, and every night after that until Lien returned in the spring, Huang traced and re-traced the generations of his tribe and he re-learnt the names of the past, which he had forgotten. It was his last great effort of scholarship.

And when the jasmine vine that trailed above the coping of the verandah was in bloom, she returned with her son. The evenings were warm now. They sat in the second gallery beyond the visitors' hall. Huang in one carved chair and Lien in the other. Beyond the dark, lacquered columns they were presented with a fine view of the garden. The columns sectioned the prospect into three vertical strophes, which might, indeed, have been an intentional triptych, a *trompe l'oeil*, or a faded mural painted upon a palace wall. A landscape haunted by the absence of figures.

Lang was seated on a pale rosewood chair a little distance from his mother. Over the seat of the chair he had spread the beautiful skin of a snow leopard. He was reading, the book laid open on his thighs, his hands covering his ears. Every now and then a gentle movement of the air carried into the gallery the sweet perfume of the jasmine. Earlier, a long billed honeyeater had swung upside down from the vine and gazed in at them, its head moving rapidly from side to side, its bright yellow eye disdainful. Then it had squawked and flown away, its direct line of flight like the dismissive gesture of a critic across the face of the garden.

Huang turned to his daughter.

She waited for him to speak. She had been waiting for him to speak about what was on his mind since their arrival the day before. For she had noticed at once that he was preoccupied and nervous and unwilling, for some reason, to be kindly towards Lang. Whose puzzled enquiry as to this she had countered with, Your grandfather is old and may be ill. It is difficult to be old.

Now that it is spring, Huang said, and the countryside is no longer at war, I shall make a pilgrimage to the shrine of our ancestors.

He had not made such a pilgrimage during her lifetime. She felt no surprise. She did not respond. She waited for what was to come next, as if he had let a stone fall from his hand into a deep well, a stone he had held all her life, and she listened for the splash in the darkness far below. In her mind she watched the black stone fall and she regretted that it could never be called back into her father's hand again. His words came then, tinkling like the lapping of water in a stone place that is never to be touched by the sun. I beg you to come with me, daughter.

Still she did not respond, but gazed into the twilit garden. She did not care for the garden. She had no feelings for it. She had approved of his renovation of it. That was all. It was not her garden. She had grown chrysanthemums in the summer and cabbages in the autumn in a garden of her own when she had been a child. A little raised garden bed that was still there in a courtyard behind the courtyard of the second entrance. She had feelings for that place. She had grown dark blooms, the deep rust of their curling petals the colour of an old fox's scalp. The colour of those chrysanthemums retained the power today to invoke summer and childhood for her. Without turning to him she said quietly, evenly, without emotion, Do you regret *everything* then, father? Is there nothing you would not wish to change if you could return to the past.

Angrily he called for Yu to fetch hot water. What is taking you so long, you old fool? he shouted.

Lang raised his head and looked anxiously towards his mother. She smiled. When he had returned to his reading, she said softly to her father, My son and I have never been parted. Not for one day. But she knew her protestations were useless. She knew there was no point in appealing now to sentiment. She knew they were directed by a far larger force than took account of sentiment. It was not her intention to meet force with force, but to do as she had always done, and to slip between the ranks of the enemy and to appear behind the lines, in a place where no preparations for defence had been made. And, as always, she had no precise plan. Her strategy relied on opportunism, her tactics on inspiration.

Huang said nothing, but he watched her covertly. He waited until she had taken her gaze from her son. Then he murmured, This is the last thing I shall ask you to do for me, my daughter, before I die.

She did not speak. His request was seamless. There was no way through it.

The black-lacquered gates to the principal courtyard – through which August Spiess had blithely stepped six years ago, going very nearly to his death – stood wide open once again. The servants and members of the household were gathered in a little crowd before them, as if there was to be a group photograph. Lang stood on his own at the front of the gathering, closest to the gates. He was dressed for the occasion in a dark green silk gown with a high collar. A pace behind him stood Yu Hung-meng. It was just breaking day and a mist hung over the roadway beyond the gates, obscuring in places the lower stories of the houses, so that their upper stories appeared to rise from heavenly clouds like mountains in a depiction of the Emperor Ming Huang's journey to Shu. Everyone's attention was fixed on

Feng's black Pontiac, which was moving slowly away along the road.

Lang's face muscles ached. He watched the car. She had promised she would wave as they turned the corner at the end of the road. Everyone had congratulated him on his manly bearing during the past ten days – ten days which blurred into a single interminable period of dread for him. Only *he* knew his bearing had not been manly. Yesterday his grandfather had solemnly presented him with a brown jade disc with a dragon carved on it. The purport of this delicate gift – a precious relic from the Sung Dynasty – had not been lost on Lang; he knew it was intended to bind him during their absence to the composure of an adult. But he had already been bound. His face muscles ached because he was bound, because he was unable to express his feelings.

As the car neared the corner he raised his hand in readiness to return her wave. But the car swept out of sight so suddenly he had barely time to glimpse the pale oval of her face behind the glass before it was gone.

A terrible heaviness descended on him.

Yu motioned to the watchman and the black gates swung closed, shutting out Lang's view of the empty road. The wooden bar fell into place, knocking like a drum in the quiet morning. Yu touched his hand. As he turned away from the gates Lang knew he was no longer the person he had been until this moment. He could not see what lay ahead of him but he knew his life – like his father's Pontiac – had rushed round a corner. He could not say what was to happen to him. Grief and bewilderment and the deep hurt of one who has been betrayed by the person they have loved most dearly, clouded his vision. The faces of the servants were turned towards him, observing him, intent upon his performance. He walked through them without seeing them.

His grandfather's refusal to take him on the pilgrimage, and his mother's collusion in this decision, was too large a detail for Lang to measure. He felt it as if it were a wall of stone pressing against his body where before there had been no wall but only the open fields. There was no way round the wall, and there was no way through it. Nor could he pretend to himself that the wall did not really exist, or that its presence was unimportant to him. The wall extended on either side of him to his furthest horizons. A forbidden kingdom lay beyond it; the kingdom of the ancestors. His grandfather had lured his mother to this place through a kind of spell, by means of a mysterious magical power, which had turned her against her own son. His mother and his grandfather had then passed through the wall together, as if they were not composed of the same substance as he, but were made of a purer material, an elemental, a more primitive, substance lacking his heaviness, his density of being. Something far older than he. As if their being was composed of a single unbroken thread, linking them to the springs of time, to the original source of being itself. He visualised this link as a continuous shining strand of existence through which the songs of the ancestors found an unimpeded passage.

How could the ancestors call to *him*? There was his divine Western dimorphism. The presence of his father in him. There was the *West* in him. His line was broken. *He* was broken. A part of him was displaced. He had become detached from the beginning. There was the vast tract of land he must always consider, and there were the oceans and the islands, there was the World and experience that lay between China and the shores of that mythical country from which his father claimed his own doubtful descent: Australia. A name. A word for a place no one had ever visited. Even Doctor Spiess knew no one who had been there. Did such a place as Australia really exist? Was there a headland rising abruptly out of an empty ocean signifying its beginning?

Until the return of Lien and Huang, he boarded in the care of the second gatekeeper's daughter-in-law. A room had been prepared for him in the quarters of this family, who had served the Huangs faithfully for generations. The old man's son had been killed fighting the Japanese. But his daughter-in-law had given him two grandsons, Shu and Shin. Shu was seven and Shin was nine. Both boys possessed long sad faces, which had nothing to do with their grief at losing their father, even though in this particular feature they resembled their grandfather.

On the second day they permitted Lang to join their favourite game of the moment, which was the conflict between the Communists and the army. Lang was distracted from his suffering and loneliness at once by the bloodthirsty nature of this game, and he decided, as soon as the rules were explained to him, that he would take the part of the Generalissimo himself. Though forbidden till this day to play such brutal games, Lang required no further coaching. The territory was familiar to him the moment he entered it. In the dust by the second gateway, wearing white gloves and a grey cloak which fastened at his throat and fell straight from his shoulders to his heels, he thoughtfully inscribed his strategy with a long golden sliver of bamboo. Then he disposed his forces around him. Shu and Shin were abashed and looked more glum than usual. The game, it seemed, was more serious than they had realised. Lang was not merely to be their playmate, he was to be their master. They had generously offered to share their brotherhood with him, and he had responded by taking their liberty. He did not wish to be their brother. They were rebuffed. They dared not complain.

Lang ordered the little red gateway to be opened. The theatre of operations was to be extended. It was forbidden for the boys to play outside the courtyard. This day they watched their grandfather hurry to open the gate for Feng's son. Lang told them to wait, and he went out and stood in the road. On his own he began to feel there was a kind of power in his grieving solitude, a kind of exaltation raising him above the level of other people. He saw that there was something beautiful and sad about his condition. He felt it in the way the others observed him from a distance. He gazed along the road towards the wooded hills. He would let his mother see this new quality of his life when she returned. To shame her and make her sorry, he would display it to her, the way certain scholars displayed their erudition to shame their competitors. He would let her see how lonely and sad and changed he was. From the far side of the road the toffee

·

apple man stared past him. Fetch Yu, he called to Shin. And when Yu came to the gateway, Let us each have a toffee apple.

The toffee apple vendor arrived as it was getting light each morning and stood against the wall across the street from the second entrance until it grew dark. In each hand he held a bamboo pole with dozens of holes in it, and into each hole he placed the stick of a toffee apple, until the poles bristled with the candied fruit like toy trees. He didn't call his wares but waited silently, his lacquered apples shining and glinting and easily visible from one end of the dusty street to the other. Few people passed along this road, and quite often he had sold no toffee apples by the time the sun went down. But whether business promised to be good or bad he came each day and he waited. It was his place. He was like a spider waiting at the centre of her sticky web in a lonely corner of the woods. Sooner or later, if not today then tomorrow, someone would stop and purchase a toffee apple from him. Today he sold three. His expression did not change. It was all the same to him.

During the days that Lien and Huang were away, Lang did no study, but played all day with Shu and Shin. Taking their cue from his behaviour, the servants decided that it was a kind of unofficial festival time, and they also did hardly any work. Some of them even took this opportunity to go off and visit their relatives. Yu sat in the sun against the wall of the storehouse every day and smoked cigarettes and dozed and gossiped with the daughter-in-law and the gatekeeper. Every so often he looked up and checked on Lang to see that all was well with him and his two playmates.

Four days after Lien and Huang left to visit the shrine of their ancestors the household once again assembled formally in the principal courtyard and waited for Feng's black car to appear round the corner. Once more Lang stood alone, dressed in his green silk gown.

•

He was trembling. He had not expected to feel so upset. He wondered if she had changed. Might she have partly forgotten him? He didn't think of his resolve to show her how sad and lonely his life had become. He watched the car come through the gates and turn slowly and come to a halt in front of him. His mother's face gazed at him through the window. He had ceased to breathe. As she stepped from the car he ran forward and clung to her and sobbed and begged her never to leave him again. This was not how he had pictured himself behaving on her return.

Huang, who appeared refreshed and in a confident mood, gazed upon this unseemly public display of emotion with serene detachment, which the observant members of his household rightly interpreted as a sign of his profound displeasure. *He*, they saw to their delight, was the one who had changed. He had regained his self-assurance. He was, it appeared, going to forget all about his past eccentricities and pretend from now on that he had always been an orthodox Chinese gentleman. Shu and Shin looked mournfully at each other and giggled, gratified to be the witnesses of Lang's disgrace.

Lien held Lang tightly against her body and she whispered to him, I promise you my darling, we shall never again be parted. Forgive me. You can have no idea how terribly I have missed you.

The assembled members of the household looked at Madame Feng and her son with great interest. They were impressed. No such scene as this had ever before been witnessed by them. It was a wonderful, shameless display. Clearly Madame Feng and her son were not even going to pretend any longer that they were not half-western devils. Yu told the servants to get on about their business at once. The holiday is over, he shouted angrily. And when they moved reluctantly, he struck them sharply round the ankles with his stick.

Three months passed. Lien and Lang had been back in Shanghai for more than six weeks. Then, to her surprise, one day Lien's maid informed her there was a telephone call for her from

Hangzhou. It was Yu. He had never before used the telephone. He shouted his message and hung up. Huang Yu-hua is dying, he had screamed. If you want to see him alive you must hurry. When they arrived in Hangzhou late that same night, Yu hurried to meet them. He was calm and grave. As soon as I told him you were on your way, he informed her, Your father recovered just enough to sit up and take a little soup from me. He will not receive you in his bedroom. He says you must wait until he is strong enough to receive you in his study. A week of uncertainty went by, while everyone crept about the house conversing in whispers and expecting any minute to hear the news that the Lord of Death had carried off the old scholar. Then, on the seventh day, just before noon, when she and Lang were reading together, Yu came into Lien's apartments and announced sombrely, Your father awaits you for the last time in his study.

Lang's hand tightened in his mother's.

Yu seemed embarrassed and unhappy. He did not look directly at Lang. Your father does not wish to see the boy, he said and he made a little gesture of defeat and left them. How else could he have expressed it? Huang's instructions to him had been explicit. Lang was never to be admitted to his presence again under any circumstances. Feng's son (he did not say, my daughter's son), the old scholar had confided to Yu one night, is a demon. The faces of the two old men were only a few millimetres apart, their watery eyes glinting and shifting in the smoky lamplight like the eyes of fearful chimpanzees, a profound and nervous suspicion animating their depths. He is a supernatural projection of his father, Huang assured Yu, speaking in an appalled whisper. I was beguiled by the subterfuge. You have only to look into the boy's right eye to see his father's thoughts there, mocking us and our Chinese way of life and waiting to see us all destroyed. Feng, Huang confided, looking around nervously at the black hole of night through the open casement, sees everything through his son. Yu was dismayed. No doubt it was true. He had heard of such things. Yu helped his master to dress, the dry silk rustling against their dry fingers.

Lien sat opposite Huang in his study and took the cup of tea

Yu passed to her. I am dying, Huang said. There is very little of me left. I possess just sufficient strength to pay my respects to the ancestors one last time. Perhaps, he added archly, I shall die while we are at the shrine. It would be convenient for everyone.

In the gallery afterwards Lien asked Yu, How am I to tell my son? He will believe I am betraying him. But how can I refuse my father's dying wish?

Yu folded his hands into his sleeves and gazed thoughtfully towards the plum tree, which was in full summer leaf, and he reflected on her double question, the dilemma of a mother. Then he sighed and sniffed and offered the conclusion, If you do not go with your father this last time, then you will have the rest of your life to regret not having done so and there will be nothing you can do to redress the wrong you have done him. On the other hand, if you do go with your father on his last pilgrimage, you will have the rest of your life in which to regain the trust of your son and to redress the wrong you have done him. This is merely an observation, he added.

Lien thanked him and apologised for forgetting to bring cigarettes from Shanghai this time. We left in such a hurry, she explained. I'll send you some when we get back. They looked at the garden. Neither had anything to say. The moment was one of uncertainty between them. She knew that Yu would never be able to advise against her father's interests. For herself, she had seen the limits of her loyalty to her father. That out of this there had arisen an estrangement, no matter how slight or how temporary, between herself and Yu greatly saddened her. She had always confided in the old man as in no one else. She offered him a cigarette and lit it for him. Sometimes Yu, she said, my spirit leaves me, and I feel a terrible tiredness which I cannot resist. I can't remember at such times what it is like to feel well. Have you never felt this?

Yu had never lived for himself nor considered the state of his own spirit. He cleared his throat noisily. Do you remember, he said, how your father took the pole into his own hands that night and drove our boat across Xihu Lake, as if he were a young man, keen to impress us all?

There they were again. This time gathered together in the soft light of a summer dawn, drawn up like a little grey army waiting for the order to march, Lang at the front on his own, in his green silk gown with the high collar, the captain of the garrison.

This time he did not wait to see her wave from the corner. Even before the black-lacquered gates had swung closed, before the great teak bar was dropped into place by the strong watchmen, while the car was still visible, Lang turned and ran. He ran as hard as he could. Startled servants skipped aside to let him through. Dust and small stones were scattered by his slippers. His green gown billowed like a wizard's cloak behind him and walls and doors and copings and lacquered columns swept past him as he ran through the house.

Breathing heavily, he stopped at last in the middle of the raised garden bed in the courtyard behind the courtyard of the second gateway. He had lost his cap, and his spiky black hair stood upright on his scalp and quivered, like the raised crest of an aroused fighting cock. Dust motes and straw swirled around him in a golden mist, glittering in the bright dawn and sprinkling the shimmering green of his silken gown. He faced the storehouse, through which the throng of servants shortly followed him.

When they saw him standing there, all green and gold in the morning sun with his hands on his hips in the middle of the garden bed, a warlord or a bandit, they hesitated and fell back. It appeared to them that he would ask something of them. They milled about in the entrance to the storehouse like sheep confronted at a gate by a dog.

Lang stood upon his mother's childhood garden bed as if he stood upon her history, just as August Spiess might have imagined him; a being efflorescent with destiny, a *lang tsze*, a traveller at the instant of departure. Although August Spiess was not here to see Lang at this moment, there was a sense in which the doctor's presence was engaged. For it was because of August Spiess that Lang did not feel himself at this moment to be utterly alone, with no alternative, except his father's, to his mother's world of the ancestors, and that he knew his own perception of the world was shared by at least one other human being whom he trusted and admired. Had he felt himself to be completely alone, then he would almost certainly have behaved differently, for he could not have possessed the confidence to seize the moment as he did. Of course, poised on the rostrum of his mother's garden, which offered him the necessary elevation from which to look down upon Yu and the servants, he did not see precisely what this moment was that he had seized. He did not see what it contained for him, he simply seized it. Or, rather, he was seized by it. The moment seized him the way a young bird in its first year of life is gripped at a certain season by the inescapable desire to leave the place where it was born and migrate to a place where it has never been before.

To set out, to depart from the old way, was for Lang the inescapable imperative of the moment, not to reconcile the opposing positions of his parents. He did not think of an end to the journey, any more than the migrating bird thinks of the end. His desire was to set out, not to go somewhere in particular. August Spiess alone had offered him a resolution to the dilemma of his dimorphism. Without considering it, without being exactly aware of what he was doing, it was into this proffered interstice between the way of his mother and the way of his father that Lang at this moment inserted himself.

He went into his grandfather's empty study and stood by the writing desk, uncertain of what he intended to do next. He turned and looked at Shu and Shin. They, who had never been admitted to this part of the house before, stood in the doorway holding hands and gazing at him with fear, knowing themselves to be beyond the reach of assistance. Come here, he called to them softly. And when they did not move, he said, Do you think the watchman will beat you if I command him to?

The boys shuffled forward, stopping at Yu's blue screen, their bare toes curling against the flagstones, gripping the cold, reassuring slate. Come and stand beside me at this table, Lang ordered them, and he patted the glossy wood on which he and his grandfather had worked in harmony as master and pupil.

When the boys would not move he went over and grabbed their arms and dragged them to the table. He held them and looked into their terrified eyes, searching for their courage, for their capacity to be his lieutenants, to be his witnesses. For that was what he needed. He needed someone to see what he did. He needed recruits, whether they were willing or not, who would carry around in their heads an awe of his purpose.

Listen, he said to them, drawing them close until he smelt on their breath the sour pickles they had eaten with their porridge. I have a new game for us. I shall instruct you in its rules. It shall be a secret between us. If either of you ever speaks of it to anyone else I shall tell my father, the great merchant Feng Three, and he will come and destroy you. It is called the ancestor game, he said, inventing the name and finding himself pleasantly taken with it. He had no idea what the rules were, but he felt confident he would be able to improvise well enough until he could either discover the rules or invent them. He felt very pleased, for he had made a valuable discovery that belonged to no one but himself.

Next to Huang's study were the scholar's sleeping quarters. Separating the study from these rooms there was a vestibule. Lang had never been beyond the vestibule. He had never seen the place where his grandfather slept. He did not know what he might expect to find there. He did not know *why* he now decided to go in. He ordered Shu and Shin to wait for him by the table, and he went through the vestibule and pushed aside the curtain.

The room was dimly lit, dark, the casements closed. Lang took an uncertain step forward. The air was thick and stale and sweet and difficult to breathe. The smell he understood to be composed of a mixture of the odours of the old man's body and the unguents Yu administered to him as remedies for his innumerable ailments. Lang at once signified this repulsive odour as the smell of death and the ancestors. That, intuitively, was the sign he attached to it. It possessed a quality both intimate and unclean. It repelled and frightened him. He almost turned back. He had smelt it before, but thinly and from a distance. Here there was a reek of it. Here was its source.

·

As his vision adjusted to the gloom, he saw that, as with no other room in the house, what he looked in upon here was clutter and disorder. There were chests and vases and pieces of furniture, and articles of clothing and pots filled with scrolls and piles of manuscripts, and books heaped one on top of another with scarcely room for a person to walk between them. Here, Lang realised, was the place in which his grandfather had passed almost every night of his life since the age of twenty and into which he had thrust the unsorted memorabilia of a lifetime. In the language of war, which was the language that most appealed to him in the present circumstance, he viewed his impromptu invasion of his grandfather's privacy as a reconnoitre behind the enemy's positions. He might have been, it began to seem possible, looking for a weakness to exploit in the defences.

There had been no formal declaration of hostilities, however, and the situation in this regard was therefore unclear. He did not possess a strategy. He was guessing. He scarcely knew himself to be at war yet. The material of his journey, of his campaign, was, he understood, to reveal itself to him as he proceeded to advance into it. The ground was new to him. His purpose was a mystery. He was aware only of having transgressed a formal boundary, of having crossed a border, and that he could not, therefore, know what rules now applied. His invasion had been intuitive and inspired. He did not know what he was looking for as he stood there gazing in upon the hoard from his grandfather's past. He did not know until he saw it. Then he knew at once.

A large, unglazed earthenware pot, a vessel more than a metre tall and almost half a metre in diameter, which resembled a family's rice jar, stood against the far wall beneath the shuttered casement. In this jar, like iron blooms arranged in a vase, was a collection of halberds and lances and swords. He stepped over a pile of books that lay at his feet and made his way to the pot. Alongside it on the floor was a bundle of leather hauberks and leggings. Here, then, was the paraphernalia of war, the arms of an old bannerman of the scholar's clan. Here were the defences of Huang and his ancestors. Lang selected a short, stout sword from the pot. He lifted the weapon above his head and drew the blade downwards through the air in an arc before him. It was not a masterpiece of the swordmaker's art that he held in his hand, but was a crude and poorly balanced piece. Its double-edged blade was blunt and pitted with rust. The guard, which had loosened with age, was a hammered bronze crosspiece, and the grip was made of unpolished pearwood. But it was a sword. He turned and retreated with his booty, his heart beating quickly with excitement.

As he re-entered the study from the vestibule he made a whooshing sound through his pursed lips and cut a wide diagonal slash before him. Shu and Shin drew back. He laughed and slashed the air again. The brothers eyed the point of the sword. He lowered the weapon and considered them. It had been his intention to also arm the brothers with swords from the pot. Now he changed his mind. Come! he commanded, gesturing at them with the blade. Let us return to the courtyard of the little red doorway, where I shall instruct you in the rules of our new game.

He concealed the sword in the front of his gown and led the way back through the house. The weight of the cold weapon against his warm skin, as he strode through the long gallery beside the faded pillars, excited in him a feeling he could not name. He saw, or imagined he saw, that what lay before him now was a kind of hidden doorway in his memory, a doorway he had not noticed before – this door opened easily at his touch, and as he went through it a mood of intense optimism and expectancy took hold of him . . .

Beyond the forgotten doorway, in his memory, there lay an extensive country, of which he knew himself to have long been the princely ruler. Had he left this place only yesterday, or had he been absent for many years? He could not tell. It was familiar and unvisited at the same time. An impatient warhorse waited for him, ready saddled and richly caparisoned. Thrusting his sword into the jewelled scabbard at his belt, he mounted the steed and rode confidently into his homeland, certain that as soon as he was recognised by the inhabitants he would be given a joyful welcome. Secure upon the back of his fine horse, which responded alertly and with an eager obedience to his commands, he gazed about admiringly at the countryside. Soon he began to recognise within himself, as if in response to the richness and beauty of the landscape through which he rode, the elevating certainty that he was a good man. Had he not always known this, but not always remembered it? He knew that if he could but once discover the wisest and the most just course in life, then he would possess the courage and the will to follow it. And is this not what it means, he asked himself, to be a good man? He was moved to a powerful emotion by this rediscovered knowledge, to a feeling of intense self-love. He spurred his horse forward, impatient to meet his subjects. On all sides the trees grew tall and the flowers blossomed thickly among the rich meadow grass. In the distance the sun glinted on a broad river and in the pastures contented herds of red cattle and flocks of dazzling white sheep grazed upon abundant herbage. Fat geese flew high overhead in the blue sky and in the fragrant trees birds dipped their bills into the blossoms and called merrily to each other.

It was not long before he came to the outskirts of a town. The imposing dwellings were constructed of expertly faceted stone. Wooden fences surrounded well-tended orchards and gardens and vineyards, in which every imaginable variety of fruit and vegetable ripened gently in the sun. Lang marvelled at the wealth of his kingdom. On all sides there was evidence of good order, abundance and wellbeing. He entered the town, certain in his mind the inhabitants would rejoice to see him and that he would find his name revered among them. The prospect of their homage made him feel generous and he puzzled over what gift he might justly bestow upon these people in honour of his visit, for it was evident they lacked for nothing.

As the iron shoes of his horse struck the paved roadway, the hard sound echoed between the buildings on either side. But it woke no response from them. Freshly painted doorways in bright reds and greens and the gleaming windows impressed him with the certainty that here lived a civic-minded and industrious people. The street, also, was clean and well-maintained, and was broad enough to be the principal thoroughfare of an important provincial town. Lang kept to the centre of the carriageway, sitting straight-backed on his aristocratic horse, which arched its neck and champed its silver bit and tossed its head proudly, as if it understood perfectly the importance of the occasion. Lang expected at any moment to be greeted by a fanfare of trumpets and to see a crowd of happy people pouring out onto the street shouting his name and making him welcome, eager to begin the great festival in honour of his homecoming.

But no trumpets sounded and no one came. And he rode on from street to street for an hour or more without meeting a single human being. At last he abandoned the middle of the road and reined in at the open doors of a hostelry. His friendly hail to the innkeeper brought no response, so he leaned from his horse and looked in to the interior. All appeared to be in order. The glow of charcoal fires reddened the sides of a row of iron braziers; and blue and white bowls of steaming rice were set ready for hungry travellers upon a freshly scrubbed table. Hot vapours billowed from the cauldrons and the ovens and there was a delicious smell of roasting pork. Lang called again. But again received no answer. Indeed, the echo of his voice, like the echo of his horse's iron shoes, seemed to him to be unnaturally magnified in the silence, almost, indeed, as if the stones mimicked him.

All day he rode about the fine town, calling out and searching in vain for someone to whom he could make known his name. When at last the sun was setting, the low orange-tinted clouds casting a fiery glow over the buildings, and a keen wind had begun to blow through the alleys and along the boulevards, he entered a deserted square. He had not seen this place before and wondered how he could have missed it. On the far side of the square the lofty granite walls of a castle proclaimed the residence of the military governor. And standing proudly in the centre of the square was the only human likeness Lang had seen all day. It was an equestrian statue of noble proportions, cast in bronze and set upon a marble plinth. Eager to discover what important person was represented here by this mounted figure, Lang spurred his horse towards it. On reaching the statue he saw at once that the towering bronze was a likeness of himself and his horse. He circled the statue, searching in vain for an inscription on the plinth. But no gilded script celebrated his name and noble lineage in chiselled stone. The statue was as mute in respect to an acknowledgment of him as was the town itself.

Determined to rouse the governor and to receive from him the princely welcome that was his due, Lang rode up to the stout gates of the fortress and, drawing his sword, hammered on the wood with the pommel. A deep booming, like distant thunder, rolled back and forth within the fortress each time he struck the heavy baulk of timber. Never had a place sounded so empty, so uninhabited and so desolate as this. Dismayed, he knew at once there could be no friends, no hope and no encouragement within. He knew, at last, that there was no one here to greet him, or to whom he might make himself known. Fighting back despair he struck the gates with the blade of his sword. Sparks flew from the iron rivets and his horse shied in fear.

Why are you riding about the place making this terrible din and waving that sword around, as if you expect to have to fight someone any minute? The voice was that of an old woman. Its tone was contemptuous. When even the most slow-witted stranger, the voice continued, can surely see that we've been at peace here for ever. What a fool you must be!

Lang was surprised to see a tall figure dressed in a long cloak standing in the shadow of his statue. He sheathed his sword and greeted her, apologising generously for not noticing her sooner. I am delighted to meet you, he said, for it seemed to him that where there was one person, no matter how poor and unimport-ant, there were likely to be others. He felt greatly relieved and was on the point of asking the woman where everyone had gone, when she came towards him.

She appeared to be in no way awed by his mounted superiority and princely bearing, but laughed and gestured threateningly at his horse, making it shy so violently that Lang was very nearly thrown to the ground. As it was, one of his stirrups flew up and struck him a sharp blow on the knee, making him cry out from pain.

Well! the advancing woman shouted at him, throwing back her cloak and revealing her nakedness, slashing the air just before the horse's nostrils with her whistling bamboo, and laughing mockingly. Have you lost your tongue? Now that you've found me, don't you want to tell me your name? She challenged him, Tell aunty your name boy! And she danced nimbly from one side of his horse to the other, jabbing it in its sensitive flanks and haunches with her sharpened bamboo.

Lang fought to control his terrified horse and he opened his mouth to shout his name aloud. But he did not know his name. He had forgotten it. His mouth remained open but no sound came from it. He searched in the darkness of his memory, but he could not find his name there. It was gone. No hint of it remained.

His horse reared high on its hind legs and retreated in terror from the old woman's stick, and she continued to press her advance upon them steadily, crying all the while, They've stolen your name! They've stolen your name! Over and over again, as if it were the greatest joke she had ever heard. Then, as unexpectedly as she had appeared, the woman ceased her attack and turned and walked away into the gathering night.

Lang galloped after her and placed himself in her path and drew his sword and demanded, Tell me at once who it is that has stolen my name or I shall cut you down. But all he heard in reply was the barking echo of his own question, flung mockingly from building to building around the vast empty square, and all he saw was his own shadow before him, gesturing at him upon the equestrian statue, and sweetly in the air about him he smelled the odour of old men and the ancestors, and he knew at once that he was in his own tomb, and had been greeted by Shinjé, the Lord of Death herself, the only other inhabitant of the place.

Clutching the sword beneath his gown, and with the disgusting smell of his grandfather's bedroom still tingling in his nostrils,

Lang emerged from the darkness of the storehouse into the bright sunlight of the courtyard of the little red doorway. He paused and looked about him, and he noted that the servants were considering him warily. It is as well for them that they do so, he thought, for I am master here now. Aside from this under-current of anxiety, the courtyard had a normal busy morning feel about it. Behind him, within the shadows of the storeroom, the straw rustled beneath the bare feet of Shu and Shin, who waited nervously. Lang continued to observe the activity in the courtyard.

He knew the journey had begun, his travelling, his campaign, his going from one place to another, and he knew that it would only be halted again by death. He was determined not to let anyone see how afraid he was. Lang Tzu, he whispered, saying aloud to himself the name his worldly friend, August Spiess, had given him on the day of his birth.

Let us go then, he said to the brothers, and sit over there under the roof of the second gateway and consider our strategy for the game. But still he did not move. He was not certain yet what he would tell them. Not everything, to be sure. He turned and faced them, placing his hand on his diaphragm, where the pommel of the sword pressed into him, and he said, First we shall each swear on this blade an oath of loyalty to the others, and shall promise to keep our secrets no matter what. The brothers' eyes were lucid and dark, uncomplicated and afraid in the shadows under the eaves of the storehouse.

That night Lang did not sleep in the room at the gatekeeper's but returned to his own bed in the empty quarter of the house. He felt alone and thought he could hear strange noises in the garden. But his newly acquired dignity would no longer permit him to sleep at the gatekeeper's. And anyway, he didn't want to go back there. Having crossed one boundary, it seemed it was necessary to cross other, even more dangerous, boundaries. He couldn't go back. Evidence previously invisible was becoming visible. Possibilities, he foresaw, might prove to be limitless. A method, indeed a critical method, was needed to deal with them.

·

But he had no method. Evidence for hitherto undreamed of possibilities was mounting up in an unsorted heap around him. Interpretation was vital if he was not soon to be overwhelmed by the accumulation of indiscriminate detail.

As he lay there, unsleeping and for the first time alone, startled by the familiar screech of the night heron, he felt more and more beleaguered and confused, until at last he found he had retreated in his thoughts, without consciously thinking about it, to the only place where he ever truly felt at home – on the train. Travelling between Shanghai and Hangzhou, a journey he had made hundreds of times, snug and secure and alone with his mother in their private compartment, he was in the only place he had ever been able to call his own.

His first memory in life was of the flat countryside south of Shanghai passing slowly before his gaze. With his nose pressed hard against the cold glass, knowing his mother was sitting just behind him reading or writing letters, he watched the fields going by, and the two-storey houses of the wealthy farmers and the peasants walking along the rows of cabbages ladling nutrients from their earthenware jars, and the dark invisible sound of the train's whistle drawing them on towards the southern hills. In the warm comfortable privacy of the compartment with his mother, beyond the reach of his dangerous father and not yet confined within the encircling walls of his grandfather's house, somewhere between the painful contradictions of his Western life in Shanghai and his Chinese life in Hangzhou, there he had always felt truly at ease and secure and happy. Travelling, he and his mother had belonged to each other, and to themselves.

The voice which now matter-of-factly informed him that being at home while travelling was merely another aspect of the precious gift of dimorphism, of his *lang tsze*-ness, was that of his friend August Spiess, his ally and his teacher, who by his own unexampled persistence in the extraterritorial region of the International Settlement demonstrated that nothing can be one thing without partaking of its opposite; the steady wisdom of the doctor, who belonged in no particular place himself, rescued Lang once again from confusion, and probable defeat.

·

Boundaries, the doctor continued, pacing to and fro in front of the windows and pausing every now and then to gaze at the traffic on the river and to shake his head in wonderment at the industry of humankind, exist to be transgressed, they are there to facilitate crossings, not to frustrate them. It is not, he went on, fingering lovingly the worn pages of his precious volume of Goethe, in those places whose exact frontiers have already been defined for us, but in the regions of uncertainty where definitions have yet to be located, that we must find our place.

The transgression of boundaries is my established custom, Lang thought to himself, feeling certain that he had been the recipient of a revelation of inestimable value. I am an adept. There is no one better fitted than I to destroy the stronghold of the ancestors, those dead who will not die but who persist in asserting an influence upon the living.

He knew now that it must be the boundary between the living and the dead that he had to deal with next, and that his visit into his own hinterland, into his tomb, where he had gone on his supernatural horse, his making visible to himself a truth that was not to be discovered in the objective facts of his history, his forward patrol, his simple little fiction, had been but a necessary preparation, a hardening of his resolve, for this journey into the vast shadowy province where his mother had been lured by his spellbound grandfather, the place where gods, ghosts, ancestors and innumerable other forms of phantoms and uncategorised demons met the living face to face.

Before he went to sleep, when the dawn was just beginning to lighten the sky over the hills and the air had grown suddenly colder, Lang knew what he must do. He wished there had been some way, before he actually did it, for him to tell Doctor Spiess.

A preliminary reconnoitre revealed Yu dozing in the sun against the wall of the storehouse, trying to keep out of the biting wind that had sprung up. The gatekeeper and his daughter-in-law, the mother of Shu and Shin, were occupied at the gate with a vegetable seller.

Urging the boys to keep up, Lang hurried through the house. At the south end of the gallery he posted Shu and instructed him to screech like a shrike if he should see Yu coming. Shin he posted outside the door of his grandfather's study.

Lang went in alone. A thin trace of the smell of old men and the ancestors lingered in the undisturbed air. He realised he had lived with the smell all his life, the way the zookeeper in his house must live with the smell of the animals, even when he is eating his evening meal. Lang swallowed and cleared his throat.

Below the bookshelves, next to the cupboard in which the precious collection of teas was kept, the assortment of boxes labelled with his mother's familiar script and lined up in order according to the qualities of their contents, there was a second cupboard.

Lang knelt on the cold flagstones and opened this second cupboard. Two large drawers filled the space behind the door. Each drawer had a plain bronze handle. He pulled the lower drawer until it caught and was prevented by something from coming out any further. He reached in to the drawer and pressed upward against a lightly sprung board at the back. The drawer was released at once and slid out easily the rest of the way. He laid it aside on the flagstones. Now he reached his arm into the deep cavity left by the drawer, a cavity deeper than the drawer itself which, on being removed, had proved to be twenty centimetres or so short of the full depth of the cupboard. With difficulty, owing to its bulk and weight, he withdrew a bundle from this secret place and laid it on the flagstones before him.

The bundle, which contained Huang's book of the ancestors, was wrapped in white Hangzhou silk and was tied with a ribbon that had also once been white, but which had become stained and dull and frayed with age.

For some minutes he knelt there staring at the bundle, half-hoping he might shortly hear Shu's warning screech and be prevented from having to go through with it. Would Doctor Spiess have scorned his fears as empty superstition? Would the doctor have possessed the power to dispel this cowardly disquiet?

Like butterflies blown into the shelter of the garden by the fierce wind, small stray sounds from the outside world floated over the wall and entered the study. Lang's attention was drawn to them: a street vendor calling his dried fish, the wheels of a cart crunching the gravel, and then, far away in the distance a steam train crossing the iron spans of the Qiantang Bridge blew its whistle, one beseeching cry that made Lang long to be safely on board.

The shrike did not screech.

As if the hands that did it were not his own, Lang watched his fingers struggle with the unfamiliar knot that held the ribbon in place.

Bent close and scarcely breathing, he parted the silk and let it slip from the bundle. He started back with fright. A face had gazed at him from deep within the uncertain depths of the bronze cosmic mirror of the Huangs. He had forgotten the mirror guarded the book. He was so startled to see the blurry features staring at him that he did not immediately recognise them as his own. One pale eye gazed through him with a kind of blind inward and immortal sight, as if it observed him unfeelingly from a remote place and time. The lips were thick and purplish and were parted stupidly. He did not dare to look again. Was this the face of his father, after all, gazing at him mockingly from within the citadel of the Huangs? Could that possibly be? He experienced the shock of a paradoxical enlightening misunderstanding: Are all fathers, all ancestors, one?

The specular impression arose and was dispelled within the second or two that was required for him to register the fact that it had been his own reflection he had glimpsed in Huang's ancestral mirror, and not a supernatural projection of his father. He remembered being told by Yu that a brother of Huang's had once looked into the mirror many years ago and had discovered that his face was not reflected there. Shortly after this the brother had died. The mirror was a powerful conduit for the supernatural. It had been with the family of the scholar since the Tang dynasty mirror master had cast it for his ancestors in the eighth century.Its interior, within which the mysterious reflections were held, was the antechamber to the signs within the book. The mirror was the residence of the ever-changing image behind the script. Lang recalled Zhuang Zhu's familiar lines: *The mind of the sage perfectly calm, like untroubled water, is like a mirror which reflects heaven and earth and all beings.* As with all such cosmic mirrors of any significance, this one, Lang knew, possessed the power to reveal not only such things as infidelities and the causes of sickness, but also contained within the cunning harmonies of its light and shade the more disquieting power to show the true form of those beings who dwelt within the borderland between the living and the dead.

Taking elaborate care not to catch a further glimpse of his face in it, Lang turned the mirror over and laid it aside on the silk. The back of the eight-lobed bronze was decorated in relief with the representation of two other-worldly birds and with eight entwining bouquets of vineleaves. The two phoenixes confronted each other, portrayed in sensuous, undulating movements, engaged upon either the ritual of courtship or in preparation for battle.

Lang wrapped the mirror carefully in the silk, and then he reached for the heavy volume, his hands small and smooth and seemingly too delicate to possess sufficient strength to lift the great book.

Three days passed before he found an opportunity to carry out the next, far more dangerous, phase of his plan. He had begun to grow anxious that he would not be able to have done with it before his mother and grandfather returned, when a fortunate change in the weather occurred. The day before Huang and Lien were due back from the shrine at Nankangfu a terrific storm broke over the lake and sent Yu and the other servants scurrying inside, where they stayed. This was the opportunity Lang had been waiting for.

Lashed by the rain and buffeted by the gale and scared half to death by the cracking lightning that broke loose from the black clouds above them, Lang and Shin slipped out through the little red gateway. Shu ran and secured the gate from the inside. He was to remain behind and to open it for them at a prearranged signal when they returned.

Once outside the walls of Huang's house there was no need for Lang to urge Shin to keep up with him. The terrified brother stuck so close they very nearly tripped each other as they ran along the road. There was no one about. Everyone had sought shelter from the storm – everyone, that is, except the toffee apple man, who stood at his pitch, unmoved by the downpour, gazing absently before him. Lang felt himself observed by the vendor.

Clutching their bundles to their chests, Lang and Shin hurried along the road beside the lake, making for the nearest of the hills. The low clouds bore down on the lake from Huang Shan and the cold wind and rain whipped the water into a frenzy, as if great fish were struggling beneath the surface. The pleasure boats tied up to poles stuck in the mud bumped against each other, making knocking sounds like bullfrogs courting. Lang glanced towards the dark sky and he saw a deep green cavern within the belly of the cloud above him.

At the end of the road they turned from the lakeside and ascended a steep hill by a stone path that rose through the forest in a series of stages. At the end of each stage a shrine with a statue of the Buddha inside had been carved from the native rock. Around them the forest trees groaned and twisted and thrashed in the storm, as if their roots were on fire and they sought to tear themselves loose from the soil.

When Lang and Shin turned the corner of the last stage Lang stopped so abruptly that Shin ran into him. An old peasant was sweeping the path ahead. She had her back to them and was bent forward swishing her broom savagely from side to side and debating fiercely with herself. Suddenly she stopped sweeping and turned and confronted them. Ah! she cried shrilly, like the cry of a shrike, on seeing them close behind her in the lashing rain. Where are you boys running to? Are you demons? Menacingly, she descended a step towards them, brandishing her broom.

Lang felt Shin clutch his gown and heard him whimper. The old peasant laughed, What is that you've got there? Let Aunty have a look at your treasures!

Lang stood his ground, his left hand searching for the pommel of his sword, which was concealed beneath his padded gown. She is only a path sweeper who is too mad with old age and boredom to possess the sense to seek shelter from the storm, he assured himself. But for all this, his heart was beating quickly and his belly was light with fear.

So! the old woman cried, standing on the step above him and looking down upon him with cunning, amused and avaricious eyes, neither old nor young but flickering with the unsteady light-and-shade of other-worldly thoughts. You have robbed a poor widow of her precious heirlooms! And murdered her too, I don't doubt. Show me what you've got in your bundles or I shall strike you from my path. She lifted her broom and advanced upon him.

It seemed to Lang that he observed the scene from a little distance, that he saw himself draw the sword from his gown, as if he were detached from the events taking place on the path, as if there were two of him, one calm and able to reflect upon the scene, the other no longer in possession of feelings but engaged in the action. He seemed to witness without emotion the surprise and then the terror in the old woman's eyes as she saw the steel blade dance towards her through the streaming air. He seemed to see her struggle to retreat, to see the sole of her sandal catch against the projecting lip of the step behind her, to see her lose her balance and snatch helplessly at the air, to tumble sideways from the path on to the steep rocky hillside, to observe her as she leaped and rolled and clutched at the branches of the trees, to see her fall, down and down through the awakened forest, her black rags dancing like so many extra limbs to the madness of the storm. And he seemed to hear her shrieks taken up by the noise of the storm, echoing within the booming clouds above him, as if they were howls of a vast unbridled hilarity, a laughter more wild and strange and more possessed of a triumphant irony than any he had ever heard before. As if it were he who were falling, not she.

And when she was gone from his sight, the noise of the storm rolled back and forth against the hillside, as if it searched for her, like a parent searching for a lost child.

The path was empty. He turned to Shin. The boy was crouched with his hands over his face, soaked and shivering. Get up, Shin! Get up! Lang ordered him. Shin took his hands from his face and gazed at the sword, which Lang still carried in his hand, and he picked up the bundle containing the bronze mirror and slowly got to his feet. You haven't seen a demon, Lang reassured him and laughed, but his laugh was thin and unsteady.

He went on, keeping the sword ready in his hand and scrutinising the path ahead. He would not have been surprised to see her there again, standing before him, blocking his way and waving her broom at him. Had he struck her? He did not know.

When he reached the spine of the ridge the path divided in two, one branch continuing up the ridge towards the temple of Lin Yin where he had once been taken, and the other descending he knew towards the river. He took the lower branch and a minute or two later came out at the bottom of a gully, where a stream of clear mountain water disappeared into a dense thicket of tall bamboos.

He pushed his way into the swaying poles, which moved back and forth in the gale, as if he were forcing his way through a chorus of tall singers linked arm in arm and harmonising a song of many parts. He emerged suddenly from the bamboos onto the flat, grassy margin of the Qiantang River.

The margin was exposed to the full force of the wind. Waves lashed the pebbly shore. He placed the book on the grass and weighted it with the sword. When Shin came out of the bamboos he took the mirror from him and instructed him to prepare a fire.

With the wind tearing at his gown so that he was forced to lean into it in order to advance, Lang approached the river. The farther bank was a darker slash upon the dark horizon. Behind him the bamboos clacked and clicked and cracked against each other.

Lang waded into the water until the waves were breaking against his chest and he could scarcely keep his footing on the slippery stones and then, like a drowning discus thrower, he hurled the cosmic mirror of the Huangs as far out into the current as he could. Briefly, the ancient eight-lobed bronze spun through the air, the phoenixes alternating with subliminal rapidity with the polished circle of the mirror, then it plunged beneath the surface of the wind-torn water.

Lang struggled back to the shore. He did not look over his shoulder. He was satisfied that he had blinded the mischievous supernatural eye of his grandfather's ancestors. He was shivering.

On the shore Shin was busy building a fire from slivers of tinder-dry bamboo, which he was resourcefully stripping from the inside of a dead pole he had felled and split. Lang knelt on the grass and untied the bundle.

His grandfather's sacred book of the ancestors lay before him, Huang's churinga, his connection with the spiritual life of his tribe, his consecrated text, in which he had his place and without which he would be displaced and cast into an alien landscape whose features he would not be able to name, the book without which Huang would be a stranger on this earth.

The waves broke with a rush on the pebbly shore, and the wind snatched the spray into the air. Lang crouched over the book and watched his chilled fingers struggle with the gold and crimson embroidered phoenix bands which held the boards in place. He laid the book open at the first page. Drops of rain and wind-driven spray fell upon the text. He placed the blade of the sword across the book to keep the pages from being torn away by the gale and he bent close to inspect the early script.

Here was the first entry in the old book. It was written in the flowing *ts'ao-shu*. The entry had been made by the Sung poet and calligrapher Huang T'ing-chien. Lang was so moved by the indescribable beauty of the hand that he gave an involuntary groan. His affection for the painted word had been kindled in him by his mother even before he had learned to talk. His love of writing was his first love. There was nothing he could ever love more, no matter if he lived to be a hundred years of age, than the painted word upon the page.

Huang T'ing-chien, the eleventh century literary painter, the first recorder of the ancestors of the twentieth century literary painter Huang Yu-hua, had left a poem in the margin. Affecting a certain superficial clumsiness in order to eschew the appearance of being merely a skilled professional, and in order not to vulgarly display his erudition, Huang had painted beside his exact genealogical entries two lines, consisting of the heaviest question followed by the lightest answer: *To what can we liken human life? Perhaps to a wild swan's footprints on mud or snow.*

So entranced was Lang by Huang's calligraphy that he forgot where he was and what he was doing. His mission departed from his mind as he contemplated the running characters on the page. He was not satisfied with the literal meanings alone, those hinges that held the characters in place next to each other, but entered each character in search of the implicit thought which it contained from the remotest past of civilisation's beginnings. With the trained discipline of a scholar, and the passion of a lover, he sought the primal literary reflection enfolded within the shape and structure of each ideograph. He travelled within the residences of the origin of thought itself, the black figures on the page, and gazed about in wonder at what he saw there.

He was bewitched by the marks of the scholar, the indelible trace upon the face of eternity which had brought history into being. Such painted signs as these, for Lang, were no less than thought itself, uttered in the eternal silence of the cosmos. For once uttered, the question endures: *To what can we liken human life?*

It was the crackling of the fire that roused him from his last meditation on the art of his tribe. Half-naked Shin danced in the yellow flames, his body steaming, unloading another rattling armful of dead bamboos on to the blaze. The fire roared and crackled, the bamboos exploding with the sound of musket fire, the sparks and flames driven flat by the gale.

Lang tore Huang T'ing-chien's page from the book and impaled it on the point of his sword, and he thrust it into the orange heart of the fire and watched it burn. Page by page he burned the book, and finally he burned the boards. And when there was nothing left to burn he stood and gazed into the coals until they were reduced to a cold grey circle of ash in the green grass. In his head all he could hear were the ringing and whistling sounds of silence and emptiness.

PRESENT REALITY

An infamous decade was coming to a close and a new beginning was expected eagerly. Four years after Lang burnt Huang's book of the ancestors, the disintegration of China seemed about to enter its final phase. In the first week of June 1937, Lang's father, Feng Three, was passed detailed and highly secret intelligence by the Japanese high command concerning the initial phases of their master plan to destroy the national morale of the Chinese people and to subjugate China under the rule of a new Nippon empire. Feng was given this intelligence, which he did not find unexpected or surprising, a month before the Japanese provoked the incident at Marco Polo Bridge which gave them the excuse to begin their military operations in earnest; operations which were to keep the Japanese people continuously at war until the Americans dropped an atomic bomb on the city of Hiroshima on 6 August, 1945 and another on the city of Nagasaki three days later, and the high command was finally forced to abandon the military option.

In 1937 there was to be no unaccountable withdrawal from Shanghai by the initially victorious Japanese army after thirty-four days, as there had been in 1932. This time, like the Mongols in the thirteenth century and the Manchus in the seventeenth century, the Japanese were not coming to China simply in order to plunder and humiliate, they were coming to colonise, permanently. They were coming to re-write history. Their means, as with the great Khans, was to be military conquest, the traditional and only honourable means by which a proud and ancient nation might seek to achieve ascendancy over its neighbours.

The Japanese policy – if such an organic bridling of a nation as this was can be signified by so rational an epithet as policy – aimed to achieve the practical realisation of a dream, upon which they had been meditating for centuries. Their mission was to turn a vision into tangible reality. Their mission, and it *was* a mission, was to turn thought into actuality. And for this the only suitable instrument with which the centuries of their civilisation had provided them was war.

Though their governments and the representatives of their press did not outwardly share their enthusiasm for the Japanese plan, most of the British, the French and the American business-men who were operating out of the International Settlements in Shanghai, and who enjoyed the uncertain benefits of extraterri-toriality, considered the Japanese policy to be reasonable and desirable, and they looked forward impatiently to its swift and successful realisation.

Feng also welcomed the imminent takeover by the Japanese. Indeed he had been positioning his interests for it ever since Chiang Kai-shek had come north in 1927 and set up his government in Nanking – 1927, that inauspicious year of the birth of Feng's only living son.

There were no Shanghai capitalists of the old comprador caste, indeed, who did not welcome the Japanese. Those who had been clever enough or lucky enough to survive Chiang's terror and his pillaging of their fortunes longed to see an end to his omnivorous militarism and to see it replaced with the orderly and reliable management of China's commercial and industrial resources under a strong central authority able to deal effectively with the threat which warlords and Communists posed to the re-establishment of economic prosperity.

Among the numerous contenders for power, only the Japanese, it seemed to the commercial interests of the day, were suitably equipped, positioned and motivated to achieve the nearly impossible task of bringing the whole of China under the control of one strong central government. No matter that a few Western journalists and official spokesmen and women, and one or two intellectuals, raised their voices against the injustice of the approaching takeover, for Western commercial interests gener-ally, as for the Shanghai capitalists (and for Feng among these), the Japanese bid for power was the only one to which they were prepared to lend their support, either implicitly or actively.

When he returned to his villa from the privileged briefing with General Sugiyama, Feng went directly into his private office and reached for the telephone. He asked the operator to connect him with a Hangzhou number, and while he waited for the connection to be made he gazed thoughtfully out of the window.

He was now nearing his fifty-second birthday. His features had scarcely aged during the past ten years. Contrary to his vengeful and piratical appearance, Feng's fortunes lay not with a capacity for sudden violent action but with his patience, with his capacity to wait, concealing himself, until the moment had matured and his raptor instincts need no longer be contained. He had no patience with the fiction of the noble arts of war. If a violent conflict were unavoidable, then he looked for a brief and conclusive engagement.

The coincidence of his son's coming of age and the end of Chinese history had not gone unnoticed by him, despite his outward devotion to practicalities. There was a fatefulness about the conjunction that could not be ignored. And although he did not dwell on the likely significance of it, it did register with him sufficiently to cause a flickering uneasiness to rise and fall beneath his conscious preoccupations.

He was prepared, on the grounds of sound strategy, to embrace both his son, whom he scarcely knew, and the new empire of the Nippon. There were aspects of both which he disliked, but he recognised that it was not a perfect world and was prepared, therefore, to work with imperfections. The Japanese and his son were both necessary to him, the former to ensure his personal continuation and the other to provide the future means for passing on what he and his father, and *his* father before him, had spent their energies accumulating – wealth and power, the fragile assurance of a lineage, in a word, a name.

Though C. H. Feng loved neither the Japanese nor his son he did not consider trying to do without either in his enterprise. As for the Japanese, he would have felt easier with them if they had been merely opportunists rather than visionaries. 'I cannot but feel that some power even greater than God has inspired our men,' General Sugiyama had remarked to him with tears in his eyes less than an hour ago. A power greater than God? It had made Feng feel terribly uncomfortable. He had not known where to look. Sugiyama's remark had made him clear his throat and fidget. It too nearly resembled the superstitious idiocies much loved by the old China. Feng wanted stable government from the Japanese, not mysterious spiritual intensities. A power greater than God! He kept hearing the general's voice saying it.

A voice was struggling to reach him through the wash of static. He realised it was his wife. He shouted his instructions to her, ordering her to begin preparations at once for her final departure from Hangzhou. He didn't attempt to explain why it was to be final. And she didn't ask him. They both knew the time had come for her to hand over the son to the father, that the moment when the pledge must be redeemed would not be postponed. They both knew the world was about to change. They both knew that if she had not accomplished her purpose with the boy in the ten years he had given to her, then there were but a few moments left to her to complete the task.

They didn't have much to say to each other. The truth was obvious. It voiced itself in the extended silences between them. Then at last, in case she should happen to consider delaying her return, he passed on to her the highly classified information that the Japanese planned to land a large military force at Hangzhou Bay, with the intention of by-passing Shanghai and striking directly along the axis of the triangle at Chiang's seat of government in Nanking. (A manoeuvre, in the event, though indeed planned, which was delayed until November, by which time the Chinese city of Shanghai – though not the International Settlements – had been almost completely destroyed by three months of the most vicious and intense fighting that either the Japanese or the Chinese were to engage in during the entire war. To the great surprise of the English and the Americans, who had long ago dismissed the fighting abilities of the Chinese soldier as negligible, the Han died in their thousands as heroically as any warriors in history in a stubborn and inspired defence of their ancestral homeland.)

Hangzhou is no longer safe, Feng shouted at her. You may

bring your parent and his servant with you to Shanghai if you wish. He meant it. The offer was a genuine one. He wasn't sure whether he heard her thank him for this or whether she said something unrelated. The waves of static crackled and hissed and approached and broke on a pebbly shore and receded again. He hung up.

He frowned hard at the telephone, as if it had offended him, his lips pushed out like those of a wooden African idol. He had been caught off guard by an uncertainty. Children were surely akin to insects. They changed swiftly and unrecognisably from one form to another. The metamorphoses of larvae. He was not sure, now that he was to be brought face to face with it, what he might expect from himself. He could not place within himself the certainty that he *was* a father. There were the two dead sons reposing side by side on their white sheet and there was the ideal son of his innermost companionship. And now there was to be the real, the actual, boy who would be returning from Hangzhou within a day or so. (His numerous daughters Feng did not consider as having required from him real fatherhood, but a kind of careful guardianship, which he was certain he had fulfilled. His affection for certain of his daughters, as for his first wife, was deep and abiding.)

Just as he was beginning to touch on this interesting question, the question of what he might locate within himself of fatherhood if only he were to search, a question, indeed, concerning his own nature, Feng did a very characteristic thing. He abandoned the enquiry before he had properly got it under way and turned his attention to the business of the day.

It was not a simple absence of curiosity about himself, however, that prompted Feng to lose interest in this inward line of thought – in certain matters he was prepared to examine himself minutely – it was a distrust, rather, of the associative processes of thought on the abstract level, a distrust, indeed a fear, of where he might be led by such enquiry. It was the abstract, not the inward, that he spurned. If he had been a European navigator in the fifteenth century, Feng would not have discovered the New World. He would have sailed his craft always within sight of familiar features on the landward side. He would have kept within sight of features that he could confidently put a name to. The empty horizon was a nameless horizon and did not attract him. And whenever he happened inadvertently to glance towards it, as now, he sensed the threat its namelessness presented to the particular configuration of familiar elements which determined the direction and conduct of his life. The risk 'out there' was too general. It was not calculable, its boundaries were undetermined, and it was not acceptable to him. After all, one might find nothing in that direction. The abstract horizon was an horizon of absence for Feng, for that which has no name may not exist, may be, indeed, a mere illusion. There could be no guarantee that the empty horizon would not remain empty if one ventured over it. So he had chosen to stay at home, bounded in his thoughts as well as in his body by present reality, by the familiar.

August Spiess had written in his journal that Feng was too large a character to be dealt with in its pages. But the truth was rather the opposite. Feng was limited, and his limitations were largely self-imposed.

Among the business of the day to which he now returned his thoughts, from this inadvertent glance towards the nameless terrors of the abstract horizon, was the mundane but pressing matter of his son's education. He had never consulted Lien about his plans for the boy's schooling in Australia. He was not vindictive. Ten years ago her challenge had dismayed and surprised him, it had caught him off his guard, but he had observed it until he had felt reassured of countering it. He had not reacted to her challenge, then or since. He had done nothing. There had been nothing *to* do. He was certain, however, that she had come to an understanding of the direction of his intentions, even as he had himself. It was even possible that August had disclosed his exact plans to her once they had been formulated. (He had been kept informed of the occasional correspondence which had passed between his wife and his friend since the birth of the boy. He did not object to it. He did not feel threatened or betrayed by it. And he did not mention his knowledge of it to either of them. For it had been one of the many silent conduits of information he had relied on for his exact knowledge of his environment. It was only the unknown that troubled Feng. The known, he believed, might be controlled, and therefore used to further his purposes.)

August had agreed enthusiastically to accompany the boy to Australia, and to remain there with him long enough to see him happily settled at boarding school and established in a useful intercourse with his Australian relations.

I shall miss you, August, Feng had been moved to admit on seeing the unexpected ardour of his friend's desire to be of service. He had expected to have to convince. He had not really meant that he would miss him. It was not that, but he had not known how else to express the emotion his gratitude had aroused. I envy you. I wish I could go myself. And he had talked at length of Australia and his grandfather and had produced a large, square, sepia photograph from a drawer in his desk.

My grandfather's house in Melbourne. They examined the photograph together. An imposing two-storey brick villa set in newly landscaped grounds, the trees and shrubs no taller than the people. A European woman in an elaborate white dress, ornamented with much passementerie and variously hued trimmings, posed elegantly on the verandah, her hands clasped loosely before her, her gaze direct and filled with assurance and authority. Behind her, in the shadows, a nanny held a toddler by the hand.

Standing on the gravel path below the woman was a Chinese of about forty years of age. He, also, was elegantly attired, his London frock coat of mid-thigh length was held open by his having his hand thrust into his trouser pocket. By this means a good expanse of double-breasted waistcoat of the same light colour as his trousers was revealed. On his head he wore a tall glossy top hat and in his right hand he carried a slim cane. He was looking directly into the camera with his good left eye. Over his right eye he wore a patch. Above his hat someone had unnecessarily inked a small X. My grandfather, Feng disclosed with awkward pride, placing his finger under the image of the man.

They looked at the photograph a while longer and August asked questions. My aunt, Victoria, his youngest daughter, still lives at the house. I shall write and tell her to expect a visit from you. It will be a great adventure, August. Beneath the photograph was the simple copperplate inscription *Coppin Grove, 1876.*

THE GIFT OF DEATH

Huang did not recover from the mysterious disappearance of his family's ancestral cosmic mirror and the book of the ancestors. These ritual artefacts had been entrusted to his care when he was a youthful scholar of twenty. They had been in his keeping for more than fifty years. He took the blow of their loss as though the gods themselves had judged him unworthy and had removed these sacred objects from him and set him adrift. His subterfuge, his making a son of his daughter, had evidently angered them so deeply that they were determined to permit him no reconciliation with his ancestors. Despite his visits to the shrine, he was not to be forgiven. This was their answer to his attempt to reform himself. It was finished. It was the end of the family. His life's course had been irremediably perverted by a selfish illusion. He feared death now more than ever, for he believed it certain he would be transformed into a disfigured ghost for all eternity.

He waited. He did nothing. He expected to die. He was expected to die. But he lingered, paused between life and death. He was silent. No one could guess the extent of his surviving capacities. He suffered Yu to dress him and to bathe him, to feed him and to massage his joints and muscles and to apply remedies to their pitiful aches and pains. But nothing could penetrate to the anguish in his spirit. There was no balm for that. He was a man condemned by his own tribe. His gods had pointed at him and cursed him. Their Word had fallen from him. His end would not be sudden. He withered, like an old tree whose tap root has been severed by a blow from an axe. He was to be culled. He was to be unlinked from the continuum. He could feel the busy fingers of death within him unpicking the brilliant cope of being. Gaps, like empty sockets where eyes had once glowed with understanding, had begun to appear in his memory of the poets. With horror he observed the steady progress of death and could do nothing to abate it.

When she could no longer hear his voice she hung up. Feng's order to leave Hangzhou had numbed her. She had no counter for it. She saw that her father was weeping silently, the tears running freely down his face, his gaze unseeing, his body motionless as ice. If it had not been for his tears she might have thought him dead.

She called to Yu and offered him a cigarette. He came out from behind his blue screen and stood by her at the open casement. She lit his cigarette for him. They smoked and looked out on the formal garden. The day was hot and still and heavy. At length she said, I have lost.

Yu said nothing. He puffed his cigarette and closed his eyes and felt the pleasure of the dark smoke curling through his lungs. Then he groaned and coughed and ventured the reply, One cannot claim to have lost until one has ceased to fight. In order to succeed, it is simply necessary to survive one's failures.

She laughed despite herself. Haven't you something better for me than the wisdom of old men, Yu?

You are young, he said. It is a temporary setback.

Feng will send my son to Australia. It will be ten years before I see him again. By then he will be a man. In Australia he will learn to despise China. It will turn him against me.

Yu said severely, No one, not even you, can predict the future with certainty. To speak of ten years hence with such confidence is not the thought of an intelligent person. Ten days even! Who would be foolish enough to say what is to happen in ten days? Remember your demon! What has happened to your demon? Slap his face and wake him up. Why look to the moment of your son's return to China in ten years? If you must look into the future, why not look twenty years into it, when he will have been home already for ten years? Why not thirty, by which time you will have both forgotten the influence of Australia? You are young. You are not yet thirty. It will all pass quickly. Do you remember the pain you suffered at his birth ten years ago? Well that was yesterday. I remember that night as if it were last night. Ten, twenty, thirty, years! What is the difference? Feng will die. Men die. He will fall from favour. It is not the wisdom of old men to say that you must deal with each day as it comes to you and not with all your days at once, but is merely common sense. It is extremely foolish to give up on a day when things are going so badly for you. At least wait until tomorrow. Who knows, perhaps the Communists will shoot Feng before he can send your son to Australia. This is not the time for you to tell me you have lost. We all lose. That is not the point.

Yu suddenly fell silent, as if he thought he might say too much. He gazed at Huang. When does he tell you to return to Shanghai?

He has given us three days, she said.

They looked into each other's eyes. Ah, three days. He was dismayed. He would never see her again. The two old roosters with the golden chick. It was all only yesterday.

She didn't mention Feng's invitation.

Once we did not smoke our cigarettes in his presence, Yu said sadly. Where has our respect for him gone? They looked at Huang, silent and tearful in his scholar's chair. After a minute Yu said, Why don't you turn your son against Australia first? All the greatest battles of history were fought in one day. You have three days.

All civilised people know there is Heaven and there is Hell, but only a fool expects to encounter enlightenment in the darkness of Hell. The blind storyteller gazed around the scholar's study with an expression of extraordinary arrogance, an air of superiority which betokened an inspection of decidedly inferior persons.

Were there others about the place, then, Lang wondered, besides himself and his grandfather and Yu? For surely such a large expression could not be intended solely for them? Were not invisible presences concealed in the dark corners of the study and beyond the casements in the gallery, and out beyond the gallery in the garden itself, squatting artfully to blend their shadows with those of the rocks? Other listeners to the story? Did they also fear the seer's contempt as he did?

Lang did not question that the quality of sight vouchsafed the blind man was more penetrating and far-seeing than that of ordinary mortals such as himself, who could see no further than the four walls that encompassed them, or to the nearest horizon, but not *through* the walls or *over* the horizon, and, indeed, into the past and into the future as the storyteller could; for, being blind to the obstruction of material objects, the features of present reality did not impede his view. Lang gazed at him with a mixture of fear and expectation.

It is too dark in Hell to see anything much at all, the blind man went on in his contemptuous tone, as if he were speaking to idiots. That is why, once you have arrived in Hell, it is so very difficult to find your way out of it again. Nearly impossible. Hell is a destination. It is not a place on the way to somewhere else. Hell is not for travellers but for those who have done with travelling. One does not pause there, but stays there forever. That is the horror of it. Naturally enough, it is situated neither quite in the East nor quite in the West, but is located in an indeterminate place somewhere between the two. Hell is a paradox and is unresolvable and those who dwell in it suffer the continuous pangs of desire and loathing in equal proportions.

He completed his prolegomena and sucked phlegm from his nostrils into the back of his throat and loosed it with careless accuracy into a turquoise jar before his chair. He held out his teacup to be refilled. His torn sleeve fell away, revealing a forearm that resembled a darkly roasted shank of sinewy meat, the leg of a half-starved billy goat. Yu came forward and filled the cup to the brim with the steaming fragrant brew. Neither Yu nor Lang thought to question the storyteller on just how he came to know so much about Hell. His words did not invite questioning. He possessed the confidence of his words. He was their intimate and knew them well.

Lang watched the blind man noisily suck the tea, and he drew the snow leopard's skin closer around his shoulders and curled his legs under him more tightly on the ample seat of the chair. The summer evening was mild. It was not for its warmth that he wore the leopard's skin, but the reassurance of its familiar touch. No doubt there was to be in the story some relief from the meanness of familiar things, and perhaps an element of instruction also. That much was to be expected from a storyteller. It was certainly for this reason his mother had invited the blind man to sit with them this evening. But the storyteller's choice of words made Lang suspect that something more was intended than mere distraction and homily on this occasion. He felt himself personally singled out for the blind man's rhetorical attention. The 'indeterminate' location of Hell could scarcely, it seemed to him, have been an entirely gratuitous choice of phrase. He pulled the snow leopard's fur around his shoulders more snugly because he knew the storyteller could see into the secrets of his inner life, and there was a coldness, a cruel detachment, in the blind man's gaze.

The storyteller banged his empty teacup on the table beside him. Huang's head jerked upward, his eyes wide with alarm. Now to our tale! How can a starving orphan boy become a great and powerful merchant of the living cargo without the intervention of demonic forces? the blind man asked with an artful flourish of his pink tongue. The boy in question was ten years old. He had just reached his majority when we encounter him on his journey. He had been travelling for several weeks after his mother and father and his sisters and brothers and all his relatives in the village had been put to death by members of The Society for Peace, who were waging a war at that time against the opium smugglers of Nanhiung-chou.

Just as a corpse left unburied for a few days seethes with a mighty colony of maggots, so the Middle Kingdom seethed with war and banditry and opportunism in the aftermath of the first opium war, and in the West it was the year of revolution. The World had forgotten peace and the victims of war were to be seen everywhere.

Starvation and wounds had made the boy so weak that he could scarcely stand. But for some reason unknown even to himself he kept going. He did not give up. His perseverence was unnatural. It was inspired and feverish, not reasoned. He travelled, poor fool, as if he believed there was to be a bountiful end to his journey. But how could that be, for there is a bountiful end to no one's journey who travels alone. He owned nothing but the filthy rag that covered his privacy. In his delirium he had even forgotten his name, and as he was the sole survivor of his clan this was probably just as well for him.

Anyway, one road let him to another as it invariably does, until he reached the great highway that leads to the sea. On this mighty road the crowd of lost and disconnected refugees moved like an endless flood that is fed by a constant deluge high in the regions of its catchment. The noise was of a thousand voices calling to lost loved ones and for the assistance of the gods. To keep themselves and their sons alive many parents butchered their daughters and cooked the flesh by the roadside. And such was the extremity of the case that no mother attempted to hide this act from those who passed by. And none of those seeing it paused to remark on it.

On the wharf that stretched out over the sea at the end of the road, the Lord of Death waited, observing her pilgrims with great interest. When she saw the nameless boy coming towards her, she perceived at once that there was something about him to be valued. It was this: although the world of the living had rejected him so completely that it no longer even deigned to favour him with a name of his own, he had not given up the quest for meaning. He had not succumbed to despair. Though nameless and without a family he did not consider himself to be without worth. Rarely had Shinjé seen such a wilful desire for life as this. She saw that such intuitive determination might be put to work, and she decided to recruit him to her cause.

The sea lay before him. He had come from the wooded mountains and for the first time in his life he gazed upon a horizon that was without vertical features. He was so impressed by the magnitude of what he saw, so attracted by the vertiginous magnetism of this horizontal depth that he forgot his hunger and his wounds and he stood on the wharf gazing in wonderment upon the twinkling expanse, which heaved and undulated and rippled, and seemed to tremble with a deep responsiveness that made him sway towards it. The hidden illumination of the sea bewitched him. Even the air seemed lighter and to wish to lift him up.

And while he stood there Death observed him. He possessed a short, muscular stature and his face was ugly, his thick dark lips hanging open loosely with a kind of stupid vacancy. Where his right eye had been, inquisitive flies probed the rawness of the socket. But the Lord of Death was not recruiting him for his looks, but for the strength of his intuitions.

How was he to go forward? was the question that held him. How might such a place as this be entered? How did one navigate upon it without rivers to navigate by? Where might one go if one did venture into it? It was just a feeling, but he was sure the wharf on which he stood could not be the end of his journey. There was more, he knew.

While he stood there, observed by Death, pondering the way forward, all around him exhausted travellers were lying down and dying. The sight of the sea seemed to convince *them* they had reached the end. Some walked into the waves with their children in their arms and didn't look right or left or alter their expressions as the water closed over their heads. They were glad the tortures of the journey were finished. They had, indeed, foreseen no other destination for themselves than death. They were content to know their bones would lie close to the soil in which the bones of their ancestors lay.

The port was Amoy and the date, according to the new calendar, was 1848. The Lord of Death assumed the disguise of a Western devil by the name of Captain Larkins, and in this manifestation she strolled over and stood next to the boy. Moored to the leeward side of the wharf was the Captain's ship, the *Nimrod*, which it was his intention to fill with a living cargo of recruits from the Middle Kingdom. It was a unique venture, for his contract was to supply the pastoralists of the British colony of New South Wales with indentured labour; a plan certain to have far-reaching consequences for everyone concerned.

Standing beside the boy the Captain gazed upon the sparkling swell. What do you see, young man? he enquired pleasantly.

I see the hide of a sleeping dragon, the awed boy answered without hesitation.

And what do you desire from the dragon?

I desire to be a rich man like you, sir.

That is an easy matter to put in order, replied the Captain. All you need do is to forsake the ways of the Middle Kingdom and sail with me and my crew on the good ship *Nimrod*, yonder, to the colony of New South Wales, and you shall never know poverty again.

The boy looked at the ship. So that is how it is done? he said, seeing the sailors readying the white sails. But will the dragon not object to carrying us on its back?

Indeed, the Captain said sadly, remembering the good friends he had lost at sea over the years, he may well object. But then again, he may bear us safely to our destination. No one can foretell the moods of the dragon. He turned to the boy, Will you take the risk of being devoured by the dragon and sail with us?

I am ready, the boy answered.

At this the Captain produced a form of indenture from one of the large side pockets of his blue jacket and he led the boy to the gangplank, where there stood a writing table with quills and ink laid out. First, the Captain said, we must have the permission of your parents.

I have no parents, the boy replied sourly.

No parents, Captain Larkins wrote neatly in the space on the form for 'parents' permission'. And what about ancestors? he enquired with silky good humor. Can a gentleman of the Middle Kingdom willingly forsake his ancestors, forever?

I have no ancestors either, the boy said, his good eye flashing with truculence and a note of contempt in his voice.

There's not much point in being Chinese if you've no ancestors, is there? the Captain observed sympathetically. You are better off being something else. *No ancestors*, he noted on the form, though there was in fact no official space for such a piece of information as this. No ancient deaths, at any rate, he said cheerfully, trailing along clinging to your shirt and holding you back. He smiled, You will find it an advantage in New South Wales. There is one further question. What is your name?

The Captain and the boy looked into each other's eyes.

There's no need for you to say it if it distresses you, the Captain was quick to offer, by this time sensitive to the boy's uneasiness with these questions of identity. There's nothing to be ashamed of where I come from in not having a name to call your own. There are plenty of people in New South Wales with new names. He opened his arms encouragingly and grinned, Don't be downcast! It's to be a new start. A vita nuova. The Italian poet first saw 'the glorious lady of his mind' at the age of ten. The auspices are with you. Jack's as good as his master there, you'll see.

The Captain became serious and considered him gravely. But we must be careful in this. A person's name is an important feature of their character. One is known by one's name. We can't call you Dante. Your nose isn't right. And a name has to be right. It won't stick if it's not right. It will come adrift when you are most in need of it and leave you wallowing in the doldrums while your more tenaciously named rivals progress. A good name is essential. Our bodies are buried in peace, but our names live forever. Is that not so? the Captain asked rhetorically, adjusting the text of the apocryphal Ecclesiasticus to the occasion, as if there were something of the liberty of a poet in him.

In order to signify the solemnity of the moment, he paused for a considerable time. To be renamed is to be reborn, he said at last. I shall call you Feng, the Phoenix. Is that not a fine name for one who is reborn?

Feng was moved by gratitude. He felt the name fall about his shoulders and clothe him with identity. He thanked the Captain and said he would never forget the gift.

Well, anyway, Larkins responded gruffly, not unmoved himself by the sincerity of the boy's thanks. A man who is going to be rich needs a name with a bit of mythology in it. And in the place on the form for the name of the indentured party he wrote, *Feng, the first of his line.*

Despite her ancient grip on her sons, China could not withstand the departure of Feng. He shed her as naturally as the awakening serpent sheds its former skin when it is touched by the warmth of the spring sunshine. He slipped silently away from her shores and did not look back, for he had left nothing behind. Ten thousand years of China's history had bequeathed him nothing. He had made his bargain. He held in his hand the twelve silver dollars that had been paid for his Chinese soul. He was no longer a man of the Middle Kingdom, but was a Western devil now, like the Captain on whose ship he had taken passage.

'Travel is a good thing; it stimulates the imagination. Everything else is a snare and a delusion.' So wrote the great French novelist and so it seemed to be to Feng and the other one hundred and nineteen indentured men and boys on the *Nimrod*; so it seemed also to Captain Larkins and to his sailors, as their ship feathered southward through transparent seas.

They rode high on the curving bosom of the swell, a small black ship skimming the outer membrane of an inward-plunging universe. Feng hung over the side and gazed with rapture into the crystal sphere that drifted beneath. And when he had forgotten the existence of land, and that there was to be a destination to this voyaging, in the middle of a starlit night, with no wind stirring the sails and the ship lifting and falling on the slumbering ocean, her copper-sheathed keel hanging suspended in the silvery light above six kilometres of clear tropical water, Feng started awake with the terrible pull of the deep within him. It was the voice of the dragon speaking. On the deck lay the sleeping figures of his companions. He heard their groans and pitied them, for he saw that he and they were merely human beings.

This should have been a warning to him of what was to come. But he soon forgot. Once the journey ended, it was as if it had never been.

.

At seven o'clock on the morning of 8 December 1848 the *Nimrod* docked at the Geelong wharf in the Port Phillip District of New South Wales, and Feng said goodbye to Captain Larkins. It was a fine summer day and the settlement looked cheerful and promising.

Feng was the first indentured man to step ashore. After a consideration had been exchanged with the Captain, an allowance being made for the missing eye, Feng's new master took him to his property, Ballarat Station, situated in the middle of this sheepman's paradise.

Feng cut off his cue and threw away his rag and, with his twelve silver dollars, he bought from his master's store a red woollen shirt, a pair of moleskin breeches, tan English boots and a broad-brimmed cabbage tree hat with a blue ribbon fluttering from its crown. And when he was got up in this outfit his master gave him an axe and a sugar bag of stores, and he sent him off with two dogs and four thousand sheep.

In an Arcadian grove on the edge of the plain, Feng found a likely spot and there, according to the fashion of the times, he camped while he felled a mighty redgum and built a one-roomed dwelling for himself from split slabs and bark. It was not many months into 1849 before he had become so accustomed to the uneventful routine of shepherding on the peaceful downs of Ballarat that Feng found it very difficult to recall the details of any other life. With his new name and his new clothes and his new country, he knew he ought to be content. A righteous man, he saw, might live well and decently in this society by the simple code of fallen Adam, a code he had been willing to adopt. Why then, he asked himself as he stood in the entrance to his hut one wintry morning as the sun was rising over the plain, should he feel this continuous niggling discontent? It wasn't even as if he was lonely. For he had made two firm friends, both shepherds and like himself in more than that.

Dorset, the younger of the two, rode a lively chestnut thoroughbred and wore a hunting pink riding coat, which had been fashioned for his shoulders by a tailor in London's Saville Row. His elegant breeches were made of velvety buckskin, and his boots had been stitched on his own last by Prince Albert's bootmaker. Though a shepherd by trade these days, Dorset was a fine gentleman to see. On his head he wore a black box hat and in his gloved hand he carried a plaited quirt.

Patrick Nunan, however, who hitched a ride on Dorset's horse, sitting double on the chestnut's rump with his long arms clamped around the red coat and his deeply recessed eyes twinkling with fear and amazement from within his wild orange hair and bushy beard, was not to be mistaken by anyone for a gentleman. Patrick was a man of the people.

In tandem on Dorset's horse, these two galloped over from their huts every Saturday night and sat at Feng's table on blocks of redgum and played euchre and talked of their ambitions and their dreams by the yellow light of a tallow wick until it was breaking day and time again to go shepherding.

Feng boiled a joint and baked fresh bread and built up the fire for the occasion, and Patrick regularly managed a half pint of rum. And on this liberality their discontents were dispelled and they grew gentle and gracious and generous with each other. At times, between the cards, they spoke of their pasts. Or Dorset did, for he liked to tell a story more than the others. He was fifteen years of age, he claimed, and had been taken from the side of his murdered mother at Broken Bay at the age of three on the twenty-second of June 1837, the very year her gracious majesty Victoria was crowned the Queen of England. And he would add to this, God bless her. As a curiosity from the ends of the earth, he was shipped to England that same year, where he lived in opulent splendour with a great and whimsical duke until he was fourteen and the duke died suddenly. The dead duke's son was not whimsical but determined to be a politician, and he shipped Dorset and his chestnut horse back to Australia. So here I am lads! He spoke English with the refined accents of an aristocrat and had been the intimate of many notable personages of London society.

As with Feng, Dorset possessed only one name. Which seemed to be a common condition among those who had become severed from their tribes. He sprang from a proud nation, he claimed, and quite as ancient as the Han. A nation whose unbroken filial piety and veneration of ancestors had never been surpassed, he asserted, for the elaborate purity of its pervading ritual. But I, too, my dearest Feng, have joined the devils, as you see. And am I not as free a man as you are yourself? Deny me that if you dare! I challenge you! But Feng declined the invitation, for he saw how Dorset cherished his freedom as dearly as his benighted brothers and sisters cherished their humbler places among the fast vanishing clans.

Patrick Nunan said less and listened more than Dorset. He was forty-two years of age. An old man, but no less free than Dorset for all that, according to his own sketchy account of it. He would say little more than that he had been born at Bertraghboy Bay on the rainswept Atlantic coast of Ireland. Though he did talk on occasions, it was often to himself. And frequently with a suddenness and a sharpness that disquieted his two friends. He had spent a good deal of his life as a solitary shepherd. And this, it appeared, had startled him into a kind of soothsaying for which he was not entirely responsible. One evening, with an unexpec-ted clarity that suggested another life way back beyond the shepherding, a life in his youth, he said, I have a daughter with the nuns in Melbourne. It was my dream to take her back to Ireland. There is something in my past, however, which is an impediment to this. I will not discuss it with you. After which, angrily flicking the cards face up onto the table one after the other, he relapsed into his mumbling predictions of disaster.

They communicated in a language of their own invention. They dug about in likely corners of Gaelic and Fukienese and English for this and that part of speech, and constructed a lingo comprehensible only to themselves. They waved their arms a good deal and grimaced elaborately whenever called upon to argue a fine point of philosophy or metaphysics, readily enlisting the aid of twigs and leaves and potato peelings and bits of wool, and whatever else came to hand, and arranging these in suggestive configurations on the table, the cards forgotten while they admired the eloquence of the illustration. Delicately one might reach forward and realign a twig a tiny, but significant, fraction. Which action was certain to draw either an exclamation of assent or disagreement from the others, and the argument would either rest there or flare again. They became masters of linguistic make-do, their discourse rose upon it as it was elaborated, and they enjoyed between themselves friendship and understanding and harmony.

Until the eighth of May 1850.

It was to be one of those days when certain lines of evolution in human affairs, lines hidden beneath the everyday and which have their origins in events aeons past, converge and collide. We are not speaking here of Armageddon, or even of Gettysburg or Waterloo (nor of even so modest a show as Bakery Hill) but of a brief shower of sparks and a little debris. Nothing for history books. Two men died, were killed, in fact, by other men; a few others seemed to understand something about themselves which they had not understood before, and one was deflected from his station toward a destiny greater than he might otherwise have supposed himself fitted for.

Monday the eighth of May 1850, then, on the pastoral holding of *Ballarat*, in the province of Port Phillip, in a society predicated upon the inseparable concepts of dispossession and punishment. The facts are important. The shaping spirit of the story is not my own.

Though there was no one there to witness it, the first sign appeared early that morning. The frost was on the grass when Patrick opened the hurdles and let out his flock. As he watched the sheep streaming across the paddock, an involuntary sooth-saying shout rose in his throat and he cried out. The Day of the Apparition of Saint Michael the Archangel! It was.

Winter had arrived early in the district. By noon the temperature had risen no more than two thin degrees above freezing, and a veil of high grey cloud had covered the sun. A south-westerly, bringing freezing air from the Antarctic oceans, had begun to blow across the plain. It was a day when everyone who could find an excuse for doing so remained indoors.

It was not possible to get out of the wind altogether, but Feng found some shelter from it among the thicket of wattles in the lee of a stony gully. He sent the dogs round the sheep and lit a fire and he wrapped himself in his cloak, a dismally inadequate garment he'd sewn together from sugar bags. The rising gale thrashed among the clacking sticks above his head, and flurries of sleety rain stung his cheeks and sent shivering spasms through to his bones. He lay on his side and curled up close to the fire, and he hugged himself and closed his eyes against the driven sparks and thought of his hut and his hearth and his friends.

The wind grew stronger as the day wore on, until it was moaning and howling through the gullies and shaking and rattling the wattle scrub, as if the earth were trying to shake something loose from its hide. Ash and smoke swirled around the sleeping form of Feng beside his fire. He groaned and his body twitched as dreams swept through him.

A tall, full-bearded Koorie warrior stepped out of the trees. He held his spears lightly, their shafts resting on the gravel. He examined the sleeping figure of the one-eyed boy from the Middle Kingdom wrapped in sugar bags. The Koorie did not stay long. As he turned to leave, his silvery-grey cloak of possum skins swirled out around him and was caught by the wind like a sail.

Slowly, Feng opened his eyes. He did not know where he was. He stared in puzzlement at the circle of cold white ash where his fire had been. A feeling he could not put a name to told him that while he'd slept the world had changed. On the far side of the remains of his fire, no more than a metre from him, there stood the iron-shod hooves of a horse. As he realised what he was looking at, the hooves stirred restlessly, shifting the little stones about. Feng raised his head.

A dozen horsemen were ranged around him, their coats snapping in the wind, their uneasy mounts tossing their heads and snorting and laying back their ears, frightened by the thing that moved on the ground before them.

Amazed by their presence, Feng examined his audience. He knew every one of them. Each of them, he saw, carried a rifle. Two wore sabres and another had a coiled rope fastened by a thong of redhide to a D on his saddle. In the first seconds of waking, as he lay on the ground with his head raised a little, Feng noticed something else about the group of horsemen, something which sent a quiver of deeper alarm through him. He noticed that each of them was either a landowner or the son of a landowner. All of them had cheerfully passed the time of day with him on occasion. Some had enjoyed the hospitality of his hut. On meeting him, every one of them had been accustomed to greet him in a friendly manner and to offer him their trust. He saw now that this group of men had become strangers to him. He saw, by the manner in which they were regarding him, that they no longer knew him nor trusted him.

The world *had* changed. He had understood at the moment of waking that he was no longer in the place where he had gone to sleep. And he had understood, also, that there could be no regaining that former place. He knew there could be no going back to it. He had closed his eyes and a catalyst had been slipped into the mix of their new society and had caused this group of men to separate out and to form a single body united by a common identity and a common purpose. While he'd slept something had awoken in these mounted men the knowledge that they were of the same tribe. Some event had threatened their species and had stirred within them the latent memory of ancestral bonds, and, in becoming the familiars of each other, they had become strangers to him. Feng knew all this at the moment of his awakening. He knew it intuitively.

The master of Ballarat Station touched the trembling flanks of his horse with his spurs and the unnerved beast stepped forward smartly, striking the white ash into Feng's face. The man leaned from his saddle and looked down at his shepherd – the wind seemed to hold its breath – and he asked in a low and intent voice, articulating each syllable with great care, Where is Dorset?

And as he asked his question the others in the circle leaned forward in unison to hear the reply, as if this were a dance which they had rehearsed, a familiar rite requiring from them particular responses. They eased themselves forward, the leather of their saddles creaking, their eyes fixed upon the crouching shepherd on the ground, the shepherd who had become a stranger, his ashen features those of a clown, a familiar made strange, a creature – though scarcely a fellow-creature now – who had been transformed and rendered anonymous by the white ash and whose body had been concealed within the dun hessian cloak, so that he resembled more a sheep than a shepherd. The demon of the land made visible. No more the cheerful and reliable Feng, the amiable one-eyed boy, but an alien in their midst. As if for them his truer form had been revealed by this disguise.

Feng got unsteadily to his feet, unsure of what he might expect, and rubbed the ash from his good eye. In his make-do patois he told his master as best he could that apart from the dreadful wind it had been a normal day so far and that Dorset was almost certain to be found tending his flock.

No thanks were offered for this information, but they looked at each other with questions in their eyes then wheeled their mounts and crashed away through the sticks.

When they had gone Feng called his dogs and sent them to gather the mob, and he drove the sheep back to the hurdles and shut them up. His master had lingered a moment to instruct him urgently, Until we take the murderer, life and property cannot be considered safe.

Confident in their ignorance that an innate, a primitive, if not indeed a savage, faculty had survived his long exposure to London society, the corps of mounted landholders sought out Dorset and asked him to track the killer for them. Dorset firmed his black box hat upon his head and steadied his nervous thoroughbred with a gentle hand and replied at once, To be sure gentlemen. Anything to oblige ye. And in his hunting pink he led them for three days through the thickest coverts of scrub and up and down the steepest and stoniest gullies. For is it not, he proposed to himself in the absence of any personal knowledge of such matters as these, to such unhallowed places that desperate fugitives will resort when pressed?

But all to no avail. He was dismayed but not downcast by this result. Indeed the unseemliness of his persistently cheerful manner was the cause of some resentment among the serious men he led. With frequent pauses to stare in puzzlement at some mark on the ground, and murmuring about a damned devious fellow, he did his best. But it was not good enough. The truth was, he could not read the land. The signs among the leaf litter meant nothing to him. Indeed he did not even discern them. Like the white devils who followed closely at the heels of his horse, Dorset saw on the ground only fallen twigs and bark and leaves and shaley outcroppings of rock and such like. He had diverted the fashionable salons of Regents Park with the pathos of his readings from Racine's great tragedy *Andromaque*, but in the text of his motherland he was illiterate. He had lost his link with her. He was a free man.

He did not fail to find the culprit because he was unwilling to find him. On the contrary, he desired fervently to demonstrate that he was as free a devil as any man present, that he was a colonist of no uncertain loyalty, that he was a founding member, no less (if not quite a founding father), of their new society. For he understood that it was a society which was to depend for its cohesion not upon ancestral bonds, but upon the principle that all persons are born free and equal before God, that he or she enters the world unblemished, that each, indeed, bears his or her own vita nuova inscribed for life upon the quality of their particular demeanour. He understood that the essence of freedom is in dislocation from one's origins, that freedom is to be judged for oneself and not for one's tribe. He understood that freedom is identity for the individual. And, as he rode about the place in his futile search for the murderer, he did not expect this to change suddenly.

He would gladly have snatched the shivering culprit from behind a bush and presented him by the scruff of the neck to the glowering potentates who rode behind him. Here he is, gentlemen. Your murderer. A rabbit from my hat. How's that for black magic? Do with him as you will. Hang him! For Dorset identified his own interests with theirs and believed in British justice as unreservedly as any Port Phillip gentleman. Indeed he considered himself elevated from barbarism by it and protected from arbitrary violence by its vaunted impartiality.

The fourth day of the hunt dawned to a steely sky. The landholders and their sons woke cold and dispirited and aggrieved. Three nights camped in the low scrubby forest, which flourished on the outcroppings of quartzose sandstone south of the main station, without either adequate cover or decent food, and with not a sign yet to indicate that they were a yard closer to their quarry than they had been on the day they set out, had brought them to a vengeful state of mind.

An elder son squatting beside the fire and observing Dorset saddling the chestnut thoroughbred was the first to voice a certain opinion. Turning to Feng's master, their acknowledged leader, and indicating Dorset by pointing at him, so that no one might mistake his meaning, this young man enquired in a voice loud enough for everyone to hear, Cannot you see the plain truth of this matter, sir?

Though he understood it, and even harboured some sympathy for it in the privacy of his own mind, the master of Ballarat was disinclined to be moved as yet in his opinion on the point that was being made. Let us mount up and follow Dorset, he said, tossing a stick on to the fire and turning away from his youthful interlocutor. So that is what they did, for a fourth day. They straggled along unwillingly, an increasingly mutinous group of men, a little behind Dorset's red coat, which a man was heard to observe was surely a kind of costumed mockery on such a one as the black tracker.

By the time the evening drew on and the hunt was abandoned for the night no further advanced than it had been that morning, the elder son, who had voiced his opinion at the beginning of the day, had drawn around himself a band of followers. With him at their head these young men rode up to Feng's master in a close body and voiced their grievance, respectful still but insistent. We are mocked, sir, and must settle this matter. It cannot be allowed to proceed for another day.

Hearing the complaint, others joined them, a few to listen, more to murmur their agreement.

They were deeply tired. They were hungry. They were saddened and angered and, to a degree, as settlers they were demoralised by the brutal murder of their confrère and by their seeming impotence to avenge the crime. They were beleagered and were not in a state of mind that lent itself to cool judgements. And so they made a mistake; a true error of judgement. For they judged Dorset not as a man like themselves, not as a free man, but as the son of his ancestors. They had not understood that Dorset, the individual, was unable to read the text of the landscape of his forebears. They believed in his innate ability to read it. And they concluded, therefore, that he was misleading them. That he was, in fact, leading them through the hills and mocking them in their ignorance of such things – they were content to admit to the possession of no such innateness as his for themselves.

They knew, in a general way, that Dorset's Australian country-men held to the belief that the land is pervaded by good and evil spirits who can be influenced and controlled by select persons among the clans. And believing this of his countrymen, they believed it also of Dorset. He was the land's familiar and they were interlopers. He was playing with them. He was subverting the legitimacy of their grip on the land. It was a point upon which they were particularly sensitive. They 'read' allusions to their act of dispossession everywhere, for they more than half-expected retribution to sweep them from their hold on the country yet.

The poor quality of their judgement concerning Dorset's relation to his ancestors, based as it was on an assumption of innate differences and on guilt and a certain superstitious fear of losing what they had gained by illicit means, misled them. It offered them uncertainty and fed their paranoia, and it made them draw more closely together to find comfort and support in each other.

And in doing this they forfeited their freedom to make judgements as individuals and they became a tribe themselves, bound by a common ancestral imperative. The transformation had begun four days ago. Feng had witnessed it when, as one, they had leaned from their saddles to inspect him.

It was growing dark among the trees, but still none of them dismounted or looked to prepare a camp. They were gathered in a clearing among the low scrubby woodland at a point where two gullies ran together. The prospect faced them of a supperless night, for they had used the last of their provisions that morning.

Dorset alone had dismounted. Handing the reins of his thoroughbred to the son of a landholder, he had walked a little way up the right-hand gully and had gone in among the open timber. As he went on he looked left and right, now bending to pick up a likely stone and weigh it in the palm of his hand, now moving on a pace or two before squatting to brush thoughtfully at the ground litter with his fingers, the pale doeskin glove held in his other hand.

The close-knit rank of mounted men observed his progress. Their weary horses spoke for them, blowing and shifting bruised hooves on the stony ground. Then a man's voice broke the uneasy hush. In the gathering darkness it was not possible to identify the speaker. With the tone of one who believes himself robbed, the voice said, He does not lead us to the murderer because he is in league with him. There followed a little rustling. Then the voice went on, Or he is the murderer himself.

After this the silence between them went much deeper. Something in the men subsided at these words. An unstable level within them, which had resisted until this moment, collapsed and sent a tremor through them. They drew into themselves. They shrugged their coats more closely around their shoulders and, becoming heavier and more anonymous, sat lower in their saddles.

Slowly the silence deepened, until each man knew his thoughts were overheard by the others.

In the rapidly failing light Dorset's red coat moved about ahead of them among the trees like a target. The red coat of the fox, it might have been. The dismounted huntsman himself become the hunt's quarry. The red coat focused the attention of the mounted men. It was all they could distinguish in the gloom. They saw nothing else.

As they watched, the silence settled within them onerously,

became horizontal and colder, reducing them to a simpler stratum, embedding them into a single mass, as if they had been a bank of fog forming in the cooling air at the junction of the unnamed gullies, fog in the stillness hanging between the darker earth and the lighter sky. *They* were simplified. Their elementary notion of Dorset as the quarry reducing them to its own elementary level and beginning to direct them towards a mode of action which, as free men, each one of them would have condemned as arbitrary and barbarous.

Not more than thirty metres from the rank of horsemen the true quarry observed the scene. The Koorie warrior in his silver-grey possum cloak was invisible to them, however. He wasn't a spirit. He was real enough. A solid, physical man standing among the trees. He was not invisible to them because he was insubstantial but because the horsemen were not looking for him. They did not know how to look for him. If he had moved, a horse might have detected the movement out of the corner of its vision and reacted. But even so, there were other movements in the bush which the men discounted. Parrots walked about above their heads on the branches of the trees and were not interpreted by them.

Without making a particular effort to conceal his presence from them once he had concluded that they could not possibly be looking for him, and curious to know the actual nature of their purpose, the Koorie had visited the meandering party of horsemen a number of times during the past four days. He observed them now with a quickened interest. He was their audience. Though they would never acknowledge it, he was the only theatre of their history. They might have sensed him, but that is all, as an eerie kind of absence.

Dorset was returning through the trees, coming down the gully whistling and slapping his quirt against his boot in time with the tune. He was wondering what to suggest next. When he reached the place where the two dry courses met he stopped abruptly and strained to see what it was that had alarmed him. Something had made him pause. He had sensed a movement towards him through the darkness. He stood still, undecided, his quirt poised, his lips pursed, the rhythm of his song interrupted.

Well gentlemen, the villain has left no sign here for us to follow, he called into the night, his educated English accents too thin, however, too high and too refined, the cadence of his speech too uncertain, to impose itself upon the dark bush with conviction. His words remained with him. They went nowhere. They died in the weighty silence. He sensed the mass that moved upon him and his skin prickled with fear.

Feng was cooking a shoulder of mutton in the pot above his hearth. It was Saturday again. The mutton was for their supper after the cards. He had seen no one and had therefore heard no news since the previous Monday, the day on which he had woken to find the world changed and himself confronted by the group of horsemen, the day on which he had risen from the ashes of his fire to answer the inquisition of the landholders.

As a wife whose husband has gone into battle waits for confirmation of the dread within her, Feng went on behaving as if nothing had changed. But an expectant space had opened around him. It waited to be named.

The dogs were barking. He finished peeling an onion and dropped it into the pot with the simmering mutton, and he crumbled in a good measure of salt before going to the door to see who was coming.

It was Patrick. He was on foot. When he saw Feng at the door, Patrick waved his arms and broke into a run. Feng went down the track to meet his friend. He did not hurry. Patrick was out of breath. His long orange hair and straggles of his beard were wetted to his neck and brow. A grey slick glinted in the corners of his cracked lips. He clutched Feng's coat. His eyes were dark with dismay. They've done for him laddie, he gasped.

They reached the junction of the two dry gullies in less than an hour. The place was still and quiet and pervaded by an eerie kind of presence. The heavy green parrots walked back and forth along the horizontal branches of the gums, cracking seed cases. Ants had pioneered roads across Dorset's red coat.

Feng saw his friend lying on his face in the stony bed of the dry watercourse and in his mind a stricken voice, which he did not recognise as his own, cried out, Dorset, this cannot be! He went to his friend and would have embraced him and raised him back to storytelling and to whistling and would have told him of the shoulder simmering on the fire for later. But it was two days on and the black corpse was bursting from the seams of its garments and was no longer Dorset.

Feng sat on a fallen log in the bed of the gully and wept. He knew now that when the world had changed, heaven had become hell. Patrick cradled him in his arms, as if he were his child, holding Feng's small body tightly against his own broad chest. He promised, by the Holy Mother of God, that he would not rest until he had brought upon the potentates a terrible vengeance for this crime.

But this was not Patrick's first loss. And even as he uttered it he knew his promise was a kind of rhetoric and that the meaning of his words did not lie in violent reaction against the landholders who had murdered Dorset. To kill one of *them*, he knew, would only increase their numbers. He understood the social nature of the fracture line which separated himself and Feng from the potentates. He had seen the like of it before and knew that individuals cannot be brought to account for such phenomena as these.

They went to Patrick's hut, the closer of the two, and fetched a mattock and a spade. They took turns to break the ground, while the other stood by to shovel out the meagre spoil. It was hard going. There was no topsoil. The ground was dry and tight and would not yield, but bounced the mattock back at them, jarring the muscles of their arms and shoulders. This ground had never been broken into. The ring of the iron mattock striking the stones and the dry scrape of the spade filled the clearing all day.

What have you found? Feng asked, leaning forward to better see the object which Patrick had picked up from the bottom of Dorset's half-dug grave.

Patrick crossed himself. Mother of God! he breathed, awed and gazing in wonderment at the thing in the palm of his hand. It is gold! A lump of purest native gold!

Feng reached for the nugget and took it in his hand. The weight of it was unexpected. It pressed upon his palm with a softness in its touch that tugged at him. As if it were the touch of a woman, arousing in him a desire more potent than any he had known before. The gold took him and woke his senses. He did not take the gold. His grief parted, as if grief were a curtain to conceal a vision, a memory, it might have been, a luminous reality beyond the everyday, and he saw his city, Amoy, transformed. And there on the wharf himself and Captain Larkins – as if every moment that has ever been is preserved and continues to exist somewhere, enriched by subsequent events. What do you desire from the dragon? the gilded Captain asked once more.

Perceiving the mesmerised expression on Feng's face, Patrick leaned over and delicately retrieved the nugget from him. We shall be rich men, laddie, he said, pocketing the gold and resuming his mattocking with a renewed will. It is the good Lord himself who has placed this wealth before us so that poor men may yet have the power to see justice. The rhetoric of Patrick's vengeance was perfected in the gold.

In the days and weeks that followed they tried the ground all round the lonely spot where Dorset lay, but they could not find a place to put him. Wherever they opened the earth they discovered gold. Dorset's motherland resisted his interment. She refused to take him back. There was to be no reconciliation between them. She offered the inducement of her gold rather than receive him to her bosom. He had declared himself free and free he would remain.

Meanwhile, he rotted. They could no longer consider moving him in one piece. We'll let him down where he is, Patrick decided aloud. But they found gold under him too, glowing with the fierce yellow eyes of a wild creature, not more than a handspan beneath their mate. Patrick declared that the bush, with its parrots and its sheep and its mysterious feeling of absence, was volunteering itself at last as a prospect for the serious concerns of civilisation.

.

The winter went by and the spring came on, and still no solution was found to 'the problem' of Dorset, as they soon came to refer to the shabby remains of their friend. By now the junction of the two gullies was knobby with heaps of mullock for acres around, as if the continent here had been provoked to a terrible case of boils. And all the while the little hessian bags of nuggets were added to daily under the hearths of Feng's and Patrick's huts.

On each occasion that they struck into the ground afresh, the question hovered over Feng and Patrick as to whether they were still looking for a place to decently dispose of the corpse of their murdered friend, or whether they were simply digging for gold. Dorset was there as a daily reminder of himself, but little by little his red coat became not so much *him* as a memento for them of a less serious time than the present.

And anyway, he got so dried up and eaten into and fallen apart and dragged this way and that by the wild dogs that it was no longer possible to see a direct resemblance to their mate in the remains. To save what was left of it from an absolute dissolution Feng hung the red coat in the fork of a stringybark one morning. The natural solution had presented itself.

If we cannot let him down then we shall set him up, Patrick declared, retrieving Dorset's skull from the bed of the gully nearby and placing it on top of the coat. There! They stood back and admired the memorial. We'll make it official then, Patrick said. And they clasped hands and swore an oath of eternal mateship on the matter. And so the lonely unnamed space where the gullies met became a place, Dorset's Gully, to which memories might be firmly attached and future references made as to the occurrence of certain facts of history.

Feng and Patrick grew so accustomed to working under the heraldic banner of the red coat and the bleached skull – propped in the fork of the stringybark for the parrots to puzzle over, as if this challenging totem guarded the pockmarked landscape – that it became the preservation of Dorset, rather than his disposal, which grew to be the source of their new anxiety. The ritual objects of skull and cope assumed a sacred and precious quality for them. Indeed, it seemed to Feng and

Patrick that good fortune might very well depend upon them.

The friends neglected their shepherding as much as they dared and enjoyed fifteen months winning gold undetected from the rich alluvial gravels of Dorset's Gully. Then, in August 1851, John Dunlop and James Regan's find in the White Horse Range nearby was reported in the *Geelong Advertiser*. The biggest gold rush in the history of the world descended upon Ballarat Station, in what had ceased to be the sheepman's paradisial province of Port Phillip, in the meantime – indeed on the first of July – and which had become the colony of Victoria. It was not many days before the aptly named Commissioner Armstrong rode up to the camp at Dorset's Gully at the head of his squad of black troopers and demanded to see Patrick's and Feng's licences to dig. The friends agreed the time had come to lift their treasure from their hearths and quit the district.

When the last moment came, it was Feng who voiced their dilemma. We cannot abandon him here, he said, and he fetched Dorset's skull from the fork of the tree, where wind and rain and the scouring brilliance of the summer sunlight had burnished the bone to a pearly gloss, and from the rotted coat he took the six gilt buttons and carried these relics in a sugar bag to his hut, where he transferred them to the more seemly container of an empty tea box from Ceylon.

Wherever Feng ventured during his life after this, on his journeyings to and from the Southern and Northern hemispheres, he kept the skull and the six gilt buttons from Dorset's coat close beside him. He guarded these objects so carefully and so possessively, indeed, that his motive for guarding them was taken, by those he most trusted, to be a superstitious dread of losing them, a dread, indeed, of the power these objects must possess to direct his destiny. It was rumoured the box contained the skull of Feng's first, his earliest known and aboriginal, ancestor. Feng's true and secret quest in life, it was often claimed by certain of these lieutenants, was to find a place where he might at last inter this bone and erect a fixed shrine to his displaced forbear.

Those of a more cynical turn of mind were inclined merely to observe that, as death was the daily companion of his affairs, the merchant of the living cargo could scarcely have carried a more fitting badge of office than the death's head.

The blind storyteller hawked and spat confidently, missing the spittoon by a metre or more. He banged his cup on the table beside him and shouted imperiously for tea.

Huang woke and stared about him in terror, certain his house was being overrun by Feng's bandits from Shanghai.

In the quiet that followed the storyteller's forthright request for tea, Lang listened to his mother whispering with Yu behind the blue screen. He strained to hear what they were saying. That she had chosen to remain invisible during the telling of the story had distressed and angered him. He felt both afraid and betrayed. For she had knowingly withdrawn the reassurance of her presence from him just when he was to be most in need of it. He was too scared, however, of what had been implied to attempt to interpret just yet the full meaning of her unprecedented action.

He feared, indeed, that she had judged him to be entirely of his great-grandfather's party. Had she not begun to see him as just such a fearful hybrid? During the telling of the story, that is how he had seen himself. During the telling of the story he had *been* his great-grandfather, the first Feng, the friend of the inept black tracker and the ape-faced Irishman. It was as if his great-grandfather's past now resided within his own memory. The skull and the buttons, to be sure, were not a book and a mirror, but they replaced too neatly those ritual objects that he had destroyed to be viewed by him as anything but their intended parallels.

Lang knew himself to have been accused. History had been made to accuse him. It might be possible to fish about in the mud at the bottom of the Qiantang River for the cosmic mirror and, with luck and perseverance, to recover it. But the book was gone forever. Things can return unchanged through water but they cannot return unchanged through fire. Fire transforms everything. His guilt could never be purged by returning what he had stolen. The unravelling of his own destiny, he had been warned, was to lie with the fiction of the skull.

·

He did not dare to look directly at the blind man, who he knew saw everything. Who he now knew had watched him tear Huang T'ing-chien's ancient poem from the book and feed it to the flames beside the clacking bamboo forest, just as he had watched Feng rise from the ashes of *his* fire in the shelter of the wattles on Ballarat Station. *To what can we liken human life? Perhaps to a wild swan's footprints on mud or snow.* He would never forget Huang T'ing-chien's question. He wanted to look at the blind man, but instead he looked at his grandfather, whose features were wild and staring and dishevelled, as if his worst old nightmares were about to break cover and play their demonic scenes across the surface of his polished skin.

Lang feared the magic arts of the storyteller, and secretly he envied him his possession of them. What he feared and envied was the blind man's ability to dwell at will within the past and to rearrange it – *as if every moment that has ever been continues to exist somewhere, enriched by subsequent events.* He dreaded the consequences of the storyteller's ability to recover and to reconsider those moments, to offer them up as judgements. What do *I* desire from the dragon? he had asked himself during the story. And to this question he had replied, with a singular passion, I desire to possess the storyteller's magic arts myself!

While he drank his tea the blind man kept a curtain drawn across the past. There was no way to see through it. Lang stole a glance at him. A power greater than memory sat smugly behind the face, which shone in the lamplight, the waxed and painted features of a demon in the temple, blindness a shuttered casement preventing those outside from seeing in, blindness a transfiguring cloak, an attribute of the gods, draping his being, a woodenness and a stillness in him like a presence. He was elsewhere. He was absent. He was not with them in the study. He did not see what they saw.

How to invoke his powers? How to pull aside the curtain without his help? Where was the key, the sign, Lang asked himself, that he must learn to read? Or was he to be forever like Dorset, illiterate in the language of what has befallen? Feng might have urged him to aspire to a reading at once. Feng, indeed, might have been his only friend, his alter ego, and have urged him to recast the past for all their sakes. The lieutenant of the Lord of Death in the unimaginable Australian bush. The traveller eternally setting out and returning. The lost Phoenix in the darkness of Hell clutching the skull and the coat buttons of his lost friend! Lang juggled the images, willing them to fall into a revealing configuration like the sticks and potato peelings on Feng's table, longing for them to *become* an ideograph, to form a word. But they remained apart, detached, incomprehensible and disconnected. Bits and pieces lacking the linking threads of structure. He could see no further down the track of the story. To enter those indeterminate places, those revealing boundaries between definite locations, which invited his enquiry, was it not enough? What prevented him from seeing as the blind man saw?

A warm night wind gusted through the open casements, lifting the silks and filling the hushed room with a troubled whispering. The old scholar gripped the arms of his chair and called shrilly for Yu to close the casements, his voice thin with panic and enfeeblement.

Lang observed him with a mixture of bewilderment and sadness and disgust. No sooner had the study been closed up than the air began to stink. It was old men and death and the lamp oil and the stench of the unwashed storyteller. Lang watched Yu assist Huang to his feet and together fumble their way unsteadily to the cupboard below the bookshelves.

He watched the old man approach the empty secret compartment, and he felt the massive wound he had inflicted on Huang. The emptiness. The absence of vitality. A literary painter no longer. The struggle now to keep breath in the body.

Cursing Yu and whining with irritation, Huang at last found what he was looking for. In his right hand he clutched a hornbill phial no larger than his thumb. He waited, impatient and fragile, bracing himself against his writing table, while Yu fetched a bowl and filled it with steaming water. The little phial lay in the palm of his trembling hand, translucent in the lamplight, the soft colour of amber, a shape with shoulders and a rounded cap, a glowing figurine; not something from this world, but a relic from another world. A votive offering recovered from a tomb in a remote province, sited there undisturbed for five thousand years in the darkness, lying with the bones among carefully crafted effigies of owls and frogs and lions and phoenixes, among jars and dishes and ceramic vessels incised with mysterious figured signs that pleaded with the powers beyond the grave.

Lang watched Huang unstopper the phial and pour three drops into the bowl. The air in the study was cleansed in a moment with the spring perfume of jasmine blossom. He remembered the honeyeater that had swung from the vine and had screeched at them and flown away that summer evening, its flight direct and dismissive across the garden, and he thought, with astonishment at his own audacity, perhaps we are ourselves those powers beyond the grave, the gods and the demons, to whom the pleas of the ancients were addressed?

All civilised people know there is Heaven and there is Hell and that harmony rules in Heaven and discord rules in Hell, the storyteller shouted.

They looked at him. He directed his gaze to a point above their heads among the shadows in the high corner of the study, and he waited. When he had assured himself of their attention, softly he drew aside the curtain . . .

The *Nimrod* stood at anchor off Williamstown among more than forty ships of sail and steam in Hobson's Bay. Captain Larkins stepped into the waiting cutter and was rowed ashore. As the little boat drew near the busy strand he was gratified to recognise Feng and two companions waiting for him among the crowd. It was no surprise to the Captain to see Feng transformed from a wretched indentured coolie into a gentleman of means, for he carried with him a letter in the side pocket of his blue jacket in which the circumstances of this feat were neatly recounted in all their details.

It took a few minutes for the sailors to pull to the shore. The Captain used his opportunity to study the group that waited for him. Feng, the shortest of the three by a half-head, stood between his tall companions. He wore a black frock coat and high collar with a large scarf-necktie and a tall top hat. On his left stood a more modestly dressed man of middle-age. All that was visible of this person's features beneath his low-crowned wide-brimmed hat was the spiky rosette of a startlingly orange beard.

A more interesting figure for the Captain stood on Feng's right. This was a young woman. She kept still and erect and straight and seemed to wait for his arrival with an intention and a purpose. She was so concentrated, indeed, she must have been impatient to draw him on to the shore. She was dressed in a handsome riding habit of a deep black-green. It was of a rich material and cut in the very latest fashion, the single-breasted jacket tight-fitting and forming a basque with its skirts. The jacket was trimmed with a profusion of metallic buttons and the open cuffs showed off the pearly cambric sleeves of the habit-shirt beneath. In her right hand she carried an American quirt with a braided lash about two feet long. With her left hand she alternately gripped and released the shank of this item in time with the strokes of the oarsmen. The Captain perceived in her a quality that he thought military and impatient. That young woman has an eagerness, he observed to himself, to get on with this matter without delay.

Having spent most of his life out of the company of women, the Captain did not consider himself to be a great judge of women's temperaments from first appearances. As with horses, in whose company he had likewise spent very little of his time, he generally considered a closer acquaintance to be necessary before judgements might fairly be made. On this occasion, however, he felt that his impression of the young woman who stood beside Feng was not due merely to her attire. To be sure, he cautioned himself, she could not have projected such a vision of herself to him across the space of twenty or more yards of water if she had been dressed in the limp look of mantled cope and Quaker bonnet, as were the other women who passed along the strand on the arms of their companions, or, even more slopingly, a pace behind parents.

He held himself most properly as the cutter neared the shore, sensing he was to be questioned by her and perhaps tested in his views and opinions by her on the cause of their common interest and, more particularly, assessed as to his fitness for what lay ahead. He felt himself, indeed, to be mistrusted by her on principle. It made him nervous to have her gaze fixed so unflinchingly on him. She must be certain to find some thing amiss. He looked elsewhere.

On the roadway behind the group an open step-piece barouche waited. The groom, who stood beside this well-proportioned and functional vehicle, held the reins of a saddled bay gelding, whose polished coat gleamed a deep red-gold in the sunlight. The attention of this watchful animal was fixed upon the young woman, its fine head turned in her direction, its ears pricked forward at the full alert, its forelegs stiff and straight. Beneath its belly in the shade sat a heavy bloodhound, its coat the colour of fresh liver.

The unwavering attention of the group on shore impressed the Captain considerably. They seemed to place great importance upon his arrival.

It was Miss Nunan, Feng confessed to the Captain when the introductions were being made, who acted as my scribe in the matter of the letter. She placed her gloved hand on Feng's sleeve and pressed his arm and she smiled a little inward smile, giving the Captain to understand that she had appointed herself Feng's protector.

Mr Feng has promised me he will learn to read and to write during his voyage with you to China, Captain Larkins. She looked directly into the Captain's eyes, as if she searched for a thought in him which might wish to conceal its presence from her. Perhaps she detected it, perhaps she did not. At any rate she made a sound denoting her satisfaction and continued. You must see to it that he keeps his promise. Indeed, Captain, you must be his tutor yourself.

Captain Larkins felt it was necessary to bow. I shall be honoured ma'am, he said, accepting both her commission and her ascendancy.

It seemed appropriate to everyone that he had used a form of address usually reserved for married women to someone as young – she was not yet twenty – and as obviously un-married as Patrick's daughter. For it was clear that she was the mistress of her father's affairs already and hoped soon to be entirely the mistress of Feng's affairs also. No one disputed, by an action or a word, that it was she with whom the Captain should consider himself to be dealing.

In the evening the four of them dined together in the private dining room of the newly built *Nunan Family Hotel* in Swanston Street, in the heart of the growing metropolis of Melbourne. In the lamplight, among the gleaming silver and polished glass, Feng seemed a boy beside her, the heavy baluster of his wineglass too large for his hand. The Phoenix Cooperative Society of Victoria, they chorused, raising their glasses and drinking deeply of the rich red claret. The bloodhound by the door raised his head and growled and fixed his sorrowful bloodshot eyes upon them.

After the toast Patrick rose and embraced Feng, clasping his friend firmly to his chest. God go with you laddie! he whispered hoarsely, exhaling a hot and reeking breath of pipe tobacco and wine fumes on to the back of Feng's neck.

Miss Nunan said it was time for a solemn presentation. She left the room briefly and returned carrying the tea box, which was decently clad in a purple drawstring bag that she had sewn herself. Feng was moved and rose to thank her. When he'd said his piece he raised his glass and looked at each of them in turn, his left hand firmly upon the purple-shrouded box. Dorset! he proposed, with a sudden excess of emotion, as an officer at the table of the Governor might have proposed to his exiled compatriots, 'The Queen!' They raised their glasses and repeated after him, Dorset!

When the *Nimrod* sailed into the Formosa Strait, two days before she reached the entrance to Huetan Bay, Feng detected the stench of Amoy carried on the warm wind from the land. The ancient smell of China came out to greet him. It recalled to his mind not his childhood, but the boiling down of old ewes for tallow on Ballarat. The smell settled heavily on him and on the crew. And as the ship sailed more deeply into it and it became thicker and more pasted to the back of their throats, the sailors became quieter and more thoughtful than they had been when they were on the open sea. It was as if the slumbering giant of China was breathing upon them. They feared to wake her, in case she should destroy them by one of the hideous and sudden means she had long reserved for the destruction of foreign devils.

In the port Feng saw that nothing here had changed. It was he who had changed. He stood at the rail and watched the throng of workers struggling past under their huge loads, silently suffering the blows and the abuse of their masters. And he looked down on the diseased and the dying and the silent dead. And he saw the stately mandarins in their brilliant gowns go by. And he smiled and was reassured. Here was the teeming shoal he had promised his partners they might drop their nets into with no risk to their capital, and from which, at little cost to themselves, they might draw a large fortune in steady increments.

Runners were despatched throughout the city and to the mainland to inform the people that a once-in-a-lifetime opportunity to improve their family's fortunes was to be offered at noon the following day by a wealthy merchant from the Colony of Victoria, so-named in honour of her gracious Britannic Majesty the Queen Empress.

A little before noon the following day Feng peeked through a porthole in the Captain's cabin and saw that several thousand mistrustful peasants were assembled on the wharf, their attention resentfully concentrated on the *Nimrod.* He understood intuitively that they had come not because they really believed they were to be offered a chance to improve their fortunes, but from a desperate conviction, a kind of superstitious dread, that if they did *not* come then, against all the odds of an eternally hostile universe, his offer would turn out to have been the one genuine philanthropic offer to be made to their caste in more than five thousand years. For others there was the inescapable parallel of Feng's arrival with that of Zheng Chenggong, the pirate's son who had returned from over the seas to lead the revolt against the Manchus from Amoy two hundred years earlier.

For one reason or the other, Feng's summons could not be ignored. The catch was, of course, that *having* attended they felt even more convinced than ever that it was to be just another hoax and that they were once again simply to be used to further the ambitions of a pirate or a warlord.

So even before they set eyes on Feng many of them had privately decided that a reasonable outcome to the day would be to see him cut down. They hated him on principle. Working simply to pay taxes imposed on their family's meagre holdings for the next generation, and miserably certain in their hearts that their desperate need had once again rendered them vulnerable to the deceitful blandishments of the mighty, they consoled themselves with the rationalisation that their real reason for answering Feng's call had been not a naive hope of some improvement, but a desire to witness first-hand (with any luck) the assassination of a wealthy man.

As the noon bell struck, flanked by Captain Larkins and followed by the ship's mate, who carried a naked cutlass and led a detachment of six sailors, each armed with a smoking musket, Feng staggered on to the foredeck of the *Nimrod.* He was dressed in his elegant frock coat and shiny top hat. The reason he staggered was that he was clutching a weighty object to his breast, as if it were a new-born child composed of lead.

As Feng came before them at the rail the crowd saw what it had expected to see. It saw, on the high deck of the foreign ship, a short (indeed a foreshortened) Western devil of extraordinary ugliness, a man not much taller than a dwarf with half-Chinese and half-Western features and a sinister black patch over his right eye. The peasants saw the corsair and freebooter they had been expecting to see and they began to jeer and to heckle and to toss cabbage stalks and other handy refuse on to the deck of the *Nimrod.*

With an effort that made him grunt, Feng hoisted the great *Dorset Nugget* above his head. The midday sun shone on the polished gold and an anguished sigh swept the crowd. It swayed like a field of Wimmera rye struck by the first gust of an approaching storm. Feng felt the power concentrated in his hands, as if he held aloft the molten sun itself, and a spontaneous shout rose in his throat and burst from his lips. Gold! he bellowed, prophesying.

Then he began to explain himself. In the hills of Ballarat, he shouted, there is enough gold for every one of you to pay his taxes for a generation and to dress his family in the gorgeous style of the mandarins. *The Phoenix Society*, which I represent, is willing to extend a line of credit for the cost of passage to Australia to any would-be gold seeker who is prepared in return to pledge to the *Society* his family holdings in Amoy and Fukien. At this stage we have only the one ship, so places can be guaranteed to no more than the first hundred and twenty successful applicants . . .

Feng intended to go on to explain that if the initial contingent of living cargo proved to be profitable to the *Society*, then of course there would be many more voyages, indeed enough for everyone. But his arms were getting tired and he paused rather too long after the word 'applicants' while he adjusted the position of the nugget.

The peasants closest to the ship heard him say there would be only a hundred and twenty places so, without waiting to hear more, they rushed forward and started fighting their way up the gangway to make certain of a berth among that number for themselves. Those further back in the crowd, who had not heard what Feng had said, assumed the ones at the front must have decided to grab the gold and be done with it. And not wanting to miss out, they too rushed the gangway.

Someone screamed, a shot rang out and an excited farmer set alight a faggot of rice straw he happened to be carrying and tossed it on to the deck of the *Nimrod*. Seeing the shower of sparks and flames, the crowd roared its approval and surged forward to join in the sack of the ship and the slaughter of her crew of hated foreign devils.

Captain Larkins saw that Feng was looking stunned by the turn of events, and he grabbed the nugget and placed it safely between his own boots on the deck. He then drew his new revolver from its holster. It was a fine English weapon which he'd purchased in Sydney on the way out. Seeing how things stood, the mate closed ranks and gave his men the order to fire-at-will, while he himself commenced to chop off clambering fingers and hands with his cutlass as they appeared over the gunnel. The deck was soon slippery with blood.

Though in possession of the advantages of efficient weapons and a defensible position, the crew of the *Nimrod* were so hard pressed that none had time to attend to the fire started by the blazing faggot of rice straw, and this soon began to take hold on the pitched timbers of the deck. Smoke and flames billowed around the struggling group of men, and those at the centre were lost to the view of those who fought on the periphery. Excited men ran backwards and forwards in and out of the smoke, shouting and firing their guns and stabbing with their bayonets, and they went sliding about out of control on the slippery deck, bumping into each other and grabbing at anything for a hold.

Feng, the last person to be seen with the gold by the crowd, found himself in the very eye of this mêlée. He felt helpless, unable to defend himself, and completely at the mercy of events. A peculiar feeling of relief swept over him, an immense resignation stilling his mind, and he found himself encompassed by a spectacular quality of silence and calm. Time ceased to pass for him. He subsisted in a profoundly peaceful enclave of meditation, oblivious to the rain of blood.

Death might have taken him in this condition and he would not have felt her touch.

When the shouting and the shooting ceased as abruptly as they had begun, Feng was the only one to step out of the smoke unharmed. Like Shadrach Meshach or Abed-nego coming out of the fiery furnace, he was a man returning to present time with a new set of instructions for living.

He looked about him but said nothing.

At the still centre of the violent skirmish he had not heard the clamour of competing noises, but had been aware only of a continuous, single resonant note, the mantic sound of silence.

In that silence the unspoken had greeted him. His new instructions for living had revoked the power of words – which had very nearly been the cause of his downfall – in favour of what might be exposed in the absence of words, the tacit. The interstitial place between one thing and another, where implication replaces explication and inference webs the darkness. He saw the power of the mysterious and the troubling in the perceptual habitat of silence and, in electing to become the silent stranger henceforth, he became the sinister stranger. Like the Western phoenix from Arabia, Feng was not consumed but changed by the fire of battle. He would say no more.

When his conscious mind re-engaged with temporal events he saw that the crowd of peasants had fallen back on to the wharf, where they were now lined up along either side, leaving a cleared way down the centre, towards which they were kowtowing.

Galloping full-tilt down this open aisle, with no care for the stragglers scrambling to get out of their way, were the Governor of Amoy and his military escort, their trumpets blaring and the hooves of their horses sounding a concert of drums on the heavy timbers of the wharf. The Governor's spy had returned to the residence and uttered the one transfiguring word: gold.

Feng stepped over the mate who lay moaning at his feet, hacked and bludgeoned (it had been the mate who had expertly defended him), and he grasped the ship's rail just as the Governor's cavalcade came to a crashing halt below him.

Like the folded imago of a silken butterfly emerging from its chrysalis the gorgeous mandarin was eased from the trembling curtains of his huakan by the hands of his retainers. Once stabilised upon firm ground this personage turned his gaze upward. Feng bowed. He did not kowtow in the servile oriental manner, which must imply submission, but inclined his torso stiffly from the waist in meagrest salutation, as he had seen the gentlemen of Port Phillip do, careful to keep his chin thrust forward and his head held high so as to conserve his dignity and to imply an elusive but incontestable cultural superiority. It was a good bow from such a short man and did all he required of it. It was a bow that offered nothing.

During his taxing meeting with the Governor in the wounded Captain's cabin later, Feng kept forgetting to listen to the loquacious and greedy old mandarin. *Tell him nothing!* belled the message in the darkness of his incurious brain as he absently caressed the velvet cover of the tea box, which lay on his lap like a favourite pekinese, and he thought dreamily of the cosy parlour of the *Nunan Family Hotel* in Swanston Street, and sought vainly to stabilise a fugitive memory of Mary's red hair, which had glowed once like mahogany in the firelight.

He roused to the Captain's promptings for brief moments and nodded sagely, avoiding the Governor's gaze, which trembled with conjecture and greed – whether to sequester the *Nimrod* and her precious cargo at once, or to seek a share in her future bounty, was the question exercising his brain.

Instead of speech, from Feng's throat there came a sound repeated ten or twenty or even more times, a sound denoting comprehension and a need for further deliberation. Hm-hm-hm-hm-hm, he went, varying the tone the pitch the timbre and the cadence. And that is all he did, but did it respectfully and enigmatically. The Governor, meantime, reading into these sounds the inferences his greed inspired in him. Feng had achieved inscrutability, which is to say, he could no longer be read with certainty.

He felt incredibly old. As if during his 'absence' in the heat of the battle he had been whisked through four decades of life's experience. He scarcely heard the Governor's voice except as a sing-song tone in the background. He was thinking of his home in far away Victoria and wishing for the day when he might return there. Australia, he was heard to murmur more than once, his fingers idly playing with the purple nap of the velvet.

At which the Governor leaned towards him, his features contorted with the effort of listening, anxious to catch the precise intonation of the cabalistic phrase. *Astray Li Ah*, the old mandarin mouthed, his gaze fixed on Feng's full dark lips, certain that here was an invocation to the powerful demon in the mysterious velvet covered box. A kind of *abracadabra* to unlock the source of Feng's indifference to danger. For how else, but with the protection of his demon, Li Ah, had Feng survived the attack of the peasants without suffering so much as a scratch? The Governor decided it might be as well to proceed with care and to cultivate this man's trust.

My Dear Mary,

The return expedition is assembled at last. One hundred and twenty new members of the *Society* sail with Captain Larkins and his crew on the morning tide. They are but the first of a great number. There are Captains who do not deserve their rank, but our friend is not among them. I should be very content if you and Patrick would confirm him as the Admiral of all our sea-going affairs. During these past difficult months he has ably seen to the charter, the provendering and the crewing of ten ships in addition to his own. These, fully loaded with gold seekers, are all to shortly follow the *Nimrod*, now quite literally the flagship of our fleet, for you will identify her by the phoenix on her masthead when she draws in to Hobson's Bay.

The members of the *Society*, our gold seekers, have been selected with great care. Each man has a family and some small holding here. None are free, as I was. Their families have pledged to repay the value of the passage at the rate of two English guineas per new calendar month, or its equivalent in silver coin, whether the member find gold at Ballarat or not, and on default of such payment the entire outstanding amount to fall due immediately, the same redeemable by the *Society* from the family here in Amoy, whether in kind or in land or in property or in trade, or in labour if need be when no other form of goods are obtainable.

Sheng Fo-sheng travels with this advance party. You may trust him. I have his two sons in my service until his return. Sheng speaks several words of English and is experienced in the ways of the comprador through his activities as an agent in the coolie trade for many years – a trade we have soon put an end to with our offer of gold (our offices in the city and throughout the province are besieged by those who must see

.

250

the hills of Ballarat or die attempting it). Sheng is to be stationed in Ballarat at the camp he will set up there. He has instructions to take account of all the needs of members; of their supplies, their gold, their health and their recreations, and of their dealings with Commissioner Armstrong and with the Protector and all the other colonial officials. In the event of the death of a member, Sheng will, at a cost to the deceased's estate, ship the remains to the family in Amoy, or wherever else in the province they may have had their home. You may with confidence make Sheng privy to everything that concerns the *Society*, except the knowledge that he is never to return to China. He will be of use to us only so long as he does not know this. His greatest desire must be to execute faithfully the functions of headman of the *Society of the Phoenix*. His one thought must be to do this well. All the commerce should therefore pass through his hands and be accountable to his manner of dealing with it. For in the quality of his service will he endeavour to deserve his eventual liberty from us and a reunion with his sons. Likewise, so long as Sheng remains in our service in Australia so will his sons continue to be our diligent and loyal servants here in Amoy, or in whatever other place I care to appoint them our representatives. Treat Sheng with every considered respect and provide him liberally with every luxury he may require to sustain the dignity of his office, so that he is kept in mind every day of our power over him.

I have been fortunate to recruit as the General of my militia one Sa Ho-ang. This fierce young man was until recently a senior officer in the Governor's personal bodyguard and is highly respected and feared by the Governor's men, who consider him ill-used and are ready to favour him with their loyalty still, even though he is no longer of their number. The cause of this is that their master took Sa's beautiful second wife by force to be his concubine. Sa stands behind me and he smiles and readily makes a most servile obeisance to the Governor whenever I meet with that resplendent gentleman. But I think that in his heart he waits for the day when he will exact his vengeance for the theft of his wife. This warrior was

·

as delighted to enter my service as I was to have him in it. If it had been by our careful arrangement, indeed, we could scarcely have come to serve each other's aims more thoroughly than we do. The situation here is charged with many such intriguing matters. Dangerous opportunities abound.

The Americans, the English, the Belgians, Danes, French, Germans and the Dutch are all in Amoy in great numbers and are gathering up immense fortunes as speedily as they can. They speak with excitement of the port of Shanghai to the north as a new El Dorado waiting to be plundered once Amoy has been thoroughly looted. I shall visit that city on the mighty Whangpu River as soon as I have completed the establishment of our interests here. I believe, however, that we shall monopolise the trade in the living cargo from Fukien to Australia without too great a struggle, for none of these other commercial folk see their way to setting up a society such as ours. They are envious of my quick success with it and wonder how it may be emulated. Thus I find myself the object of their most assiduous attentions and am invited to dine at their consulates on the island ten times a week.

It was nearly dawn by the time Feng finished the letter to Mary. He was working alone in a square tower which topped his villa and overlooked the harbour of Amoy. The tower occupied almost the same dimensions as had his hut on Ballarat Station. The unpolished wood floor was bare and the furnishings were a plain deal table and chair. Besides his writing materials the only other items on the table were a lighted oil lamp and the velvet covered box containing Dorset's skull. Feng knew he could be seen for miles around sitting in his lighted tower, yet he felt concealed there.

He picked up the letter and read it through. When he had finished he sealed it with his seal. A heavy mood had descended on him. He listened to the slap of the naked feet of a squad of the *Society's* militiamen trotting past in the street below, their captain calling and the chorus of their response. It was nearly dawn. His collectors were beginning their day's work. For even before the first ship had sailed with its cargo, there were those who were already unable to meet their obligations to the *Society* on behalf of a son or a brother. Somewhere not far off, in one of the narrow twisting streets of Amoy, a small merchant or a shopkeeper would be raising his head from sleep and listening to the approaching chorus.

Feng sat on unmoving in his tower as the sky began to grow light. He was listening to the silence.

Lang opened his eyes. Yu had come from behind his screen and was helping the blind storyteller from the room. Lang looked at his grandfather. The old man had woken, weeping, from his sleep. He closed his eyes again and tried to think himself back into the story, but all he could see was an image of his weeping grandfather.

VICTORIA

Victoria Feng, the last child and ninth daughter of Mary Feng (née Nunan), sat writing at a plain cedar table in the gazebo in the garden at Coppin Grove. Her mother had died seven years earlier and the last of her eight sisters had married and left home the previous spring. Victoria looked older than her thirty years. She was extremely thin, her long black hair was untidily caught in a loose bun at the nape of her neck and she was dressed in a simple muslin gown of a steely grey, the colour indeed of a wintry morning sky. The gown was soiled and showing signs of wear and neglect.

She wrote, then paused and considered, then went on. And every now and then she looked up from her work and seemed to follow with her gaze the flight of a bird across the garden. Her right hand steadied the sheet of paper and her left, for she was left-handed, manipulated the pen, the instrument of her craft. That is how it appeared. She wrote with care, as if the shape of her words mattered as much to her as their meanings, as if, indeed, their meanings might very well be located in their shapes.

She hesitated and crossed out phrases and re-wrote them and sometimes she uncrossed the crossings out and re-established the original phrase.

On it went, rising from her pen, this composition, gathering in flocks of words beneath the oriental temple roof of the gazebo, and flying off into the hot garden, a migration of signs, certain textural cadences going down sombrely towards the turbid river, where there was a little jetty and a boat, and others, more wild and lighter, streaming away like black native bees towards the remnant of bush which flanked the lawn on the southern side of the garden, and escaping shrilly into the dazzling light there among the tall skinny gumtrees and the dry crackling ground litter.

The afternoon was windless and hot. It was February 1908 and the end of a very dry summer. Victoria laid aside another sheet filled with her writing and, placing it on top of the others, she weighted it with a round stone. She took a new sheet and dipped her pen into the blue and white porcelain inkwell and she bent over the paper. She hesitated, her lips compressed with thinking, then she went on: 'After absences lasting more than half a year he came to me each time as if from a strange apartment which communicated with the part of the house in which I lived by a hidden staircase or passage. When he was absent from us I spent many hours searching for the entrance to this secret way and often imagined I had found it. For a time after his departure I learnt to dull the sharpness of my grief with a resort to the fantastic, and in my daydreams I joined him in a land of pure imaginings which, for me, must lie beyond the hidden doorway. Together he and I, like the mythical Feng and Huang of the Chinese other-world, the heavenly emissary which appears when the land enjoys the gods' favour, journeyed side by side and danced our benevolent dance in perfect harmony upon the land which blessed our presence.'

She stopped writing and looked up from her work as if she had heard a sound from the house, perhaps hearing her name called. She looked up this time not at the garden but towards an upper storey window of the house. Standing at the window, not looking down at the garden or the gazebo but gazing into the distance towards Richmond and the smoking factories and crowded workers' tenements, was the figure of her half-brother, her father's only son from his Shanghai marriage to a Chinese woman, the man who was to become at any moment the second Feng.

Victoria stared at her half-brother until he moved away from the window. He looked so much as her father had when she had been a girl that she easily imagined him actually to *be* her father standing there at the window. Soon he would go away again. Perhaps he was already leaving. She snatched up a new sheet of paper and began writing hurriedly:

Feng, the Merchant of the Living Cargo, the mighty Phoenix, lay in his bed dying. He was struggling to accumulate a pool of clarity within his failing consciousness large enough for him to draw from it a thing of great importance for his son, who had travelled all the way from China and now stood at the window waiting. At last Feng managed to emit a feeble groan. This sound drew his son to his side. With a small rush of breath, already soured by the stench of carrion, Feng whispered, Tell them nothing! and then tried to thrust the velvet covered box at his son. But he found he could not move it.

Feng's great energies were spent. The tea box on his chest weighed as much as one of the iron anchors of the old *Nimrod*. It crushed the breath from him. He struggled against it. He seemed to struggle for years and years, for decades, but really it was only for a moment. He lay upon his back and gasped and strove alone in the gathering darkness to pass the talismanic skull of Dorset to his son. But the harder he struggled the heavier the box grew. He could not move it.

As the box crushed the life from him, Feng began to imagine he was once more seated at his table in the lantern roof of his villa in Amoy, listening to the *Society's* collectors hurrying along the dark streets before dawn. Yet even while he was imagining this, and he imagined it with an incredible vividness, he knew he wasn't really in Amoy but was in the house at Coppin Grove.

He was so puzzled and so confused and so nauseated by the contradictions of it all that he began to weep. He despaired. There was no one near him. The maelstrom whirled him away helplessly and he knew it had all been for nothing. I am a dead man, he thought with horror as Shinjé drew him into the void.

The second Feng eased his father's fingers from the box and drew the blanket over the old man's head and went downstairs to tell his father's Headman, who was waiting in the hall.

Sheng Fo-sheng, Headman of the *Society of the Phoenix* for the past half century, stood at the edge of the crowd and watched with disgust as Feng's coffin was lowered into the grave. He held his breath while the priest swung the smoking thurible over it and uttered his mysterious incantation. Each time a spadeful of earth landed on the coffin Sheng felt the thud in his own heart. He watched the white devils bind the bones of his master into the soil of Hell.

When they had completed their barbarous ceremony he turned away and walked quickly along the gravelled path, ignoring the fearful cries of Feng's disfigured ghost. It was time to go home to his two sons.

Victoria didn't blot the page. The ink was drying today as soon as it touched the paper. And she didn't re-read what she had just written. She put down her pen and rubbed her hands over her face and blew out a big breath, and she jumped down from the gazebo and walked quickly across the lawn and in among the eucalypts. In a few days she would begin her life quite alone. She wanted to cry, but held back her tears until she was out of sight of the house.

INTO REGIONS OF UNCERTAINTY

He had never thought of his father as 'father' but as Feng, a dangerous entity who might confront them without warning and inflict some unspecified damage on their lives. He had always been afraid of his father. There had been no other emotion. He believed all sons were afraid of their fathers. And were afraid, too, of having one day to become like their fathers. Until the ancestors had revealed themselves to be the true enemy, his father had been the 'enemy'. The 'enemy' had always been located in Shanghai. In Hangzhou Lang had considered himself safe.

In Shanghai, however, it had never been a matter of going to war against the enemy, of looting and burning and drowning in order to have a decent existence. It had never come to that. Feng was indestructible; everyone knew it. There was no point taking him on. He was not vulnerable to sudden assaults. The strategy had been to keep out of his way as much of the time as possible. The strategy had been to render oneself invisible to him. To render him and his world, indeed, invisible to oneself. To hope, secretly, that he would forget about one.

For ten years, it seemed to Lang, the strategy had worked.

It was early afternoon on a day towards the end of September 1937. It was almost three months since Feng had telephoned Hangzhou and told Lien to abandon the old house and return within three days to Shanghai.

Lang was looking out of one of the tall windows in the grand upstairs drawing room of his father's villa – the same room in which, almost eleven years earlier, Lien and Feng had had their meeting to discuss the question of her visiting her father in Hangzhou. He was wearing a grey English worsted suit and a droopy silk bowtie and he was reflecting unhappily on an angry exchange he'd just had with his friend and tutor, Doctor Spiess. His emotions were unresolved, a mixture of guilt and fear and anger. He was thinking about what had been said and, in particular, was regretting his parting words as the doctor went down the stairs. It will be your own fault then, he had shouted over the bannisters, if you get yourself killed for nothing! And he was trying not to admit to himself how unimaginably terrible the death of the doctor would be.

Doctor Spiess had left only moments before to make his way to the Chinese city. Every afternoon at this time for the past three months the doctor had set off for the front, which was only a mile or two down the road. And on most of those afternoons

Lang had stood by the window just as he did today and waited for the doctor to wave to him from the corner. Sometimes, after the doctor had gone, he had felt so afraid and sorry for himself that he had sat by the window and wept.

Today he did not weep, but he continued to stand by the window long after the doctor had disappeared round the corner. Things had come to a head. He had said things he had not meant. Now he was trying to keep alive a faint hope that if he stayed by the window he would see the doctor hurrying back any minute, waving and smiling. I've changed my mind! You are right, of course, my dearest boy. It's selfish of me to go there every day. And far too dangerous. Anyway, what difference does the little I do for them make to the outcome of this war? Let us forget the fighting and read some more of Rilke together. Poetry is more important than war. 'How shall I hold my soul so that it does not touch yours? How shall I lift it across you to other things?' *Wie soll ich meine Seele halten, dass sie nicht an deine rührt? Wie soll ich sie hinheben über dich zu andern Dingen?*

Although it was only just after three in the afternoon, there was a kind of twilight outside. Heavy smoke from the ironworks and from the steamers and from the naval guns was bellying against a dark overcast of rainclouds. The river and the waterfront were illuminated in a coppery light, as if a great Bessemer converter were discharging its load of molten steel nearby. The solid structures of the buildings along the waterfront and the ships on the river, and the river itself, were rendered in a variety of soft, metallic hues which made them look like lurid shadows cast up against the more solid, the darker, sky. They had lost their detail, they had become a painter's idea of a city under siege. Lang observed that the people on the street below his window no longer strolled; they were not at ease, but hurried, fugitive figures eager to be gone from the scene before some terrible event unfolded and engulfed them.

He was alone in the large room. He had turned off the lights after the doctor left so that he could see outside better. Every minute or two the house vibrated, as if an earthquake was taking place. There was a peculiar and sinister calmness over everything, in which small events continued to unfold. A British cruiser had begun manoeuvring to a new station in the middle of the river, the moving sailors on her deck tiny. He watched her making a pale bow wave as she turned against the thrust of the current. Less than two kilometres downstream, out of sight, the Japanese battleships continued at regular intervals to fire over the Settlement into the Chinese city – where the doctor had gone. Each time the ships fired a salvo of shells from their big guns the window pane in front of Lang rattled and the floor trembled. An earthquake.

Don't be afraid of Australia, the doctor had said to him when they were walking together in the park one autumn afternoon, a day when the sky above Shanghai had been clear and blue and people had seemed to have all the time in the world to stroll and to feed the ducks and to sit and gaze into space. Long for something you can't name, the doctor said, and call it Australia. A thing will come into being. See a golden city on a plain, shining in the distance, and be certain the greatest prize existence can bestow on you is to belong somewhere among your own kind. Let it be Fairyland, an other-world. A land imagined and dreamed, not an actual place. The ancients of all nations understood that we don't belong anywhere real. They understood that the mystery of life, the paradox of our existence, is located in that charged space between the present reality of our individual life and the dream of the immortality of our species. It's the Phoenix, among the mythical beasts, which embodies this paradox for both the occidental and the oriental worlds alike.

They're one in this, as they were once together in most things. It's said to have been an oriental named Phoinix, after all, who founded the greatest travelling nation of the West, that of the Phoenicians. It was he, also, who first introduced the written word to Greece! To Greece! Imagine that! So, nothing is discrete. It's all linked if one bothers to look closely enough. The ancients quarrelled with their fathers, too, and left home and founded nations. What has changed? We've confused ourselves by allowing it to seem that intractable differences divide East from West.

Almost as if a law of nature had decreed the separation. But that wasn't always our view.

There's nothing for you to fear in the blind storyteller's words. He accused you of nothing. You accused yourself. He didn't understand what he was saying. He meant nothing. He doesn't deal in meanings. He didn't need to understand. He was the mouthpiece. That's his craft. Forget him. He has long ago forgotten you and is telling another story today. He's not important. It's up to us, dearest boy, to interpret the story for ourselves. In order to live on, we know the phoenix must periodically die. We know that. The phoenix, therefore, is both the mortal individual and the immortal species in one. It is the emblem for all living creatures, not only our own species. It is a peculiar creature resembling nothing actual. And that's just as well.

Art is a phoenix. Art annuls the sterile dichotomy Life/Death and makes for contradiction and fertility. It is both life and death. It shoots out from between the named and the known like a startling and mysterious flame, confounding the familiar. Art is our dispute with present reality. It seems not to arise from among our common associations, and to mock what is most dear to us. We resent it. It affronts us. Art utters a word and the thing so commanded to exist struggles into being. We think how ugly, how disgusting and how disfigured it is. But we cannot rid ourselves of it, and eventually we grow accustomed to it. Then, at last, we call it beautiful and fall deeply in love with it. But we cannot own the thing art has brought into being, nor say to what nation it belongs. Art belongs to no nation. Art is the displaced. It is not validated by nationality. That is something else.

You are unnamed and must therefore go unrecognised in China. You are literally un-familiar here. But in Australia, which is I believe a kind of phantom country lying invisibly somewhere between the West and the East, you may find a few of your own displaced and hybrid kin to welcome you. China is not the place for you. I've known it ever since your birth. In this one instance, though he doesn't understand your purpose and would have no sympathy for it if he did understand it, I'm with your father and against your mother. If you really are determined to be an artist, Lang, then Australia is the very best place for you. I couldn't recommend anywhere more highly. There's nowhere better. You'll be able to imagine it into being for yourself. You'll be able to make it visible. Think of that! You couldn't do that with Paris or Berlin or London, now could you? Or even with Hamburg. There must be plenty of work for artists to do in such an uncertain place as Australia. No end of it, I'm sure.

A sound behind him interrupted this half-recollected and half-imagined conversation with his friend and Lang turned from the window to see who had come in to the room. His father was standing in the lighted doorway to the hall. Feng was just standing there, not moving, silhouetted against the streaming electric light from the hall, as if he had not yet quite made up his mind whether he would come into the room or would continue on his way without speaking.

Lang waited. He might have been waiting for the thunder after lightning, counting the seconds, measuring the distance from himself to the centre of the storm. The thump of the Japanese naval guns continued at intervals to transmit a delicate tremor through his body, as if this were their principal purpose and death and destruction merely incidental side effects, consequences too remote to be bothered with. Normality squeezed itself into the intervals between each salvo, the foghorns of lighters and merchantmen on the river taking up the echoing spaces.

Waiting, he became conscious of the smell of coalsmoke. The smell of coalsmoke lingered everywhere in Shanghai. It could not be kept out of even the most sequestered European salon. From his earliest years, the smell of coalsmoke had been the smell of Shanghai and of his father's dangerous world. Arriving at the busy railway station, returning from the jasmine-perfumed air of Hangzhou, the smell of coalsmoke had always greeted them. It had subdued their spirits and silenced them as they stepped from the train, their little journey together in the precious seclusion of the compartment over, Feng's respectful watchful Russian waiting for them beside the Pontiac. They no longer belonged to themselves. Coalsmoke was the permeating breath of a dark clamorous world of heavy industry and war, a world, ironically enough, in which the ancestors had lost their sovereignty long ago. There was no debate on that. It was an iron world in which ghosts had no place. His father, the 'enemy' whose attentions he was forever trying to evade, was a kind of prince in this world.

As his father started towards him now from the doorway, it was not simply a man, or a parent, whom Lang saw striding with decisive steps through the coppery light, it was a kind of legendary being possessed of an absolute authority to dispose of and to direct his life. Feng, the Third Phoenix, the old enemy.

Lang held his arms straight and close to his sides, his thumbs brushing the worsted nap of his trousers, his fists clenched. He knew he had been seen, had been selected now, and was no longer to be overlooked, but was to be set on that path designed to make of him the Fourth Feng. That was the reality he would dispute. He thought of his mother as he had seen her this morning, restless and sad and ill in the next room, grieving for her father and for Yu and for all she had lost of China, and he knew there could be no help for him from her. The Japanese guns bellowed and recoiled and the flash lit up the sky. He felt the tremor pass through his bowels.

The black weave of his father's coat brushed against him as Feng leaned to look out of the window. Feng made a noise in his throat, as if he detected something of particular interest out there in the smouldering light, something detailed and observable among the wallowing structures of the city. Or it could have been that he made a judgement on what he saw. I thought you might have been able to see the American flagship from here, he said, as if he felt the need to give a reason for coming into the room and looking out of the window.

The grey ships passed slowly up and down through the iron gloom as if they were not real now, at this moment, but were impressions from voyages made long ago, offsettings on the memory of the river, like the engravings of the parts of the human body that had left their ghostly imprints on the facing pages in Doctor Spiess's anatomy books.

You can see the *Augusta* from the roof, Feng said and turned. Have you been on the roof?

They looked at each other.

No sir.

Well come on then, Feng said impatiently, leading the way. It's time you joined us up there.

Lang followed his father. All civilised people know there is Heaven and there is Hell, the blind storyteller had said, but he had not revealed how to distinguish one from the other.

THE LOVERS

FROM THE JOURNALS OF DOCTOR AUGUST SPIESS,
TRANSLATED FROM THE GERMAN BY HIS DAUGHTER, GERTRUDE SPIESS:
MELBOURNE 1968

The Esplanade, St Kilda, 1 December 1937 For certain people
exile is the only tolerable condition. For these people, to be in
exile is to be at home. But how is one supposed to understand
this? I have reached the age of sixty without having yet decided
whether I may safely assume a complexity in others as
capricious as the grounds upon which I base my own actions,
or whether I might consider others to be constant to some
permanent arrangement of preferences about what they want
from life. The 'truth', I suppose. What they believe to be the
truth, at any rate. Their basis for action.

I have discovered motives, my own and everyone else's, to
be impenetrable. Terrifying possibilities at times flicker across
my mind, like faint and mysterious messages transmitted long
ago from a remote region of the interior, where a great battle
has been being waged day and night for centuries, possibly for
ever. These messages flutter into my brain like exhausted
doves returning to the dovecote. I fear I may not decipher
them for years, or never. Are they cries for my assistance? *What*
are they?

Whenever I feel this uncomprehending fluttering in my
brain, I know that a loss of detail and incident will shortly
follow it. That I shall experience an opening up, an incredible
clarity of mind enabling me to see with disturbing lucidity far
into the vast oceanic depths of eternity, to see into that by
which we are encompassed, as if I stand on the brink. And in
this undistracted state of mind, that I will see there is nothing
in those depths. That there is no outcrop of facts or feelings to
which I am safely anchored. That I shall see, in other words,
that there is nothing there. Which is, of course, to propose that
there is nothing here either. That, indeed, there is nothing.
That there *is* only nothingness. Vacuity. Space unoccupied.
Space, no matter how richly charged with metaphor, not even
booming faintly with the music of the spheres, nor resounding
eerily to mysterious mantic chants. But an unechoing infinity in
which *here* is exactly equal to *there* and the one has cancelled
out the other. A pressure mounted against my eardrums
rendering me deaf to all messages. A tension within my skull
rendering me insensible to productive thought. In this state of
mind, what am I able to call into being but despair?

Is it despair? Does one call it by that name? Does one search
the holy scriptures, as my dear father would and say, This is
that which the writer of Ecclesiastes spoke of when he wrote,
Therefore I went about to cause my heart to despair of all the
labour which I took under the sun? Or does one assume the
cold and diagnostic mode and find through lengthy scientific
enquiry that a parasitic amoeba inhabits one and drains one of
the will to live?

Under the influence of this condition of mind I know myself
to be detached from the strivings of the rest of humanity.
Under its influence I could not muster the will to pilot a ship
against the current of the mighty Whangpu River, or even into
this tideless port of Melbourne, but would let it drift. Under the
influence of this mood I am dislodged from the continuum of
past and future. I do not care. I am rejected, even, as unworthy
by the fastidious hand of Providence. Under the (blessedly
temporary) shackles of this mood I am a solitary being whose

endeavours are unrelated to the fulfilment of the world's ancestral dreams. I *call* nothing into being, indeed nothingness. I am a being without meaning. I am set aside from the great project. And, anguished beyond belief, I ask myself, why should this be? And I have no answer.

Then, when I am miraculously cured, the terrible question ceases to bother me. I wake in the morning and smell roasting coffee beans and see the sun sparkling on the little waves in the blue bay beyond my window and I am redeemed, the foolishness of the night forgotten.

Before I go out to the café this morning to drink coffee and to search the newspapers for some reference to how the war is going in China, I must insist that no interpretation of history can fail to reflect the condition of mind, as well as the state of knowledge, of the person who proposes it, whether that *historian* is sick and bitter and bewildered by the way life has dealt with him, or whether he is filled with hope for the future and emboldened in his judgements by the validations of earlier successes. The true facts of history, then, what are these? What can they possibly be? Before I walk along the esplanade this morning on my way to drink coffee and to read the newspapers, I must insist that all histories are nothing more than mere fictions. In that case, however, and how much less palatable this possibility is to me, might not all our wonderful fictions be nothing more than mere histories? God forbid that Werther and Lotte should turn out to have been only *real* after all! To live in a world without histories is one thing, but who would wish to endure in a world without fictions?

·

The Esplanade, St Kilda, 15 December 1937 I brought an armful of books to the drawing room on the first floor of Feng's splendid villa every Wednesday before lunch, and we sat together at the circular Italian table with its intarsia scenes of hunting and we studied German poetry and history and discoursed upon the anxieties besetting his life. After his return to Shanghai from Hangzhou, with his mother, in June, after their final retreat from that troubled redoubt of Classical values,

·

we made little progress with his schooling. His state of mind was often so knotted and confused that I could not offer to answer his questions but could only sit in silence and squeeze his hand in mine and wonder at the fate of this boy, who seemed destined to become the loneliest man on this earth. Madame Feng entered the darkening room one afternoon, for we had not bothered to put on the lights, and found us thus, holding hands and sitting without speaking in the gloom, given over to our state of deep reflection. You are like lovers, she said, contemplating us from the doorway and not putting on the light or coming into the room, as though she feared to approach too close to us, in case she should confirm for herself that we were no longer quite of her world. And after that, and always with a kind of sad, amused irony, she referred to Lang and me as 'the lovers'. She told her maid, They sit together in the dark whispering philosophical secrets to each other. I observed her fade and withdraw and become increasingly detached as she saw that she could not follow us into the reality we had begun to construct for ourselves. Hangzhou was destroyed and Shanghai was burning. The end of China's history had arrived. She delivered him into my hands and from then on faced her own future with a kind of bitter amusement.

He begged me not to continue my dangerous work at the front in the Chinese city. You don't care for me as much as you care for those wounded peasants! he accused me one day when I was preparing to leave. And when I refused him he became hysterical and dragged at my clothes and screamed at me that I didn't really care for him. So I didn't go into the city that day but remained with him. And when I'd calmed him and promised him that I would never abandon him, hugging him tightly to my chest and telling him again and again, and close to tears myself, that he was more precious to me than if he had been my own son, in order that he might understand why I went up to the front line and did what I could for the wounded, I recounted to him the story of my beating and its sequel.

When I left your maternal grandfather's house in Hangzhou

.

and set off alone in search of the Sung kilns of Fenghuang Hill, leaving behind me my uneasy audience in the principal courtyard, you were a baby, not more than a month old, I said. And I told him how the Communist students had attacked me and how I had been saved by his mother, who had arrived with the Russian chauffeur in the Pontiac.

Several months after I'd returned to Shanghai, one day when I wasn't thinking about the incident on Fenghuang Hill but was busy with patients in my surgery, your father came to see me. He had never come to my surgery unannounced before, so I knew something extraordinary must have happened. He was very grave and serious but a bit excited too, as if he were impatient to let me in on a great surprise. He asked me to go with him at once. He would not tell me where we were going. When the car turned in to Guizhou Road and I saw the Laozha Police Station ahead, however, I began to fear the worst. We drove in through the gates of the station, which stood wide open. It was obvious we were expected, for the Municipal Chief of Police, Alistair McKenzie, who was a friend of your father's and of mine also, was waiting for us. Without a word of greeting, he took me by the arm and led me to the cells at the rear of this grim building. In the open, against the far wall of a small courtyard, there was an iron cage. In the cage were a dozen young men and women. They were naked. They had been horribly beaten and tortured and some were unable to stand without the support of the others.

As Alistair and your father and I came out on to the little verandah outside the guardhouse the young men and women in the cage turned and looked at me. They did not speak or make any sound, but just looked at me. The policemen who were guarding them made various humiliating comments, but the prisoners didn't seem to hear. Alistair pressed my arm and said, Here are your assassins, August.

One by one, as I watched, the prisoners were taken from the cage and shot.

For twenty blissful years I had lived as if the condition of extraterritoriality were a kind of literary conceit. A literary conceit which had, by the most magical accident of cultural displacement and imagination, by a unique conjunction of sublime European wit and the colonising instinct, become a reality. We seemed to live as people outside history. Each one of us an actor who wrote his or her own lines as the play progressed. We were not ordinary human beings but a privileged community situated among the stars, inhabitants of the empyrean. We were gods who dwelt in the sphere of purest fire. Life was all imagination to me. I was drunk on it for twenty years. I spent my time at dinner parties and at the races gazing at my fellow extraterritorials with a kind of muted adoration, as if they moved in a story which I told myself.

After Fenghuang Hill and Laozha Police Station I saw that we were a part of the tragic history of China. And I could stand apart from it no longer. My beautiful illusion of a civilisation that floated in a kind of detached element of imaginative zeal was shattered. It fell to pieces and I knew it could never be put together again.

Lang, who had been sitting in my lap all the while I was telling this story, jumped up and strode over to one of the tall windows, where he stood looking out and saying nothing. What is the matter? I asked him. In an unpleasantly forthright manner that was brutal and which shocked and hurt me, he replied, Why don't you just go back to Hamburg then?

I have to admit that what follows is an imaginary conversation. I regret that it never really took place. It is a discourse that made its progress through my mind later. I was distressed by the manner of Lang's question and for the moment could think of no reply to him. It was not an unfamiliar question to me, but I had never imagined that he, of all people, would ask it of me. I suppose, really, this is one of those so-called *conversations* which can never really take place because they do not belong to present reality but belong to our reflections on reality, to our *speculations*, in the strict sense, as to what reality might be. I suppose, in truth, it must be admitted that what follows is a literary conversation.

When I was a boy growing up in Hamburg, I *said*, I believed that one day I was to become a playwright. Doesn't every young person secretly cherish some impractical ideal concerning their future. My father would have disapproved of this ambition so I never disclosed it to him. I used to go about secretly imagining what it would be like for me when I was grown up and had become a famous Hamburg playwright. Of course, if it was to be congenial to me as a successful playwright, then the Hamburg of my imaginary future could have no place in it for my father. I had to tamper with reality, therefore, in order to contemplate my solemn and romantic destiny with pleasure. I gazed upon the future guiltily and in secret, like a voyeur gazing upon the scene of the crime he plans to execute. I loved my father, indeed I still love him, and I did not like the fact that I was required to remove him from the scene in order to enjoy my future. Yet I was unable to resist the allure of this peculiar freedom nevertheless.

It was a landscape that I looked upon. It was a magical landscape which waited for me to enter it. I perceived it then, of course, not as a sexual landscape, but as a painting by Claude Lorrain, as indeed the enigmatic landscape of metaphor. I was familiar with the paintings of Claude and knew him to have been the very first European artist to have applied his talents entirely to landscape paintings. I knew, what is more, that he had hired other artists to paint the figures into his otherwise completed pictures. There, go ahead and do what you like with this place I have created, Claude seemed to say to me. So I accepted his invitation and painted myself in. I had also learned from my tutor, a minor Prussian nobleman who was a fierce defender of something which he called *the irrepressible genius of the Germanic soul*, that while the French venerated Claude alongside Poussin as one of the very best of their artists, in reality, *historically* so to speak according to my tutor, Claude had actually been a German who had imagined into being the ideal landscape for the German soul to take up its residence in. My tutor justified his opinion concerning Claude's nationality by pointing out that Lorrain was part of the Empire when Claude was born, and that furthermore, Claude had been unable to speak more than a word or two of French and had done no work in France but had spent his entire working life in Italy. The Prussian's arguments did not convince me that Claude was a German but rather that he had not belonged anywhere in particular.

In his peculiar detachment from any real place I sensed in Claude a spirit close to my own ideal. He painted landscapes which were the dwelling places not of his fellow citizens, of whatever country, but of gods. He was what my father called a *Stimmungsmaler*, a painter of moods, a painter whose scenes play upon the open mind of the onlooker. A painter of pictures which invite the onlooker to inhabit them himself. A painter, indeed, of landscapes of the mind, lit by a golden Italian sun and veiled in the mists of a northern vision. They are pictures of no real place. As one stands before a painting by Claude, the hero in the picture is not Juno or Proserpina, but is oneself. The temple in the middle distance is a shrine dedicated not to a god of the Classical pantheon, a god of one's remote ancestors, but to the worship of oneself, to the worship of the god within oneself, the god by means of whose powers one imagines oneself into being. When I was a boy it seemed to me that all I had to do to fulfil my most secret and cherished dreams was to accept the invitation to become the heroic figure in my own Claudean landscape. This I did and have not undone till now.

I have often been asked, my dear Lang (I went on in my imaginary conversation), and quite as rudely as you asked me a moment ago, why I have not returned to Hamburg. The enquiry has usually implied that my interlocutor believed I *ought* to return there. In response to this rhetorical insistence that I don't belong, I have usually replied with the very first thing that came into my head. I am not known for my wit and have never striven for irony. Oh well, I have usually cried cheerfully, in response to this question, I shall you know. I probably shall, just wait and see. Something like that. Anything at all. A more elaborate lie only if I've been pressed. The more hard-pressed the deeper the lie. But never, before this, have I replied with the truth. I have never confessed to anyone until this moment, in which I freely confess it to you, that for more than twenty years the International Settlement has been for me the Claudean landscape of my youthful dreams.

That, then, was the imaginary conversation which never actually took place. What really happened was the following. When he asked me why I did not return to Hamburg, I replied superciliously that there were a number of reasons but I did not care to discuss them with him just then. And I at once insisted that if I were not going into the Chinese city, then we should get on with some real work for a change and not waste any more of each other's time. I got up and switched on the light and opened our book and ordered him, in a schoolmasterish tone, to translate after me Peter Hebel's *Auf den Tod eines Zechers*, knowing full well that he would be completely at a loss with Hebel's Alemannic dialect.

I walked up and down the room with the book open in my hands and listened to his hopeless attempt to make some sense of the poem. Then I confronted him across the table and said spitefully, *On the Death of a Drunkard*, my dear Lang. Is that clear? *Auf den Tod eines Zechers*, never forget it! 'They have just buried a man I knew, it is a pity about his special gifts. Search as you will to find another like him, he is gone, you will never find one.' It is a memorial, my dear boy, to a man who wasted his life. And I placed the book on the table before him and with a disdainful emphasis I said, Have the poem translated for your next lesson. Then I left him. And as I walked home through the streets, in mitigation of my cruelty I began my imaginary conversation with him.

•

Before the middle of November the battle for Shanghai was over. The great city and its industry was a smoking ruin. We had not seen the sun for months for the pall that lay over us. The Settlement was crammed with more than a million starving and wounded Chinese seeking refuge from the Japanese. The streets everywhere were crowded with them day and night. They lay against the wall of Feng's villa when I arrived in the

•

mornings. Through his great influence with the Japanese, Feng
made arrangements for Lang and me to get away from the
stricken port on the SS *Wangaratta*, which was one of the last
ships they permitted to leave.

After three months of uninterrupted bombing and shelling,
Shanghai was eerily silent during these days. We talked in low
voices. We were more on edge than we had been during the
height of the fighting, when we had often been forced to shout
in order to be heard. It was as if men waited now for the
judgement of God on their fierce proceedings. Even the
metaphysically inspired General Sugiyama was subdued. After
generations of plotting and dreaming, the prospect of the total
success of their plan to conquer China seemed to daze the
Japanese. During the first moments of silence after the battle
they did not dare to whisper the word victory in case God
should answer them with another word.

It was only three days to our departure. Madame Feng's
appearance during this time reminded me of the Chinese
officers I had seen who had been captured and were being
held in compounds by the Japanese. I thought her exhausted
and thoroughly demoralised by the completeness of her defeat.
She had succumbed once again to a recurrent infection which
has troubled her since Lang's damaging birth, so I saw a good
deal of her. I visited her every day and did what I could to
relieve the symptoms, which were extremely uncomfortable for
her. She was grateful to me for smuggling to her the Chinese
remedies forbidden by her husband. I believe she also found
my persistence amusing. As she had never extended the least
show of intimacy to me since the day of my beating, I was
surprised and moved when she took my hand in hers one day
and smiled at me in a gentle and forgiving way and said, You
should not lose your faith so easily, Doctor Spiess. China will
defeat her enemies. She will win. Have no doubt of that. She
withdrew her hand then and with great intensity said, One day
the old values will be restored. Once again I was reminded of
how easy it was for me to underestimate this woman's strength.
Before I left she laughed and chided me, You will never

understand us doctor. Her illusion that the past will return isolates her tragically.

•

During this peculiar period of hiatus in Shanghai, a moment that hung between the defeat of what had been ancient and had become terrible and the beginning of something new that might in the end become just as terrible, Lang and I went on meeting regularly in the antique drawing room. At our next meeting after the Hebel incident we embraced each other warmly and each of us begged the other for forgiveness. Once again, even more strongly than before, I experienced a mysterious gratitude for his existence, as if in each of us a voice must cry out *without you there is only silence*. I was reading Holderlin's lines to him – 'The land with yellow pears and full of wild roses hangs down into the lake, you gracious swans, and drunk with kisses you dip your heads into the sober water' – when he interrupted me with the question, Do you think a Chinese can be an artist any longer?

•

The Esplanade, St Kilda, 16 December 1937 My journal cannot be a map after all, joining the beginning of my journey to the end of it. Such a celebration of travelling is possible only for those who are certain of a place to which they will return and there receive the welcome of a true homecoming, to those, that is, who have as their destination the place from which they first set out. The mapmaker is neither a refugee nor a colonist. The mapmaker must leave no gaps. He must not lift his pen from the moment he sets out to the moment he returns or his map will be of little use to those of his countrymen who would follow him. I am not a mapmaker and *my* countrymen are those who, like Claude Lorrain, are detached from place. I am at liberty, therefore, to lift my pen, to leave a gap and to pass over in silence our last days in Shanghai and the misery of their parting. I shall bury it in the silence of the empty page.

There is a duplicity in this travelling for me, however, for while I rejoice here he despairs in Ballarat.

•

I returned from that city three days ago to my rooms overlooking the bay on the first floor of this pleasant house to find that Miss Cheong had made everything cosy and welcoming for me, and I began at once to think only of myself. I cannot, however pass over Ballarat in silence, but must set it in its place here.

The 'aunt' of whom Feng spoke, being a grand-daughter of Feng One and of his Irish wife, Mary Nunan, is in reality his aunt once-removed. She and her family are clearly not without certain expectations in this affair, but feign perplexity and discouragement. Lang, they wish to imply, is like an exotic and rare disease that has been visited upon them as a sign of displeasure from their offended God. A burden from which, however, if they endure it without complaint, they may be delivered eventually with due recompense. His claim upon them is one of kinship, and this, they make plain, cannot be refused.

Ballarat might be Hangzhou, for there is a fine lake with views to the hills, situated on the north-westerly margins of the city. After that, however, one ceases to think of the City of Heaven and begins to think of other things. The Hallorans live in a plain, single-storey wooden house among others of its kind, in a street that seemed strangely deserted. From the windows there is a view of neither the mountains nor the lake, but only of more houses like their own facing them across the way.

With an affected show of ceremony Mrs Halloran, attended closely by her husband, Frank, and by their three sons, ranked in age from twelve to sixteen, ushered Lang and me into a small, dark and desolate room situated immediately off the central passage and just inside the front door. This room, a kind of ante-chamber to the rest of the house, is surely as seldom visited by the members of the household it serves as is the grimmest Hangzhou reception hall by the members of the household *it* serves. Indeed the purposes of both are clearly identical, being not so much to admit guests readily to a degree of warmth and intimacy with the family as to keep them for a period of probation at a safe distance. Lang and I sat on a sofa facing Frank Halloran and his sons. We avoided each other's eyes, for there was no ritual with which to disguise our unease. On each darkly upholstered chair, yellowed antimacassars gleamed like pale beacons in the gloom, fading beams from a bygone age, offering us no hope at all. Mrs Halloran absented herself to prepare a meal of grilled mutton chops and sundry boiled vegetables, the health-giving properties of which she celebrated in detail to us before going, as though she believed Lang and I had narrowly survived a famine.

When we were at last called to dine and the heaps of steaming food were set in front of us in the kitchen, for the house is without a dining room, it quickly became apparent that Mrs Halloran and her lusty family were to be shamed by our incapacity to eat the meal. Lang hung his head and could do nothing, not attempting so much as a mouthful. I struggled on alone long after the family had finished theirs, conscious of the extreme unease, the suspense, the crisis of anxiety, indeed, that my lack of a genuine appetite for the food had brought on, conscious, as I swallowed heavily and with unusual noises that I do not normally make while eating, that the dignity of the Halloran family now depended on my performance.

It became an agony of chewing and swallowing. How I wished Yu had been the cook! Then they would have witnessed a performance of banqueting sufficient to satisfy the proudest host. Without wine to assist the process, chewing continued to be possible after swallowing ceased to be. Swallowing is more akin to our heartbeat, to the unconscious and therefore uncontrollable functioning of our vital organs, than it is to the readily directed motor operations of our jaws and limbs. When I could no longer swallow I ceased to chew. There was nothing else for it.

Like relatives gathered around the sickbed of an expiring loved one, the Hallorans gazed at me with fading hopes, their eyes mutely pleading with me, is there nothing more you can do for us Doctor? I laid my knife and fork solemnly upon the considerable pile of uneaten meat and potato and pumpkin and indicated, by my calm but resigned expression, that the unfortunate outcome had been beyond the scope of my profession to prevent. Death comes to all of us. Amidst a silence that seemed about to bring on church bells, Mrs Halloran rose and removed the cold remains. It was plain from their expressions that the Hallorans had failed one of life's essential probationary trials – that of the feeding of guests.

While we drank tea Mrs Halloran questioned me. Had I, she asked, found her own aunt, Victoria Feng, to be in good health? *We* hear nothing from her, she added pointedly, looking to Frank for confirmation of this. Her unstated question, it appeared to me, was, why has Miss Feng not been called on to support this boy? Where is *her* contribution? Her connection with him is altogether more direct than ours and her resources more adequate. We do not mind, but.

Undoubtedly it is a constant uncertainty hanging over the Hallorans as to which branch of the family Victoria Feng will bequeath her considerable estate and the valuable property at Coppin Grove. I replied that I'd not yet called on Miss Feng but would be doing so on my return to Melbourne. Mrs Halloran made a noise in her throat, which I shall not attempt to interpret here. She drank her tea and clattered her cup on the saucer and she drew a deep breath and looked at her boys and shook her head and let the breath out again through her nose, her lips remaining throughout tightly pressed together. At this Frank advanced me a little smile. It seemed I was to accept that there is much I do not understand. Indeed that is so, I am sure, and equally sure am I that there is much *they* do not understand. But it will never be my intention to enlighten them. The gulf between us is too vast. I have no wish to bridge it.

They elicited no word from Lang, the forlorn cause of their perplexity. He had sunk into a state of deep despondency where the mediation of words was of no use to him. He could not be reached. I felt myself to be accountable for his despair. I could not bear to think of Madame Feng, alone in Shanghai, thinking of him.

Our arrival in a body at the great red-brick school, where the Hallorans' three sons attend as day boys, was the occasion for another species of mystification and anxiety. The tall Head Brother, swaying forward in his sombre cassock, led us from his office into the garden, which was as large and empty as a field. Here he pointed to a row of recently planted pine trees. What had these trees to do with us? I was not to discover the connection. The Hallorans, I perceived, however, felt themselves favoured by this excursion. The brother required us to admire his trees. And this we did. They were not interesting trees. They were not trees of distinction such as the scholar Huang might have admired and wished to see in his garden, but were saplings, thin and rather forlorn and lacking in character. We stood before them as if reviewing an unhappy parade of cadets. The Brother kept his hand upon Lang's shoulder, possessing him as one might possess new property.

While we gazed obediently towards the row of ordinary pine trees bordering the immense lawn, Mrs Halloran sought to describe to the Brother the actual nature of Lang's kinship association with her family. She revealed it to be an attenuated association and not exactly one of blood. Or was it? This point did not emerge absolutely but was left to be inferred from the general body of her evidence, which was extensive. The thoroughness of this woman's genealogical dissertation, the sheer abundance of detail in her divulgement of the family pedigree, greatly impressed me. She might well have begun *Unto the woman he said, I will greatly multiply thy sorrow and thy conception; in sorrow thou shalt bring forth children.* Though a poor cook, she is undoubtedly a distinguished matriarch, the keeper of a thing which is of a primordial nature, a thing sacred and extensive and complex and Biblical and reaching into the archaic origins and virtues of the Hallorans' Australian genesis. A book of the ancestors which she carries with her in her memory, a consecrated grid of knowledge devolved upon her through the delivery of her kind. Who begat whom and where and in what circumstances of ease or deserving need these consecrated couplings and joinings and procreatings took place.

It was a criss-crossed membrane of life and death laid solemnly upon the landscape for many miles around. A map for those who could read the signs posted against its legend. Here was an oral tradition quite as exacting in its rigour as the literary tradition of China. A mistake would have been unthinkable. A mistake would have been blasphemous. There was poetry in it, too. Stories of romantic interludes and tragedies and brave deeds. The ingenuity and enterprise of the Hallorans had persisted through fires and droughts and floods and wars and sudden death.

Slowly the family emerged.

While she spoke a light rain began to fall on us. No move was made to take shelter. The Brother's thin fingers tensed and relaxed, kneading Lang's small round shoulder, while he gazed upon his trees and from time to time confirmed with a movement of his head or a click of his tongue that he was attending to Mrs Halloran's unfolding. Once he interrupted, his thick black eyebrows coming together in an unbroken line across the upper portion of his face. Wasn't it Jack and Molly Keenan's girl, then, from Mansfield, who married the Costin boy? His puzzlement was sincere. No, oh no, Brother. There was shock in Mrs Halloran's response. If you'll forgive me, Molly was an O'Brien. Her father was a carter in Benalla. The O'Briens were all carters. The youngest, Terry, God rest his soul, did not return from the Dardanelles. His name was put by mistake on the memorial in Yea, if you'll remember. There were letters in the *Courier* when the council voted not to have it changed because of the expense. It is still there today. The Brother's eyebrows remained joined. Was it *Joseph* Costin, then who was here? he persisted, the drizzling rain settling on his tight curls and forming a shimmering membrane of lace over them, a mocking portent of priestly office for this male eunuch, the brother who would not become the father. It was *one* of the Costin boys took out the Donovan Bursary in thirty-two, I know that, Mrs Halloran. He turned squarely towards her. She waited for him, respectful but knowing better. And you know Molly Keenan only passed away at St Vees in July? Yes, yes she did. Mrs Halloran had known this and was able to confirm it. Respectfully she continued. Molly's own mother was a Macey. There were nine of them. The brother's fingers tightened on Lang's shoulder.

A Halloran and a Feng, at last, were to be seen embedded in the landscape by each other's side, overlapping just a little. An X placed on the genetic map signifying a boy from China. Mrs Halloran returned to it, eventually, and reminded us, who had quite forgotten by then why the excursion had been begun, that this was the very place from which she had set out, ducking her head at Lang and placing him, a solitary disfigured member of her tribe, on the extreme periphery of her vast, breeding landscape, placing him, indeed, on its horizon – almost *over* it. In her oral book of the ancestors the concealed argument had concerned the question not of the primacy of either the male or the female line, but legitimacy of descent. It had concerned what had *befallen*. Kinship, no matter how extenuated, was the singular quality that could not at last be resisted.

The Brother's fingers dug into Lang's shoulder, restraining the would-be escapee. I was repelled. The rain will do the trees good, the Brother murmured, and led us back into the building, where a bell was ringing.

Standing between the watchful Brother and the three large Halloran boys in the arch of the doorway, Lang looked small and misshapen and startlingly oriental, a miniature, a diminutive caricature of his father. He did not weep or protest when I let go of his hand, but gazed at me with hurt and disbelief.

I have abandoned him in the golden city of his ancestor.

·

The Esplanade, St Kilda, 20 December 1937 The cause of my duplicity, that I rejoice in St Kilda while he despairs in Ballarat,

·

is that I have encountered here a delicate and compelling paradox. This place is at once familiar and strange to me. It is as if I have long been expected. Miss Cheong on her knees scrubbing the front steps smiles and says nothing and seems to know what I must do. My arrival from China has fulfilled in her a secret and long-cherished hope. We are friends without needing to speak of friendship. It is a game between us. I may not ask for directions and she may not offer them. I must locate the clues and decipher them myself.

Early each morning I am enticed awake from an untroubled sleep by the sounds of the trams and the workmen going along below my window. I get up at once. I am eager. I do not wish to waste a moment of the day. It is with a feeling of mysterious joy, with a conviction that I am abandoning my onerous, mundane responsibilities in order to pursue a higher purpose, that I set out each day on my quest to solve the mystery of my presence in this place.

Here I am, then, freshy shaved and wearing my linen suit and new straw hat with its cerise band, which exactly matches the silk handkerchief in my breast pocket, and I am coming down the ochred steps of The Towers with my cane in my hand. I bow to Miss Cheong and bid her good morning. On the last step I pause to admire the sunlight sparkling on the blue waters of the bay. Then I turn left and stride towards Acland Street, swinging my cane as I go.

Within the confines of this narrow street the air is rich with the appetising aromas of freshly roasted coffee and baking bread. The pavements are crowded with hurrying people. The shops are all open, their windows filled with every kind of fruit and meat and sweet delicacy. Along the centre of the roadway, trams go up and down ringing their bells. I enter this street and I am at once elevated by its life. It does not matter to me that I do not know where I am going. I am here, that is what matters.

As I walk along I am accompanied by the intuition that at any instant an old friend from days gone by, someone I have not seen since my youth in Hamburg, will hail me from the passing crowd with a shout of delighted recognition. August

·

281

Spiess! It is you! My dear fellow, you have arrived at last! We have been expecting you. And he will place his arm in mine and will insist I go with him at once to meet the 'others', where we shall celebrate our reunion in grand style.

No one calls to me. But the intuition does not fade. At any moment I shall chance upon a familiar circumstance and a lost memory will be restored to me. I shall know at once where I am. Meanwhile I remain invisible to my familiars. With my memory restored my full presence will be restored also, and I shall really be here.

I pass the open door of a café. The hubbub inside rushes out and surrounds me. Fascinated, I pause and listen. The isolated phrase *Licht und Schatten* is carried to me with a peculiar clarity upon the medley of voices. *Licht und Schatten*, 'light and shade'. I look into the crowded café. Men and women sit at tables drinking coffee and reading the morning papers and loudly discussing the affairs of the day. Others silently eat breakfast. As I gaze in at them, the detached phrase in German striking my attention, familiar yet strange, *Licht und Schatten*, these people in the café seem to me to be at the very centre of a perfect civilisation. The steaming cups of coffee and the rustling newspapers and the shouted orders and the appetising smells and the eager exchange of views engage me in a kind of metaphysical delight. It is as if these folk possess a precious secret, a secret I am certain I once possessed myself. Shall I possess it again? I go in to the café and sit at one of the tables and I order a coffee. Something priceless and secret lies close to me.

Without thinking, I have given my order in German. No one is surprised by this. The two women who sit opposite me do not interrupt their conversation. The young waitress wipes the table in front of me with her cloth and goes at once to fetch my coffee. August, I whisper to myself, this is not a dream! I know that nothing will surprise me. The mystery, the intuition of the familiar made strange, persists and deepens, and I know that I am about to decipher a vital clue as to my whereabouts.

Unrecognised, and therefore unseen, I eavesdrop on

·

delicious intimacies and sip my coffee. I am at the centre of the world. I am in the secret place I once knew in my imagination. There is no nostalgia in what I feel. I cannot say this is a European city. It is not a European city. For where is the grand public architecture memorialising mighty regimes, the tyrants and emperors, the conquerors and princes from whose ambitious struggles this State was fashioned? There are none. There are no bronze equestrian monuments here. There are no palaces, no citadels, no open squares for armies to parade their force before a sullen and resentful populace. Here lethal princes have never immortalised their conquests or themselves in stone and bronze. If there were to be a revolution in Australia there would be nothing for the people to tear down, for they have put it all up themselves.

As I eavesdrop I quickly come to understand that these folk have never known the shadow of the prince, but are accustomed to live without the expectation of the tyrant setting forth from his fortified walls with his men-at-arms to renew his arbitrary demands upon them. The speech and the gestures of these people are without a care for the censure of any person. They do not confer closely and in whispers, but shout their opinions for all to hear. They do not watch their fellow citizens in case they are betrayed, for there is no one to whom their fellow citizens might betray them if they wished to do so. Everyone is a prince here and Australia itself is their citadel.

These folk reside beyond the reach of history. Here extraterritoriality is the status quo. Here there is no pre-existing law that waits in the hinterland to reassert its rule against their occupation. Unlike the Han, who labour impatiently beyond the boundaries of the International Settlement for the day when they will expel the foreign devils from their native soil and reimpose the hegemony of their own fiat, the indigenous inhabitants of this place are so thoroughly dispersed from their lands and discouraged from revolt that they have ceased to possess a jurisdiction to be reckoned with. Clearly, possession of ancestral links to the land confers no special privileges here, as it does in Europe and elsewhere. Here to have arrived a week ago, as I, is to be more privileged than to have arrived a thousand years ago.

There is no nation here. Here the displaced are in place. This is not a community that has been wrestled into being through the fierce valour of warriors set one against the other for generations, but a community engendered domestically. Such is the architecture which dominates all styles, in buildings and in conversations. If the people of Australia were ever to set up a memorial bronze, it would undoubtedly depict Mrs Halloran descanting upon her theme of procreations.

While I drink my coffee, the mystery is dispelled and the enigma of my intuition partially resolved. Have I not arrived in such a place as our youthful ardours in Hamburg once directed us to dream of? A kind of children's land, where it is not necessary to be afraid of the dark?

·

The Esplanade, St Kilda, 27 December 1937 It is the free-standing two-storey house I saw in Feng's photograph. It is constructed of red and yellow brick and is situated on a commanding hill among other large houses of its period. This style, I have observed, represents the acme of Australian domestic architecture. Deep, ornate verandahs on both floors shelter a solid square core of building.

Miss Feng's home is set in the midst of an extensive neglected garden, in which mature elms and aspens and other European trees shade wild areas of unmown grass. As I walked down the pathway towards the front door, I entered a place of calm and seclusion, a place even of some concealment. There was no one about. A dog barked repeatedly farther up the hill. I might have been in the countryside. I pulled the bell and knocked upon the door, but no one answered. As I waited within the cool shelter of the verandah I was feeling nervous and expectant and uncertain of how, or even if, I was to be received, for she had not responded to either of my letters, in which I had requested permission to call on her. Did this woman really exist, then? I wondered. Or had she died or moved away years ago? Or was she, perhaps, a ghostly

·

inhabitant of an Australia imagined into existence merely to gratify Feng's own peculiar needs, a kind of private and mental refuge for him from the harsh immutable realities of China, from whose weighty history his predecessor had been cast up as a disinherited superfluous and eroded being? If Mrs Halloran had not herself asked after the wellbeing of her Aunt Victoria, I might have abandoned the case.

Getting no response to repeated hammerings on the front door with my cane, I ventured to the side of the house and looked out on to the wilderness of garden. Stout aerial cables of Chinese wisteria looped about my head from the balcony above, and at the bases of the supporting columns great stone pots, one broken open and its earthy contents spilled out, nurtured thick clusterings of hardy blossoming geraniums. Three steps led to a weed-infested path. I saw that this was the aspect of the house in the photograph shown me by Feng. I was standing in the very place where the woman in the elaborate white gown, his grandfather's Australian wife, Victoria's mother, had stood. I remained there for some while, spying upon the sunlit garden from my place of concealment, and trying with little success to reanimate in my imagination something of the old days here as they must have been. The sunlight was extraordinarily clear and sharp and the shadows cast on to the black and white tiles of the verandah by the wisteria formed a dappling about my feet, like the stilled reflections of water in a painting. Eventually I was put in mind by this of the enticing and suggestive phrase I'd overheard from the footpath outside the café, *Licht und Schatten*. The aptness of this slight, but real and present, connection encouraged me and I took it, along with the geraniums, for a favourable sign.

I'd noticed some way out from the verandah where I stood, perhaps thirty yards distant, a kind of knoll, a prominence which had attracted my attention. Apprehensive that I might be observed and taken to be an intruder, I started down the steps and set off across the open area of dry grass towards the mound. I was like an explorer on a level plain who has perceived a hill in the distance and is drawn towards its superior elevation in the hope that if he ascends it he will be granted a superior understanding; surely the hope of all ascents since that of Moses in the wilderness of Sinai.

I had gone no more than half a dozen steps out from the verandah when a gazebo situated further down the hill towards the river came into my view. Convinced by now that the house and its wild garden were without occupants, I was startled to see a woman seated at a table within this oriental and picturesque construction. She was writing. She had not seen me. I advanced towards her down the gentle slope. I had arrived to within a few yards of her, and was on the point of calling out to her in case my sudden appearance should startle her, when she looked up.

She looked up the way one does when one is deeply engaged with a composition. That is, she looked up suddenly and in mid-sentence, her mind yet balancing the weight of the work-in-hand while her eyes examined her surroundings, as if she believed the word or phrase that was to serve her was to be located not within her memory but on the outside, among the world of material objects.

She looked up from her work directly into my eyes. She might have been appealing to an imaginary companion, to a fanciful amanuensis whom she was accustomed to have by her side at all times, for she showed no surprise at seeing me standing before her in my pale suit in the bright sunlight, my hat held respectfully before me with both my hands. Indeed it was as if she expected to see me there, had even *called* me into being, willed my existence in her garden for no other purpose than to serve as her literary consultant in this particular instance – and what when she has done with me? Shall I not vanish once again? Will I not be sucked back into that limbo from which she has granted me a moment of reality? So concentrated and intense and so searching and familiar was her gaze that I felt it was I who was the fiction. If her attention should wander from me then I should cease to be there. She would have her word, would have drawn it in with her to *her* place, and would possess no further use for me or for her garden until the need for our presence ripened in her again.

She resumed writing.

Hot, metallic bird calls clinked in the willows beside the river and the sun burned my scalp. The air shrieked faintly with insects. I watched her complete the sense of what she had in mind. She wears a simple grey dress of a light cotton material. It is soiled and frayed. She is slight in build and exceedingly emaciated, her skin loosened on her frame and aged and wrinkled far beyond her years. She is tanned to the leathery complexion of a peasant. I know her to be fifty-nine, a year younger than myself. In her gaze, where her intelligence and energy are concentrated, I had detected a family peculiarity, a likeness shared by Feng and Lang, a manner of looking at one as though one is on the outside, located among an arrangement of objects, and they, the observer, are far away inside, inhabiting a more entirely immanent reality than one's own. Her appearance is unexpectedly oriental, as that of someone of unmixed Chinese descent, and is not at all the look of the Eurasians one is accustomed to see in the International Settlement. This impression is no doubt due in part to her weathered and emaciated condition. In China she would never have been considered beautiful, even when she was young, for she possesses the much despised single-lidded eye.

I coughed. I insisted on my presence. I am really here, I wished to say. Looking away has not got rid of me. She ceased to write and straightened up, working her scrawny arms back and forth to loosen a cramp in her shoulders. And she smiled. You're Doctor Spiess, she said. And you've come from Shanghai as a companion to my relation. It's very good of you to call on me Doctor. Won't you come in out of the sun?

Perhaps I should come back when you've finished writing? I suggested.

I'd like to know when that might be, she said, a little ironic.

I went up the steps into the gazebo. Flakes of desiccated paint crumbled beneath the grip of my fingers on the rail.

There wasn't much spare room and I was required to stand beside her desk, as if I had been called up to her to account for myself or to be examined by her. A word, Doctor Spiess, she asked, that one might use in place of pilgrim? She waited, then looked up at me and smiled, offering me reassurance, her eyes sharp and black and observant, reading my features with open and unabashed interest.

I saw that here was a woman to whom it would not be possible to tell a lie without finding oneself immediately detected. It seemed to me that if I were to tell her anything at all, then I should tell her everything. I at once drew encouragement from this conclusion, and made the decision to go in boldly and to hold nothing back from her. Why, if pilgrim will not do for you, there is no other word in English that will, I responded. Bunyan used it up so entirely that you'll never get it back from him. You must either use pilgrim and allow for there being something of Bunyan in your use of it, or leave that region of conjecture alone. Unless you would go back before Bunyan to the Latin root and tease something out of *peregrinum*, which signifies the stranger. If you wish to save yourself that trouble, the Chinese possess a useful phrase. Though I dare say it may not particularly suit you.

She laughed and said, You have the advantage of me with going back to Latin roots, doctor, and she invited me to sit in a cane chair which stood to one side of her writing table. I imagine you could do with a cup of tea? she offered. I said I'd be very glad of tea, as the walk across the bridge from Richmond and up the hill had made me hot and thirsty. She didn't move but continued to look at me. And what's this phrase in Mandarin, then?

There were books and piles of papers and tea chests with dirty crockery and cooking utensils on them, and there was an untidy camp bed and other items of furniture spread about the gazebo's octagonal floor, as if she must camp out here. I made space on a teachest for the volumes that were on the chair. The boards of these books were curled from exposure to the weather.

.

I settled myself into the creaking chair. The phrase, I said, is *lang tsze*.

Lang tsze, she repeated after me, taking the tone just right and leaning towards me, small and light, sitting above me on her tall narrow chair and waiting for me to elaborate, an eagerness and a suspense in her that made her youthful.

I felt trusted by her and as though much was expected of me. It refers to a son, I said, who has gone away from home, who has gone away and gone astray, who has abandoned the customs of his family, that is. There is something of the prodigal in it, though that is not an exact parallel. He has abandoned his family and his duty towards them, let's say, but he may return to them one day enlightened and redeemed. Is that not a kind of pilgrimage?

O yes, of course, that is a familiar story, she said with so much impatience that I hoped I'd not disappointed her. She gazed out of the gazebo towards a belt of thin native bush, which I saw forms a narrow corridor of wilderness between the bank of the river and the continuation of the road above.

I do not wish to figure life merely as a journey, she said emphatically. As a travelling to a sacred place of understanding and returning fulfilled and forgiven. I know nothing of such things! The somewhat contemptuous tone in which she said this made it apparent that she felt herself to be correcting in me a rather too literal misunderstanding of her purpose in asking the question.

She turned to me. I don't travel, Doctor Spiess. I'm not a *lang tsze*. I was born in that house. She lifted her arm and pointed. And I have gone no further than this. I have never left home. Travelling does not interest me. I have spent my years imagining China from this garden in Kew. How should I *imagine* China if I were to visit it? It's not visiting I care about. It's not China but the imagining that interests me. A Chinese would recognise nothing of home in my stories. You're right, however, about *peregrinum*, if that was your word. It is to live among strangers that I know about in my work. That is the part of the pilgrim's experience I care for. I write of what it is to live among strangers, Doctor Spiess, I do not write of what it is to be enlightened and redeemed. I leave that to the Bishops.

•

We talked all afternoon and into the evening. She drew my story out of me by insisting there was a story *in* me to be drawn out. I could not resist her expectation. And she was a very good listener. So I told her everything. It was a joy to do so. Every word delighted her. Suspense transfixed her. We laughed often. And whenever I would have passed quickly from one incident to another she would not permit it, but insisted on hearing every detail. So with her I gazed once again from the casement in Hangzhou at the winter-flowering plum tree, in that sad original of all formal gardens. And once again I banqueted in the cold guest hall upon Yu's splendid dishes, transformed briefly into an enigmatic sign by my silvery fur coat. And, with emotion, I told her of the night Madame Feng and I had struggled to deliver Lang into this world. The wrong place for him, I said. A disintegrating world.

When I was silent at last she rose and heated more water in the billycan on a kerosene stove. I fancied we were both listening to the peculiar silence of the evening, intimate and entirely familiar to her, new and strange to me. I felt at home with her in her gazebo, which is surely an explorer's camp situated far out on a great plain, with only the stars to drench it in their flames at night and the path that shines in the darkness, pointing towards the remnant of native forest. Hers is not a world of solid objects, but is a transparent reality without a hard surface. There are levels, some deeper some shallower, but all permeable.

She stood beside my chair and poured fresh tea into my cup from the steaming billycan. There is a place, she said, where your plays have written themselves. That is the manner in which she speaks, saying such things so casually and with such assurance that one 'sees' the place she speaks of.

We did not leave the gazebo. It is her home. I am confident

•

she will set about writing me and the people I have spoken of into her work. I believe I can see the means of her remaking of us as her own. I and Madame Feng and Huang and Yu and Lang and Feng, and even Mrs Halloran, will all surely come to serve her in the examination of lives lived among strangers. As I spoke I saw her attention collecting us, for in a way I understood she was not listening to me but to herself, listening to her own voice all the while in a far off place of deep enchantment.

THE LITTLE RED DOORWAY

On the morning of 10 September 1976, a violent equinoctial storm passed across Melbourne, travelling from the south-west to the north-east. A one-hundred-year-old elm fell on a house in Glenroy and power lines were brought down. There were no reports of injuries to persons. There is often savagery in Melbourne's climate at this time of the year, yet it always seems startling and unanticipated. Radio and TV presenters spoke that day of *freak* weather. It is as if we persist, despite repeated experience, in referring to a northern hemisphere tribal memory for an expectation of a gentle spring, in which *The first butterflies appearing on those warm afternoons of late March and early April when the blackthorn hedges turn white and the dandelions open their saffron heads, enrich the spirit and elevate the soul.* And they do, but not in Melbourne. It is as if we are unwilling to let go and to reconcile ourselves to a fierce spring, to a spring in which raging Antarctic storms wrench trees out by the roots and fell power poles. And there are just enough of those 'warm afternoons' for the delusion to persist that it is they which represent the true norm, if only things *would* return to normal.

On this day Gertrude's important, her first, one-woman show was to have its official opening at The Falls Gallery. For Gertrude, therefore, unquestionably, but also for Lang, and even for myself in a private way, 10 September was to be a day of special significance. For the three of us, the triangle of us as Lang would have it, it was to be a day on which certain critical, and irreversible, reckonings would be inscribed. The Falls Gallery is in Richmond, within sight, just, of the hill around which Coppin Grove makes its elegant half loop, before it becomes Shakespeare Grove and eventually rejoins Isabella Grove.

At a little after seven in the morning, the storm winds struck South Melbourne and woke me. It was my empty garbage bin crashing on to its side on the concrete landing of the outside stairs that actually woke me. I came up through layers of sleep and broke the surface like a slow giant whale returning to the wind and the waves from a secret rendezvous in the deep, where everything is still silent. I lay there with my eyes open, listening to the bin rolling backwards and forwards on the concrete with a mild thunder and puzzling what the sound might be, the dreamless emptiness of my sleep hanging beneath me, still asserting the pull of the deep on my mind.

Then the telephone rang.

I reached over the side of the bed for it. There was a familiar pause after I'd said hullo – his deliberate heightening of the anticipation. Have you got the storm over there yet? I asked.

In an awed, husky whisper, he confided, Mao's dead, Steven.

For 10 September 1976 was also the day of Mao's death; or rather, if it was not quite the day on which he died, it was the day the news of his death was announced in the world's press.

I was looking at Gertrude's translation of her father's journal. I'd left the last volume on the floor beside my bed after reading late. It was open at the last page. I had begun to realise something about it which had not occurred to me before. I said carefully into the telephone, I suppose that's good news then, is it?

There was a very long pause. I heard him light a cigarette and turn aside from the phone to cough. I read August Spiess's words about Victoria, indeed Gertrude's words: *As I spoke I saw her attention collecting us, for in a way I understood she was not listening to me but to herself, listening to her own voice all the while in a far off place of deep enchantment.* But I wasn't thinking about the meaning of the words this time. This time, as I read, I was thinking about something else, about the thing I'd begun to realise about these translations.

Lang said in my ear, anxious and testing for a reaction, They might let me go back now.

This surprised me. It even shocked me a little. Privately I'd wondered more than once if he'd ever considered the possibility of going back, eventually, if the regime were ever to become more open to the rest of the world. It wasn't out of the question, after all, that his mother might be still alive – Madame Feng, Huang's beautiful Lotus, aged and alone somewhere in a transfigured Hangzhou or Shanghai, holding firm still to her hopes for a revival of ancient values, still out to defeat Feng, dreaming of her son, that he might return shining from the West, like General Koxinga, and save the Middle Kingdom from the demons of the Lord of Death. If she'd survived the war and the Revolution and then the Cultural Revolution – one upheaval after another – she'd only now be in her seventies. A reunion was still possible. It was not out of the question. His *voicing* of the idea of a return to China, however, seemed fanciful to me. It did not come from a part of Lang which I'd taken seriously. I said doubtfully, Would you go back though, if they'd let you?

It's the first chance in thirty-nine years, Steven! What was the matter with me? Hadn't I been doing my sums? Hadn't I been paying attention all this time? What could I have been thinking about? Hadn't I realised this was all serious for him? I felt rebuked, and guiltily reminded of the fact that I'd not yet let him see the *Reflections*, even though Gertrude had read them a while ago.

I was afraid of his opinion of them; and even more of his claims, of what his opinion and his claims might do to my possession of these unfinished pieces. Given half a chance he might yet make good his claim upon them. What had just begun to seem possible to me might be lost to me once again if I were to let him loose on the work before it had reached some sort of conceptual certainty. The voice, with which I had at last begun to replace the ranting chant of my father's ghost, might be silenced in me once again. Nothing was decided yet. Nothing was fixed or clear, or definite enough, or strong enough yet to be called my own with any assurance. Gertrude had embraced me and had generously understood all this and been careful to say nothing. Her acknowledgment had been important to me. For she was, as Lang had observed so often, the only real artist among us – she had made something her own. Lang might rage and denounce the work as spurious and he might successfully challenge me for repossession of his memories against my fictions.

Why shouldn't I go back? he asked into the silence, which was crackling with the static of the storm, his voice thick with suspicion, trying to read my features through the phone, trying to hear what I was really thinking.

What I was thinking was of Melbourne without him, without access to her garden at Coppin Grove and to the suggestive memorabilia, and to his difficult drunken realities. I'd miss you, I said, claiming to be without ambivalence, claiming that life would not be less problematical without him.

No you wouldn't, Steven! He chuckled throatily, sounding a bit triumphant. No you wouldn't. You wouldn't miss me. He read out a few lines from the *Age*, in which the journalist claimed no foreign dignitaries were to be invited to attend Mao's funeral. I told you you'd get it wrong! He laughed and wheezed and choked. You'll never understand us. They're keeping it in the family! It's going to be strictly a family affair, Steven. We're the only ones who can do that.

After forty years hadn't the connection atrophied? I know, he'd told me, there'd been nothing all this time. Not a message. Not a word. No news since his arrival at St Patricks in Ballarat. The possibility that somehow he might have contrived to retain the option of going back to his original homeland, *because there really is something different and special about being Chinese*, something which I'd not understood and never would understand, offended me. I felt jealous of the possibility of it, no matter how slight or illusory it might really be. It was as if he were taunting me with his possession of a certainty he knew I wouldn't be able to match.

·

Are you still there Steven?

I'm thinking, I said. The garbage bin rumbled back and forth. He was beginning to enjoy himself. I decided to get off the phone and asked him what time we were to meet later. We arranged that I would pick him up from Coppin Grove at five. He suggested we have a drink at a pub in Bridge Road before going on together to Gertrude's show. I hung up before he could begin developing his theme.

The part of him I'd not taken seriously was his foreignness, the possibility that he might really be a *peregrinum*, a stranger among us, a genuine *lang tsze* who could return home enlightened, redeemed and reconciled, no matter how long he'd stayed away. In seeking to confirm my own unclear sense of Australianness, what I'd never considered was the chance that Lang might not see himself as an Australian at all. I began to test an image of him as a *foreigner*. I let the word sidle into my mind and accompany the image: foreigner. On the face of it a descriptive appellation, an appeal to neutrality, a form of applied classification, indicating something neither good nor bad but simply other. Yet applied to him I recognised at once that it was sinister. As a tag it was coercive of categories. It dismayed me to see him so described. I resisted it. An intimacy was available to me . . . I approached the house and entered the hallway. Having come from his bedroom at this hour, or from the kitchen, he would be facing the front door. In the large mirror at the far end of the hall there would be my reflection, standing as Sickert might have had me stand, against the light, looking in at him. As if I really were emerging from the hidden inner garden. And there would be a reflection of his back. At this hour he would be wearing a pair of loose yellowed drawers with button-up flies. Apart from these, which he would have slept in, he would be naked. His body, which I love with a strange, resisting tenderness, is small and hairless and exceedingly pale; his skin untouched by sunlight. A network of blue veins is visible, rising to the opalescent surface then diving deep into the interior. His musculature is poorly defined. His is an almost adolescent body and not unlike that of his great-aunt's in the portrait of her as a child, which now hangs to the right of the front door – outside the front room where the other portraits hang – and which cannot therefore be viewed by someone standing, as I am, in the doorway itself. He is hunched over the telephone and he is shivering. His tight black hair is standing straight up on his scalp, like the closely shorn mane of a hunter. Its appearance is surprising, giving him the look of someone belonging to an elect caste. It is his most striking feature.

I worked steadily all morning, systematically examining each page of the journals. The entire text is in Gertrude's careful, rounded handwriting, done with black ink and an old-fashioned split nib, yet throughout the seven volumes there is not one crossing out, nor a single revision in the margin. For a handwritten manuscript this is remarkable. But is this a handwritten manuscript? Or is it something else? The seven volumes, all small folio, are uniformly bound with green cloth-covered boards. Every page is numbered at the top centre, and at the beginning of each new section there is a bracketed note giving the actual date of its translation. A rectangular label on the front cover carries the volume number and, simply, A. I. W. Spiess. Altogether there are four hundred and sixteen pages.

It is a beautiful thing. A unique set. The easy flowing text is clearly not a first draft but is a painstakingly crafted transcription of a highly finished translation. These books are not the product merely of a dutiful impulse. There is a larger and more considered purpose than that in their creation. Gertrude's intention in completing this massive task cannot have been simply to produce an English language version of her father's journals. I felt convinced of this.

I found the dates instructive. The bracketed date of the translation of the first section of Volume I was given as 14 December 1964. Only a month after her father's death at the age of eighty-seven, when Gertrude herself would have been eighteen. The final date, bracketed before the last entry in Volume VII, was 15 May 1968. Three and a half years later. From the age of eighteen to twenty-two, then, during most of the period she'd been a student at art school, Gertrude was working on the task of making these journals, translating, redrafting and transcribing them. In a handwritten manuscript of over four hundred pages the absence of corrections would indeed be remarkable, but in a finished work of art the absence of such obvious signs of revision would not be. I had assumed, until this moment, that she had given me the journals to use as a source for my own work. Now I began to see that this may not have been her motive at all.

Mounted on the inside back cover of Volume VII, the last volume, was a black and white snapshot. An elderly man in a panama hat and a pale crumpled suit and a young Chinese were holding hands with a little girl who stood between them. The young Chinese was Lang. He was in his early twenties. He had a cigarette stuck squarely between his lips. The cigarette was so bright it looked as if it had been superimposed on to the photograph with white-out. Since that day he appeared hardly to have changed at all. I'd never seen a photograph of him before. The little girl was trying to drag them forward and they were pretending to resist her. Behind them was a kiosk at the end of a pier, and then the sea. I felt as though I should have known them then, and I wondered who had taken the photograph.

My journal cannot be a map after all, joining the beginning of my journey to the end of it. How could he have been so certain he would never revisit Hamburg, the place of his origin? Had he really *been* that certain. How much latitude had the translator exercised with his original text? To what degree had her hindsight led her to modify her father's thoughts? Could she, indeed, have resisted tampering with them, still loving him, grieving for the loss of him? *I have discovered motives, my own and everyone else's, to be impenetrable.* What was the German for this? How had he actually expressed it? Would another translator have rendered this thought as his daughter had rendered it?

As the day wore on and I progressed more deeply into my re-examination of the journals, I became increasingly convinced that in these books Gertrude had embarked on a fictionalisation of her father. Perhaps at first not with that intention. Perhaps at first simply smoothing out a difficulty or making an image turn more surely. But before very long beginning to enjoy the practice of the form and to do it with increasing flair and assurance as the work proceeded. Finding herself required in the end, if she were to realign the warping of the structure which her infiltration of the text must have induced, to take the work through several painstaking drafts. And by this process, little by little and with subtlety, replacing the presence of her father in the work with the presence of herself; accomplishing a reverse colonisation to the one with which the chanting spectre of my own dead father had threatened me; the living child, in her case, fittingly taking up and renaming the spaces of the dead parent; making herself at home while making *of* herself an artist.

With the new expectation in my mind, with a mixture of feelings, with curiosity and excitement and a certain envy, I began my re-reading in Gertrude's voice of what I had read once as the authentic journals of Doctor August Spiess. As I opened the first volume I recalled Gertrude's enigmatic smile, as if we were about to share a secret, as she placed the seven volumes in my hands, and at last I understood it: *9am, 18 December 1927. Hangzhou, at the house of Huang Yu-hua the literary painter! I am elated and exhausted. That I am here at all seems still to be a dream . . .*

I was late. It was after half-past five. The instant I stepped out of the car I knew he wasn't home. The front door was closed. I knocked, knowing there would be no answer, and went round the side without waiting. The flywire door to the kitchen was swinging backwards and forwards in the wind and the kitchen door itself was locked. I peered through the window. My reflection peered back at me, anxiously – another me trapped inside his house, inside his powerful cosmic mirror, lying at the bottom of the Qiantang River. Mutely we gazed at each other through the greasy lens of the glass, strangers, familiars. It was the window through which Gertrude had framed her image of us at the end of summer – two friends in white shirts sitting in the sun in old-fashioned cane chairs, while the rest of the world moved on. I shielded my eyes. Inside the kitchen there was only the usual mess. No signs of flight or panic or rage. I stepped back on to the grass. I knew no neighbours would bother me if I were to break in. Even if I were to set off one of the alarms, howling among the quiet groves of Kew, no one would bother me.

A stealthy movement behind me made me turn. The poplar was thrashing about in the wind. Numerous branchlets with one or two pale new leaves attached had been torn off in the storm and were scuttling about the lawn like shimmering green crabs. I could just make out the ornate wrought-iron finial on top of the gazebo, angled a little to one side – sinking towards the west – a high note of Victorian style pointing at something that was no longer there. Pointing at nothing. A finial indeed. It was spring but the garden had acquired an abandoned air.

It was now after six. There was less than half an hour before the opening of Gertrude's show. I drove quickly yet I wanted to go back and really break in to his house. To search for something. Something to provide me with the certainty that he was not his father's son, that he was not the Fourth Phoenix, who must one day feel compelled to burn our books and cast our mirrors into the stream.

He wouldn't be at all upset. He'd be delighted. He'd even be disappointed if I hadn't actually purloined an item or two from the alluvial congeries of memorabilia on and underneath his dining table. It would excite him. It would be a *real* move in the game. Steven! Steven! Steven! he'd cry, It's you! *You're* the thief! It's you I've been setting my alarms for all these years! And I didn't recognise you! I *invited* you in! I thought it was Tom Lindner and his lot I had to look out for but it was you! I could hear him choking with mirth, the jaundiced vision of his pale eye confirmed, mocking us both; mocking the seriousness of everything, revitalised, able to believe once more, for a little while, in the elevating power of prophetic irony . . . Let's have a drink! Struck by an idea. I tell you what, why don't we get the lotus cup out and have a look at it! You still haven't seen it, have you? Snuggling against me as he urges me to go further with him. You do *want* to see it, don't you? You remember I told you about the little red door? The second gateway? Dragging me along with him. The rain and sun eventually weathered my mother's new coat of paint to the colours of autumn in the forest. I had a recurring dream on the SS *Wangaratta* when I was coming to Australia. August and I used to talk about it – we'll get the cup later. Last night I had the dream again. Just like that. A dream from my childhood! What do you think of that? What does that *mean*, Steven? Shall I tell you what it was . . . ?

The traffic in Bridge Road slowed almost to a standstill. There was a line of trams banked up one behind the other. I'd begun to see that the garden at Coppin Grove really was depleted and used up; that she was no longer there, that she was in me. The focus of our affairs was moving, to the gallery, to Gertrude and her drawings. That's where it was about to break the surface. If I were to return and steal Victoria's portrait now it would be merely a nostalgic memento. The lights changed twice without anything moving . . .

I got back to Hangzhou, somehow. It had been difficult. I arrived there on my own. Maybe I was still a boy. But perhaps not. I can't be sure about that. I'd been travelling for days, for ages and ages, to get there and I was worn out but in a state of elation. It was real. There was no feeling that any of it might be a dream. The instant I turned the corner at the end of the street I could see the little red doorway with its upturned roof. The toffee apple man was there at his post across the road, his apples trembling in the sunlight. I ran up to the doorway and hammered on it with my fists and yelled out, Mother! Mother! Mother! I kept banging and yelling, It's me! I'm home! It's your son! But no one answered. After a while I realised I could hear these deep booming echoes, just as if someone was striking the temple drum up in the mountain at Lin Yin. But inside me. It was the first inkling I had that none of it was real, and that it was all a dream, this heartsickening booming. I stopped hammering on the door. There was no one there. The place was empty. They can never know I returned.

·

The traffic came to a stop completely. Nothing moved. I wasn't going to be there with them for the precious bit of ritual at the beginning – the opening ceremony; the moment when she would become fully visible to us in the presence of her drawings. They are, or might be, standing on their own at the far end of a long gallery, their backs to the door through which I will soon enter. They are looking at but not discussing three large black and white drawings, which hang on the end wall. A bold, symmetrical arrangement – windows looking out onto a darkening landscape from the lighted hall – the three large drawings are heavily worked, richly textured, complex and full of concealed narratives and fugitive figures (as I have been told in the article in the fine-art journal they will be). I will know soon if they are also graphic realisations of her own journals, the journals which she has *made* her own; something the article could not have told me. She is wearing the expensive black gown she was wearing in the clever photograph. Lang is small and shabby beside her – a demon with blue smoke rising through his electrified hair. (It surprises me to reflect that the dream of the red doorway is not his dream, but is my own.) I remember that the last volume of her journal begins, *For certain people exile is the only tolerable condition.*

They are examining the uninhabited tryptich before them: a divided landscape waiting to be inhabited, the principal characters withheld by her until this moment.